THE ALTERED

MG HARDIE

MoorRey Publishing

ISBN 978-0-9968296-5-6
Ebook: 978-0-9968296-7-0

The correct citation for this book is The Altered, United States, 2019.
https://mghardie.wixsite.com/the-altered-ones

The universe had more dimensions than I was able to perceive. I never conceived of living amphibiously in two worlds. Having aided in destroying the world, I had been invited to have a front row seat to the apocalypse. If I am insane, this insanity has brought me closer to reality. The whole world, all of it, is made up by amino acids inside brains. We all have an innate skepticism towards any system, don't we?

I was one of 10 billion, now it's just me…

CHAPTER 1

Nine months ago, Devon discovered that humans were not alone in the universe and his family was killed for it. He mourned for his family alone. Devon had been altered. Devon's abilities grew but he was no match for these unseen creatures and he did the only sensible thing he could do, run.

Devon ran from Them. He hid from Them, but he would never escape. He returned home. In the debris and rain soaked rubble that was once his home, he found a half burnt stuffed butterfly. It belonged to his one year old daughter Brianna, it was all that remained. Devon attached the butterfly to his backpack.

Devon's mind was once comforted by the concrete, metal, and glass erections that protruded into the heavens. It was the buses and trains that crisscrossed cities that captured his imagination. He only wanted a promotion because he tired of the intense competition for languishing parking spaces. Not long ago he thought long lines and traffic jams were all about him.

Now, Devon knew something deeper and darker lurked underneath all of it. As his abilities grew, he saved those that needed saving, sometimes even from themselves. Yesterday Devon spent seven hours performing multiple organ surgery. Today, he stood in a courtroom representing a teenage defendant.

"We request probation, your honor," Devon said straightening his tie.

"Probation denied," the judge proclaimed.

In court cases where there is any doubt, the people usually side with a group, a gender or the uniformed. The police, the city council, the district attorney say they want to make the community feel safe; they just don't want it too safe. Some policy choices develop from care and concern, but most are unconcerned about collateral consequences.

They make these government decisions complete with a headline that makes the choice seem rational. Robbery is the largest group of offenders; to Devon this indicated a lack of resources.

When you only have a few hours to investigate a case and ten minutes in a courtroom, to prevent your client from spending a decade or more in prison, you use whatever advantage you can.

However, The System must be fed, or maybe just the judges. It was ten cases before Devon realized that judges who aren't hungry are more lenient. So Devon moved his court cases to the early afternoon. Doing this gave him more favorable rulings.

Most of Devon's involvements with people were short-lived, no one mattering more than a day. Because of vivid, lucid nightmares he was scared to close his eyes; because of powerful otherworlders he was afraid to open them.

In these dreams he could see his wife Sarah, he could touch her, but she wasn't there. At the end of the dreams, she would squeeze his hand, softly say "good-bye", and then her face twisted in a woeful grimace as a fiery whirlwind carried her away.

Devon woke up from these nightmares drenched in sweat and soaked in fear. Still every night he got up and put on his uniform of shadow. His muscles twitched from training; still he spent hours patrolling the streets and climbing buildings.

In city after city, Devon exposed academic, legal and political con artists. He revealed scams and busted up human trafficking rings. Devon despised prosecutors that made careers by overcharging and wrongly prosecuting the less fortunate, low information citizens. This was his duty and he went about it one state, one city, one person at a time.

Not far away, an engineer pulled the emergency brake handle. The train shuddered and the brakes slammed shut. It was too late. At 10 a.m. a passenger train traveling from New York to Miami, carrying 147 people collided with a freight train, near The James River in Virginia. A railroad track switch was locked in the wrong position causing this locomotive to barrel into a stationary 5,000 ton freight train.

The train screeched and hissed as passengers were thrown from the back of the car to the front. The lead passenger car derailed first and slid a thousand feet across gravel. Six passenger cars followed the first one off the tracks. Two railcars flipped and were flattened.

Tables, chairs, and people tumbled into each other as though they were inside a dryer. Inside the carriages, luggage and various objects became projectiles. The train windows shattered as the train twisted. When the sliding trains came to a stop shouts and panic turned into chilling silence. Soon an incoherent din filled the cabins as injured passengers fumbled for something, anything.

Blood mixed fuel leaked into gravel. Disoriented passengers were trapped inside the metal carriages. The ripping metal of slowly flipping of a derailed car turned the silence into screams and shouts of, "We're dying", and "Help me."

Within ten minutes of the collision Devon arrived. He pulled thirty injured, but alive people from the wreckage. Ten people were killed; one hundred and twenty people were hospitalized. Devon exhaled deeply and scanned the wreckage for more survivors. It was time for him to go as rescue crews started to arrive.

Devon thought this accident was caused by otherworlders, but it wasn't. These people weren't targets. A System had done this. This System targets everyone. It will be said that this collision, these deaths could have been prevented—if only the administrators had allowed some new device that linked satellites with computers to monitor trains, to be implemented.

From this incident an alphabet named program would filter from the top down and into every vehicle. This all would be done efficiently and without emotion, this is the nature of The System. The System changes reality by laws, by entertainment, by violence and by accident. The System programs interactions between people.

The System assisted by the media produces feelings of self pity. It uses human memory, words, ideas, facts and events to trigger embedded traumas. Inside dreams it projects artificial images. It manipulates symbols and standards.

The System distorts social values. It suppresses true feelings and logic in order for people to lose their true self. The System runs all other systems. The System grabs babies in their crib; assaulting them before they are born. It herds people into organized easily monitored groups. It creates beings with a conformity coerced by corrupted consent.

The System protects those that wear corporate logos and it promotes those that promote it. The System was everywhere and it controlled everything. Devon was the one thing The System didn't planned.

Thirty minutes after leaving the derailment, Devon returned to a small storehouse near Glenn Allen. His clothes smelled of fuel, his face was marked with ash and today was a good day. A meeting with Prime, the leader of these otherworlders, three months earlier, extinguished much of Devon's anger.

Under Prime's orders, otherworlders caused natural disasters that ravaged Devon's world. These beings had killed Devon's family and were from a twin Earth. They can't be seen because they exist in dark matter. Devon had been altered to survive. This altering caused him to evolve. He only returned home when he had evolved enough to fight these invaders.

As Devon traveled the planet he was careful of the video strips designed to pacify the masses. These otherworlders could see Devon, but The System no longer could. To remain anonymous Devon concealed himself with rafters, rooftops and darkness.

Devon left the storehouse, and in no time was on top of the James Monroe Building looking down on the people filled streets. His eyes swelled with tears, tears that were reminders of a simpler time when his wife and daughter were alive. Devon looked down at the stuffed butterfly as these thoughts floated through his mind.

"Look at them scurrying along..." Devon whispered to himself. "We humans are bacterium on a galactic grain of sand that is in a space sized ocean. Animals adapt to the natural environment. Human beings, change the natural environment to make ourselves live comfortably."

When the streets were dark and silent, Devon practiced cutting street lights on and off by a simply touch it. He did this by controlling the electrical current flowing through his body. It was a neat parlor trick. The more he moved the more static electricity his extremities produced. He generated what's known as an electrostatic force. This small electric field also allowed him to adhere to structures. He could climb structures without grabbing or digging in his nails.

The charge he generated is the same charge produced from rubbing feet back and forth on carpet. It is a stronger form of static cling that comes from alternating positive and negative currents. Devon could achieve this effect through layers of clothing; this made patrolling the streets easier.

Even though, using this static electricity drained him, he occasionally caused people's beloved electronic devices to temporarily malfunction. The hours of depression that followed could be called entertaining.

At night Devon traveled in sewers and on buildings. On rooftops is where footsteps and screams blended with the crash of knocked over metal trash cans. Through the noise, he heard a baby crying.

"Why is my night filled with the clank of bracelets?" Devon said to himself. "That's the sound of a crowbar repeatedly digging into someone's abdomen. That's the wood clank of a bat as it bounces on the pavement, and the rattle of a dragging chain. Through these sounds I can hear shotgun blasts barking in the distance.

"This building is dominated by the clash of perfumes. I can hear cats tumble through the garbage, beyond that I can sense small changes in air density, bone vibrations, temperature variations. I can hear a car accelerating two blocks over..." Devon said to himself as he overlooked the city.

These otherworlders didn't want our water or our resources. Occasionally one of them would scowl at Devon, but they kept their distance, they had an understanding. These otherworlders, like to be called Them.

The males wore black and each had shiny golden seals...one seal...three seals... Prime had seven worn, unpolished seals on his coat. Aside from grotesque facial features, hulking frames and translucence skin, each otherworlder had moving lights along their fitted trench coats. These lights and patterns varied from Them to Them.

The symbols showed whirlwinds, fire, earth, or waves, all of these symbols glowed with yellow, blue, green or red luminescence. These symbols related to the abilities of an otherworlder. Tornado caused tornadoes and Eruption caused eruptions and so forth. The intensity of these lights increase or decrease during their missions.

The females are smaller than the males although most are six feet tall, Devon's height. They have light tattoos on their shoulder, and they wear a variety of elegant garb. They appear with the up-dos, natural curls in soft waves and a variety of ponytails and twists. Devon had seen a few of them sleeveless, midriff showing and with elevated back collars.

The females moved gracefully as if floating, often not moving limbs not necessary to the mission. Their light gowns flickered with soft light. They illuminate when they connect with a subject. The level of the color on their dress intensifies based on contact with their subject.

More females walked around with humans. They usually engage when a person is sleep, altering thoughts and priming future actions. If their target wakes up, they might feel as if an intruder was in the room. At their most intense these otherworlders might be glimpsed from the corner of an eye.

Out of the corner of one's eyes, the shape of something is worthy of a double take but is registered as a figment of the imagination. The human brain discards this millisecond appearance as too much information.

These beings are stronger and had long fingers, but were biologically similar to humans. Once an otherworlders energy is expended they jump over a building, fly away and disappear into a rift.

In the United States, there are sixty nuclear power plants, ninety-eight nuclear reactors and 100,000 cell phone towers. Radiation creates these rifts that lead to overlapping worlds. Otherworlders use these passages between worlds to come and go on this plane as they please. These radiation created rifts are not visible and they were not visible to Devon until a week after he had been altered.

Each rift had a particular sheen, each extended into a three-dimensional plane, each a different color and size and each was mathematically generated by intentional radioactive expressions.

"There's an otherworlder now…" Devon said to himself before he moved to the nearest rift location. Devon had been told that no human could breach the fissure between Earths and that no human could survive crossing this border between worlds.

It was no hallucination that nine months ago Devon Heathrow was dead. It was not an imagining that he had stood in a great chamber on the edge of one of these rifts. Right now he definitely had one foot inside of this rift. It was clear that anything was possible.

The rift is a million twists of emptiness, fastened together with ragged bits of improbability. The rift was a furious snapping empty convexity, with no real sides or bottom. The rift very existence was an ominous warning.

Perhaps living with the consequences of his actions and being alone drove him to enter the rift. Perhaps he wanted to destroy himself, perhaps to discover himself. "What's on the other side?" was the question that burned inside of him.

This rift was mathematics visualized; mysterious in its movement. It was an iterative algorithm in spherical form. It was the same calculation applied over and over, an infinite self repeating complexity and all of it generated by one equation, $E=mc^2$.

The rift was hot. It was a hole ripped into the fabric of what was. It hugged the earth in a place that seemed out of time. Devon was now inside of the swirling darkness. Heat engulfed his face, his heart pounded like a wild animal bent on escaping his chest.

He wiped sweat from his brow and tried to calm his breathing. Now two steps inside and the pressure on his body doubled, when the pressure tripled Devon was hurled from the opening.

Devon landed hard, moaned and closed his eyes—not that it made a difference. A cold hand wrenched at his stomach, pushing its contents up. He rolled over to combat the nausea and passed out.

For six months Devon roamed familiar streets in uncharted territory. He posed as a janitor, lawyer or doctor; this pretending made it easier for him to assist the most vulnerable. Each field he endeavored took a week or two to master, and each time he pretended his knowledge, skill and awareness grew.

Devon returned home and discovered why his wife, Sarah and their one-year-old daughter Brianna had been murdered by these beings. This discovery caused Devon to track down otherworlders. Some fought valiantly, others he managed to kill. Devon's actions caused The Council to have Commotion hunt him down.

Commotion's silver eyes peered at him, through the wet darkness. The two destroyed a swamp as they battled. They brutally clashed in a swamp until Commotion submitted and offered Devon the meeting, in Alaska of all places.

He was the only person who could see these beings and he knew no one could perceive the threat the way he did. Humans viewed the otherworlders uses of power as acts of God, forces of nature and chance. These happenings were anything but random occurrences.

Getting to Alaska took several hours even with Devon riding on top of airplanes. Once Devon landed, he ran the frozen tundra; the sun urged him forward. He ran until he stood before the glacier covered mountain that was faintly outlined by rift radiation.

This place was on the edge of the rift, exactly where Commotion said it would be. Devon felt strange as he stepped beyond the great doors high on top of the glacier.

Inside the chamber, the architecture was indescribable. The materials it was made from were strange; origin of these materials was unknown. Inside the inner chamber were vast walls with intricate designs. Each forward step brought Devon a growing sense of unease.

In the main chamber, rational thought left him. In was there that Devon stood face to face with Prime, the leader of these otherworlders. Prime showed Devon around the chamber and viewing screen upon viewing screen of humanity's destruction. Prime's message was clear; everything would be laid to waste.

In the cold whiteness, a council of faces sat in judgment as humanity was put on trial for its crimes. Inside that glacier and in front of those faces Devon had been mankind's representative.

Their ruling to continue their plan caused Devon's eyes to produce a golden outline as he angrily challenged it. As he did, Prime flipped a gold seal on his coat, and the walls of the glacier became transparent.

Outside of the glacier, ice fell and electricity arced out of the largest rift Devon had seen. From a rift stepped Prime's best equipped acolytes, each one larger than the next. They growled and stretched their bodies like beasts just waking from a long sleep.

As each stepped out of the rift, powerful trumpet like roars were heard. These were by far the loudest sounds Devon had ever heard. They weren't the midnight roars and loud booms of industrial drones that permeate the walls of cities. These sounds came from within a crying Earth.

These horrifying sights were the answer to Devon's objections. Devon realized two things: One, humanity's survival would require courage, something he did not know if he possessed. Two, this had been the longest conversation he had in a quite some time. The thought of him single handedly taking on these otherworlders was suicide.

Devon had been altered; he had abilities, he had adapted. The terrifying prospect of preventing the destruction of humanity loomed before him. He swallowed any remaining fear and turned back to the faces.

"My wife and child weren't left behind, they were murdered …murdered!" Devon said, his gaze firm and sentiment lingered. This display caused the council to confer with Prime.

Prime turned with an imperceptible smile on his face. Devon's passion caused the council to reach another decision. Maybe it wasn't a smile on Prime's face. Maybe the look on Prime's face was pity; after all, Prime's faith in humanity hadn't been shaken, Devon's had. Prime flipped a gold seal on his coat and his acolytes reentered the rift.

Prime told Devon, the new role they wanted him to play in their plan. Devon was to give them an answer in a year's time. During that time Them would continue their missions and Devon would not be harmed.

Devon left that place and continued his litigating, doctoring and pursuit of the scientific method. Devon wasn't really a lawyer, doctor or a scientist and he was no hero. He didn't volunteer to become a hero and he had no qualifications unless rage counts.

Devon could no longer hold Sarah or Brianna, yet the world kept spinning. His only comfort came from having late night coffee with

Gina Lawrence, a few months ago. How he felt no longer mattered, so the lies he told himself just to keep going had to be brilliant.

Devon continued to save those he could. He could be found power jogging through a jungle, cloaked in a ripped tank top and artfully distressed cargo pants. You might have found him covered in a blaze of blood, dirt and sweat after a saving people from Landslide on the edge of Xinmo, a village in Sichuan Province. In clashes like these he was thought to be a victim.

Everyone slept, except for him. In fact, billions of people were sleeping right now. Devon had nightmares, horrific memories brought to life. Devon awoke from smoke, splinters, blood and screams to sweat soaked sheets and darkness. These nightmares were like an alarm clock, waking him up in time to put on his uniform of shadow.

It's time to wake up, Devon.

Devon's eyes slowly fluttered open. He lay face down in the dirt outside of the rift. Some world saver he was turning out to be. The Earth had rotated considerably while he was passed out. Exposure to rift radiation caused a cascade of free radicals to wreak havoc on his body.

Devon's inability to fully enter the rift was the only time he saw failure as liberating. The first time he was expelled from a rift, it took a week for his strength to return. Each time Devon tried to enter a rift he was expelled with an overwhelming urge to drink as much water as he could find. This thirst was followed by a persistent, low hum in his ears. When a week of recovery turned into days, he would eventually be granted access.

Devon believed that if he could get to the council that would change everything. To face these monsters on their turf he would have to train like never before and prepare for the unexpected. The completion of Devon's new plan included something too risky to talk about.

Devon permanently took off his white gold wedding ring and he would no longer solely wear long black trench coats. He would now wear various colored coats, lined with viscose fabric for a touch of royalty. Devon's arsenal of trench coats would make a 90s R&B singing group jealous. Devon finished his outfits with boots, a hoodie and black gloves.

Today, as he put a small white stuffed rabbit into his backpack, he told himself, 'It's not too late,' and he sped off towards his destination.

CHAPTER 2

Mr. Joshua Dougan was Devon's best friend in college. He knew everything about Devon. Four states and half a day later, Devon reached Salem, New Jersey. Devon cautiously descended two flights of stairs, two steps at a time into the basement of St. John's Episcopal Church. He headed to the corner towards the storage room. This room had been rented to Joshua Dougan.

In college, Joshua approached Devon in the quad as if he had somehow skipped the balled-up phase of concentrated masculine insecurity. Joshua tossed his empty soda can into a recycle bin. His suit, a little too loose fitting; his northern accent didn't quite go with his environmental awareness. His body language said minimalist, his mood said impatient and his hair didn't look quite right.

Joshua's parents hated each other too much to stay together. He was abandoned right after he was born. He was placed in an adoption center and was never adopted. He would call several group facilities home. In one year, he moved fourteen times and missed 212 days of school. Devon remembered the old photos of Joshua. In those photos

Joshua always wore a brown tattered sweater and worn blue jeans, a uniform, considering how many times he wore it.

Joshua didn't go to dances, the prom and he couldn't have a girlfriend. He would occasionally say words like 'awkward' when nothing was. This challenger of authority was put on several ADHD medications.

The fights were frequent and the beatings he received were bad, but it was the periods of hunger that bothered him the most. Nature took his last bit of hope when he realized he would grow no taller. Joshua had an attitude. He didn't want to end up being that person in their forties, who still acts like they are in their twenties, obsessed with popular culture of their teens.

He was impulsive, brash, a self professed loner, but he put on epic parties. He sipped slow, lived fast and he'd try anything once. He had spent the better part of his life eating large helpings of too-the-fuck-bad. He once bought a thousand dollars worth of heroin. He was so shocked at how little he received for his money that was the last time he used drugs.

Devon left school in his third year. Have a white mother and a black father left Joshua an out of place novelty. Joshua's minority heritage somehow became more important than who he was. It's funny how the things that mark a person as different are more notable than the parts that are the same as everyone else.

Joshua had been the situational minority, his entire life. His existence was a black and white assault on cultural confusion. He was the subject of philosophical think pieces in some of the courses he took. He hated those annual TV specials that ask 'why can't we all get along?'

Joshua had been called light skinned, biracial, mixed and other less flattering things. He really just wanted to be called Josh, JD or Big Poppa.

He was an average student who would have fared better if he applied himself. When Devon met him, freshman year, they were easy lays for things like fantasy sports, gaming and coding, things that held no commerce in pre-twenty social circles.

After Joshua's condo was ripped apart by explosions and otherworlders fighting with Devon, his small startup was hit with a virus that destroyed the servers. The authorities charged him with fraud. Joshua managed to make off with a quarter million dollars.

Devon slightly opened the door of the church storeroom. It was five minutes past midnight. Devon slowly entered the dark room. Three steps inside the room he saw an otherworlder, a female. Its hands were open. Its arms extended and the light tattoo on its arms was subtly glowing.

Her corset-styled armor and chiffon-lace skirt draped her sides. It looked more like a dress than a battle garment. Her short jagged hair moved slow and graceful as if it were underwater.

"Please stop..." Devon quietly said stepping out of the shadows. The being's eyes shifted and she turned towards Devon, her glow lessened. She narrowed her brow as she looked at Devon.

"You must be Devon," the being said.

"Please stop..." Devon repeated.

"I have my mission..." The being said turning towards Joshua. Her tattoo of light pulsated towards the sleeping subject. She was stimulating clusters of cells within him. She hacked into Joshua's dream. Joshua turned over several times. Devon quickly grabbed the being's arm and pulled her away from the bed. Her glow immediately stopped.

"How dare you!" She said standing erect. She had a lanky 6'1' frame and two small lateral scars alongside her head. Her eyes were large almond shaped, silvery pools full of infinite darkness. She wasn't beautiful, but she could be called attractive. Devon put out his hands in an effort to calm her down.

"It was told to us that you would not interfere and we would not kill you. Is this not correct?"

"It is..."

"Then why?"

"He's a good friend of mine, my only connection to the past."

"We need his mind."

"Surely, there are others..."

"I have heard about your tenacity and determination."

"You have?" Devon said as the being walked around the front of Joshua's bed and looked him in his eyes.

"We all have. Have you made your decision?"

"I have not."

"Is it fair to say that you'll return on subsequent evenings as you have done tonight..."

"It is."

"You would risk everything for a friend?" The being said her stance softening.

"I would."

"I will report this mission as a failure."

"You know who I am. Who are you?"

"I am Will Power."

"What were you doing to him?"

"Planting feelings of unhappiness when he's away from electronic devices."

"For what purpose?"

"To motivating him to create programs that maximize timelines this will move artificial intelligence forward."

"Will you get in trouble for telling me your mission?"

"...the mission was a failure."

"Can you undo what you've done?"

"Once the human mind has a hold of something letting go is not easy... Do you trust me to try?"

"I do now."

Will Power slowly glided next to Joshua's bed and reengaged with Devon's friend. The light pulses were now slowly going in the opposite direction. There was a strain on Will Power's face. Joshua squirmed in the bed as her lights rapidly flashed. Will Power stopped, breathed heavily and leaned over. Devon reached out and she took his hand.

"Are you alright?" Devon asked.

"I've never done that before..." An exhausted Will Power said.

"How is he?"

"Your friend has a dark past."

"He's stubborn, I know."

"I did what I could... I erased the last two months of motivations. We won't be bothering him anymore," she said floating towards the door.

"Thank you."

"It was an honor to meet you..." Will Power said. A gentle breeze slightly shifted the curtains; Devon's attention was drawn towards the noise. When he turned back around Will Power was gone. Devon took his coat off, pulled up a small chair, sat in the dark and waited.

In the distance soft thunder was heard. Near the wall was a straight-back wooden chair. On the table was a laptop, two energy drinks, half a cup of espresso. The contents of this cup made the room smell like old coffee.

Near the dresser cluttered by virtual reality goggles, a half a bottle of sleeping pills and a smartphone was a waste bin full of torn lottery tickets. Devon tapped gently on the dresser.

Joshua's eyes took the scenic route in his skull before opening. Before Joshua moved, he spent half a minute staring at the black dots on the ceiling. He kicked one leg out of his blanket, revealing his coffee cup themed pajamas. He slowly put his feet into the brown slippers next to his bed. He wiped his eyes, turned on the nightstand lamp and questioned the accuracy of the clock next to it.

Joshua looked around the bedroom with wide frightened eyes. He became alarmed when he saw Devon looking at him, chewing on a cracker.

"What the hell are you doing here!?" Joshua said, jumping up.

"Is that anyway to greet an old friend?" Devon said with a smirk on his face.

"I don't know what you are!"

"Until last night you had a being attached to you. That being had been engaging with you nightly... putting thoughts in your head..."

"What!" Joshua said as he nervously looked around the room.

"I got this being to leave you alone."

"How exactly did you do that?"

"I flashed my designer smile and she left..." Devon said smiling at Joshua.

"None of this is funny..." Joshua said walking around rubbing his temples. "So what... I'm supposed to be thanking you or something..."

"How do you feel?" Devon asked.

"Tired and motivated. Do you know that for the last six months I burned though all my cash and I've been hopping from church to church fixing computer problems, installing software?" Joshua said ending his frantic pacing to sit on the edge of his unmade bed.

"I know. Will Power told me."

"Will Power..."

A mechanical chirp came from Joshua's smartphone. Joshua's synapses fired with the promise of possibility. This digital slot machine's handle issued promises based on what could be, each time you look at it. The sounds, the colors told your mind that you had a chance at something—anything. Joshua's arm instinctually reached for it.

"Don't pick it up..." Devon said.

"But it might be..."

"...It's listening..." Devon said placing his finger to his lips. Joshua's kettle drum heartbeat went back into a semi resting mode.

"I thought I'd be safe in a church," Joshua said picking up yesterday's espresso.

"Why?"

"You know...the demons."

"Them aren't demons."

Joshua sipped the espresso; the day old taste of the dark liquid caused him to sigh. "Demon, Them—what's the difference? You are different. I mean I'm not bigger than you anymore. Remember rush week freshmen year? We were so wasted. You went back to the dorm with the ugly one," Joshua said with a chuckle.

"We remember rush week very differently," Devon said.

"How so?"

"Rush week, we were the ugly ones," Devon said. The two men smiled and hugged each other tightly. "Joshua it's good to see you."

"It's good to be seen."

"So you just collect junk and old computer parts..." Devon said looking over at the scraps of broken equipment in the milk crates that populated the corner.

"If it's useful it's not junk. Churches don't have big budgets, so I help out where I can. I am modernizing the ministry and they give me room and board. I figured, where better to be than a place of worship when those demon things of yours come-a-calling."

"I am glad you never put the Whitman glasses back on..."

"I was tempted to."

"So you still have them?

"Yes, I have been trying to duplicate the technology. I was able to make the chipset smaller. See this, I created a smaller eyepiece that will be more powerful," Joshua said putting down the Whitman glasses and proudly lifting his bulky prototype out of a crate and handing it to Devon.

"When will these be done?" Devon said examining the device.

"At the present rate of funding—about three years."

"The otherworlders will never allow you to complete this."

"They are stopping me from doing this. They are preventing me from doing that. I feel like I can do whatever I want."

"That's the point."

"For me to feel free?"

"Convincing you that you are free."

Joshua snatched his prototype from Devon, cleaned the lenses and placed it neatly in his top drawer. He put it next to the dusty wall cross he had taken off the wall.

"I don't feel like I'm being controlled," Joshua said.

"You didn't know one had been with you this whole time until I told you."

"What are you talking about? These are my ideas; no one put them into my head."

"Are you sure?" Devon said causing a gold ring to outline his pupil. "I can tell her to come back..."

"Naw...it's cool," Joshua said looking over his shoulder.

Joshua slowly made up his bed. He used his arm to push all the trash off his dresser into a mesh waste bin.

"I haven't seen you in six months and now you just show up out of the blue." Joshua said.

"It's not like that," Devon said.

"What's it like..."

"It's worse, because now I have abilities."

"My anti-troll feed filter must not be on. No...no...we are not doing this again. It was nice seeing you and all, but you need to leave," Joshua said pointing to the door. Joshua would rather roll into one of his digital selves than have this discussion. In his digital world he could be wherever and whatever he wanted to be.

"Josh wait..." Devon urged.

"No, you wait..." Joshua said turning towards Devon. "The last time I saw you half a city block was leveled, so why should I give you the time of day?"

"I looked for you for months. It took some time to find you. You took yourself off the grid."

"Not off enough, obviously," Joshua said facing towards the door of the room.

"You're my best friend," Devon said. Joshua turned away from the door and approached the larger Devon.

"No. I was your best friend until fire demons tried to kill me and destroyed my condo, there's a deposit I'll never get back."

"That's not fair, Josh..." Devon said.

"Oh yeah, and your eyes, started glowing... there's no coming back from that."

"I have more control now. I've been around the world since then."

"How do I know those flame things aren't right behind you?" Joshua said in an animated way.

"Running can't be easy, when you don't know what you are running from."

"It hasn't been! I only had those glasses on for a few minutes. I saw those creatures hitting you with punches of fire. I could feel the flames. I saw the paint on the walls melting, the wood cracking and the metal bending."

Joshua wasn't the kind of person to notice the first or last raindrop, but he noticed all the raindrops in between. Unfortunately, Joshua had put on the Whitman glasses and in doing so he invited otherworlders into his life and mind. Joshua's raised eyebrows, full arm swings and body gestures showed he needed someone, anyone to talk to.

"Two days after that explosion, I still thought I was dreaming," Joshua continued. "I thought I had lost my mind. Not a day goes by that I don't think about it. I also saw you fall off the balcony—fourteen stories straight down."

"I almost fell."

"I thought you were dead for sure."

"I was saved by thoughts of everything I lost. It was those thoughts that sustained me these six months."

"How did you survive that explosion?"

"It took me a week to heal."

"A week..." Joshua said incredibly. "I ran down to the fifth floor and people in the halls were screaming, 'We're all gonna die!', 'We're all gonna die!' and I was one of them. For three days my ears rang with the emergency alarm—three days. I haven't stopped running."

Devon walked over and picked up Joshua's smartphone. "The application we created in college identified a subject's environment and detected moods," Devon said. "The key was that our design notifications steered lives. It filled up lives with noise. It worked because humans are persuadable at every level."

"That's called engagement," Joshua said.

"We called it a tool, but not all tools are a net positive to lives. Our application was one of the thousands that fought for attention, every second— all you had to do is download it."

"That's because we told people that our app was worthy of attention."

"Do people even have a choice?"

"Of course people have a choice..." Joshua said taking his smartphone from Devon and placing it back on the dresser.

"If it is a choice driven by hidden programming is it unfree will?" Devon said pausing for a moment. The look on Joshua's face told him that it was okay to continue. "Underneath all programming, there is a something called The System that colonizes minds.

"This system can act through a device to create unintended thoughts complete with auto play, ads, filters and videos, to which the youngest of us are most susceptible. These devices have everyone, anyone competing for more screen time."

"What System? You helped me with the app."

"Instead of using set times for our measurables we placed them at crucial and random moments, that was my only real contribution. This would force a person to see our content or they pay the premium to see them less."

"Hey, that was a great idea."

"It's wrong," Devon said.

"It's just business."

"When people look up from their devices, they are unhappy. They are unhappy because simply being human injures them. Is that just business? Are we responsible for that? Children that can't put words together can download apps, go into debt and manage devices powerful enough to launch spacecrafts into orbit."

"Everyone is persuaded by something, they don't need to be aware of it," Joshua said.

"Just exploited…right."

"When you are creating a digital mousetrap, there is no such thing as ethics. Capitalism has no time for morals, that's just not reality. You wanted reality, that's why you got married. That's why you took that broker job, right? I mean, I don't think I could settle down like that."

"Love makes you do things you swore you'd never do. Love is LSD."

"What?"

"Loyalty, Sacrifice and Discipline."

"The startup's gone, the application's gone, so …"

"There's more…" Devon said.

Joshua tossed the empty espresso cup into the waste bin and picking up an energy drink.

"Do you really need that?" Devon asked.

"It's a sickness," Joshua said opening the small can and taking an intentionally loud sip. "Did you really travel the whole planet in six months, with no money, chased by those things?"

"That's a story for another time…"

"That's a story for right now!" Joshua said.

"I wasn't because of anything noble. I was running the same as you, only faster."

"At least you knew what you were running from." Joshua said as he fluffed his pillows.

"I have seen the sea change from morning to night." Devon began. "I have been one thousand feet underwater in the vastness of the undulating nothing. I have seen the most amazing creatures. I saw

Octopi with fins in miles upon miles of quiet, solitude. My craft has been chauffeured by dolphins.

"I have been places where birds seem to soar for weeks and volcanoes taller than Everest rise from the ocean bed, but still far from the sun's power. Their eruptions shake the planet, heat water and cause the winds of the Earth to circulate.

"I have inhaled salt air, marveled at shoals of fish. I have paid enough attention to know that the ocean and the sky are but inverted and that we do not walk, but are one of the many creatures that swim through the air.

"I have witnessed Shearwater birds swim sixty feet underwater and then take off and fly through the sky. I have seen creatures in the waves that defy explaining. I have silently viewed the Coral Triangle. I have experienced the ruggedness of the Azores, the cold of Ellesmere and the isolation of Tristan da Cunha. I have swung on vines in the rainforest and traveled the Gobo and Sahara Deserts.

"I've been in the middle of an all out war and I have won battles by simply showing up. I have survived in bottomless caverns. I have seen cathedrals so beautiful another language would need to be created just to describe them. I have had discussions with the most brilliant minds on the planets. I have even befriended a Bengal tiger and I believe that there is a purpose for all this."

"A tiger… That's quite a journey." Joshua said looking through his crates. "Joshua turned and put the energy drink down. Joshua suddenly seemed sad. "As amazing as all of this is and it is amazing, it still doesn't explain why you are here now?"

"I'm here because; it's time to stop running."

CHAPTER 3

The past crept in on Devon like steam moving up a mirror. Devon could smell his wife's lasagna as he moved around the storeroom. Joshua's voice faded out of Devon's mind. Devon's mind took him to the nightmare.

In the nightmare Devon could feel his wife's warm cheek, he could smell her scent. The lasagna slightly burned around the edges comforted him. In the nightmare Devon happily interacted with his dead family, like one would in temporal lobe hallucinations.

He wanted to live there, until these dreams became heart stopping, bone crushing, blood dripping, gut-wrenching nightmares. Devon took one more look around his mind before Joshua's voice rushed back into his ears.

"I'm still trying to wrap my brain around all of this..." Joshua said.

"I start at the new beginning..." Devon said recalling the events that had lead to all of this.

"By all means," Joshua said sitting down.

"Six months ago, I stumbled across a plain looking unmarked package in the bushes outside my front door. Inside that package were those stylish high tech glasses. I turned the glasses on at lunchtime and two huge men seemed to appear in the courtyard. I overlooked this. I finished eating and went back to my office..." Devon said recalling the nightmare he was presently trapped inside of.

As Devon drove home, he put on the device so that he could call his wife. He uttered the phrase, "Call Sweetheart." A few seconds later, the rural landscape began to change, the sky darkened. Shrubs began whipping around the road, Devon's eyes tightened as he and his wife spoke.

"I have something special for you this evening," Sarah said gifting him with a smile on his eyepiece. "Is that right?" Devon said.

As Devon sped down the two lane road, the tall trees began to sway, and from those trees, two dark, tall, well dressed men descended into his path. Devon swerved the car, barely missing the two gentlemen; he turned his head, to yell, "Lunatics!"

"...is everything alright?" Sarah said through the device.

"Yeah...the weather is getting weird," Devon said.

Two miles down the same road, two men emerged again from funnel clouds into his path. This time, Devon pressed down hard on the brakes, the car screeched to a halt. With the motor still purring, the two men approached Devon. Earlier, at lunchtime, when he saw them in the courtyard, he didn't notice their faint halo, now he did.

Devon couldn't make out the red symbols that moved along their clothing and the device's facial recognition gave him nothing.

"Devon...Devon...are you there?" Sarah's voice whispered into his earpiece.

When Devon pressed the floating 'End call' symbol the men faded away in a visual ripple. The running engine kept pace with his heart. He removed the device and stared off into the distance. Somehow this incident and the ripple in the square were related. Devon exhaled hard and checked his head to see if he were running a fever.

He placed the device in the backseat, tightly gripped the steering wheel, pressed down hard on the accelerator, and continued home. Once home he hurried inside, leaving the device in his car.

"Baby, are you alright?" Sarah said when he came through the door.

"Yeah, there was just something strange in the road. I'm fine."

Sarah hugged him tightly; she could tell that he was troubled. Brianna ran over and held onto his knees until he reached down and picked her up.

"Da-dee's home..." Brianna said as night fell and cold descended on the Heathrow's, fairly secluded, three bedroom house. Devon washed the dishes, emptied the trash and then he sat in his car trying to make sense of these vivid hallucinations. Devon took the wrapper off a small pastry and lit an awful smelling cigar.

"It must be vacation time," Devon sighed. Just then, the device in the backseat began to hum. The sound froze Devon. He slowly looked into the rearview mirror. He could see the powerful green illumination as vibrations cause the device to dance on the seat. Devon grabbed it, put it on and quietly said, "Hello?"

"They are more than you'd imagine..." a harsh voice said through the device. Devon listened with growing horror, not at what the voice was saying but at its grinding emptiness. It wasn't a machine generated voice; it wasn't a human voice either

Devon pressed the end button and sank into his seat. He cupped his head with his left hand in frustration. The wind began to whip around the Heathrow's home. Caller ID on the device gave him locations from Guatemala to Siberia. Devon sat back and looked out the window of his car toward his house. He noticed two large black crows perched on his stucco roof. The hum of the device once again shattered the night's silence.

Devon touched the device, and yelled, "Who the hell is this!"

"Them are more than you'd imagine," the harsh voice said.

"Them...who is them?"

"Look up," the voice echoed.

Devon's eyes panned up to the roof of his house where he saw the crows. He could now make out the form of two well dressed men gazing down at him, their silver eyes cut through the darkness.

"Them..." the voice on the device cracked.

The two men stood up and dropped down to the ground without so as much as a thud. Cold air vapor bellowed from their mouths as they approached him.

"... and you know the rest," Devon said wiping his eyes, his thoughts returning to the room with Joshua. "It wasn't until later that I realized the glasses were meant for Sarah."

Joshua fumbled with the glasses as he picked them up. "These were for your Sarah?"

"Whoa...wait...wait...d...do... don't turn it on. I told you they are everywhere," Devon said emphatically.

"Why Sarah?"

"Remember that bio-chemistry class I accidently enrolled in... that's how we met. She lectured the class on pyrosequencing. She worked for the Whitman Foundation." Devon said sighing. "Sarah was always better at figuring out things that I was, she would have had answers to all of this by now."

"She really lucked down with you..."

"She saw things in me I didn't see in myself. I didn't deserve her. I only dated two women in college, that lying, soul-sucking, psychotic, sex kitten, meat grinder in a poodle skirt Brandie Randolph and Sarah Macintosh."

"You dated more than two women in college..."

"True, but no one else is worth mentioning. Sarah was the best instinct I have ever had in my whole life."

Who exactly are Them?"

"These beings have studied and observed us through the gulf of matter. For decades, centuries and millenniums, these beings have listened to our prayers, our hopes, and our dreams. They have walked side by side with us."

"That's not so bad…"

"Myths were created around the interactions between our two kinds. Middle Earth does exist. Winged fire breathing creatures do roam the plains. Leviathans lurk the depths and there are many things that go bump in the night…"

"….that's not so good…"

"These beings use energy to create happenings here that are part of their mission."

"Happenings…"

"Happenings are events that sometimes take a destructive form and other times they are seen as coincidence or luck but are all part of a larger mission. Throughout history sometimes these happenings, were called witchcraft and other times they were called miracles. The otherworlds were not aware people prayed, hoped and dreamed for all the wrong things.

"These beings were with us through two evolutionary shifts, an ice age and countless world wars, but now our kinds are at odds."

"So, get governments involved."

"I forgot to mention that these otherworlders can't be seen."

"They can't be seen… I saw that demon blow my door off," Joshua said with a smirk on his face.

"You had the Whitman glasses on, so you were able to see them. They exist in a dark matter Earth that is superimposed over this one. They can enter this plane through passageways called rifts. These rifts are usually near large radiation energy blooms. The more we experiment with radiation, the more entry points are created.

"Their facial disfigurement is the result of radiation from going through these rifts. When an otherworlder goes through one of these doorways they absorb energy. They use this energy to complete their mission and then they return to their side. Their strength diminishes slowly the longer they are out of their world. The radiation they absorb also causes the silver tint in their eyes."

"I saw that."

"They have what you and I would call honor, only it's not a word or a phrase to be put on a t-shirt. The males wear fitted trench coats, a uniform emblazoned with lighted chevrons. These lighted chevrons designate their abilities."

"Abilities?"

"The Happenings, remember. Among other things they can create or enhance natural disasters."

"And that's their mission?"

"Unclear..."

"So we check the weather channels and avoid places where natural disasters occur. I assume they use natural disasters as cover."

"They do, but they can also create fires and explosions. They can briefly change the weather, change a mind or cause an accident."

"So there is no way to avoid them..."

"Not when you can't see them."

"But you can...right?"

"One of these beings altered me, to save my life. The side effect of this altered was that I am evolving. I am becoming stronger, smarter. When these beings realized I could see them, they came after me and that's how my family was killed. They murdered my family. They destroyed your condo. Everywhere I went, Them weren't far behind."

"So that's why you disappeared? The one you drove away from me... you said those are different."

"The females are smaller. They can use the energy to create a breeze that passes through a room to scatter papers about. They can randomly knock a book from a table, cut off a television or caused a faucet to leak."

"So they can be around anytime?"

"Yes."

"And they see everything?"

"Yes."

"Even when I'm in the bathroom?"

"I suppose."

"Or whatever I might be doing under the covers in my bed in the middle of the night because I haven't been with a woman in a while..."

"Who's to say they weren't causing you to do it," Devon said with stifled laughter.

"See...you made it gross."

"No, you made it gross."

"The females have the same odd shaped head and silver glowing eyes as the males, but they aren't as grotesque," Devon said.

"That's comforting..."

"The human mind has different frequencies during the day. When people sleep it is easier for them to engage and implant suggestions, thoughts and ideas."

"So they're like guardian angels?"

"They can make you go right when you were going to go left. Their missions are not always successful because the human mind is complex. The females may seem less destructive, but they are perhaps more dangerous."

"So we stay away from nuclear sites, right?"

"Nuclear devices have been used and tested all over the world, even in the atmosphere. They mostly use cell phone towers..."

Joshua looked at his cell phone and gulped hard. He stood up, walked over to the smartphone and turned it off.

"Portable Babel towers," Devon muttered.

"So we've invited our enemy right next to us," Joshua said lowering his voice. "Can our statespeople reason with these beings, can't you?"

"Humans aren't ready to see the connections between people, actions and policies. It is hard for people to accept that there are powers outside of their control that dictate actions. The unknown frightens them."

"It frightens me." Joshua responded. "So what's their problem?"

"They hate our kind."

"Why?"

"In their world, our nuclear testing rains down radiation on their people... many have died."

"Oh, my."

"What we have done has caused death, mutations and other horrors. Some days they can't be outside unshielded, other days their eyes burn even while indoors. Their children are born deformed. For decades they didn't know we were responsible. Now they curse our very existence every time their skin inflames, flakes or peels."

"I can see how that would be a problem. So apologize. Did you tell them we're sorry and that we'll fix this?"

"Yes."

"And?"

"They threatened all of humanity."

The blood vessels in Joshua's eyes swelled as his mouth fired off questions: What are they made of? How do they do what they do? Have you fought one of them? Joshua was no longer scared of Devon. The only thing that would satisfy Joshua burning questions was the truth.

"This is going to be a long night." Devon sighed. "Joshua the truth isn't pretty. It took me so long to approach you because I had to synthesize a particular substance and that took months."

"What substance?"

"Hypernium."

"What's that?"

"A substance created by Doctor Noah Whitman, a scientist formerly employed by the North American government."

"The guy who made the glasses?"

"Yes."

"So what's he doing now?"

"He's dead."

"Otherworlders…right."

"A single strand of Hypernium appears flexible; however, as you bend it the stronger it feels. The more molecules there are, the stronger it becomes. In its solid state Hypernium is nearly impervious. This is the substance that is within me."

"So you have more?"

"I do."

"You said you have been a surgeon?"

"In several countries," Devon said, pulling out sunglasses he had created. "These glasses are embedded with infrared lights. This creates noise around the eyes and nose." Devon put on the sunglasses, "Take some pictures of me."

Joshua grabbed his smartphone, turned it on and took several pictures of Devon. The images were all distorted. After Joshua managed to close his mouth, he said, "You know how much money we can make from this?"

"There's more…" Devon said.

Joshua's eyes widen further and then Devon showed him retro-reflective tactical goggles, which had a heads-up display. Devon pulled a red umbrella out of his backpack and handed it to Joshua. Joshua got up and twirled the umbrella. Around the edges LED lights turned on as it spun. "This confuses the most advanced surveillance tracking systems," Devon said.

Devon collapsed the umbrella and pointed to his clothes. "I can regulate my body temperature. My pants, shirt and sweatshirt disperses body heat this shields me from thermal imaging. I called it Stealthware."

From the top of his backpack, Devon pulled out a smaller container and opened it, "Surveillance dust and thermite bombs," he said. Devon put down a green soda can size device next to Joshua, "This is an MRI device."

From the bottom of his backpack, Devon produced two flat black devices and he attached them together with a snap, "This is my favorite... the polymer replicator." Joshua touched the device, he held it. It wasn't heavy and it was smaller than a high-end handheld computer.

"I created my ReActive Electro polymer, R.E.A.P, with that," Devon said proudly. REAP is flexible, extremely strong and becomes translucent when an electric current passes through it. I put it on everything, like my motorcycle helmet."

"Motorcycle... You have a motorcycle?"

"Yes."

"Aren't you afraid you'll be attacked by them?"

"Not anymore. I still have to be careful not to draw too much attention to myself."

"So you made all of these?"

"Most of it, some I acquired in other ways. There is something else…" Devon said. Devon pointed to the TV on the wall and a small spark of electricity jumped from his hand. The TV turned on and Joshua fell down on the edge of his bed with his mouth open. After two minutes of silence, Devon caused another spark to jump from his hand and the TV went off.

"You know I have some ideas," Joshua said looking at Devon.

The items Devon presented looked like the contents of a buried treasure chest to Joshua. Joshua smiled as he sat among the items like a kid who had just opened his Christmas presents.

"You always do," Devon said. "If you have time, I'd like to show you something."

"Time is the one thing I have."

"Good, I hope you're hungry because I made lasagna, put on something warm."

CHAPTER 4

Outside the church is where Devon would introduce Joshua to his second favorite thing. Joshua hurriedly stomped up the stairs. Devon zipped up his sleek orange outfit; it was close to noon.

"What in the world is this?" Joshua said as Devon mounted a titanium, carbon fiber, aerospace grade steel, one-fourth ton rolling vibration with wheels.

"The Soul Stirrer," Devon said with a smile. He patted the motorcycle like it was a family pet.

The Soul Stirrer was a twenty inch, three hundred millimeter tire, water cooled hybrid twin engine motorcycle. It ran off lithium-ion batteries, JP-8 jet fuel, propane or olive oil. The aluminum-magnesium tubing of the bike's frame routed the exhaust. The Soul-Stirrer was quieter than most conversations.

This bike covered larger distances and handled off road as easily as it did the street. Its max speed registered as a time of day. When Devon rode at these speeds his eyes strained to see the centerline. He was always trying to provide a margin to test his reflexes.

At night, when things got dangerous on the road, he created a small electric current to activate the bike's electroluminescent yellow pin striping. The Kevlar yellow and ballistic black motorcycle had no auto drive and no networked computer; it was safer that way.

Devon didn't cool it down on curves when he rode towards the horizon, through the valleys and around farm country. He explored places where the road rose through unpopulated woodlands and down through the gaps in the hills. Devon's memory usually faded along the roads that flanked the mountains, if not there, the rivers that crept alongside canyons produced amnesia.

On the Soul Stirrer, Devon could travel from Los Angeles to New York in twenty four hours. There was nothing like the sun at his back and the wind in his face, as he tore down a road. On windy days sand blows across the highways, appearing as drifts as thick as an oil slick.

Devon pushed the needle towards one twenty, one forty, one fifty. At these speeds, even with his improved hearing, the only sound was the dull roar floating back from the mufflers.

Devon's steel horse chewed up mile after mile of gravel, stone and mud roads equally. Devon rode through the rain, the wind, and the heat as he let the beast wind out. Devon bent dangerously over curves and rolling hills and all of it—breathtaking.

"Get on," Devon said handing Joshua a helmet.

Joshua put on the helmet and got on the back of the motorcycle. Devon shifted gears and in thirty minutes they were out of the city. In two hours they were northwest of the state. They rode half the night to a rundown out of the way town. Devon parked at a motel in the middle of the town. Devon looked at Joshua as he got off the motorcycle.

"I don't have any questions," Joshua said. There was something about the stillness of the moment. They walked into the hotel and then to the fire escape. They climbed four flights up the ladder towards to the roof. Devon used his hand to break the roof access lock.

"You just go around breaking things?" Joshua said incredulously.

"I always pay for them. I brought you here so that you understand what I have been doing. Now sit here and watch that building across the street through these," Devon said handing Joshua some binoculars. Devon pulled out a dagger and checked three guns before putting them into holsters.

"That building there?" Joshua gulped. Devon sheathed his dagger and nodded.

As Joshua picked up the binoculars, Devon jumped off the roof. Joshua ran to the edge of the roof and looked down. He saw Devon quickly run into the building. Joshua's heavy breathing was the only sound heard.

The sun started to fade as Joshua anxiously looked through the binoculars. He looked at the building as his eyes searched for Devon. He saw nothing. He put the binoculars down and rubbed his face.

Once again, he looked at the four-story building, searching for his friend. He brought the field glasses into focus and there was Devon on the bottom floor, issuing an overhand left to an unknown foe, followed by a front dropkick. Devon skillfully flipped a small shiny blade from hand to hand while taking on three other attackers in the dimly lit tan hallways.

Devon kicked a goon against the door of an apartment, followed by a flying knee which knocked him through the door. He followed this with a backhanded uppercut shot to the head to the other goon inside the room, rendering them incapable of retaliating. There were over a dozen more hostiles in front of him.

Joshua looked though the building and blinked rapidly, he couldn't believe what he was seeing. This was more interesting than watching the white wine drunks show up for Sunday matinee church. Each time Joshua put the binoculars down to wipe his eyes, it was as if he had tapped the refresh button as the attacks renewed.

This hooligan's mistake was trying to surprise Devon. His entire point of view was dominated by Devon's fist. It landed on his jaw with a huge thud. Devon's force was 6'2" 210 pounds multiplied by how fast his legs and arms reached a destination. Devon wasn't using his full force; he was measured with his strikes.

Joshua grimaced as a blazing roundhouse from Devon sent an assailant failing down the dirty hallway. Devon stepped on to the second floor of the building and slammed his foot into this gunman's rib cage.

This guy was well trained. He refused to go down; another kick from Devon snapped his ribs and he doubled over as pain exploded through him. Devon simply pushed him over.

Over the last six months, Devon had fought through several slurred speech masses that may have been otherworld-aided, but more often than not they were full of alcohol. He learned a lot; his attention to detail and observations were unrivaled.

Spatial physics, probability calculations, coupled with his knowledge of human abilities, limitations, and movements created forethought. He could see what was coming before it came. This allowed Devon to be a whirlwind of movement too fast for the eye to follow.

This building teamed with highly skilled defenders. He could hear them loading their weapons through the wall. Devon shot a back kick into this professional trouble maker's midsection with so much force that he slid on the floor to the end of the hallway. His body flopped over with a wet, fleshy thud as it hit against the wall.

Another assailant fired a fist into Devon's side, this fighter recoiled his hand as if he had hit a bag full of sand. Devon crashed a terrific right cross against the attacker's chin, followed by an uppercut to the liver of the gunman behind him.

On the third floor, Devon avoided a brutal combination from a highly skilled assailant. Before the attacker could bring his hands up to defend, Devon drove his shoulder into the guy's chest, slamming him into the wall, where he landed a dozen punches.

Devon opened a door and motioned with his hands. A dozen bruised and battered occupants ran out of the room and down the hall. Devon stopped one and presented them a handful of cash, a map and pointed down the hallway toward the exit. They didn't look back.

There were sparks and then the lights went out, leaving the building dark. Devon ran his hand along walls to determine how many people were inside a room before he reached through a wall to exact justice. Inside the room, flashlight beams and several shaky red dots scanned the area; as the room's occupants tried to avoid this black and orange leather clad ghost.

Devon descended from the ceiling to deliver a palm strike to the nose, which exploded, erupting blood. A kick sent a two hundred and forty pound sack of meat and bone through the thin wall that divided rooms. The remaining roughnecks jumped to fight and one by one they were laid out in a similar fashion.

On the fourth floor, the red emergency light cut through the darkness. Two bruisers aimed guns at him. They fired, they missed. Their bullets only raked the walls. Devon ran up the wall and from above them he twisted the guns from their hands. He threw the weapons at the henchman trying to escape out the door. The guns hit him in the head knocking him out.

Devon stood there among the moaning, as dropped flashlights slowly rocked to a stop. Devon climbed out of the window, up the wall and leaped from one rooftop ridge to another.

Joshua was terrified by what he had just seen. He went down the fire escape as quickly as he could and tried to keep up with Devon, but Devon was nowhere to be found. The approaching sirens caused Joshua to panic more and he went back to the motel. When he rounded the corner, he saw Devon sitting on the motorcycle.

"So…so this is what you do?" Joshua said trying to catch his breath.

"I don't enjoy hurting people. I made sure that no one died. The authorities have tried to shut these traffickers down, but they are well connected and well financed. Whenever they get compromised they easily change locations and set up shop somewhere else.

"I have helped from a distance, but still their operation grew, so tonight I acted. Some people got hurt, others will be charged but the organization is in shambles. Those that were abused will now have a chance. Sometimes, terrible things have to be done," Devon said holding out the helmet and motioning for him to get on the motorcycle.

"So, you are just some kind of uncaped crusader…" Joshua said putting on the helmet before he hopped on the bike.

Six hours and four states later, it persistently rained on Red Level, Florida, a small coastal town. What was once thought to be a just a storm had turned into a hurricane. When they got off the motorcycle, they were drenched. Devon smiled and walked across the street as traffic lights violently swayed. Joshua put the Whitman glasses on.

The moment Joshua saw Hurricane land in the middle of town; a seldom seen fear stirred inside of him. It was the confused kind of fear a just born baby experiences when they see indescribable shadows and hear indistinguishable sounds, monstrously amplified by hopelessness.

The destruction perpetrated by these otherworlders was secondary to lacking the skills to explain what he was seeing.

"So th, tha, that's Them..." a frightening Joshua uttered as he sought shelter beneath a store awning.

"That's Them." Devon responded and he walked into the street.

Hurricane was in the middle of the swirling winds, his arms outspread as drops of water flew sideways around him. Hurricane's silver ringed eyes slowly turned to Devon. A cold chill ran down Joshua's spine and left his body. Joshua dove onto the ground as wind punched Devon in the face, knocking him out of his shoes. Joshua got up and ran at fear-for-my-life speed, but he was still being pushed backward by the winds.

The wind chevrons on Hurricane's coat illuminated and then a surge of water came. A frigid wave took away a hundred people as Joshua propped himself against what looked to be the oldest building in the city. When the wave subsided, Joshua trudged down the street in chest high water.

Joshua picked up a little boy clinging to broken furniture and went inside the nearest building. They went up to the third floor with the boy. Moans drifted up from the floor below them, the boy refused to let go of Joshua's hand.

After the first wave subsided, Joshua could see the dead and injured floating. The second wave swept everything away, even the moans. Roofs were full of earth, felled trees, boats, belongings and corpses. The boy went to sleep and Joshua covered him.

A wet and shaking Joshua took off the glass and went downstairs where a golden eyed Devon waited. They got into a small boat that had floated four miles inland. Every time a floating body bumped the boat, Joshua's stomach emptied. Devon paddled through the town, lifting bodies into the boat and Joshua covered them. They had filled three boats with bodies before the waters subsided.

In the muddy street, people reemerged, and then a building exploded. A flaming pole crashed down dragging wires to the pavement. Bodies were flying through the air. A woman ran towards them, where her clothing was been torn away, Joshua could see the pattern of her dress burned into her skin.

Closer to Joshua, a man and a woman had smudged and scorched faces. People reached out to him. Joshua's eyes turned to their hands, where strips of bloody skin hung like gloves turned inside out A panicked Joshua ran blindly as cries filled his ears. Dust filled the air and lungs, as disoriented people stumbled past him—Joshua could only look away.

The Soul Stirrer was partially buried in the mud but was unharmed. It took them ten minutes to clean it. They took one last look at the devastated city before Devon throttle the engine and they disappeared into the night.

They made their way to Fort Calhoun, Nebraska. This was a town that could be walked from end to end in ten minutes. As they walked through the town the landscape grew darker and the sky became erratic. An otherworlder floated over some buildings and landed in the middle of town.

Joshua put on the glasses as Devon made a makeshift barrier out of large cinderblocks. Joshua's bubble of sarcasm, pretense and indifference was shattered immediately the moment Tornado's feet touched the ground. He directly took cover behind this barrier.

Tornado's eyes glowed silver and winds whipped around him as he moved his hands back and forth. He summoned a funnel cloud down from the sky. A twister quickly formed and sucked debris half a mile up.

Loud, monstrous, two hundred miles per hour winds tossed vehicles a hundred feet away. Tornado caused wind to pretzel telephone poles and peeled away highway asphalt. Tornado commanded walls of air to punch houses, uppercut trees and slam buildings. The grocery store, the gas stations and the school were gone in a matter of seconds.

Joshua looked away for a moment and then he turned back to the continuing horror. Devon slowly walked through the destruction. He ducked flying vehicles and other items that would be found later somewhere in the woods. There were unmoving bodies lying in the red mud as the earth tightly hugged those that had fallen.

Tornado's eyes lost their glow and the funnel cloud started to disappear. As the winds died Tornado looked at Devon and grunted, and then he jumped over a building and was gone. The tornado had ripped several houses off their foundation and left two miles of destruction. Joshua's hand shook as he took off the glasses. He cautiously came out of his hiding place and joined Devon as he walked through the destroyed town.

In the distance, explosions from propane tanks were the backdrop to the toxins from household chemical mixing into waterways. Crying people walked through the broken town picking up their belongings amongst the shredded wood. Another explosion rocked a nearby building, forcing Devon and Joshua to the ground.

Devon recovered immediately. Joshua's ears were ringing, his lungs refilled after five seconds of silence. The returning noise sounded like a shredded bow being drawn slowly over the untuned strings of a broken violin.

The building the explosion came from was still standing; damage to the structure was minimal. Joshua lay on the ground wishing he was somewhere else as the winds lightly swirled above him. Devon picked up Joshua and pushed him towards the door of the building. Devon kicked what was left the door open and Joshua followed Devon inside.

"What is this place?" Joshua asked.

"An office building of some kind," Devon said, as they made their way through offices. In the fourth office on the left, there was a small black device sitting on a desk. It was making a sizzling sound.

"Hmmm," Devon said walking over to the device.

"What it is?" Joshua wondered out loud.

Devon got closer to the device and moved the components around.

"Looks like an advanced electromagnetic pulse device."

Joshua's foot hit something on the floor. A man lay face down on the floor. Joshua jumped back and immediately threw up. "Is that man dead?" Joshua said pointing to the body. Devon nodded and continued to examine the device.

"You can't just sit still while these things wreak havoc…" Joshua said, his voice pitching towards panic.

"I can and I will." Devon responded.

Joshua went into the hallway were another man lay on the floor. Joshua hoped the figure lying on the ground was asleep. Joshua knelt beside the body. There wasn't much left of his face and the remaining skin was covered by burn marks.

The man's pelvic area had been crushed. His chest exploded. His legs were fused together, in a half melted way. Joshua backed up against the wall and threw up again.

Joshua eyed Devon with a nervous glance. Devon looked like he was standing guard as if he expected something or someone to come back. The look on Joshua's face said what his mouth couldn't.

"It was Them."

Devon moved the light from his flashlight to the wall, just above Joshua, where blood had splattered.

"I think we should go," Devon said.

"What are we even talking about this for?" Joshua said, already heading toward the exit. Outside a cell phone tower had collapsed on the roadway.

Joshua's reality had been turned upside down. People say the villains are the Americans, the Chinese, the Russian, the Iranians, even the Canadians, they never say it was Them. People say things like, "The snow caused the wreck", "The rising water damaged the house", "The schedule was altered due to rain" and "The cold air killed." People said these things unaware of just how accurate their words were.

As Devon and Joshua headed to the outskirts of the city they didn't speak. Joshua watched Devon clean and double checked the Soul Stirrer.

"Are you all right?"

"Yeah… so, another version of this Earth exists and it overlaps and occupies the same region of time and space simultaneously, just like a quantum state."

"It is a world nearly identical to this one. The quantum forces responsible for creating this shared existence are also responsible for causing quantum interactions between our worlds. "

"Just so that we are on the same page… This system is a computer program."

"The System is not a computer program it's more than that. The System is without form. Every moment, every breath contains a choice. But life is imperfect. We make the wrong choice. Were it not for our minds we would end up in a state of perpetual regret."

It's terrifying enough to consider that every thought we have, every choice we could possibly make, branches off into a new world and now we have to deal with these things…"

"Things can get a whole lot worse."

"So not only are we not alone in the universe, we are overmatched in every way and you want me to volunteer to save humanity?" Joshua said finally.

"You could say that."

"Will it hurt?"

"It will."

"How much pain are we talking about?"

Devon finished wiping off his motorcycle and said, "Imagine laughter being taken out of everything, that kind of pain. You have a choice. Every day, every minute and every second I have to live with what I did. I lost my family because of it."

Joshua could see that Devon was in a sadder state. "Devon, you're too hard on yourself. You're blaming yourself for things that were beyond your control."

"That's exactly what Prime said," Devon responded.

CHAPTER 5

"Where to now?" Joshua said.

"That's the question, isn't it...the now...what about now. If we take the road to the right, you go back to fixing computer problems and you never speak of any of this again." Devon responded.

"And the road to the left... Adventure?"

"That's a road of sacrificing ego and pride for the greater good. Down that road is a mission to save humanity at any cost. Down that road things will get ugly before they get beautiful. Down that road there is no private sector, no awards ceremony and no retirement plan. Down that road things are always harder than you think they are going to be.

"The long road to the left is where you get bathed in a whole new world of pain and discovery." Devon said.

"This is some sales job you are doing here," Joshua said.

While they spoke, this Nebraskan city had changed from day to night. The temperature dropped to the mid 50s. Joshua respected Devon but his reality had changed.

The things these otherworlders could do didn't fit the laws of physics; Them were never supposed to be in this world. Joshua saw their size and the scale of their wrongness. Could he just go back to the way things were yesterday?

The choice that loomed before him caused his hands to shake. The gold of Devon's eyes was gone but it was clear that Devon was more than man. Joshua watched anxiously as Devon prepared the Soul Stirrer for departure.

"It was important that I tell you these things." Devon said. "It was important for you to see these things. This is not something to undertake lightly. We can go to the right and you can go back to recording your Shakespearean readings of TV show theme songs."

"They're dramatic readings, Gilligan's Island is my most viewed video," Joshua sighed.

"I just want you to understand." Devon said.

"So you can train me and we can go to the other side and stop the end of the world… and we're doing this together….right"

"Right…"

"I'll take the road to the left."

Devon slowly nodded and gave Joshua his helmet.

"Do we get to wear uniforms? I want a red eye mask," Joshua said getting on the motorcycle.

"No," Devon said. He throttled the engine and they went down the left road. Joshua held on tightly as Devon shifted into the future. The vibration of the bike relaxed Joshua and he began to put the day's events behind him. Devon cut off the bike's glowing yellow striping and rode two states northwest in the dark.

Joshua woke up somewhere near the mountain range. They were north of Malmstrom Air Force Base in Montana. Devon drove the Soul Stirrer, right into the thick brush. This brush-lined path led to the side of the mountain. Devon got the bike off and walked up to side of the mountain. When Devon got closer, the camouflaged door slid open.

"So you've been here before?" Joshua said getting off the bike.

Devon nodded, and they slowly entered the underground laboratory. This place is where Devon had been changed. Devon had been to this base before; he had to make sure that he wasn't crazy. He also had to use the particle accelerator to create more Hypernium.

Hypernium has an affinity for red blood cells, which quickly deposit it into the body's tissues, where it bonds to the bone and becomes bone. It wouldn't register it as metal.

Joshua passed the personality assessment protocols and Devon analyzed the data from each workup, every examination showed green Devon shined a penlight into Joshua's pupils.

"There is a lot for us to go over and not enough time to go over it," Devon said turning the lab's filtered air on.

"We are doing this together, right?" Joshua nervously said looking up at the empty viewing gallery. The room smelled stale, sterile. Joshua put on a white hospital gown and sat on the operating table. The table was cold, hard and unforgiving.

"You might feel like you are dying." Devon said.

"Might?"

"I haven't done this before, but I know how it goes. It's not too late to change your mind."

"Humanity needs me, right? I saw what Tornado and Hurricane did. You are going to need a lot of help to stop them,"

Devon organized the surgical tools on the tray and prepared to put Joshua under for the procedure.

"Don't put me under," Joshua quickly said.

"The pain, remember?"

"I don't want to wake up changed. If you wanted to spare me something, it should have been the night full of Wilhelm Screams." Joshua said his stomach still turning from the images.

The intensity of florescent operating lights caused Joshua to squint. He turned his head to shield his eyes. Devon put on a surgical mask and pulled green gloves over his hands. He injected a liquid into his friend's side for the pain.

A steady, obnoxious beep rifled through the darkness over the movement of forceps, clamps, scalpels and retractors. Devon tried not to alarm the patient, but the patient was alarmed. In between beeps, Joshua wondered if he would survive the procedure. He flinched as incisions were made to his sides and legs.

The margin for of error was narrow; the balance between success and failure was precarious. The most minuscule hesitation in adding Hypernium could spell disaster. Nerve irritation caused Joshua's eyelids and facial muscles to twitch.

A wave of excruciating pain ran through his body but even that was muffled by curiosity. Devon snapped joints into place, reset ankles and lassoed his spine into alignment. No traced of a limp would remain. Devon drew black marks where he would make adjustments.

Joshua felt raw. He closed his eyes and took four long measured breaths, holding each in for a five-count before letting it out. "I'm not dead...but I feel like it," he said through slurred speech.

Devon stepped into the light and lifted a syringe filled with an effervescent green liquid. The syringe and the unknown substance caused Joshua's eyes to dart around the room looking for a way to escape. Looking into his surgeon's face, Joshua couldn't tell if he was angry or not.

A large syringe of full spectrum antibiotics and pain killers was slid into Joshua's right thigh and its contents slowly injected. Joshua felt something that could best be described as pain but was something more than pain. Joshua winced as the warmth moved throughout his body and the pain became a memory.

Hypernium is liquid as long as the temperature is kept at twelve hundred degrees Fahrenheit. Once the temperature is reduced, there is a ten minute window, where the metal can be poured and molded.

Once it cools it cannot be manipulated further, even in temperatures beyond its melting point. Hypernium occupied a spot on the periodic table that has yet to be determined.

"Hypernium crystallizes with no observable molecular patterns," Devon said as he began to operate. "Whitman knew his research would be used in the building of military machines, so he didn't turn it over to the government. There isn't much of it left."

"How did this Whitman die?"

"You don't want to know."

Joshua strained his neck to see the tools that Devon was using. Devon was careful not to show him these tools. Joshua should have been unconscious, but he wanted to hear more. Devon placed a clear piping tube into Joshua's side.

"Them are dark matter beings that can only be seen with a subflux disturbance. This disturbance is created from the radiation of a rift. The Hypernium allows me to engage with them. The Whitman glasses produce a small sub-flux disturbance."

The electronic monitor beeped softly in the darkness. Joshua's body swelled as the Hypernium worked its way through his blood vessels. The operating table read the patient's vitals as the surgeon shifted instruments on the operating tray.

"Is this how you were changed?" Joshua asked.

"My legs and arms were broken and my spine was cracked. Dying is not something you want to experience," Devon said, his hand hovering over the instruments. Joshua gulped hard and kept his eyes straight ahead. The sound of the instruments struck Joshua with panic. Not the panic of fear, but the general kind of panic that is present when faced with uncertainty.

Devon penetrated Joshua's left thigh with a large, glowing object and the room filled with steam. Joshua watched dark lines spreading underneath his skin as if it were cancer that quickly metastasized. He could feel the liquid forcing its way through his body.

"Oooooowww," Joshua said. He started to violently cough; he was choking. Devon had hit a nerve. He administered a second intravenous push for the pain.

"They call us OMB's," Devon continued.

"OMB's..." Joshua said still coughing.

"Other Matter Beings, sometimes they refer to us as human." Devon reached down and touched Joshua's arm. "Skin is durable; internally it is surrounded by tough and dense connective tissue. This will be your first line of defense."

The operating table beeped out Joshua's rising beta waves. His heart began to quickly pound, any faster as if it would explode. There was a lot of blood, but Devon continued to operate. Seeing gauzed soaked with his blood made Joshua to faint. Joshua quickly regained consciousness as Devon continued his story.

"The human body is designed to withstand certain tolerances, conditions. What I am doing will remove these constrictions. Three percent of the human body, the brain, uses twenty percent of the body's energy. Energy creates heat that the body uses for certain healing activities, neural transmitters and protein synthesis. These all require energy.

"Hypernium will modify your frame. This will free you from environmental impediments and increase energy synthesis. You will become smarter. Your cartilage, muscles and residual concussive damage will heal as you evolve.

"Avoiding bullets, bending metal and jumping across a street, still sounds incredible even after I've done it. Being impossibly strong can be a hassle. I have broken my share of faucets and doorknobs before I mastered using my strength. You will become more durable and your bones denser. The way you move will change, with increased speed seconds will extend." — Slice— Cut.

There was a sputtering sound as the final drips of fluid drained from its container and into Joshua's body. Devon continued to adjust Joshua. Devon finished the fluid transfer and removed the tubes from the patient. Joshua could see the steam and feel the heat. Joshua's pain threshold had been passed some time ago. Devon administered another intravenous push.

Joshua started to wheeze as the bone numbing liquid continued to flow. Devon gave him nitroglycerin to keep his arteries open. The voice of the operating table announced, 'Heart rate...not good.' Joshua's arm, neck and shoulders started to tingle and his chest constricted.

The Hypernium had reached Joshua's heart. His hands made fists so tight that his nails dug into his palms. His body violently shook and then he flat lined. A single deafening tone filled the room as Devon's eyes widened.

"I've killed my friend; I should have spent more time as a surgeon," Devon thought as he began chest compressions. "It has almost been a year since I was changed. It's been three months since I entered the outskirts of the rift and now, I am removing my best friend's hand."

Devon was always putting syringes into the chest of someone he didn't know. Joshua Dougan had to be brought back; there were no other sane choices. CPR wasn't working. Devon quietly said a prayer and the room dimmed as his hands began to glow with an electrical charge. He placed his hand on Joshua's chest. Zap, an electrical current passed into the patient. The heart rate monitor beeped softly, steadily.

Joshua inhaled violently. His neural scans resembled explosions in the sky. Joshua wrinkled his forehead underneath the intense light. Devon sighed heavily as he leaned against the operating table, his brow glistened. "Vital signs stable," the operating table's voice chimed.

Devon applied soft cybernetic patches to stimulate the patient's muscles. The epidermal patches eavesdropped on the language of his internal systems and whispered data to the floating monitors that chirped in the darkness.

Devon lifted a multi-spectral imaging device and scanned Joshua's body. The scan showed the bonding process was nearly complete. The swelling had gone down as Joshua's cells bonded with the foreign element. The reading from the scan made Devon's lips form something that could pass for a smile. Joshua could see and hear, but he couldn't move.

"Hypernium molecules are bonding with your bones and the calcium molecules in your blood. Here is what I know; our two dimensions are conjoined. They share properties such as gravity. They are sister worlds.

"Right now, we are surrounded by radiation. It's everywhere from the three-day dose in an x-ray to the three-year dose from an abdominal CT scan. Light itself is radiation, intense light can damage skin.

"Because of radiation cell phone towers were placed on mountains far away from people, but now these towers have become more and more common in the suburbs.

"Once on this side otherworlders utilize happenings, like landslides, tornados, floods, avalanches and freak downpours as part of their missions. When the moving ground reaches out and pulls someone in, when the wind drops a roof on someone, when a wave drags someone under; there is no answer to the question why?

"Female otherworlders move keys, lock and unlock doors, knock a book off a shelf and they can whisper into minds. They can't control thoughts, but over time they can change actions."

Joshua's face showed that he was exhausted, the bonding was over. His eyelids began to lower.

"You'll wake up to a different world." Devon said.

Joshua's eyelids covered his eyes and he rested. Devon cleaned the lab and took Joshua to his nearby hideaway to recover, a barn.

Three days passed before Joshua opened his eyes again. His mind was bombarded by 1's & 0's as light flooded into his eyes heavier than before. He saw Devon lifting bales of hay, moving shoeing equipment and pushing around a tractor. Joshua's heartbeat made a gong-like sound. Joshua's fever had broken, he moaned and drifted back to sleep.

The sound of water from a running faucet prompted Joshua to open his eyes. He saw Devon washing his hands in the sink. Dirty, dark beads of sweat raced down his arms. Devon's clothes were burned, the smell of fuel floated through the air. Through the mirror, Joshua saw Devon's face covered by black soot. Joshua's head still throbbed. The incoming light made him turn his face to the side.

"Is something on fire?" Joshua whispered.

"I was..."

Joshua gulped, half turned and went back to sleep. The next day Joshua was again bombarded by motion. His senses were overloaded by simple gusts of wind. Joshua was awake but he didn't open his eyes. He felt the clothes on his skin. He twitched at every sound. He reached down and touched his knee. He lay there, discovering that humans have far more than five senses.

Everything felt different, alien. He slowly opened his eyes. He was alone in the barn. It was dark; night had fallen. Every hair on his body tingled. His fingers glided over his legs, his waist, his stomach, his chest, his neck and his face.

His pulse was loud, but his panic was finally under control. Joshua bit into his lip to make sure he was alive. His excitement showed from underneath the blanket. Normally he would relieve himself and roll over. Joshua laid there until his excitement waned and he went back to sleep.

The squeal of wooden doors informed him that Devon had once again returned. Joshua had enough strength to sit up on the couch. "So, you just left me," Joshua said rubbing his eyes.

"It wasn't like you were going anywhere," Devon said handing him a cup of water. Devon helped Joshua clasp his fingers around the cup. Joshua sipped from the cup; much of the water escaped his mouth. He allowed the cup to fall to the floor.

"Basically, I have to relearn things I learned as a baby..."

"Start slow, things come back fast."

"How long was I out?"

"Four days."

"Four days?"

Joshua rubbed his eyes and examined his hands and arms for the dark lines. He pressed down on his legs and examined his wrist, his abdomen and his chest as he looked for any trace of the procedure.

"How do you feel?" Devon asked.

"My back hurts... My front hurts."

"What do you remember?"

"Not much..." Joshua said, clearing his throat. "I remember the operating room and then I found myself standing in a beautiful green forest. I looked out over pastures filled with flowers with trees, fields, animals and faceless people. Snow capped mountains were in the distance. There was mist rising from the surface of a nearby river as fish glided beneath the water. Colors were everywhere, yet everything was bathed in a white light, even the sky."

Joshua's body was recovering faster than his mind did from the operation. Joshua's worry extended beyond the cellular ink used to restore him. His vision was erratic. He tried to offset the effects by keeping his eyes closed. He didn't move until his head stopped spinning. When the visual randomness subsided, he tried to stand. Joshua stumbled and fell back onto the sofa.

"Crawl, until you can walk," Devon said.

Joshua shakily stood up. He slowly shuffled around the barn. His muscles burned and he groaned with each step. Joshua reached out and nothing was there. He tried to prevent himself from falling but he fell flat on his face and passed out.

Joshua opened his eyes and let out a loud moan. Devon picked him up and put him on the couch. He placed a steaming blue bowl of soup in front of him.

"Eat some soup." Devon said.

"Uuugh…" Joshua said, tasting the soup and wrinkling up his nose. "What is this?"

"Leek soup."

"It tastes like regret," Joshua said putting the bowl down.

"Eat to eat, not to critique," Devon said.

As Joshua put the bowl down, he noticed that a subtle blue wave danced across the back of his hand. Nerves shot through him as if he were a bouncing knee.

"What's happening?" Joshua asked.

The skin is the largest organ of the human body. A chemically inert, usually stable pigment known as melanin within skin cells and is responsible for the skin's color and shade. Melanin appears as a layered painting at the surface of the body and it easily bears dark or light colors.

Both Charles Darwin and Aristotle before him noted the color changing abilities of reptiles, octopus and certain fish. What just happened to Joshua would be considered drastic by any standard. Pigments inside Joshua's cells had begun to move.

This was a temporary rudimentary change in color and it was purely accidental. Humans have one class of pigment cell; Joshua's body was developing another.

"You will be able to change your skin tone a little," Devon responded.

"And you can do this?"

"I can."

Joshua reclined on the couch looking at his hands.

"I'll be back," Devon said, grabbing his coat and heading for the barn door.

"Can you bring me a double bacon cheeseburger?"

"Not a good idea."

"Come on," Joshua pleaded as Devon left the barn.

Devon was gone for less than an hour. When Devon returned, Joshua was walking around like one would imagine Frankenstein's monster would. Joshua moved fast to take the grease stained fast food bag from Devon's hands.

"Thanks. My favorite," Joshua said, as Devon went around the barn making erasing every trace of their presence.

Joshua sat down. In the lower right of his plate, he squeezed out the ketchup. He put the fries left upper. The cheeseburger was front and center. It took him three minutes to set this up. Joshua picked up the cheeseburger and dug his teeth into it and slowly chewed.

Joshua put the burger down and ate a french fry. He swirled two more fries into the mound of ketchup and put them into his mouth. He took another bite of the cheeseburger and let out a large sigh. He carefully rubbed the salt from his hands and stood up.

"Finished already?" Devon asked.

"The fries taste like extra oil and the cheeseburger; there aren't even words to describe how awful it tastes." Devon slowly raised an eyebrow.

"The air doesn't feel the same. Nothing tastes the same." Joshua said.

"This will pass. I can heat the soup up..." Devon offered extending his hand. Joshua just stared as Devon chuckled.

"So what now?" Joshua said.

"Do you feel strong enough to travel?"

"I do."

CHAPTER 6

Activity at shipyards make it easy to disappear among the rows of containers. The docks were where anyone could jump off of a pier, fish and do as they pleased without being noticed. The shore men ignored Devon as if he were a shadow. There were still times when he had to approach the warehouse by stealth or leave by loose planks.

Devon purchased a 15,000 square foot climate controlled warehouse. This warehouse had four large scientific refrigerators. Certain sections could be used for growing and there was also a dirt free section for highly sensitive computer components or lab work. Fresh air filled Joshua's lungs on the ride on to this new shelter.

This harbor refuge wasn't safe; it would be a temple for the altered. Devon had several hideaways this one was near the city and close to farmland. After they arrived, Joshua explored the warehouse, while Devon made sure everything was operational.

"So...what's the first thing I need to learn?" Joshua said, feeling stronger.

"How to control your fear," Devon said.

Joshua just nodded. He slowly smiled and then he did a flip. The flip was shaky, but he landed on his feet.

"Use this," Devon said pointing to Joshua's head, "Control the shock absorbers in your legs, the spring in your foot arch and unlock your body's potential."

Joshua closed his eyes, breathed in deeply and then jumped into the air and rolled as he landed. The first time he climbed up the wall he was so disoriented that he fell to the ground. The impact of falling knocked the wind out of him. The third time he climbed up the wall, he did not fall. Joshua moved around the warehouse, his muscles almost moving on their own.

Joshua was mid-somersault when visions of disfigured faces entered his mind. His stomach contracted with fear and a buzzing noise filled his hears. The petrified look on his face reminded Devon how the presence of the otherworlders initially sent him into the same nauseated state.

"The nausea means Them are near," Devon said.

"If this is how it feels, I don't want it," Joshua responded, holding his stomach.

"Somewhere in this city, an event will occur; shortly thereafter, similar events will occur. A well known person commits suicide and the masses' thoughts, discussions and sentiments are on the incident. Days later across the world another well known person commits suicide. This is how they divide attention.

"Staging events close together would cause people to notice a connection of some sort. The few that know what is occurring profit from it and they will not allow others to evolve beyond fear.

"Why?" Joshua said, his pain starting to lessen.

"Because fear is a commodity."

"Should we stop these happenings?" Joshua said, finally able to stand up straight.

"We should definitely not. Also, riding in an airplane is out..."

"What! How are we going to get around?"

"There are other ways, now get some rest," Devon said, pointing Joshua to his sleeping area.

The following day, Devon rented a small boat and took Joshua out past the breakwaters. Devon had trained in the floating undulating nothingness. He learned quickly in the danger of the ocean. He figured that this was the best way to train Joshua.

As the boat bobbed up and down, Devon looked at the ocean with a fondness. Devon stood on the front of the boat and inhaled the salt air. Joshua sat in the back, his ribs ached from soreness.

"I was forced into the cold depths beyond the coral reefs. It's a different world," Devon said walking back to the steering wheel. "These otherworlders have more muscle mass and their skeletal structure is stronger than a human's."

"You said something about moving lights?" Joshua said looking off into the distance.

"The males have trenchcoats, with subtle black leather covering on the front and that extends to the back armor. If you're close enough, you can see latticework etched into their clothing. Their armor is flexible. It looks as though it was forged by lightning. It is embellished with finely crafted symbols. These emblems light up and move whenever they use their abilities.

"The first time I encountered Tsunami, he used rogue waves to flip over the cruise ship I had stowed away on. One hundred and fifty people died that night," Devon said. One-hundred and fifty, Joshua silently mouthed.

"I still hear the screams, "Devon continued. "Earthquake pulls apart and crashes the earth together. He moves bedrock, stone and creates fissures.

"Lightning's coat completely illuminates when he has an outburst. His coat has a cape and he can fly. Of all the otherworlders I've seen, Tornado is the most disciplined.

"What do you mean?" Joshua said and then he threw up.

"He can create small barely noticeable twisters with one hand and with the other hand he creates twisters that push the limits of the Enhanced Fujita scale. He usually comes quick and without warning. He is not like Hurricane.

"As you saw Hurricane likes to have an audience, he's a performer. Hurricane, Cyclone, or Typhoon may appear anywhere along the path of a tropical disturbance. A hurricane can unleash more than two trillion gallons of rain a day. The warmer the water the more energy a hurricane has. Hurricanes spin around a low pressure center known as the 'eye'. This is a circular wall of wind and rain, bookended by constantly sinking air.

"Some otherworlders use rivers to snatch away pets and loved ones. These beings have lorded over seasons and have devastated communities," Devon said spinning the steering wheel.

"...ThunderStorm?" Joshua queried.

"ThunderStorm comes with dark clouds, winds, rain, snow even hail. He uses storm clouds as giant capacitors. His coat has a cape..."

"ThunderStorm..." Joshua said, motioning to the sky his next words were struck somewhere between his larynx and his tongue.

Twelve miles into their journey, ThunderStorm darted in and out of darkening clouds. Joshua grabbed his ribs and proceeded below deck. Their open water training session would not escape ThunderStorm's watchful eye. The hairs on Devon's body stood at attention as he turned the boat back towards the harbor. ThunderStorm continued to darken the sky over them. The lights on coat glowed in the darkness.

"Is he gone? Is he gone?" Joshua asked as he paced below deck.

"It's okay to be afraid; it's not okay to stay afraid," Devon responded as they returned to the harbor. Joshua emerged from below, once they reached the shore. Devon wasn't being attacked anymore, but these happenings seemed to occur more when he was around.

Once they returned to the warehouse, Joshua's training started. In less than a week, Joshua was vaulting from soft objects to hard objects, walking and jumping onto rails and wall edges.

"Two foot landings reduce body stress," Devon coached.

Devon built a climbing gym by suspending ropes and ship chains from the rafters. He used pipe fittings and created bars that could be hung, dropped or swung from. He crafted railings and pipe based structures. Being altered came with less muscle fatigue, which allowed them to train longer.

"Rolling after landing spreads the impact across your body," Devon instructed.

The warehouse was versatile. Devon could convert the warehouse into an office building layout or a hotel setting. A fourth of it was dedicated to physical training and tactics. Devon turned this waterfront lair into a residential layout in the morning and into a retail storefront by the afternoon.

The warehouse had a slight draft. A draft that made its way around the traps, projectile firing devices and collapsing walls to crawl up their spines.

Devon introduced a rigid reading schedule. To Devon language was the embodiment of thought, of physical reality. Right now, Joshua was supposed to be reading, but he wasn't. Joshua had picked up a sword and began making noises while wildly swinging it.

"Swing it at me," Devon said walking over to him.

Joshua looked down, paused for a moment, and then he thrust upward. He tried to catch Devon off guard. The blade slipped past Devon's defense and came within an inch of Devon's throat. Devon didn't even blink. He laughed softly and said, "Good strategy."

Joshua struck again, cutting lazily at him. When Devon avoided a swing; he's slapped Joshua's face. After the third slap, Joshua stepped back. Devon side stepped Joshua's thrust and grabbed him by the shoulders and drove his knee up. Joshua twisted, taking the blow to his thigh.

Joshua reoriented his sword and made an arcing swing, thinking this display would prompt Devon to get a sword of his own; it didn't. Joshua launched a particularly wicked sword strike, which would have hit Devon were it not for a subtle foot shift. As the sword came down two powerful hands clamped it like sprung jaws of a bear trap.

After a few attempts to free the sword, Joshua let the sword go. He touched the darkening bruises across his eyes and went back to reading.

"Your swordplay is coming along nicely," Devon said, putting the sword back into the weapons cabinet. Devon's hand was uncut.

Devon had to squeeze decades of training into Joshua within a few months. Devon did drills three times before moving on, first a walkthrough, followed by slow movements and then medium speed.

"Constantly read the situation," Devon said.

"A few cuts to the hand are better than a knife through the heart," Devon said.

"Attack what attacks you," Devon lectured as he noticed that Joshua was putting emotion into every move.

"Reserve your power, not your skill. Create distance... always in control...always in control... options..." Devon said hitting Joshua's shoulder with a wooden ruler.

"Options? The only option I have is to get my ass kicked," Joshua said bending over breathing heavily.

"Pull out the gun and engage while rolling," Devon said.

Joshua thought for a second, and then he rolled while pulling out his gun. "Changing levels alters trajectory and creates distance and distance creates options," Joshua said.

"Always in control...now again...faster." Devon said nodding his head like a coach during a critical moment. Joshua's training ended when he was exhausted enough to sleep where he stood.

Joshua felt better in his second week of training and that's when his body began to purge. Blood flukes, tapeworms and things beyond descriptions were expelled from his body. His body violently removed the toxins he had spent over two decades putting into it. Joshua found cleaning up the warehouse to be unpleasant.

"The fly can outmaneuver any human craft ever built," Joshua said looking up from his book; his eyes were following a small winged intruder. The insect buzzed across a room unaware of the beings trying to end its existence.

"A housefly can travel at 2,300 miles per hour at twice the acceleration of gravity, it can execute six full turns per second. It can fly straight up, down or backward and somersault to land upside down on a ceiling.

"Did you know that fly receives sensory inputs from about 81,560 receptors on its body?" Joshua said.

"That many?" Devon responded.

"I counted them."

"People only accept convenient facts that don't anger their mind. Politics, journalism and faith are accepted as long as it doesn't challenge basic assumptions," Devon said handing Joshua a mop.

"So, these otherworlders want more than to just kill people?" Joshua said moving the mop across the floor.

"None of this is about what they want. Truth has to be something that is demanded, something that is required, and something that is expected. People are happily rolling in metal boxes and living in electric caves to be concerned about truth."

"And these otherworlders are suing our own methods against us?" Joshua said putting down the mop. He hung up another heavy bag and started punching it.

"Humans are putting cars into orbit not the Them," Devon said. "A person's mind may reach out in two dozen different directions; still, people follow the rules. Most minds can't be confined to thinking one way. For The System each of these acts is a small red pin in a very large map."

"What kind of actions?"

"Dropping bombs on people while they sleep, launching attacks on countries with no army, deciding who lives and who dies by a button press or pen stroke. The System keeps tabs on its enemies, so it surveils everyone. It rids the world of natural born leaders, making it easier for the masses to follow its created leader."

"How does it make sense to create leaders when you just got rid of one?"

"The System's goal is executed by roads, rules and limits. A true leader would eventually guide their followers to get rid of the System. The System doesn't just exist to survive. The System wants to grow, so it alters reality. This is usually unnoticed but when it is noticed it becomes a Berenstain bears footnote."

"So, you are just going to right all of this, who do you think you are John Titor?"

"Who's that?"

"Nevermind… And you've had run-ins with The System?"

"Indeed…"

"So why are you still here?"

"I am an anomaly, a ghost. I was something not to waste time on and now you are the same. Our existence outside of the mass consciousness will be problematic."

"You don't know how scared I was a year ago…" Joshua said.

"All things in the universe make up one organism, this organism we call life. We are simply droplets of water in a vast ocean. Man did not weave the web of life; he is merely a strand in it. Whatever man does to the web, he does to himself."

"How do we what truth is?"

"How do you know being raised in group homes wasn't orchestrated by Them? We have to view things in a three dimensional way," Devon said. Joshua finished cleaning and lay in his bed. He lay their thinking until he drifted to sleep.

The next morning, twelve miles northeast of Fairfield, fire was burning. The fire had already burned one hundred acres when Joshua and Devon arrived. They helped the evacuees, provided water and blankets. They found things like pets, medication and people but some things would never be found. Devon had seen many wildfires, but nothing like this. The blaze was so enormous that it created its own wind.

The humidity dropped and the winds increased and that's when bad things started to happen. Wildfire landed and waved his cape of living flame. His coat was ablaze with flame and it ignited the air. Devon and Joshua helped those they could as flames danced around them.

Sometimes an otherworlder such as Wildfire travels with an assistant. On this mission his assistant was named Vapor. The fire quickly surrounded a nearby a home. Devon kicked in the front door and he and Joshua went inside. A mother, father and son were on the floor in a side room.

Vapor entered the room. He was intent on suffocating the family. Devon and Joshua had other plans. As Devon and Joshua carried the family out of the house a propane tank exploded, knocking them to the ground. Devon and Joshua received first, second and third degree burns for their efforts. Joshua yelled as the sky darkened with smoke. Devon had several oxygen masks that he had taken from a fire engine. He gave these to the family.

"Go!" Devon barked.

"Thank you…what's your name…" The father said.

"Go!" Devon yelled as he covered Joshua's leg wound. The wound produced a trickle of blood and it was already healing.

The sound of a quickly approaching fire is like that of a fast moving train over wooden tracks. The shouting voices of the firemen were swallowed up by the howling fire. Wildfire touched every tree, every bush and every blade of grass. He did not welcome the presence of Devon and Joshua and he drove the temperature toward 900 degrees.

Wildfire waved his cape and ashes rained down a half a mile away. Embers floated from house to house, as if they were searching for someone. Devon and Joshua's faces were blackened and sweat ran down their backs. The fire surrounded them; it could not be outrun.

A twenty five foot rock face, patchy grass and a few spaced out trees stood between them and the flames. Devon pulled out the silica weave fire shelter that he took from the fire crew. The flames approached them as if it were an old friend. Wildfire continued to scar the earth as nearby trees crackled in flame. Joshua watched in horror as a wave of embers was sent after them.

Devon pulled out the shelter and they stepped into it. The shelter covered them like a reddening cold sore. They lay face down and as close to the ground as possible. The air is the coolest and cleanest near the ground. They pulled in their knees, elbows and feet to pin the shelter down underneath them. The first wave of heat hit the shelter. The flames pushed the covering as the noise swept over it.

"This will be a field training exercise," Joshua said mimicking Devon. "I knew this was a bad idea!" Joshua mumbled as flaming debris rained down on them.

The shelter deflected most of heat, but for half an hour they felt as if they were on fire. In that oven, Devon recalled that not long ago he hiked the entire planet, swum the deepest oceans and journeyed treacherous jungles. He had been driven by one thought; the same thought that clawed at him every night— avenge my family.

Joshua impatiently stuck his head out the shelter, causing hot air and smoke to pour in. Wildfire roared even louder. Devon pulled Joshua back inside their defensible space. For thirty more minutes they sucked in hot air as Wildfire burned over them.

It would be an hour before Joshua and Devon could emerge. Their shelter was covered in layers of thick soot and ash. Wildfire burned 300,000 acres, demanded the attention of 10,000 firefighters and had claimed sixty four lives. The flames would not be contained for another four days. Joshua and Devon had done all they could.

They returned to base. Devon cleaned up and changed his clothes. It would take Joshua two days to heal and recover from smoke inhalation. While Joshua mended Devon welded and created partitions in the warehouse for more training. Once Joshua healed, he went on a night time mission with Devon to shutdown a gun shop that sold illegal firearms.

"You just let that guy go. You could have used your surgical knowledge to torture information out of him?" Joshua said as he grabbed his helmet.

"That's not the way things get done. That's not how we stay off the radar."

"You're going to take his word for it, that he won't do it again?"

"He saw what I did to his shop and his weapons. He won't do it again. Do a little harm for a lot of good."

"I did like the way you accidentally hit him with a jab, instead of shaking his hand."

"None of this is clean. You're going to help me clean it up."

"I took out all the surveillance equipment around the dock, but I still think we need masks."

Devon looked at Joshua from the corner of his eye and said, "Get on."

Joshua smiled and hopped on the back of the Soul Stirrer. Every day they reset the facilities for various exercises, today would be no different.

While they trained, Devon only thought about Prime, The Chamber and the rift. This made Devon push Joshua harder.

"Even the good I have done has given me nightmares." Devon said as he repeatedly washed his hands in the sink.

"I'm sorry that these creatures took away your family, but you didn't kill your family," Joshua said.

"What if I did?"

"Those otherworlders killed your family. Stop beating yourself up... It could have happened to anybody."

"But it didn't happen to anybody, it happened to me."

"It was an accident."

"Was it?"

"It's not your fault...it's not your fault...the burden isn't yours alone." Joshua consoled Devon.

When the world became too much for Joshua, his mind would long for him to swipe left and double-click a situationship. Devon was full of moralism and dreary sarcasm. He was more laid back than a week in Maui. These two couldn't have been more different.

Devon bested the Delta forces, the police, Seals, Berets and the Dogs of wars. He preferred the HK 416 and firearms that use a piston gas system for the bolt carrier. Piston gas systems are more reliable, reliability lends to better accuracy.

The HK 416 doesn't kick when fired, it hardly moves. It has a high rate of fire, a shorter barrel for close quarters use, could handle a variety of ammunition and it could be fired underwater.

Every morning Joshua smiled at his AR-15, like it was a newly unwrapped present. The AR-15 uses a direct gas system. A bullet's kinetic energy is equal to half the mass of the bullet multiplied by its velocity squared. Its muzzle speed is three times that of a handgun. A bullet fired from an AR-15 can go through three inches of bone. When a high speed bullet enters a body, the tissues ripple so violently that arteries burst. The bullet doesn't have to hit it.

Devon slowly crossed over the threshold button hooking into the room along the wall. Joshua was supposed to immediately enter the room in the opposite direction, but he didn't. Joshua constantly drifted from his area of responsibility.

"Always keep your eyes on the target," Devon said pointing out Joshua's positioning error.

"OK, OK, clear the corner, stay along the wall," Joshua repeated checking his rifle's magazine.

"Breach and clear," Devon said. After Joshua mastered this drill, they moved to assault tactics. They used alternating forward movement with suppressive fire. Weapons training was the only type of training Joshua didn't complain about.

When Joshua saw one of Them, he would nearly crawl inside his skin or try to grab on to Devon. Devon had to use substantial force to control him. Joshua would soon be able to see these otherworlders without the hazy outline. If one of these beings knew that Devon had altered Joshua; they'd both be dead.

Joshua would be sent out until the sight of an otherworlder was nothing more than a shadow to him.

CHAPTER 7

Petrified, scared and usually speechless, Joshua woke up and cheerfully said, "I always wanted to have powers." This indicated to Devon that Joshua was ready to start the day's training. This morning's training would be full of scaling high walls and climbing trees until their hands hurt. Afternoon training would consist of showing Joshua how to navigate sewers, tunnel and aqueducts.

Big City's make the same decision: Move the homeless camps out of the aqueducts. In these aqueducts the homeless and disenfranchised cannot be seen or heard. The plan is to put the problem in your face. Once there they can sell the public on programs they can raise taxes they can increase the police force without push back.

You'd be surprised how many people live in the storm drains. The homeless are usually overlooked as mentally disturbed as they ubiquitously fill in the landscape. If you spend time with the homeless, you'll see how some operate more like a pop-up store.

They are ex-military, teachers, some have degrees, some are doctors and most of them are happy. They are well organized. They talk about which locations provide the most money, peak sympathy times and what storylines work the best. They discuss what signs and props work best. They make sure assigned posts don't overlap. They also have message boards and gathering places.

Homeless villages only need protection from outsiders. They have become organized and committed, but most are classified as unfit to stand trial. They have elders who solve disputes. Some of these people make a respectable tax-free, high five figure income. In makeshift towns full of colorful tents, shopping carts and no accountability it wasn't hard for Devon and Joshua to blend in.

Some within these groups have felt the pull of The System and are here attempting to fight it the best way they knew how. In places like this the hallmarks of consumerism and conformity were discouraged. Some people have died trying to escape The System.

Many feel that having a home, a job and bills tied them to a moral-less system. They view those that willingly tie themselves to such a system as mentally ill. If you speak to them long enough, you realize that they aren't disturbed, most are rational.

The System has a way of reaching people that rejected it. It reaches out through agents of authority, political representatives and wayward harassers. If The System had to, it would contaminate their water supply.

Within this group you have to stay on the move, but those trying to free themselves are too large to go unnoticed, too unskilled to combat this multifaceted enemy. Otherworlders caused fewer destructive happenings around these disenfranchised masses. Inside fragile minds the whispers of otherworlders seemed like madness.

Devon and Joshua walked over drug addicts and syringes as they practiced being invisible. The asylum was no longer a defined location. The inhabitants pop their heads out of tents to scuffle over change, but here underneath the overpasses they couldn't care less if humans weren't alone in the universe.

They sat unrecognizable on top of Ferris wheels, bridges and on high voltage wires. Joshua preferred to roam the street or the tops of buildings. He really didn't like the smell of the sewers.

"I traveled to the far east to punch rocks with my bare hands," Devon said while they were training.

"You just beat rocks like they stole money from your mother." Joshua said.

"I learned how to put a spear between a wall and my neck, with the sharp end on my windpipe, and then I pushed forward bending the spear with my throat."

Joshua stopped doing sit-ups and said, "Is there a remedial course?"

"You won't have to travel the far corners to learn this."

"How do we know when we are ready?" Joshua said.

Devon slowly pulled out a Wudang sword and said, "When you realize that you'll never be ready, you'll be ready. Now don't move." Devon started snapping the sword around Joshua with blinding speed. Joshua's remaining questions were erased by the precision of Devon's sword movements.

Devon and Joshua ran on the sand and in the snow. Joshua's training required a lot of hill sprints.

"This is a lot of running," Joshua murmured as he stopped sprinting halfway up a hill.

Devon stopped and turned to Joshua. "Running for weight loss is important. We run so that our legs are always underneath us," and then Devon knocked Joshua's leg from under him, this caused him to roll down the hill.

At the end of the second week of training Joshua entered the puzzles solving stage of his evolution.

"I saw three otherworlders at the grocery store, and one in the park. That makes seventeen for the week." Joshua said excitedly. His nausea around the otherworlders had lessened. Devon simply nodded as Joshua spoke. Joshua was the closest thing Devon had to a brother.

Joshua learned Farsi and Arabic first because they were difficult to learn. Native language speakers have a different perspective than someone who learns the language from a book or program. Today, Devon introduced a new routine, involving tennis balls. Devon would throw the ball at Joshua, the balls Joshua didn't pluck out of the air hit his body, hard.

"What do you expect from me, I was an orphan," Joshua whined as another ball bounce off of him.

"Being an orphan had nothing to do with you; it had to do with your parents. Those cigarette burns weren't your fault. The beatings and the abuse wasn't your fault. Your abuser is at fault," Devon said hitting Joshua with another ball.

"Attack the arm that attacks you," Devon said, walking by as Joshua finished his morning exercise. He placed The Iliad on the chair for Joshua to read. Joshua said, "Thank you," but he meant something else.

Devon went to one of his many jobs, while Joshua trained and explored. That evening, Devon returned and crumbled his white smock in the corner. He went to the sink and furiously washed his hands with hot water.

"Were the patients a pain in the rash?" Joshua said jokingly.

Devon looked at Joshua with frustration. Joshua's smile faded. He slowly raised his German essentials book and lowered his eyes. Learning how to mediate was especially hard for Joshua, he had to block out a city and the new wonders within his mind.

"Use a weapon as a last resort. Stopping the enemy is the goal," Devon instructed.

"How do we do that?"

"We use knowledge, language and strategy before any physical contact."

"And then?"

"We show the enemy love, turn them into a friend," Devon said. "Why are you looking at me like that?"

"Your compassion for your murderers is unexpected," Joshua said.

"I hated them. I wanted to kill all of them. I don't want you to hate them for who they cannot help but be."

"Remember when your biggest worry was how women didn't want to date you because you lived at home with your mom. It was the same women who wanted to date you when you lived at home with your wife…"

"Yeah." Devon said, lowering the 400 pounds bar onto Joshua's chest. "I understand people better now," Devon said, silently.

"I understand people less now," Joshua retorted pushing the weight up to complete the set.

"When do I learn how to fight?" Joshua asked, showing off his shadow boxing technique.

"Footwork, position, never approach in a straight line and always cover yourself," Devon instructed ignoring Joshua's question.

"We are evolving, so why do we have to work so hard?"

"We must seek out failure. Failure is where the lessons are. Failure is where we find our weakness and our strengths. We work hard so we become better versions of ourselves."

"This is my third week of practicing. When do I get to spar?" Joshua said, as while jogging on the treadmill.

"You aren't ready for that," Devon said leaning against a wall.

Joshua stepped off the treadmill. He took off his oxygen mask stepped into the arena and said, "I feel great. I feel powerful."

The arena was a section of the training area that was filled with mats, gloves and protective equipment. Devon walked into the arena as Joshua confidently bounced around.

"You sure, you're ready?" Devon said slowly approaching Joshua.

"Yes…"

Devon struck Joshua's face so hard that he went down on one knee. Devon's hand felt like concrete. A similar punch caused Joshua to run to the nurse's office with a bloody nose in the tenth grade. Joshua stood up and shook his head.

"You said you were ready," Devon said.

"I guess I wasn't. OK. I'm ready now."

A spinning back kick from Devon lifted Joshua in the air before putting him on the mat. Devon did five flips capped off with a jumping split. Joshua staggered to his feet in time to receive an immediate black eye and a split lip.

Joshua's brain said that Devon had disappeared and teleported right next to him; before his ribs were pounded with punches. Joshua turned and fired off his best combinations of punches. The first punch Devon dodged the next punch Devon grabbed out of the air and flipped Joshua onto his back. Joshua stayed on the mat for a minute.

"You said one state, one city, and one person at a time…right… Now, where did I put that book?" Joshua said getting up, dusting himself off.

"Hand to hand combat with someone who won't kill you won't get us where we need to go," Devon said as Joshua limped away. It took Joshua two days to recover from this lesson.

It was common for Devon to squeeze a week's worth of training into eight hours. Devon trained even when his muscles hurt. Devon told Joshua that everyone has a tell. A tell is a gesture or movement most people don't realize they are making. It is these slight movements that could predict an action.

Joshua altering caused him to be plagued by fits of hiccups. Joshua also developed a bit of car sickness. Luckily, he could still ride buses and the Soul Stirrer. Joshua wasn't curious about the outside world. Joshua took to hacking into systems and reading code. Devon would sit Joshua next to people, but he was mentally far away.

In the middle of stretching, Joshua stopped and said, "Yesterday, I saw a female otherworlder. You said the female ones weren't as grotesque and could pass for human. Clearly, your tastes haven't changed; my stomach turns every time I see one."

"Hmmm, sounds like time for a road trip," Devon said. The two navigated the winding roads to the South Arapaho Peak, west of Boulder, Colorado. Falling white flakes obscured the horizon; little bits of white drifted to earth on an imperceptible breeze. They trekked towards the top of the mountain.

Above them the otherworlder Avalanche loomed. He wore a smirk as he erased every trail in sight. He did so as if he were imposing judgment. Avalanche buried three snowboarders as he tore down the mountain. They could both hear the muffled sounds of other hikers above them. Joshua only saw Avalanche's face in whiteness.

Joshua's body moved slower than his mind, he was only able to see the white flurry coming towards them. The ice came straight at Joshua, it moved like it had a mind. Joshua took a step backward and slipped off the ridge. His hand dug into a boulder, preventing him from falling into the ravine. Around Joshua sliding snow filled a 50 foot chasm. Devon reached out and lifted the terrified Joshua back up.

Avalanche left an empty space in the side of the mountain as his face floated out of view. None of this bothered Devon. He had scaled

K2, the second highest mountain on Earth, unassisted. Joshua was noticeably disturbed and now he could now see the otherworlders without a grainy haze.

Devon had thought Joshua was moaning through his workouts. It would be two weeks before he figured out that Joshua was humming, not moaning. It wasn't the sound from the pressure of underwater waves impacting the seabed. Joshua started humming to increase the sensations in his face to help him focus.

Joshua's humming wasn't special, but three weeks into training and it became clearer. Sometimes he would hum a verse, other times it was an entire song. 'Careless Whisper', Devon interrupted. 'Your Love is King', was interrupted. 'One Last Cry'... Devon let him finish that one. Joshua hummed through Taylor Swift, N'Sync, Michael McDonald and the Motown catalog during indoor training. He saved Bob Marley, Prince and Stevie Wonder for outside training.

The two were inside of a library when Devon asked, "What have you learned?"

"There are people who regularly toss food on the street as if it were filth," Joshua responded. "I see people who allowed fruit and juices to run into gutters, even the underfed waste food. I have learned that people paint themselves as the victim, only so they could be the hero…if only to themselves.

"I have learned that the System uses those with the loudest voices and those with quiet ways. It uses the flashy, the flamboyant and the unsmart. It uses the educated. It uses those that are easy to control and easier to replace," Joshua said

"Usually," Devon responded.

"Coalition politics and people saying things just to be contrary…is that The System?"

"Ummm."

"Is it like the league ignoring a push off by a superstar player in the championship game before shooting the game winning shot? Does The System make you say a catch isn't a catch?"

"Those are good examples. For all of that to work, you need the team, the coaches, the referees, the announcers, the owner, the league and the network to all be on the same page."

"And no one notices?"

"No one is told to notice. All a player has to do is shut up and play, that's their role. The more you comply, the bigger roles you garner and the more money you earn. What have you noticed about people?"

"I see people setting new athletic records, not because they are evolving but because technology makes it appear they are. If anything, people are devolving. All of this is so much bigger than I had imagined," Joshua said as they entered the warehouse. Joshua resumed his weapon cleaning duties.

Joshua's body fat dipped below double digits in the fourth week of training. Other than the Hypernium effects, his body functioned as usual. Devon scheduled another field trip. As they sped west towards California; Devon told Joshua how he tiptoed on a white sand beach near a tiny tucked away harbor. They arrived just as the residents in Beachwood Canyon, Los Angles were just waking up.

Devon said he would only be gone for a minute and that was an hour ago. He left Joshua on the fifth floor of this office building. Truthfully, Joshua preferred being anywhere those hideous beings weren't.

He was just getting comfortable on the fifth when the floor started shaking. The walls jerked toward him. The dirty windows on the balcony shattered. The light poles shook. Joshua made his way to the door as things fell on him.

"Hide under the desk or run outside?" Joshua asked himself and then the lights went off. People started running down the narrow hallways and down the stairs; Joshua was in front of them. Behind him people pushed and shoved trying to get out of the building.

Once Joshua was outside, he saw Devon in the middle of the street; his eyes had a gold outline. Between Devon's feet, one crack became many, until a whole section of the curved street upended. Joshua sprinted towards Devon, but the earth reached out tripping four people, including him. Joshua fell to the ground as walls crashed down, the noise was deafening.

Devon leaped to avoid collapsing pavement and then everything was still. People were moaning, cars were overturned and eight buildings collapsed. The apartment building Joshua had been in was no longer habitable. Dark, foul smelling water sprayed from broken underground pipes and ran down the hillside as hundreds of people aimlessly wandered the city in the shadow of the Hollywood Sign.

Joshua slowly got up and nervously walked over to Devon and then an aftershock hit. This kicked him down in the middle of the broken street. Earthquake's range was quite large. Neither of them saw Earthquake. Devon could feel his presence, just as he could feel weather changes. This earthquake lasted less than thirty seconds, but it felt like an hour.

The air was thick with dust as fires raged throughout the city. Devon picked up Joshua and dusted him off. Joshua had bumps and bruises but was unhurt.

"What do you see?" Devon asked once Joshua's heart rate returned to normal.

"They can control physical matter but it isn't perfect. I liked it better when I didn't know."

"We have more work to do," Devon said as they walked back to the Soul Stirrer. When they returned to home Joshua had a renewed spirit.

"Let's spar," Joshua said entering the arena, avoiding his French lesson.

"Are you ready?" Devon said entering the arena.

"Yes," Joshua said and then he mechanically lunged at Devon.

Devon ducked under a right cross. He dropped under Joshua's second swing. Devon formed his hands as if he were gripping a tennis ball; he turned sideways and lunged at Joshua. He dug his fingers into the bicep of Joshua's swinging arm, ripping at the muscle.

Devon released Joshua and used the middle and forefinger of his right hand to rake along Joshua's nose and mouth. With his left hand, he struck Joshua's neck, grabbing the windpipe as Joshua's arms flailed. Normally you would pull it out, lacerating the throat; it would kill him. Devon pushed in; this temporarily closed the windpipe, cutting off Joshua's air.

For a time, it appeared that Devon's hands moved faster than an eye can see. Joshua's body twisted and blood shot out of his mouth. Devon stepped inside Joshua's extended arms to issue an elbow to the underside of his chin and a palm strike to his chest. This technique of rolling one strike into the next created a cascading effect.

Joshua retreated and hobbled over to the recliner. He moaned while finding his bookmark. The lesson: strike an aggressor in opposing directions. Force the aggressor's body into the next strike, so they could mount a counter attack. It would take Joshua two days to heal.

"We had some great poker games." Joshua said with a smile on his face as he sat up.

"You're only saying that because you always won." Devon said preparing the ship chains for use.

"Remember those summer classes…" Joshua asked as he wrapped his ribs.

"They were the worst…" Devon chucked.

"Do you wish you had never dropped out of school?"

"I got married. I got a real job. I had to drop out." Devon said placing his hand on his friend's shoulder. "Joshua, there's no going back. So, ask what you are going to ask." Devon said looking at Joshua.

"Ok…are the biases within people accidental?" Joshua said.

"It doesn't take much for people to think their reasons are superior, their beliefs are superior and that they are superior," Devon said walking through their sanctuary.

It was the fifth week and Joshua was now able to jump from rooftop to rooftop. Joshua and Devon ran along rooftops as softly cooing pigeons jumped out of their path.

"My hair hurts," Joshua said complaining. This prompted Devon to stop running. Devon looked at Joshua and said, "What?"

"When you said other world, I pictured overgrown amoebas, viruses and things of that nature; not these glowing eyes snarling beast that rip heads off."

"Keep moving," Devon said.

"Why does everything have to hurt so much?"

"Today's six thousand pain reminders will be tomorrow's two thousand. This isn't some Hollywood production where you don't have to earn your abilities. You'll feel every muscle, every pain, every bit of growth… appreciate it."

Their training continued and so did Joshua's humming. He hummed renditions of 'Don't Worry, Be happy', 'Sun Daze', 'Staying Alive', 'I Will Survive', 'The Walker', 'Eye of the Tiger' and 'Moves like

Jagger', Devon interrupted his rendition of the G-funk classic 'Regulate', it was terrible.

Joshua was no longer just another slack-jawed, gum chewing, apple eating asshole who wore sunglasses at night. He was I-don't-give-a-fuck casual most days, complete with ripped jeans, wrinkled shirts and general dishevelment.

"Who are the Yous?" Devon asked as they returned from their afternoon run. This was the first run Joshua had kept up with him.

"Yous are people with any number of real or imagined ailments. They explain things as if their pain is absolute. They have headaches, migraines and insomnia because they are out of place. Each minor error is a subtle mental position on race, gender and age, but most people are Not Sees."

"Not Sees?" Devon asked.

"They refuse to see. They take pride in not seeing. Their identity is rooted in not seeing. They wish violence and death upon anyone who does see. They do not see that repeated unfounded claims in the media are social engineering plans. They cannot see the systemic ground working being laid in front of them. They cannot see the System priming psyches. Not Sees are the worst kind of Yous.

"What have you learned?" Devon asked sensing that Joshua was in a talkative mood.

"I've learned that most people are drunks, procrastinators and disbelievers. You have to paint the villain green or purple or maybe show half of their face eaten away for their villainy to be recognized. They have monetized gender and they engage in recreational outrage. All influencers are complicit." Joshua said.

"That means we have a lot of work to do." Devon said.

"There are a lot of unfit minds out there. Why even try to work with the beasts? Let's just get the people to do what we need them to do." Joshua responded.

"And how do propose we do that?"

"I have some ideas."

"You want to seduce them with flashing lights, square footage, big windows, discounts, events, plush chairs and espresso. You want to promise them exquisite values and legal addictive stimulants..." Devon said.

"That's been done before." Joshua said.

"What then..." Devon curiously said. Joshua looked up his face is different.

"We hit the panic button." Joshua said with the unhappy knowledge of what he was about to say on his face. "They already fear being taken over by the other, the reds, the yellows, the browns, the blacks, the ruskies, the commies, the government, institutions, mothers, fathers, the people; we just add the unknown..." Joshua said exhausting his mental artillery.

"Trying to solve the problem from only one side enables the monster. So, what must we do?" Devon asked as he threw a tennis ball at Joshua as hard as he could.

Joshua caught the ball and said, "Rise above."

CHAPTER 8

Four weeks ago, Joshua was frightened by the reach of The System. Three weeks ago, the happening with Avalanche scared him. Two weeks ago, Earthquake left him speechless. Today Joshua was past the edge of what's known. Excitement is what got Joshua up in the morning. For Devon, there was an anticipation that pressed against his lack of sleep.

The time for extended equations, studies and detailed reports were at an end. Devon began to pack for their journey. Neither of them knew what to expect as they rode toward the rift location. This was the southern part of the nation; here there were several varieties of poisonous snakes.

They parked the Soul Stirrer and took their gear into the wilderness. They avoided three coyotes and a bear as they pushed towards a row of cellular turrets; a rift was nearby. The unexpected sound of a bird leaving a tree branch, caused an invisible menu of choice to appear inside Joshua's head, he said nothing.

Devon drifted off in thought as pine needles brushed along his face. *My former life is hazy and far behind me. My memories of it are perhaps tricks of my mind.*

Joshua and Devon had a vague protocol based on their skill sets. Joshua had been given advanced weapons and survival training, but there were still some things he could not do. Joshua thought about being altered as another pebble lodged in his shoe.

Devon sliced my femur and told me about his meeting in the chamber. This will be my first true opportunity to test my limits. Joshua's thoughts ended when the last pebble was removed.

"Okay…when we get there, do I go or do we both go?" Joshua said. The decision had already been made—they would both enter the rift. This was nervous chatter from Joshua. Most of the time, Devon just shrugged his shoulders and nodded as he appeared to consider Joshua's opinions. Joshua asked more questions as confidence was replaced by fear.

"Aren't you worried?" Joshua asked.

"I'm just anxious," Devon responded. Devon was indeed worried. This could be the first time he could fail in front of Joshua. Some time ago otherworlders had exited this rift and had moved fast westward towards their mission. It would be several hours before they returned. Joshua didn't want to have an encounter with them.

Joshua pointed just beyond the clearing. "There it is," he said. It shouldn't be there, but there it was. The rift opening was next to a small creek. Devon and Joshua stood there staring at the entry point. Once Joshua could close his mouth, he asked, "How far do you think it goes?" Devon had no answer for him; this was thin circular protrusion that you could see on either side of.

Devon crouched down and said, "Twelve feet in diameter, touching the ground at two distinct points. Facing south..." Devon continued rattling off observances to quell his fear, their fears.

They took all the typical readings, all of which told them nothing. Joshua was glad that the opening didn't appear as some ball of fire or other ghastly concoction. For half an hour, Devon's thoughts turned inward looking for explanations. Everything they had seen unto this point faded into the backdrop of this rift.

They stared into the future as sunlight slowly crept through the leaves. They could feel the rift's fluctuating energy. Devon noticed Joshua rechecking all of his gear. Joshua turned away from the rift and started walking.

"We should set up camp," Joshua mumbled. To Joshua the rift was something he feared, something he would never understand.

"Joshua when I stepped inside a rift there was a force pushing me backward, a force that increased with each step," Devon said Joshua was they walked to a small clearing. "The sound inside was like standing behind a jet turbine. I could feel the molecules in my skin splitting more and more with each step."

They set up tents and would head back in the morning. They doused the fire and quickly went to sleep in anticipation. The following morning, they rose early and ate a light breakfast. There was a noticeable chill in the air. Joshua took out his rifle and double checked his ammunition. He offered Devon a handgun. Devon declined.

Joshua would not relinquish his rifle. "Suit yourself." He walked towards the opening with his hand on his rifle.

"Joshua, you know my stance on guns!"

"That's why I have enough for both of us."

In the distance, they heard a loud sound that startled the birds from their perch. Joshua pulled his rifle out. Devon looked at him puzzled. Joshua hunched his shoulders and said, "I'm still human." Devon's expressionless face hid the fact that his brain had pulled up an invisible menu of possible responses. Devon chose to say nothing.

Joshua wanted to fight fire with fire. Devon felt a new tension between himself and Joshua, or was it just fear? Joshua had seen what these beings were capable of and he didn't want to be a casualty. Joshua gave out an audible sigh as he brushed past Devon on the trail towards the portal.

They returned to the location of the rift. It was still there. Joshua took off anything he didn't need for the trip. Devon took a deep breath and stepped inside the rift. One step, two steps—they were inside. Inside walls moved as they entered as if a membrane expanding.

The faint order of burnt matches filled their nostrils. The wall was bulging outward toward them, like a gaped mouth. The dark tunnel caused them to widen their stance and move slower.

Inside the tunnel, small colorful lights intensified around them; they could still see the forest behind them. There was a silence under the canopy of trees. A beetle slowly spiraled up toward the branches followed by dust motes. After the third nervous step they realized they had truly entered the rift.

Four steps inside, and the darkness was alleviated by the light underneath the barrel of Joshua's rifle. Devon's shadow had been swallowed by the walls. The temperature increased as the sound of their steps became muffled.

With the increase in temperature came a kind of gentle sweetness. The floor was charged with electric particles. The glassy black walls showed scarring. They pushed forward into the darkness.

Joshua slowly reached out to touch the wall. As his fingers approached the surface, the wall sensed him and a blue ripple emanated from it. There were hundreds of interconnected ripples, symbols and shapes at various intersection points and all of it written in a language they couldn't understand. As they stepped they watched ripples disappear, collide and rearrange.

Joshua's eyes were as large as silver dollars. For the time being, words defeated him. He tried to suppress the hundred new questions inside of him. He tried to take some photos of this living wall.

"Don't touch the ripples!" Devon said in the calmest a voice he could manage. He remembered that a hand swipe from Prime over the wall changed a thousand lives. Devon and Joshua watched the upstream and downstream face of one ripple collide with the wave of another. Each collision brought a different color.

"What are they made of?" Joshua asked.

"Why do they need to be made of anything?" Devon said.

"Is it magic?"

Devon just nodded. The rift's inner darkness deepened. Light from Joshua's rifle disappeared all that was left were small dots in space.

"I think it's all networked to their cognitive quantum processor," Devon said. Several moments passed as they pondered the ramification contained in each ripple.

"What is it made of?" Joshua yelled again.

"I don't know. How do you feel?"

"I feel fine. Is this what their technology looks like?"

"We should keep moving," Devon urged. Devon was enthralled and he wanted to indulge himself. His impulse to touch the ripples on the wall was larger than him. Devon now understood the ripples to be information. This slow revelation filled him with elation and dread.

Devon recalled what the wall color meant when Prime had touched it during the Alaskan meeting. The dots were green or red when a happening occurred. They were yellow when a rift location was moved and blue wherever an otherworlder was. The blues and reds on the walls were bright. The wall had a wet slickness to it.

Devon had watched Prime easily manipulate the ripples, but in this rift there were a wall cracks that halted the movement of the ripples. These cracks seemed to form stress and the passage of time, perhaps this was an older rift.

"How much further?" Joshua questioned from behind.

"Further," Devon said pointing to what looked like a rounded archway. The deepening darkness suggested downward steps. It was an act of supreme control to walk those few paces.

"You can see the precision in the creation of this," Joshua said. "What's the purpose…"

No threat had presented itself to Joshua, but it was important to eliminate the possibility. Devon let out a gasp that cut Joshua off in mid-question. "Look!" Devon said as he pointed. The path ahead of them gently curved ahead of them. Devon suddenly had an absurd memory about the pink wallpaper he had put up in Brianna's nursery. Something about this place stirred old memories inside of him.

The altering was like a drug that allowed them to cross a never seen before barrier. Right now they were lost between universes. Their minds wondered, 'How far the rift extended?' The rift was unlimited potential, but it was more than energy; it was an organism. The rift breathed and the walls were alive. The fact that it partially lit their path was a sign of intelligence.

"Do you feel that?" Joshua said, quickly turning around.

"Feel what?" Devon said. Joshua was sweating

"Turn off your light it's useless." Devon said.

Joshua hesitated to comply. Devon looked back at him. Once Joshua cut off his light, they noticed that Joshua's rifle was disintegrating. Joshua pressed down on the trigger, it wouldn't fire.

Realizing the futility in any further action, Joshua slung the rifle across his back.

With each step they got closer to the light at the end. Devon looked at Joshua's face which showed the strain of each step.

"How are you doing?" Devon asked.

A sharp grunt was Joshua's response. Thirty feet inside and a field could be seen on the other side. There was a kind of lower stepping leading to it. It was on this lower step that Joshua fell to his knees.

"You can't make it! It's time for us to go," Devon said lifting Joshua up. Devon's desperation to get to the other side couldn't hide the disappointment that surged through his voice.

"No…no… you continue. I will wait for you outside…" Joshua said breathing heavily.

"Are you sure?"

"I'll be fine…you go."

Joshua turned and walked slowly back. Devon descended the electric walkway. His final view of his world was of Joshua looking down at him with uncertainty.

CHAPTER 9

Joshua went back to wait for Devon. Devon was inside the rift, alone. After a few more steps Devon made it through the rift. He immediately fell to his knees and threw up. Beyond the darkness of the rift, the red sky was blinding. He stared into the slowly swirling vortex. Its movement mesmerized him. He ran his fingers over the nearby black grass, the plants moved slowly as if underwater.

At first glance, everything looked the same, but it wasn't. The resemblance to Devon's Earth was so striking the presence of speech balloons seemed appropriate. It was at least ten degrees cooler even though a sensation of heat could be felt. A chorus of sounds rang out in the distance.

The gravity was different. Devon fell over like a toddler struggling to walk. The terrain was familiar but it didn't feel the same. Walking calls for stepping and swinging forward. The ground on the other side gave a little push forward. Devon used the heavier air to weigh him down, so he could move.

The red sun dappled forest area wasn't empty. Two species of a large snail type creatures and a species that could pass for lizard called this place home. Devon saw what looked like dragonflies with feathered wings. Next to him was a muddy yellow rut that had collected enough rainwater to become a pond. This pond was surrounded by orange weeds.

Devon slowly waded through the pond and into the short flora that lined it. He sat near the grey tree roots at the water's edge. The yellow pond water was partially covered by something that resembled algae.

Firefly type insects slowly scouted near him. Shoe-sized white frogs slowly hopped through the brush. Devon was immobilized by all of the information.

Several trees were 100 feet high. One leaf was the size of a small house. Devon slowly stood up and everything swayed, like sea grass under a gentle ocean current. He saw small blue cat like creatures, these creatures stood upright.

Devon reached out and touched one of them. Fire outlined the creature's body and Devon received a small shock for his ignorance. Devon was fighting off competing sensations He couldn't breathe, maybe he didn't want to.

Devon noticed no physical changes from the blue creature's shock and it didn't matter; no antidote waited for him back at the camp. A black moose-like creature grazed in the distance. As Devon got closer, more of these creatures came to investigate the disturbance…him.

Devon imagined Joshua saying, "I told you to take a weapon." His instincts told him to hide in the black and grey shrubs. Near this hiding spot small blue flames slowly drift to the ground. He watched these moose-like creatures eat these fallen flames. Consuming these flames caused the creatures to become transparent.

The flora that covered Devon withdrew into itself like it could feel his presence. He scooped up a little bit of dirt and placed it into his pocket. To his left were trees. Devon plucked off a piece of bark and it ignited briefly, more little blue embers fell. There was a controlled inferno that showed through holes in the bark.

Devon heard a cry of anguish, behind him several of the black creatures were on their side. He saw no wounds; this had to be from the radiation. This sight drove his mind back to the realization that he couldn't stay there. He had been there an hour and had walked two square miles. He viewed every green rock, fire tree and orange reed along this yellow pond.

He looked up at the large leaves that covered the area. He couldn't see if there were any cities beyond where he had traveled. Devon's eyes watered and he threw up again. Devon retraced his steps along the stream next to the pond back to the rift.

Devon entered the swirling rift and came back up the walkway. He could see Joshua through the rainbow sheen. Devon moved toward the light. He could felt the pull of the rift as he searched for the strength to keep moving forward.

"Let's get out of here!" Devon said tumbling out of the rift. Joshua helped him to his feet and they made their way back towards the campsite. Steam rose from his clothes. The layers of Devon's boots had been eaten away. His suit had been eaten away and he was severely nauseated.

"What's on the other side?" Joshua asked with an expectant look. What could Devon tell him about the other world that wouldn't be considered insane? They quickly reached the campsite and Devon slowly took his gear off. Joshua checked his gear and counted the bullets in his clip; he stared at Devon the whole time. After the second gallon of water, Devon spoke.

"We have to leave." Devon said. He said this because he wanted to extinguish his own desire to reenter the rift. He knew if he stayed he might want to go back down those stairs. He unsheathed his dagger, it had been chewed up, it was unrecognizable.

"Maybe we could wear masks next time," Joshua said handing him a canteen of water.

"I'm not sure that would help," Devon said, too exhausted to laugh.

Joshua sat back down. Devon's reaction must have fell within the range of acceptable responses. Devon sat and thought he should have waited until Joshua was stronger. These thoughts distracted him from thinking about the effects, if any; the rift would have on his body.

No one has ever seen anything like this in the history of seeing. They were the first, he was the first. Devon stepped into the silence that hung about their camp with a suggestion, "We need time to think about this. So we can decide what to do next." He meant, of course that he needed time.

Devon wanted to go back, he needed to go back. Joshua wanted more than anything to just go. They ate dinner and Devon tried to focus on anything but the rift. Other than the lingering nausea Devon didn't feel any different. There was a possibility that he might be unaffected.

Joshua hummed some soulfully melodic tune as Devon sat and sketched a detailed chart of locations on the tablet computer.

After eating Joshua unconvincing said, "Tomorrow we will go back. We will go further." His demeanor was more assertive than before. Joshua's training sessions were so grueling that most evenings he went right to sleep; still nothing could have prepared anyone for this.

"Look at what I brought back," Devon said pulling out the soil sample from his pocket.

"Dirt?" Joshua said.

"True enough," Devon said, relenting for the moment. He didn't say what he was thinking: Highly radioactive dirt. Devon examined the sample under the microscope. The findings from the dirt made him more confident that no bacteria or virus could survive the journey through the rift. The cells he found were carbon based, with some irregularities. Joshua was right, it was just dirt.

Devon thought that the sample may have been corrupted, perhaps by his presence. The photos of the rift ripples came out as pure darkness. The few photos of the corridor were dark and out of focus. Devon didn't get many samples. The thought of taking samples was the last thing that crossed his mind.

"Any luck with the samples?" Joshua said sticking his head inside of Devon's tent.

"No. No luck at all,"

"So we have nothing. Now what do we do?" Joshua's tone made it clear that he hated asking.

"Did you bring dessert?" Devon asked.

Joshua nodded and smiled because words wouldn't do. "I'm not ready to go back, are you?" Joshua said. He hoped that his urging would quicken their evacuation.

"Not yet," Devon said. He hadn't fully recovered, but he wasn't ready to leave.

Devon ate around the campfire and for some reason the food tasted better than it had in over a year. The wind picked up and it began to lightly drizzle. Devon sensed the rain before it fell. Joshua saw a distorted Devon through each raindrop.

After Devon finished eating and they retired to their tents. Joshua wanted to experience the earthquakes. He wanted to walk against the hurricane. The gusting wind punching him in the gut was something he craved, but only if he could control it. If Joshua put his mind to something it became a compulsion.

What bothered Joshua the most wasn't that he couldn't get to the other side. It was that nothing he brought mattered. Nothing they took with them mattered, not the tents, the rifles, and the equipment—nothing. The rain grew in its intensity.

The calmness of Devon's return must have seemed mysterious to Joshua. Devon's continued guardedness, his need to be alone, must seem strange. Devon didn't tell him much about the otherworld only that the water was made yellow from the radiation.

Devon didn't tell him that he had looked into that bubbling yellow sludge and he saw nothing live. He didn't speak of these things because something inside of him felt they didn't deserve to be here, that he didn't deserve to see any of it.

Devon lay awake in his tent thinking of what to expect from his next trip into the rift. His mind returned to the same question: What lies in other rifts? Interrupting these thoughts was the sound of Joshua's snoring.

The morning had the scent and feel of a fresh start. When Devon exited his tent; Joshua was gone. Devon's constant need to run toward conflict grated on Joshua and Joshua's stubbornness grated on Devon. When Devon woke up his senses were so heightened that the ordinary swoop of a dragonfly came as a revelation. Was this sense heightening a side effect of his visit into the rift?

There remained only minor fatigue from his previous trip into the rift. Devon tried not to panic at Joshua's absence but there was a rising panic. He became convinced that somehow Joshua's failure in the rift had changed him.

Joshua proudly rounded the bend carrying three trout he had caught in the stream by hand.

"I thought you'd never wake up," Joshua said.

They ate breakfast and Devon put on more clothes this time. They walked back to the entrance of the rift.

"I will come after you if you don't return in two hours."

"I'm coming back," Devon told him. "Yesterday I returned in 2 hours."

"2 hours…you were gone nearly 5 hours."

"5 hours?" Devon said shocked.

"So no gun?" Joshua asked.

"I have all I need," Devon said breathing deeply. Devon pressed his daughter's stuffed butterfly into Joshua's hand for safe keeping.

"Remember the plan," Joshua said. "Get to the other side, look around and get out." That was the last thing Devon heard before he entered the rift.

Devon moved quicker through the rift. The darkness was temporarily alleviated by the flickering of orange light. Devon paused for a moment and waited for the light to return, but it never did. He wasn't far from the other side. Devon stepped out of the portal. His boot prints from yesterday were still there.

How could he have been so careless? He slowly looked around and used his foot to cover up his tracks as he walked. Across from the pond was a stream. Devon would focus his attention there. He was rewarded by a minute long glimpse of bluish otter-like creatures that were lazily floating. He made sure not to directly interfere with any being here.

There was also something else; moving slowly through the reeds. It was close to the bank in deep cover. Devon couldn't tell what it was and after a while he lost track of it entirely. These bluish creatures disappeared every time Devon moved. They had been tipped off and were laying in wait for his exit.

Devon felt like he was alone in the wilderness. When he left camp, it was nine in the morning. On this side of the rift it appeared to be one in the afternoon. On the other side the sun was red, but otherwise indistinguishable from the sun Devon was used to.

Only colors with longer wavelengths can pierce through the thickness of the atmosphere. Earth's atmosphere contains nitrogen and oxygen molecules. These atoms scatter light waves. Violet light scatters into the atmosphere in large amounts. Blue and green light scatter in similar ways; this is why the sky appears blue.

Particulates in the air and water vapor scatter blue light, leaving mostly red light. This is why the sun looks red when it is low on the horizon.

In school, Devon always colored the sun yellow, even though NASA colored it orange. The sun is not yellow. It is a white light emitting object, its frequencies are scattered through the atmosphere and it appears in a variety of colors at different times.

On the other side of the rift rainbows were red shifted and plant leaves that were black in the day were noticeably red at night. The stream Devon sat by was orange. Devon saw various sized Rorschach ink blots flying through the air. He slowly waded through the shallow orange water.

The slower movement of creature and the faded colors of plants told him that these things were dying. These creatures which would have normally attacked him on sight were mere shells of their former selves.

Devon struggled to catalog the three-talon toed flying ink blots and the pink large spider-like creatures. The blue otter-like creatures with webbed appendages and lash-like tendrils for tails floated in the stream.

This time Devon patrolled in the opposite direction and then back to the pond before reentering the rift. When Devon came out of the rift, Joshua was frantic. "Last time you were gone for five hours… this time you were gone for a day and a half!" Joshua stammered.

Devon grabbed him. He looked in his face. "Get a grip. I couldn't have been gone that long," he responded. Devon slowly looked around and took note of his moonlit surroundings.

"No…no…no. You were. I stood guard. I stood right here."

"Guard against what?" Devon said as he took off his smoldering clothes.

"Anything… does it matter," Joshua said as they hurried back to camp.

"You said you would come and get me in two hours," Devon said, replacing his eaten away boots and clothes.

"Without my gun? If you never return, if something happens to you on that side, I can't get to you." Joshua said. He finally calmed down after seeing that Devon was fine; a twinge of fear still ran through him as he loosened his grip on the rifle. Of course, Joshua was right.

"What did you find?" Joshua said as Devon wearily guzzled water.

"I saw the plains. I walked the plains but I felt like I was observing plains from a thousand miles away."

"And what else?"

"I took more samples, for all the good it will do. The next time we come back to the rift, we'll need to know more."

"Come back, what do we need to come back for?" Joshua offered. They began packing. They got on the Soul Stirrer and returned to the warehouse.

The second trip to the rift did two things. It convinced Devon that he could survive on the other side. He was nauseated but it lasted for a shorter period of time. The second thing it did was convince Joshua that he was not ready for this kind of journey. In fact, Joshua couldn't wait to get back to training.

Joshua trained harder; he also wore a sadder look. Devon trained Joshua in a sheltered way because Joshua couldn't engage with otherworlders. Now for the first time Joshua fully understood what he was up against. Joshua spent the last six months erasing his electronic footprint from the world. He sat at his desk near his laptop.

"While you were in the rift, I waited just outside. My finger hovered over the trigger of my rifle and that's when something occurred to me," Joshua said turning to Devon.

"What was that?" Devon said.

"Imagine you have an empty tube of toothpaste," Joshua said walking over and picking up a tube of toothpaste. "Instead of filling it up with water, sodium lauryl sulfate, fluoride, propylene glycol, diethanolamine and artificial sweeteners; you liberally fill it up with the notions of people. You seal it, shake it and squeeze it from the bottom.

"The more pressure you apply the more the ingredients get pushed together. The more the ingredients shift towards the conservative opening at the top. Not all of the ingredients are used, some stay at the bottom, some on the sides, but all of them are necessary for the whole thing to work." Joshua said squeezing out some toothpaste. "And like this tube, systems are just a delivery method." Joshua said opening his computer.

"Hmmm," Devon said as he looked at Joshua.

"I thought about what would happen to me if you were dead." Joshua said. "The certainty of death gave meaning to time. For me each moment you were in there held significance. Time wasn't important to you on the other side. Time is measured in seconds, minutes, hours, and years, but it doesn't flow at a constant rate. Like the water in a river rushes or slows depending on the size of the channel, time flows at different rates in different places.

"Today it is Tuesday and I could very well be experiencing this day in the past. Perhaps, we are right now living in the past and everything happening has already happened and we are somehow experiencing it as the now," Joshua mused.

Whenever Joshua was in turmoil or doubt he looked for digital comfort. He would engage in quantum physics and other things that couldn't be explained linguistically. His visuals informed how he spoke. Today he would continue to question the stability of matter.

Devon could no longer able to read Joshua. Joshua's mind was growing into his body. He had his life and Devon had his, both were intertwined. Joshua had witnessed devastation, yet all of his experiences were from a safe distance. A tornado didn't tear through a house and toss two cars because it was after him. The earth didn't destroy a city block just to pull him into it.

Joshua would have to actively participate in his learning. He will discover. He will move forward, but the mission remained. Devon knew he needed more.

Devon had traveled the world. He had learned from the people. He made mistakes, he took chances. He had been in real peril. He could have died two dozen times. Asking Joshua to do the same is something Devon would not do.

Devon had been a buffer between Joshua and everything with bad intentions. The following morning, Devon left. He only left behind a note on the comfy recliner that read, "I'll be back."

CHAPTER 10

Gina woke up and looked around her bedroom. Sunlight started to peek through her curtains. Gina pulled her long legs, complimentary arms and high insteps out of the bed. Her night was uneventful.

She flipped open her notebook computer and looked through her emails. Her eyes passed over dozens of sales. The digital offers were confirmation that she was valuable. She clicked a forty percent off lingerie advertisement. She looked at her pajamas and remembered that she hadn't bought lingerie in over a year.

The walls of her bedroom were brown, like the kitchen. The walls were bare except for shoes that hung from a single nail. Her closet bulged with tight fitting clothes, most of which she could no longer wear. A large window was in the right position for sunlight to creep into the bedroom around 6:30am.

Needles and various threads were on the nightstand next to what looked to be an unfinished green blouse. A dozen shoes hid underneath the edge of the quilt. There was a large stuffed giraffe in the corner. Gina got up, made the bed, not a wrinkle in sight.

She rubbed her stockings together, warming them with her hands before putting them on. She walked into the bathroom, washed her face and playfully twisted her hair. She mixed two scents together and rubbed it on her thighs. She quickly squirted herself with something that smelled like jasmine and wood strawberry.

Gina went into the living room and turned on the TV. She sprayed water on the two ferns that cascaded down the wall unit. When the leaves were sufficiently damp, she went into the kitchen and made breakfast. While she made breakfast she half listened to the Seattle weather forecast.

During a commercial break, she moved her neck left, then right, to stretch it. Her 5'5", one hundred and twenty pounds frame fought for the remaining bits of her youth. She had the kind of beauty that went unnoticed underneath prescription glasses and modest clothes. Her subtle curves were defined by an athletic figure, wide shoulders, narrow hips and ample breasts.

It took her forty-five minutes to look over her petticoats, dresses and skirts. She settled on a white and blue blouse, a skirt that was tight about her waist and showed from the bottom of her knees. She caught her hair in a net of velvet and squeezed into three inch purple heel. She walked pass the 'The Future is Feminine' plaque in the hallway on the way to the bathroom.

In the bathroom mirror, she looked at her smooth thin pouty lips, rubbed her cheeks. She brushed her teeth, twice. She read somewhere that successful people brushed their teeth twice in the morning. She took the makeup brush and combed backward on her eyebrows, only getting the powder on the skin behind the hair. This is how she enhanced her arches and took the focus off of her almond eyes. Gina completed the look with an eyebrow pencil and a kiss of lipstick.

Gina turned off the TV, hurried downstairs and got into her car before the street sweeper gave her a ticket for the second week in a row. She listened to the local news on the radio as she fought her way through traffic on her way to work.

She parked in her office parking space. She purchased two dozen bagels from the coffee shop and briskly walked by the disheveled man holding the *end of the world* sign outside. She crossed the street and entered the six-story building. She got in the elevator and then up four flights to her small office.

According to the flashing reminder on her computer, there were two networking meetings today. It was her turn to bring bagels. Gina did her job, she was professional and efficient. At lunchtime, she sat in the nearby park.

She watched the Mute Swans and ducks in the large pond fight for food, as little turtles peeked out the green water. Gina liked the park because it wasn't crowded. Most people need a reason to go to the park, for Gina the park was the reason. Gina finished eating and slowly walked towards her office with her hands in her pockets. Her walk was delayed, thoughtful.

The stoplight turned green for her to walk across, but she didn't move. Across the street was Devon; she straightened her skirt as the walk signal counted down. Once the signal showed ten she walked across the street. She made eye contact with Devon but didn't break her stride. Devon ignored the raised hairs on his arm.

Devon took three days to figure out what he would say to her when he saw her. He cleared his throat and said "Hi." Gina turned to him and smiled. She slowly walked over to him and said, "So you're stalking now."

"I had to see you."

"Is that right?"

Last time Devon saw Gina was six months ago, but he never lost track of her. A dozen times he wanted to go to her; in his mind, it was a hundred times. Every time he thought about seeing her; he thought about what would happen if he did.

"I am glad that you're OK," Devon said, pretending to be unaffected by the smell of jasmine. He came closer, so he could smell the hint of strawberry. These scents made him feel anxious. The mixing of scents summarized big city living. The small smile that played at the edge of her mouth reminded him how soft her lips were. Her smartly tousled ends couldn't hide her blushing face.

"Can I see you later?" Devon whispered. He didn't want to disappoint or raise her hopes, but he did want to sound serious. Gina seemed startled by this question; a piece of her thought him to be a ghost.

"Maybe," she said. She pulled the oversized black sunglasses down from the top of her head. Gina paused for a moment and said, "Seven o'clock at Coffee Net on fourth. Do you know where that is?"

Devon nodded. Gina's voice that made that one sentence sound like Christmas. The purple jacket and heels turned and went into the office building.

At 6:55 p.m., a small corner table inside Coffee Net was occupied by Devon. He placed a single green tulip on the table and waited and he waited. Devon waited an hour and a half. The purposeful click of her heels, the rhythmic sway of her hips came through the door. Gina arrived as if waiting was part of his punishment. Gina was worth the wait.

Devon stood up and she hugged him like an old friend. He inhaled her as they let go of each other. They sat there silently eyeing each other for two minutes. Gina smelled the tulip and stood up to leave. She took one step toward the door before turning around. "Where the hell have you been?" she said. She sat back down. Her phone lightly chirped.

"Could you turn off your cell phone?" Devon requested.

"You've got a lot of nerve," she said shaking her head. "You just left, didn't say a word and now you just show up" Her paused was like the hum of a tape recorder; it hung over the table. Her irritated tone made him squirm. "Say something," she said her eyes demanded answers.

"I've been gathering the courage to trust you," Devon said shyly.

"Trust me? I've been completely honest with you."

"So I'm the only one you've slept with this year?"

"That's none of your business."

"I thought we were being honest here."

"I am being honest about what I want to tell you," she said twisting her hair making sure her long neck was highlighted. She didn't know what to make of this; still she invited Devon back to her modest one bedroom apartment.

Her apartment wasn't a dive and it wasn't first class. He had been the only person she had invited to her apartment in two years. Last time he came to her apartment, it took two weeks for her pelvic area to readjust.

Devon entered her apartment; she didn't turn on the lights. He followed her into the bedroom. His eyes shifted to how she softly planted her feet. Devon smiled when he saw a six foot tall stuffed giraffe in the corner.

"I see you got the giraffe," he said.

"You're the admirer?" Gina said as Devon looked around the room.

"I didn't know you were a ballet dancer?" he said, his eyes stopped at the satin green pointe shoes that hung on her wall.

"How could you?"

"Do you still dance?"

"I have big ankles," she said with a subtle smile. Gina seemed afraid to look at the shoes. "I picked up choreography easily," she said. "I loved the pageantry, the costumes, the make-up, and the music. When I was on stage and that curtain opened... it was lights, perfect pirouettes and all five positions.

"I hit all my marks at my twelve-year-old recital. The founder of the local junior ballet company came backstage to talk to me. He critiqued my style, my technical ability and then he asked me if I wanted to be a prima ballerina? Of course, I said yes.

"That was the day he started training me to be a professional dancer. I practiced every day. I even went to summer camp, we couldn't afford it, but I went." Gina said taking the shoes off the wall. Devon sat patiently listening as she slipped on the shoes. Gina stared at the photo of her mother on the dresser. Her thoughts left the bedroom and traveled back to her childhood.

"I had just finished the 11th grade when my mother was diagnosed with stage four pancreatic cancer." Gina said. "My mom accepted the diagnosis and her fate. No more chemo, no more therapy; she just wanted me to make her comfortable, and I did. I helped her to the bathroom, brushed her hair, feed her and clothed her.

"My mom was in a lot of pain. I just couldn't sit through Calculus or Language Arts with her like that, so I didn't attend school for the last months of 12th grade. I didn't even go to the Prom. Ten months later, my mother died in her sleep; she was gone."

"A week after she left me, I was formally invited to audition for principle by the company director. I had practiced for this moment, the routine...Swan Lake. I was on stage alone; the lights were hotter and brighter than ever. I moved with confidence, grace and power. I held my breath for most of the routine.

"Rotate, fully extend the leg, arms offset center of the body, turn.... I knew what I had to do, but somewhere around spin twenty nine I lost my balance. I fell to the floor. I heard sobbing, my own. The diagnosis was a grade three left ankle sprain, a complete tear of the ligament. The prognosis for recovery was two to four months. I cried as I was carried off stage. I knew I wouldn't be closing with the fifth position for a while.

"My mother put me in ballet when I was six," Gina said taking off the shoes. "To dance professionally was a dream we had chased for eleven years. My mother believed that my connection to America was the fulfillment of her Asian-American dreams.

"I was her last hope, she'd say. No one in the family, other than my mother, saw me that way at all. If my cousins took out the trash they were spoken of as if they had split the atom. The only thing I knew how to do was sew on buttons. I was good at that.

"My relative's constant bickering only stopped for photos. They only saw me as a banana. I saw the looks they gave me when I walked by. The kind of looks that hoped the creature before them would stretch and twist until it became something else. I could never take my mother's place. I didn't speak the language, I didn't know the traditions and I couldn't fly away.

"My older sister disowned her hapalua sister. She hated America for great grandfathers, for grandfathers and for her experience, but most of all she hated America for my presence. She saw my weakness, my mistakes and my deficiencies; somehow everything was my fault.

"Did you know that in Mandarin there are over thirty words that mean "not smart", Bù Cōngmíng is the most common. That's the word my sister called me. Not smart go empty the trash, Not smart is spinning again, Not Smart make up your bed. My sister returned to China long ago. She never saw me perform; she never came to a recital."

Devon extended his arms and Gina gladly walked into them. "It took a year for my ankle to completely heal by then I had gained fifteen pounds." Gina continued. "The company founder said I was no longer suitable to be a prima ballerina. I said something like go fuck yourself, you're a shit coach and my career was officially over." Gina said.

Gina walked over and hung the shoes back on the wall. "They say I was a quiet child. My mom said that whenever I heard music, I would dance around the house." Gina rubbed her right foot remembering all the corns, calluses and toe ulcers. Her left ankle was completely healed but every now and then she felt pain.

"We weren't rich. Ballet tuition, summer camp fees, shoes, costumes and miscellaneous fees accumulated. When my mother passed away there was a lot of debt. I paid that off by working at a local dance club."

"You were a stripper?" Devon said.

"I waitressed there. Once the debt was a manageable size, I went to a little college where they let you complete business management courses online," Gina said flopping down on the bed. "Oh, how I wanted to be like Suzanne Farrell, Allegra Kent and Kyra Nichols. I should have known that someone like me could never be like them. It was stupid dream, I know."

Devon thought of his hallucinations, the fresh nightmares and said, "It's actually beautiful." Gina went into her dresser and pulled out a blue sleepshirt and then went into the living room. She quickly returned wearing the sleepshirt.

"Since you've come all this way to see me you can stay, but you get the couch and don't get any ideas. I put a pillow and a blanket out there for you."

"Okay."

"The heater has been broken since winter," Gina said sitting back on the bed. Gina looked at Devon and then slowly reclined on the bed. She laid her head on her pillow and sighed. Devon stood up and reached for the bedroom door.

"Devon— I'm a little cold, Could you cuddle with me, for warmth?" she said softly.

Devon nodded. He removed his shoes and crawled in the bed behind her. He got underneath the blanket and spooned up perfectly behind her. He wanted to lay with his back to her. She could feel his heat pressing against her. She exhaled slowly as she snuggled her backside against his body.

Devon slightly increased his body temperature to lessen the need for extra covers. Gina reached behind her to touch Devon's hip.

"Where have you been?" she said, half sleep.

"In the morning, I'll tell you everything."

She pulled his hands to other soft areas. Devon placed a single kiss on the back of her neck, a minute later she was sleep. She made a soft purring sound as she slept.

Gina's alarm sounded and she reached behind her. Devon wasn't there. She sat up on the bed and looked around. She got up, stretched and then walked into the living room. Devon spent the night on the couch. Seeing Devon sitting on her couch brought a smile to her face.

"Do you want some toast?" Gina happily said.

"I'll take a slice," Devon replied although he wasn't hungry.

Gina went into the kitchen and started making breakfast.

"I haven't slept that good in a long time," she said as she brought a big plate to Devon. She sat down next to him.

"I made scrambled cheesy eggs as well," Gina said proudly.

Devon took a small bite of the strawberry preserve covered toast.

"Go ahead and eat," Gina urged.

"I'm not really hungry," Devon said. Last night he felt like leaving and roaming the sewers, but he didn't. Gina dabbed her index finger in the last bit of strawberry preserve. Devon kissed the strawberry off her fingertip.

"You promised to tell me where you've been," she said biting into the toast. "You're in some kind of trouble, aren't you?"

"The world is," Devon said. Devon looked pensively into Gina's eyes. He sighed and said, "I've been around the world and back. A year ago, I was a junior level stock trader; today I don't know what I am. Remember when I told you that I was married and had a daughter?"

"Yes."

"They are dead because of me."

Gina's mouth froze mid chew and she put the plate down. Devon stood up and took a deep breath. He slowly walked around the living room. Gina's eyes followed him as he moved.

"A year ago, on my way to work, I found a package in the bushes outside our home. I didn't think much of it at the time. I opened it on my lunch break, there were stylish glasses were inside. I put them on. I could surf the Internet. They were voice activated, but they also allowed me to view another world."

"See now, you have to leave," Gina said getting up. "I always pick wrong. Why did you have to be a psycho?"

"Honesty, remember?"

"You've got five minutes to start making sense."

"Later that night, these beings came to my house killed me, my wife and my daughter."

"Killed you?"

"Killed me."

Gina put her plate on the kitchen counter, grabbed the largest knife she could find and started poking it at Devon's direction. "Are you leaving, or do I have to call the police?" she stated.

Devon put on his shoes and said, "I'll leave." He walked over to the open window and jumped out of it. Gina dropped the knife to the floor, nearly cutting her leg. Her apartment was on the second floor. She ran to window and looked down.

Devon was gone.

CHAPTER 11

Gina sat on the couch for five minutes, talking to herself, before beginning her day. She moved when she felt mentally stable enough to go to work. Gina was in the park sitting on her favorite bench. She sat in the shade of her favorite tree, eating a tuna salad sandwich when Devon slowly walked over to her.

"You're not limping. How did you know I would be here?"

"Stalking, remember?" Devon said sarcasm dripping from his words.

"Right...You really expect me to believe that I'm talking to a dead man?" Gina said, chuckling.

"I was brought back."

"I don't have enough mental health days to cover this," Gina said, putting her sandwich back into her bag. She shifted uncomfortably as she cleaned her area. Devon put out his hand and said, "Please...Walk with me."

She stared at his hand and looked into his eyes, and then she put her hand into his.

"I've missed this," Devon said as she stood up.

"You missed walking through the park making up ridiculous stories," she said as she walked with him.

"I'm just getting you away from other people, so I can tell you the ridiculous part."

"I thought you already told me the ridiculous part?"

"Promise me... that you won't fly off the handle like you did this morning?"

"I can't promise you that," she responded.

Devon looked around for a moment. "I was brought back by a being from another earth."

Gina turned and walk away from him mumbling, "I was in last years' woman march. I participated in the Nutella Riots. I don't need this."

Devon knew that Gina would need a lot more convincing than Joshua. He quickly scaled a tree, leapt to another tree and flipped down in front of her. Gina stopped in her tracks and slowly sat down on the nearest bench without looking.

"I wasn't just brought back. I was altered."

"So you're not human?"

"I'm human, but I am more," Devon said sitting next to her. "These beings, these otherworlders, are called Them. They are bigger, faster and stronger than humans. Their earth overlaps ours and they can enter our earth through radiation created doorways."

"So, aliens are coming here through radioactive gateways?"

"They aren't aliens. They can't be seen because they exist in dark matter."

"And they can't be seen? Got it."

"So you got it."

"No, I don't have it. There are beings here, but they can't be seen. Then how did they kill you and your family?"

"After coming through these doorways, which are called rifts, they absorb energy. This energy gives them abilities."

"Abilities?"

"Do you remember that mudslide in Oso a few years ago?"

"It was terrible, forty people died. It took them a year to dig out the roads and homes."

"That was Them."

"The mud?"

"Once on this side they can harness elements to cause a happening, an event."

"Like a mudslide?"

"Or a hurricane, tornado or an earthquake..."

Gina smirked, got up and started walking fast towards the park exit.

"You promised."

"I never promised. You don't just come back into someone life with this. If you don't want to be with me just say so. You don't have to do some Cirque du Soleil performance, which was impressive by the way and invent alien stories."

"There's more..."

"Nope...nope..." Gina said quickly walking by Devon.

"Please..." Devon pleaded.

Gina looked over her should at Devon. She sighed and said, "Come on. These heels are killing me anyway. I am going to need a drink or two if there is more to this. Don't smile because you're buying."

Devon followed Gina three blocks away to a bar called, The Executive. The bar had its melody erased by encroaching social outrage. All that was left was a stale, dependable tone that droned on, like the wind blowing across a hole in an opened soda bottle. There was nothing executive about this place; it was a dive bar with an updated menu.

It was happy hour and the bar was half full. Gina and Devon took a booth in the middle of the establishment. She sat across from Devon ordered a drink and called her office. She had more meetings scheduled, but she was taking the rest of the day off.

Gina removed her shoes and stretched out her toes. Devon lightly rubbed her feet underneath the table as pop music lightly played from the overhead speakers.

"So about this altering," she said, playing with the paper napkin underneath her third mint mojito.

"I was altered by one of the otherworlders," Devon said. I was reborn with grief strong enough to survive death. This being was out of phase. They had been on this plane too long and couldn't go back through the rift. The experience of it caused him to want to help humans before he died.

"This altering enhanced me and I have been evolving. If I had not been altered, I would have never met you."

"So Them…. cause storms?"

"They cause some natural disasters, sometimes they make you lose your keys or place thoughts in your mind."

"For what reason?"

"It depends on their mission."

"Mission?"

"They come through these rifts and carry out their mission, and then they go back."

"So when they visit, people die in natural disasters."

"Sometimes."

"So they are murderers…"

"They murdered me. Finish your drink we are leaving."

"Don't think that because we cuddled last night, and I'm listening to this story of yours that you can start ordering me around."

Devon smiled and said, "This place is about to be robbed."

"Huh," Gina gulped.

A few minutes ago, a man wearing a dark trench coat entered the bar. Devon made out the outline of a sawed-off police issued Mossberg shotgun underneath his coat. The individual took a few minutes to look over the place and now he stood in the path to the front door.

The man pulled out his shotgun and fired into air ceiling. He yelled, "Everyone shut up!" as ceiling tiles fell to the floor. "You know what time it is. When I come to your table put your wallet and purse in the bag."

"You're not getting my purse," a woman near the back of the bar exclaimed. A man sitting next to her got up, pulled out a handgun and placed it to the women's temple. "Is that right?" The second robber asked.

"Can I just dump the contents on the table?" the woman said while placing her purse on the table.

"Come over here, start with her," the second robber said.

The man in the trenchcoat finished beating a man, who tried to leave. The man was now on his way to relieve the woman of her new purse. Gina reached across the table and held Devon's hand. The robber with the handgun had visited half the tables and was now in front of Devon and Gina's table.

"Why don't you leave these people alone?" Devon calmly said. He never broke eye contact with Gina.

"Hey Johnny, we got us a hero over here…"

"What do we do to heroes?" Johnny replied.

"Bury them," his partner said. Johnny quickly walked over to point the shotgun at Devon's chest.

"I have more money in the car, a lot more," Devon said. "I'll give it to you if you just leave these people alone."

"Where's your car?" Johnny asked.

"In the alley…"

"What ca…?" Gina said. Devon's darting eyes silenced her before she could finish the question.

"Billy, rich guy here has a car out back," Johnny said, turning to his partner. "Alright, you and long legs… get up."

"Me?" Gina said.

"Yeah… you. Get up you're coming too," Johnny said, using the shotgun to motion for Gina to get up. Gina put her shoes back on and they walked to the back door exit. Billy stayed inside to watch the other customers. Johnny quickly looked around outside and once again put the shotgun to Devon's chest.

"You think I won't use this! There's no car out here!" Johnny shouted.

"I know. I just brought you out here, so they wouldn't hear you scream." Devon said.

"Hear me scre…?"

With Devon's left hand, he crushed the barrel of the shotgun. With his right hand, he punched Johnny so hard he flew fifteen feet backward. The thud against the wall and subsequent scream caused Billy to blindly run out the bar's back door. He came out looking for someone to shoot.

Billy turned to his right where a petrified Gina stood in the middle of a darkening alley. Before he could exhale, a large fist dominated his point of view. This punch sent him hard to the ground.

Billy lifted his gun only to have his fingers broken as Devon crushed the gun around them. The pain coupled with the overload of information caused Billy's brain to reset and he fainted. Devon waved over to Gina, but she didn't move. She wanted to move, but she couldn't.

"Some people don't have any manners," Devon said walking over to her.

"Don't touch me! Don't you touch me, whatever you are," Gina said.

"I told you I wasn't lying. Look, these guys won't be going anywhere anytime soon. They are damn lucky you were here, I went easy on them," Devon said picking up the bag containing the stolen items.

"You went easy on them?" Gina said her heart still racing.

"Take this bag inside, make up a story and meet me out in front," Devon said handing the bag to Gina.

"Why me?"

Devon pointed down to the blood spattered on his shirt. The sight of the blood nearly caused Gina to faint.

"Gina you can do this," Devon said. Gina took the bag and walked back inside the bar. Devon took off his shirt, balled it up and put it into his pocket. He zipped up his coat and walked around the corner.

Five minutes later, Gina emerged from The Executive's front door. She hugged Devon tight. Police cars were just arriving on scene.

"They still made me pay for my drinks," Gina said.

"What?" Devon said, his eyes widening.

"Let's just get out of here," Gina said tugging on his arm. Their hands touched and they silently walked two blocks to Devon's motorcycle. Devon got on the Soul Stirrer and throttled it. Gina stared at his motorcycle and then she looked at Devon.

Devon handed her a helmet. "It is the law you know," he said. Gina looked at the helmet and then again at the motorcycle.

"It won't bite you." Devon grinned.

"I think I'll drive my car; you follow me."

Gina got her car and Devon followed her home. Devon parked down the street from Gina's apartment building. He met Gina in front of her apartment building. They walked up the stairs and entered her apartment.

Gina took Devon's bloody shirt and put it into her washer. She went into her room while Devon waited in the living room. Gina returned with her hair let down.

"So this is what you do?" she said admiring Devon's finely crafted upper body.

"Sometimes," Devon responded.

"Them...right, or is it They?"

"Both."

"So you fight them?"

"I did."

"You did...So you can see them."

"I can."

"They are here...right now?"

"Not now, but a female one was at the bar."

"What? Why didn't they do anything?"

"Maybe it wasn't part of their mission. After I punched the Johnny into the side of the building, she left."

"They were controlling, suggesting..."

"For all, I know they could have been telling him not to rob people."

"If they can't be seen how do I avoid these things?"

"You can't."

"You're scaring me more."

"I won't let anything happen to you," Devon said.

Gina's face muscles relaxed and she was calmer.

"Give me a moment," she said.

Gina went into the bathroom turned on the shower and took off her clothes. When the steam started to creep underneath the door, she stuck her head outside the bathroom and said, "Come get in."

Devon took off the rest of his clothes and got in the shower as she commanded. She laid her head on his chest and cried as the water engulfed them.

Devon held her as warm water trickled down her back. He gently washed her. Devon stepped out of the shower carrying Gina. There was a slight creak as the floor sagged from the weight.

He entered the bedroom, slowly dried her off. He laid her on the bed and slowly massaged lotion into her still damp skin. The week old bruise on her thigh from bumping into her desk made her slightly turn when his fingertips wandered near it.

"I'm exhausted," she moaned.

Devon wrapped a towel around his waist. Gina stood up, awkwardly naked. She rubbed her waist and sighed. She walked in front of the mirror, turning this way and that. She slowly pulled the nightgown down around her. Devon's head followed her every move. The nightgown covered her but revealed the side of her breast when she moved like she is doing right now.

She smelled like chocolate. He needed to touch her; he wanted her to touch him. She could feel his want, she knew his need. Devon was altered, but this want was something she would play with at least for a while. She cut off the light and opened the curtain allowing the silver moonlight to bath the room.

The way she sat next to him on the bed caused him to swallow hard. Every time she moved she came closer to him, until their mouths touched, sealing at the soft wet corners. Devon couldn't help but kiss her back. He felt her tongue and she felt his.

All day, her eyes hardly met his but now her eyes penetrated him. His hand found her cheek. She was smooth, soft and warm. It was as if the heat had cut her shape of her out of the darkness.

Kisses had always made her drunk, they freed her. When you kiss someone in the dark, it's not like you are kissing them. You are kissing the darkness, as if the darkness had life, a shape, a taste and warmth. It's like being in a sexual position where you can't see the other person's face...it could be anyone. The towel that covered Devon started to unravel.

Gina fell back and sagged against the pillows, her eyes never leaving him. Devon was afraid to look at her, afraid of her words. He was afraid of what was next. The window rattled there was a sound of movement, it was just the wind.

"Do you mind warming me up again tonight?" she said.

"I don't mind," Devon said, once again getting under the cover behind her. His arms surrounded her until she slept.

It was Saturday and Gina stayed in bed until ten. She lay there for two hours thinking about everything Devon said. A single tear ran down her cheek to settle on her pillow. There was the sound of plates clattering in the kitchen.

Gina angrily rounded the corner. When she entered the living room and she saw a half dressed Devon preparing country omelets and pancakes. Gina took the plate from him and gave him a big kiss, her hand lingered on his chest.

"A girl could get used to this. I mean the breakfast, the rubdowns and the cuddling—not the guns, blood and aliens. The good thing is that I know I'm not crazy," she said in between nibbles.

Devon sat down beside her. He used her computer to pull up a video of a massive avalanche. Gina heard people shouting and she saw one skier rising above the moving whiteness. On another video a man leapt over abandoned cars and ran into a fast moving wildfire in Lakeport, California.

"That's you?" Gina questioned. Devon nodded his head. Gina put down her plate and angrily rushed at Devon. She pounded him in the chest until she grew tired. Devon put his arms around her.

"You know how many times in my life when I felt like I didn't belong." Gina turned away from him as tears filled her eyes. "After my mom left me... I knew how it felt to look at the danger warnings written on a prescription bottle. I knew how it felt to take a mouth full, and to not care, because you're not worth anything," she said looking up.

"You allowed me to believe that you were just another person who didn't believe I was good enough. Is there a point to this?" she said her eyes narrowing. "Why did you come back?" Her voice grew more intense.

"What do you mean?"

"I mean... It's been two days, when are you going to sleep with me?"

"Remember you said it took you two weeks to recover last time?"

"Of course, that's why I'm asking," she said.

"What's keeping you here Gina?" Devon whispered.

"Keeping me here?" Gina responded. "Well I'm alone. I'm in a nowhere job which provides for my kitchen porn, so there's that." She with a half-hearted smile. She was in the same position as most first world women. Stuck in a job she was overqualified for due to education and under qualified for due to gender.

"How would you like to be a part of something larger than yourself?"

"Six months ago, my life changed when I met you outside that theater. That night you noticed me in ways people never do. That night I broke all of my rules. I felt like I knew you that I could trust you. I only spent an evening with you. That evening I thought I was a part of something larger than myself.

"For the first time since my mother died I allowed myself to feel. So as long as you're making breakfast; I'm listening. You said you are evolving. What are you evolving into?"

"A better person."

"Bad dreams are keeping you up?"

"Yes."

"You still see her, don't you?"

"Who?"

"Your wife."

"My family... I miss them."

"You still haven't told me what any of this has to do with me?"

"I really don't know why I am here. It's just that I have spent so much time running. I have seen amazing places and unique people but the only found peace when I was with you. I was lost and being with you steadied me. Being here now just feels right. Besides I never got to properly thank you."

"You thanked me about five times that night," Gina said leading him into the bathroom where she brushed her teeth.

"The first time I tried to enter a rift; I was exposed to high levels of radiation and my skin ripped. It made me nauseous and I was disoriented. My glands were damaged and my skin pigmentation changed. I couldn't recognize my own face in the mirror. Each time I entered a rift I went further, until I finally got through to the other side. The other side is amazing…" Devon said describing his journey to Gina.

They went into the bedroom. Gina was no longer scared. Devon's eyes moved to the ballet shoes on the wall. "Do you think you can show me?"

"No… I can't." Gina waited a moment, stood up and took a few steps towards the shoes. She gingerly grabbed the shoes off the walls and held them in her hands. When she did her eyes lit up. She sat down and put the shoes on. The shoes were tighter than she remembered. She looked at Devon and stood up. Her arms lifted up and she spun around it was as she were flying.

She turned, stretched and walked around the room. She swayed her hips and Devon's eyes dipped lower as she stood in front of him. She was effortlessly flexible.

A neglected desire was aroused within Devon. It permeated his being. The image of Gina slowly spinning was burned onto his retina. Devon struggled to not allow his emotions to spill out like a hit vein.

"Me, dreaming of becoming a ballerina. I should have just gone to pharmacy school. A six-year-old, sewing on buttons for meals in a sweatshop; I just happened to look up at the TV," Gina said. She placed her feet in the third position and said, "My name is Gina Abigail Lawrence."

Gina sat on the edge of the queen size bed and slowly took off the shoes and stretched her feet. Her watery eyes glared at him, she reached over and put her hand on Devon's lap and started to rub.

"You've gotten bigger since the last time I saw you."

"A little."

She leaned over and put her lips on his. She kissed him as if she would devour him. Her breath was heavy, her mouth was wet. She moved her hand to his chest and whispered into his ear. Before he could do anything, she sat up and wrapped her hand around his manhood and licked.

Devon shuddered slightly before she took him inside her mouth. She didn't mind the salty taste. She had always preferred savory to sweet.

Wetting her lips with her tongue, she said, "Now I'm, going to show you something amazing…" She looked up at him with a curious smile. She leaned forward and ran her warm, wet tongue along his length. Devon's anticipation grew by the minute.

She slowly closed her lips around him. As she did this she thought of performing on the biggest stage, underneath the brightest lights. The subtle sounds Devon made were the rise of applause as she went deeper.

His hands softly pushed her away. She looked to him wondering what she had done wrong. Devon wore a heavy lidded expression as he grabbed her hips firmly. He lifted her into the air and pulled her toward him, it was her turn.

The first touch of his tongue to her flesh produced a soft cry that escaped her lips. Under the attention of his tongue, her soft skin hardened into a bud. He lowered her onto his lap and swirled his tongue around her nipples. Gina gasped from the pressure and warmth.

One of Devon's hands pressed into the small of her back. His other hand moved through the thin material of her gown. He pulled her close to him. She leaned back as his tongue continued its journey. She leaned back until her head touched the floor. Devon's free hand ran over her wetness.

Her moans were sonic approval of his actions. His hands held her in place; she would not escape his flicking tongue. She filled up like a river under flood; pulsing waves of need quickly filled her. This was not the gradual spring melt she had been used to. His lingering tongue pushed her dangerously near the edge. She was about to be swept over when he stopped.

"I, I can't take any more..." said she breathing heavily. Devon gently laid her on the bed. She twitched as he pulled the covers over her. Devon took her shoes and placed them back on the wall. Gina's closed her eyes trying to freeze time to stay in this moment forever.

CHAPTER 12

Gina clung to his back as he shifted gears on the Soul Stirrer. The rhythmic and constant tapping of raindrops provided their journey with sounds other than crickets and frogs. The leaves on the road momentarily parted as they sped past. Devon paid no attention to the trees, to nature, or to the way his motorcycle chewed up the gravel road and spit it back out.

Russell Maples grew in the shadow of lofty mountains. Rusted twigs lined the well kept gravel roads that led to driveways. Slender sapling rose in the shadow of every tree. Branches contorted along these roads to curve in, creating an arched rooftop of leaves.

A month ago Gina had been altered. Three weeks ago Devon gave Gina a gun to fire. She slightly squeezed the trigger; there was a flash. She immediately put the gun on the table.

Gina had no ill effects of being altered like, Joshua's car sickness, but after firing that gun her hand shook, out of synch with the rest of the world.

The morning breeze gently blew dew from the leaves. The rest was disbursed by the sun's heat. They parked three miles from their destination. They slowly made their way through the brush and into the forest.

About a mile into their journey, Gina slipped her hand into her belt pouch and pulled out a string. She smoothly fit it onto her weapon without looking. She opened the quiver attached to her belt and put an arrow to her bow.

There was a leaf sixty feet away, forty feet high on an ash pine. Gina selected this target because it looked like it was the next to fall. She nocked the arrow and felt for the wind. It was drier, the breeze was gentle, and she accounted for this. She took a step, exhaled, aimed and when she felt in control, she let the arrow fly. The arrow pinned the leaf to the tree's bark.

She had pulled the bow so tightly that lines of red and white were in her palms like she had been burned. She lowered her bow, letting it hang parallel to the ground with her right hand while the other went to her hip. Devon took two steps forward. He smiled and stared at her for a moment.

"I hope you don't think I am going to get that," he said.

Gina handed him her bow and scampered up the tree to retrieve the arrow. She heard a noise; below her was six foot, 500-pound brown bear. This mother bear was standing on her hind legs. The bear was growling at Devon. Devon was thirty feet away and shifting into an attack stance. Gina climbed down the tree quickly and landed ten away from the bear.

"I got this," she said hiding the alert in her voice. She slowly raised her hands to draw the bear's attention. She stepped sideways and positioned herself between the bear and Devon and then she yelled.

The puzzled bear lowered from its hind legs, turned and trotted back into the woods.

"How did you know to do that?" Devon asked as they continued their journey.

"I read it somewhere," she said shrugging her shoulders. She put the arrow back into its quiver. Gina didn't like guns but she kept a Glock 19 and a SIG Sauer P226 close by.

Gina liked visiting the rift late at night, because she might see a fox passing by or sugar gliders resting on telephone poles. As they walked, nighthawks gathered nearby to feed on insects and mice. She watched these creatures play out ancient rituals of predator and prey.

She wandered down a dirt trail strewn with pebbles, dead leaves, and pine needles still damp to the touch. If she stood in any one place for too long her shoes would have had velvet ants and emerald beetles crawling over them. Tall pines, with their scaly ridges of bark, rose on either side of the rift opening. This rift site was near the ocean.

The Connecticut air filled Devon's lungs as he walked into the oceanside rift. He came out near a small jetty. On this jetty was an octopus-like creature. It was eating a smaller creature. The bones sounded like a king crab shell being twisted and slowly cracked. Devon's mind was on his goal but he couldn't help but to explore this new world.

As Devon approached this creature, it flared its cuttlefish like a skirt and disappeared into the murky orange depths. Out further into the ocean a whale-like creature let out an angry. On Devon's way back to the rift, he neared a cove that contained twelve waterfalls all crashing into the rock bed.

His presence scattered hundreds of what looked like large Jersey Tiger moths. Falling water from over 300 feet sounded like a sponge being slowly squeezed. This cove was also frequented by a small lizard that walked on its hind legs, the hissing sounds they made sounded like the buzz from an old TV set. There was a distinct smell of chemicals wafting through the air, no doubt the result of radiation damaged cells. Devon exited this rift.

Devon and Gina gathered their items. It took Devon an hour to steady himself, but he was no worse for wear. The salty wind blowing off the sea, the odd interior stillness disoriented him; perhaps it was the lingering sound from the yellow crystal waterfall.

The next rift was in Buchanan, New York. This was no forgotten town. The inhabitants were inhospitable to Devon for no discernible reason. In this rift, Devon noticed that the plants seemed to face in the opposite direction of similar plants on his Earth.

Devon sat and examined the roots of these plants. The plants were parallel to the geomagnetic field. This meant that magnetic field here was stronger. The trees were dusted with yellow snow.

Near the rift was a green cow-like creature. The breath that escaped its blowhole was labored. It was dying. A creature about the size of a large cat appeared. It had blue eyes, a pink nose, rounded ears and three toed paws. The fur was thick and white. It had a single black stripe that ran from the nose to trail along its back.

Another curious creature had a feline snout, ears and whiskers. It was opossum-sized and brown. The creature had flippers, a sleek body and a short flat tail. There were several of these creatures near the lake. The large one must be the alpha; it was gray and had black crisscross pattern stripes along its head.

These creatures disappeared below the yellow foam surface of the water. The markings on their head mimicked the black reeds along the water's edge. These creatures were always in large masses and they loudly squawked when disturbed. Devon exited the rift and marked a spot on the map.

Next, they journeyed to a mountain range in Tooele County, Utah. It was basin desert full of saltbushes, salt grasses and other salt tolerant plants. This location was dominated by sagebrush and salt flats but there were also rifts present.

On the other side, Devon discovered a few scavenger species such as a large six-legged insect that had a large bee-like head. It had a brown head, a white thorax and a red abdomen. The wings attached at the thorax. Their beaks and talons were razor sharp.

These creatures lived in caves they dug out. There was a sticky substance on their cave walls produced by the females. It smelled like sour milk. These creatures didn't attack Devon and he didn't provoke them by disturbing their nests. This rift was another mark in the map.

Through a portal thirty-six miles from Phoenix Arizona, Devon saw a gargantuan insect. It had to be the size of four elephants. It had a large hard grey shell. Devon examined the shell of a dead one; it was several inches in thickness. This creature had long prongs on the side of its head, small beady eyes and six legs. Still, there was no city here. Devon marked on the map again.

They traveled beyond towns of brown roofed cabins to Morris, Illinois. The rift was not far from the rusted car wheels that were buried up to its spokes in the dirt. This rift was a secluded mountain area.

As soon as Devon stumbled out of the rift a small primate followed him. On the ground were pen-size serpentine creatures that hid in holes, waiting to dig its fangs into a passerby. This was the second rift where Devon saw the large orange four-legged herbivore and the flat red tree climbing animal. These two creatures must be common to rain forests.

Over a ridge a squid-like creatures that made a cow-like mooing sound. In a nearby field a dozen ten-eyed deer size creatures grunted as they grazed. Some of these creatures had patchy fur and stumbled around; they would ne casualties of radiation.

In the evening, the sun's red filter brought a high pitched buzzing. Small hummingbird-like creatures with the head, legs and chest of an eagle produced this buzzing. These creatures were unafraid of Devon as they pollinated the flowers; another dot on the map.

The swamp was covered in yellow fog and was home to a large number of plants, which were densely packed together. There were higher concentrations of carbon dioxide, xenon and hydrogen sulfide in rift areas like this; another map dot.

At night, the forest of Decatur, Alabama was dark, wet and very cold. Despite the rain and damp conditions it teeming life. It was like a prehistoric biological wonderland. Most of the rain water never hit the ground.

The splash of raindrops sprinkled golden rainwater on the leaves of trees, some of which reached one hundred feet high. This caused the forest to be a murky depth of shadows.

The interior of the jungle was dark as layers of leaves blocked any sunlight. On the leaves insects squirted something similar to honeydew secreted by aphids. Most of these flowers bloom at night. One plant was illuminated by a broad red band near its stem and iridescent blue near its tip.

A large group of orange plants, with spiraling leaves, folded up and disappeared down a shaft when touched. Devon poked it and it didn't move away, so technically that's a plant. The grey moss on the side of trees added to the natural ground cover.

Devon could see life flowing the plant's veins. He grabbed a large blue leaf and held it up so he could look through it. When he did this he saw a giant herd of single cell animals. Their eyes had the bubbled look of boiling tomato soup.

They were the size of a calf and if you looked at them long enough, you could see through them. There was no other sound except the sound of these creatures moving over the black grass. One of these cell animals turned to look as Devon but kept grazing. Devon watched these simple creatures for a while, before leaving to mark the map.

"What's on the other side?" Gina asked him. This question was met with opportunity. Gina had entered the rift in Connecticut and then again in Utah, each time she exited after only a few steps. Her nausea was too great, being close to the rift affected her.

With her excitement dampened, the rift had been reduced to an email; that had held her attention long enough and was now to be deleted. While Devon was in the rift Gina trained. She ran for miles and swam if there a river was nearby.

Gina liked the solitude because her body was always in some state of shock. She wore long sleeve shirts and sweatpants to hide injuries and body discolorations. Sometimes she would injure herself just to see how long it would take to mend, sometimes even after an injury healed, she would feel phantom pain for days.

She was performing physical feats in less time than it took to describe them. She already had the balance of a gymnast. She was now performing back flips and butterfly twists in succession. Gina could duplicate any physical action after seeing it a few times.

She gained bumps, bruises and cuts trying to climb every structure she could find. Her light landings on the ground, following flips, showed she had started getting the better of gravity. She had new feelings and new sensations; in some ways she didn't hate this.

She developed a wider binocular vision and spectral range which made late night practices easier. Any new revelations made her eager for Devon to return. She would often burst into tears from being profoundly connected to everything.

Gina was by the creek aiming her arrow; she didn't bother nocking it. She didn't have a target. She stood there motionless. She closed her eyes, concentrating on the sound of anything approaching. She didn't have long to wait before she heard the sound of little claws pushing down leaves.

She opened her eyes. The target was set, near the brush and seventy feet away. She took careful aim from her position, her target was still concealed. She waited until the opossum pushed its head far enough from underneath the brush to expose its neck.

There was a hard thud and the creature fell over into the soft brown leaves; the arrowhead protruded out of its body. Her arrow hit the animal before it noticed its mistake. For a fleeting moment, a harsh grin crossed her face. Gina's hand reached for other arrows. She was tracking three other targets.

Gina liked flowers and plants. She welcomed their presence. "Plants are the earth's lungs. Plants, like people have tenacity, inventiveness and an ability to adapt," she'd say. Gina marveled in the radical otherness of plants. She admired the plant's dependence on sunlight, their inability to get up and leave and still thrive.

"Seeds are merely the plant's way of adapting, splitting itself, traveling," she said to herself while looking through the microscope.

For Devon the rifts had become familiar, places he didn't need to rush from. Gina waited for Devon, so he couldn't get caught up with his explorations. Each excursion had a time limit and a draining effect. They each had a recovery time, three hours, two hours, one hour before they traveled to a different rift. Alabama would be their sixth rift in two weeks.

The samples Devon had brought back resisted any interpretation which was strange. It was strange because they found no cells in the samples; just a much lighter color of dirt.

At the time, Devon thought the sample was contaminated or evidence that organisms from the rift decomposed quickly. Another thought came to him, a thought too late to test; perhaps he had caused a reaction in the rift and to the samples. Devon had done his best to be an impartial observer, but sometimes he was doing more than observing.

Devon spent the rest of the afternoon looking at samples under the microscope on the table outside of their tent. The samples he examined told a series of obscure jokes with punch lines he didn't understand. The slides had an unusual structure, but they still fell within an acceptable range.

He had Gina look at a slide and write down what she saw. She kept squinting through the microscope and raising her head. Gina sat back raised an eyebrow and said, "It's dirt." Devon made a mental note not to take any more samples.

Later as they lay in the tent Gina stared at him; her eyes full of hunger. Devon gently pressed down the hairs on his forearm and cuddled beside her in the sleeping bag. He held on to her in the shadow of the rift before they returned.

CHAPTER 13

The warehouse was dimly lit when Devon quietly entered. He expected to see his altered friend. There was no wind, but his trench coat flapped out of respect. The warehouse was in various stages of I-don't-really-care clean.

Light was provided by several aromatherapy candles that were scattered about. Overturned champagne flutes littered the floor as "Boogey Man" loudly pumped out of man-sized speakers.

On the wall above burned, bullet grazed, knife punctured clothes hung the word 'Joshua' written in large hand-drawn calligraphy. In each section of the warehouse a voice command panel had been installed.

The windows had been replaced with larger ones, which were also computer monitors. A grand piano, electric guitars and a half finished self portrait sat in the middle of the structure, next to a server and a large yellow toolbox.

An assortment of gloves hung on the wall. Displayed on the computers were charts that graphed muscle response, elasticity and cellular regeneration. Joshua had been tracking how high he could jump, how fast he could run, how strong he was, how many particulates were in the air and from what Devon could tell; he was trying to win the lottery.

In the rear of the structure were missiles and engines parts and a forge to craft weapons. Devon walked by a box filled with solenoids, soldering equipment and drills. Another box had keypads, tubing and various wires this box sat by a hydraulic lift, a welding torch and three used fire extinguishers

Beakers labeled "Venom" and "Acid" were on the laboratory table next to the distortion glasses. This computer's algorithm was trying to locate people.

Two women moved around an emperor size bed in the center of the building. Both women screamed when they saw the well dressed Devon. Joshua quickly rounded the corner wearing a Persian orange and silver embroidered robe and blue scandals. Joshua dropped his scepter when he saw Devon. Joshua gave Devon a hug deserving of the three month absence.

"Who are they?" Devon said gesturing to the naked women.

"Great art in bad frames," Joshua said. "pozhaluysta, ostav'te," Joshua said to the ladies, which is Russian for 'leave'. Joshua poured a drink. He turned back to Devon and asked him if he wanted something to drink.

"I'm good. What did you do with all of the books?"

"I got bored."

"Really? You are still learning languages."

"Well… you kinda interrupted my final test in Russian," he said with a chuckle.

"I can always come back later…" Devon offered.

"It's great to see you," Joshua said embracing Devon again.

"What's with the robe?"

"Oh, this…it used to belong to Nicholas II," Joshua said taking a sip from his cup.

"The last Russian Czar…It's a museum piece…"

"It used to be."

The ladies took their time getting dressed, but they left before Joshua finished with his drink. Joshua took off his robe and shorts and put on a white tucked shirt, a thin black tie, slacks and black oxford shoes.

"You have had sex since you've been changed?" Joshua said as if a notion had just struck him.

"Once or twice," Devon responded.

"You've got to give her that out of town feeling, even when she's in town."

"There are too many things to worry about, pregnancy, injury and one wrong move and someone might find out that what I am doing isn't normal." Devon replied.

"Oh, what I am doing isn't normal, it's God-like. Well… I keep hearing 'oh god this', 'oh god that' and 'oh my god'. I have a growing team of partners and sometimes we partner-up, if you know what I mean…" Joshua said.

"I can see how that kind of thing can go to a person's head. This place looks like hell. Wait, is having sex all you've been doing?"

"Every chance I get. I mean sex is always amazing but now it's unbelievable. I always thought I was a stud but there isn't a word for what I am doing now."

"I know how phenomenal it is. Before I was altered, I didn't realize how intercourse regulated hormones and affected mental states. As I have evolved, I realized that regulating my body and mental clarity through sex, while amazing, is lazy. Joshua, we are trying to save the world, not get lost in it."

"I've kept up with my training," Joshua said with the look of disdain on his face. He didn't like to be scolded.

Devon looked up at the artwork on the walls and over the bed. He looked at the hanging red and green mood lighting. Devon turned off the music and opened the large toolbox marked 'Loot'. This box was filled with credit cards, money and jewelry.

Devon pointed to the sixteen guns on the bottom of the weapons locker. Devon held up the unloaded handgun that was sitting on the desk and said, "This is not keeping a low profile."

Joshua hunched his shoulders and said, "It's just me, my guns and my millions."

"Where did you get all of these guns?"

"The web, back pages, information feeds and from set-ups..." Joshua said, taking the gun from Devon and placing it into the weapons locker. "...by set-ups, I mean I took them."

"A flamethrower...really and I see you got a mask," Devon said looking at the black and red demon mask on the wall.

"Yeah... You should have seen how scared people are when I kick in a door wearing that. I don't wear anymore; you don't need a mask when you're...ummmm. Now, I just wear the distortion glasses. I've been careful."

"Careful, doing what?"

"Let me show you," Joshua said rubbing his hands together like a giddy child. Joshua picked up the distortion glasses and grabbed some gloves off the wall. He put on his suit coat and left with Devon. Under Joshua's direction, Devon drove two cities west and parked.

Joshua led Devon to the top of a restaurant. Joshua took off his coat, handed Devon the binoculars and instructed him to sit and watch.

Then he jumped off the roof. Joshua quickly pulled a pistol from his back holster. He ran past the expensive bulletproof vehicles that lined the street. Devon sat down as air vapor came from Joshua's mouth as he entered the building.

The five-story building Joshua entered had been taken over by Taylor Hooper. Taylor Hooper drives without license or insurance. He breaches contracts and he's the biggest human trafficker in the tri-state area. His clients are middle and upper class deviants. He had a small army of well paid, well trained protectors.

Taylor wasn't a criminal mastermind. He wasn't smart. He just filled a void. A void left by politics, a void overlooked by society, a void usually filled by overseas business trips. As long as the authorities received their cut, he could operate within this void. Taylor walked through the town like he owned it.

Through the large windows, Devon saw Joshua quickly empty a magazine into several people. Devon stood up, but it was too late. Joshua had cleared the first floor.

Joshua scanned left then right and started up the stairs. One foot on the second floor walkway and a thug lunged at him. Joshua calmly moved out of range, struck this attacker's throat, flipped over him and put a bullet into him before he landed.

More henchmen came into view; Joshua avoided point blank gunfire and created the necessary space to put a hole into each torso. Joshua sent bodies flying across each room he entered as profanities were hurled in his direction.

Joshua firmly gripped the pistol as he checked the blind corners. Bang, a two handed shot through the heads of two suddenly appearing thugs, a third was hit in the shoulder and fell against the wall. Joshua ran towards him as he writhed in pain. He delivered three blows to his skull and then fired an unsighted shot under his armpit to hit another man.

Joshua aimed and pulled the trigger until the pistol was empty. The last thug on the floor should have ran off or hid, but he didn't. Joshua hit him in the left temple staggering him against the wall.

Joshua grabbed the dazed thug and rolled him into a triangle choke. Joshua held him for a few seconds between his legs while reloading his gun, and then he shot the henchwoman that was creeping down the stairs. Then he put a bullet through the head of the guy he had been choking.

An errant bullet hit the transformer box and knocked out the building's power. Devon watched in infrared horror as muzzle flashes illuminated the building's corridors. Joshua didn't have infrared vision yet, but he was far from blind. He could hear breathing, heartbeats and terrified whispers in the dark.

On the next floor, Joshua picked off three other baddies with precise shots. He kicked in a door and immediately smashed the nearest guy's head on the table. He grabbed the gun hand of another thug and flipped him onto the table and used the thug's gun hand to fire at the two other men in the room, dropping both.

As light slowly filtered through the building, Joshua stepped into the hall and reloaded his gun with a flip of his wrist. Joshua fired his gun like it overslept. Joshua conserved bullets by not double-tapping the bodies he stepped over.

On the fourth floor, Joshua was out of bullets so he grabbed an assailant that was trying to run down the stairs. He lifted him and then slammed him hard to the floor. Two scruffy face assailants hit Joshua in the chest and back.

The big one was strong, but his hand came back broken, he dropped his shotgun and clutched his hand. Joshua smashed the hot polished steel against the thug's head. He fired the shotgun to blast the body of the smaller one through the wall. Within these narrow hallways Joshua inflicted maximum damage while avoiding trajectories of return fire.

Joshua picked up a rifle and fired a bullet, two heads at the end of the hall jerked back. This startled the others who immediately opened fire riddling the hallway full of holes and debris. Joshua pressed his back pressed against a corner and gritted his teeth as fifty slugs smashed into the nearby wall.

Half a dozen armed men stood between Joshua and the staircase to the top floor. Joshua frowned as tiny explosions of debris bounced from the wall. Joshua removed a magazine from a whimpering man's gun vest. He snapped the magazine in and adjusted his grip. He shifted forward around the corner and managed to land a headshot at the end of the hall. Five left.

The incoming fire slowed down, one more shot from Joshua and it died completely. Joshua quickly peered around the corner and the storm of gunfire renewed. Joshua scooted back just in time. He looked over his left shoulder to see the black fabric of his outfit stained dark with blood; it wasn't his.

He could hear them advancing on his position. Once his calculations were complete, he spun from cover and dropped two more bastards before they could catch their breath. Two more left. Joshua quickly rounded the corner before the closest assailant could raise his rifle. He put two rounds into his gut. He dropped his gun and fell to his knees, clutching his belly.

The other henchman went for the just dropped rifle. Joshua kicked the rifle away and landed a left haymaker breaking the man's cheekbone. Joshua hit him in the stomach and then tossed him down the flight of stairs.

Emergency lights came on and Joshua tucked in his black silk tie. As Joshua steeped on the top floor, two concussion grenades landed near his feet. There was a flash of light as heat filled the room. The first blast tossed Joshua across the hall. The suffocating smell of powder surrounded him as the floor shook.

The second explosion blew a hole in the wall and shattered the glass in the windows. There was silence, a moment of confusion and then the muffled sound of obscenities drifted into Joshua's ears. His lungs burned as he got to his feet. The closest henchman kicked him in the face; another one smashed his head into the wall. Joshua fell to the ground again.

Joshua looked up as one of the men took a decorative sword off the wall. The sword was thrust as Joshua. Joshua dodged this, but a chair was broken against his back, sending Joshua to his knees. Joshua kicked the sword wielding man against the wall. The sword dropped on the ground next to Joshua.

Four gangsters converged on Joshua as he grabbed the sword. He spun around on his back and separated the attackers from their ankles. A burned, bullet grazed, blood soaked Joshua stood up as the sword fell to the floor.

He straightened his clothes and tucked in what was left of his tie. Joshua's boots pressed shards of glass, splinters of wood and bone into the vinyl floor as he approached Taylor Hooper.

Taylor Hooper had already urinated on himself. His panicked eyes looked toward the fire escape, which was outside the window Joshua was standing in front of. If he wanted to escape, he would have to go through Joshua.

Taylor jumped at Joshua and began hitting him. Joshua lowered his eyebrows and grabbed Taylor by his three hundred dollar t-shirt. The shirt ripped as he lifted him off his feet. Taylor's rectum emptied ruining his leather pants. Joshua put his finger to his lips and said, "Shhhh."

Taylor tried to use his arms to defend himself but it was no use as Joshua slowly cradled Taylor in his arms like a child. Taylor could only feel pain as his ribs were crushed. All of the muscles on the right side of Taylor's torso failed simultaneously, as Joshua tightly pushed his arms together until Taylor's spine cracked. Taylor's body dropped to the floor as Joshua surveyed the carnage.

Downstairs, a large crowd gathered around police cars as several ambulances screeched to a halt. Across the street from where the yellow hallways were stained read a worried Devon paced. Devon stopped pacing and put his head down and sobbed like he had just lost a friend.

CHAPTER 14

Because of Joshua, Devon would now had fresh nightmares. The corners of Devon's lips slightly lifted and quietly scolded Joshua for this mass murder. Devon and Joshua rode back home in silence.

"I knew you wouldn't approve of my methods..." Joshua said as soon as the door of the warehouse closed.

"Your methods, everything you just did saddens me." Devon said taking off his coat.

"I did what you did." Joshua responded.

"No. What I did freed the innocent and was a step towards justice. You were just hurting people. This is not why you were altered; this is not why we trained!" Devon said turning towards Joshua.

"What? The things I always wished for now bore me," Joshua said walking around animated.

"You are creating fear. If this is what you have been doing the authorities are no doubt looking for you."

"Looking for me, they need to give me a nickname. You think the authorities find basements and hallways full wounded people and come looking for me. I always make sure that deserving people have been set up for my actions. Plus, I just erased all the video surveillance devices in the surrounding area.

"The authorities will do what they always do, which is take credit for toppling a massive criminal enterprise that operated in the city. The police will make it look a warring gang mass murder to scare the public into giving them a bigger budget.

Some will get promoted; there might even be a documentary. I can't believe you are this upset. A little part of the world is safer because of what I have been doing."

"Murdering…"

"I have these abilities, why not use them… Assembly line justice is too slow."

"Your way does not leave an environment of hope and a different way of thinking. You are creating vacuums for more misguided people to fill."

"You vigilante your way and I'll vigilante mine," Joshua said slowly walking away from Devon. "I am not like you."

"What does that mean?" Devon questioned.

"I have little desire in being a super and having below average sex," Joshua said washing his face and changing his clothes.

"This is not you," Devon said.

"You haven't been here, how would you know?" Joshua shot back. "You left and I didn't know if you were coming back. I didn't know if you were still alive. So, I handled things in my neck of the woods. Taylor was a violent psychopath. Did you see the pants he had on? He definitely had a high midichlorian count." Joshua chuckled.

An exaggerated hysterical laugh came from around a corner inside the warehouse. Gina's lightly pastel boxer braids slightly moved as she walked towards the two. Her green, fitted lace-up dress couldn't hide the sculptured nature of her body. Joshua's eyes soaked in her 5'5" frame.

"She's not bad. You know I have some ideas..." Joshua said to Devon. Joshua's voice was drenched with age old notions. His eyes revealed that any respect would not be equal. Gina glanced at Joshua and then shook her head.

"This is Gina and it's not like that. I brought her to meet you. I had hoped under better circumstances."

"The way you talked about this guy I expected better." Gina said.

"Do you want to see my highlight reel?" Joshua asked.

"I saw it," Gina responded.

"Well?" Joshua said.

"What you did was like grabbing a few poor kids to paint an urban mural on the side of an overpriced, not terribly good tasting, gentrified eatery, only to appease the residents."

"So, Gina, what's your story?" Joshua said.

"I don't have a story."

"Everyone has a story."

"If you must know, Devon and I have been installing handicap access elevators in New York subways."

"Ohhhh! Sounds real dangerous," Joshua retorted.

"Not as dangerous as what you did tonight."

"If I had done the same thing while defending a group of women or children, I would be given an award."

"People have rights," Gina said.

"Are those the people who are leveraging the state to support their deviancy or are they the people who taking away what little rights people do have?" lectured Joshua.

"Yet for all of this philosophy, women have no desire to date a violent psychopath."

"Yeah, but I dress nice. When I tell them I'm into murder and executions, maybe they hear mergers and acquisitions or maybe they are just into fucking dangerous men. Devon, this is fun..." Joshua said smirking at Devon.

"Fun, you really aren't thinking clearly," Gina said taking off her glasses and stepping closer to Joshua.

"Little girl—I've never been clearer. Let's see...you're shorter and smaller than me."

"Is that all you can see?" Gina said with a courtesy chuckle.

"I see that you've been altered, well congratu-damn-lations. You said not much Hypernium was left," Joshua said sternly at Devon.

"There was some left over," Devon responded nonchalantly.

"What does she have that we don't?" Joshua asked.

"Decency," Devon said.

"Can you blame me for growing tired of all this training," Joshua said. "Tired of all this reading and eating leek soup. I'm tired of Them, and The System and what's more I have realized that when we put out the call...no one will come," Joshua said growing annoyed.

"You don't know that," Gina said.

"Sure I do. By my calculations, we have less than a twenty percent chance of succeeding. People are too busy waving a rubber tomahawk in one hand and a league sponsored beer in the other. I've seen them cloak themselves in the American flag while brutalizing Americans.

"On social media people actually think they are talking down a product, when they're actually advertising it; and this is what we have to work with. Beings with smaller brains have lived and survived longer." Joshua said.

Joshua clasped his hands together and formed a simple hologram, a hologram he was having trouble trying to stabilize. He only managed to show a few grainy images before giving up.

"Joshua, I know firsthand that yelling at people won't change the world. The System is corrupt; the participants in the system are victims," Gina said.

"Their only super power is being a victim. They will watch us be destroyed while asking for more butter flavoring on their popcorn. How can you have any hope in the face of that?" Joshua said.

"I live with hope," Gina said.

"Gina, is it? This is not the type of undertaking for a little girl."

"Are you going to talk all night?" Gina said.

She stood in from of Joshua and bowed slightly, and then she issued a savage palm strike to Joshua's groin, followed by a back flip kick. Her tactical black boot landed underneath his chin. This jolt put Joshua on his ass.

"I'll have that drink now," Devon said walking towards the couch. Devon poured himself a scotch on the rocks and sat down.

"Working in subways must be dangerous," Joshua said holding his jaw.

He got up and lunged at Gina. Gina stepped inside his guard and landed a hard right hand. The fiercely driven fist sank into his hard tissues, causing him to flinch. She shifted her center of balance to avoid his counterstrike. Gina's dress ripped as she swept Joshua's leg, he landed on his back.

Gina briefly mourned her dress. Joshua quickly ran at her but was met with a kick to his abdomen. He stumbled backward into a pile of cables. Gina advanced and launched as series of flying kicks. Joshua sidestepped and grabbed Gina's leg. He turned and threw her through a wall and into the bathroom.

Gina landed six feet away and slid another ten. Gina tripped Joshua as he got close to her. The two fought while prone on the ground. When Joshua tried to get up Gina kicked him in the face; when Gina tried to get up, Joshua back fisted her. Devon poured himself another glass of scotch.

Gina kicked herself up and ran towards the weapon rack. She grabbed the nunchaku and swung at Joshua. Joshua knocked this weapon out of her hands. Gina picked a chrome sai that also went flying. The steel karmas were also tossed aside. Gina grabbed a double tiger head hook sword, a butterfly sword and then a dragon Kwan Dao, which was so heavy the rack wobbled as she removed it.

Gina was forced to drop each weapon she picked up. Each weapon that she dropped was picked up and used skillfully by Joshua. Gina bent and flexed, her clothes ripped and tore as she avoided being cut. Once all the weapons had been cycled through they bashed each other against furniture and walls.

Gina's fingers splayed to maximum as she caught a powerful blow from Joshua that stopped an inch from her face. Joshua followed this with a roundhouse kick that sent her to her knees.

Joshua performed a simple kata, looked Gina in the eyes and whistled the hook from a 70's tune about Kung-fu fighting. Gina scrambled to her feet and jumped out of the window and onto the sidewalk. Joshua followed quickly behind her.

Joshua nearly had her when she quickly scaled the nearest building. Gina ran quickly along the tops of structures. Joshua ran through three walls, two doors, and several windows trying to keep up with her. When Joshua climbed to the top of a building, she'd kick him in the face and he'd fall back down.

Joshua scaled a building by leap frogging off walls. He reached the top of the building without being attacked. Once Joshua was near the rooftop pavilion, he threw two concrete bricks at Gina. She dodged these but lost her balance and slipped off the edge. She managed to grab onto a pipe. She held on with one hand; dangling from a six story building. She swung and twisted until she could swing over to the broken fire escape. She climbed down and ran in the opposite direction. Joshua chased her back into the warehouse.

As Joshua came around the corner, Gina launched a series of attacks. Joshua easily pushed through her attacks, he grabbed her and lifted her over his head and slammed her down. Joshua held her neck at arm's length as she struggled in his grasp. He raised his free hand over his head. This was a powerful blow he would not be able to deliver.

Devon had grabbed his arm. Joshua let Gina go and yanked his hand away from Devon.

"I was just warming up," Joshua said dusting the glass and wood from his clothes.

"She isn't your enemy. I'm not your enemy."

"Who is the enemy?"

"Them."

Eighty two days had passed since Devon had altered Joshua and forty seven days had passed since Gina had been altered. During that time Joshua had been exacting justice and mending his own injuries. He was sloppy. A shadowy glimpse of him had been caught on video and there had been deaths. Joshua may have still been afraid of Them, but he no longer feared Devon.

"You've gone from vigilante to assassin. Being altered comes with responsibility. We don't want people to fear us."

"Hey, don't underestimate fear, it works."

"I've heard that somewhere before." Devon said.

Gina limped over to the couch and picked up her glasses. They were broken. She no longer needed them; she only wore them for the look. She got ice from the refrigerator placed it into large sandwich bags and placed them all over her body and she sat quietly on the couch.

Gina was slightly disappointed in herself. She wasn't counting on being saved. She would have asked Joshua if his scrotum still hurt, but pain swallowed any premeditated passive aggressive attempt to piss him off.

"You have something you want to show me?" Devon said to the pacing Joshua.

"I have something I'd love to show you," Joshua responded. Joshua assumed an exaggerated pose and from eight feet away he launched a superman punch at Devon. Devon bent backward to avoid the bad intent of this punch. Joshua landed and pushed his attacks at Devon. Each combination Joshua used was faster than the last.

Joshua struck Devon with a blow that felt like a bat had hit him. Surprised that he had struck Devon, Joshua grinned and danced around. He did three flips in succession and fired three consecutive kicks to Devon's face. Joshua grabbed Devon's shoulder and ripped his shirt.

Joshua fired off an overhand punch, which Devon narrowly deflected. Joshua struck from the left side, again Devon deflected the punch. Devon threw an overhand punch, which Joshua redirected so he could kick Devon in the face.

Joshua's satisfaction with his success, almost caused him to miss the moment to counter, but counter he did. Devon leapt out of range. This time Joshua wasted no time patting himself on the back, he continued his assault. Devon was hit with a right cross that cut his lip.

Devon intercepted Joshua's next kick and spun him like a corkscrew, sending him to the ground. Devon launched himself high into the air to land with a crashing knee which Joshua avoided by rolling. Devon's knee cracked the warehouse floor.

Devon overwhelmed Joshua from all angles. This caused Joshua to think. Joshua jumped and Devon jumped. Seven feet above the ground

Devon kicked Joshua in his side. Joshua landed hard and rolled into his loot box.

"You are stronger and faster, but too reckless not to be noticed," Devon said as he tossed Joshua into the server, destroying it. Joshua quickly got up used his palm to deliver a blue shock to Devon's midsection. Devon dropped to one knee.

"Hmmm…that's new," Devon grunted. Joshua followed this with another electrical push which sent Devon flying backwards into the training partitions. Devon grunted, his eyes had a faint gold outline and he rose to his feet as if he were levitating.

"Tonight, you barely left before otherworlders came. You aren't ready for that type of attention, we aren't" Devon said dusting off his clothes.

"I don't have any family or kids. I've been alone my whole life I've never had anyone… except you…but then you left me. You never really came back." Joshua said quickly approaching Devon.

"Don't do this…" Devon pleaded.

Joshua threw a strong, swift punch at Devon. While Joshua's arm was fully extended; Devon moved his head to the side and registered a grin. Devon put his right hand next to Joshua's face and frozen pink lightning jumped between his thumb and index finger and then there was darkness.

Not only did this pulse overload the circuit breakers it flung Joshua to the other side of the warehouse. Static came from the speakers and broken monitors partially illuminated the floor as the backup generator turned on.

Joshua was on his knees panting heavily. His eyes erratically searched the warehouse for Devon. Devon had altered his skin to match the darkness and became invisible. Gina squinted to follow the action; her infrared vision was not fully realized.

Joshua ran as the shadow behind him punched holes through hardened brick and plaster. A kick sent Joshua flying a dozen feet, against the wall. A storm of punches from this shadow snapped his head back. These were not the cordial arsenal of haymakers that were used in earlier training. These lessons would do more than blackened Joshua's eyes.

"There has to be a reason I'm alive, there has to be a purpose for this," said the shadow before it jumped into the rafters. Joshua followed the shadow, the shadow outmaneuvered him. This shadow covered one hundred feet in what seemed to be four seconds.

When Devon's pigment changed back and Joshua landed several bodies blows to his midsection. Devon absorbed these hit and redirected the energy back into Joshua's hand pushing him backward. Joshua slowly fell from the ceiling struts like he was in a western getting shot off his horse.

Joshua landed on the concrete floor with a thud. They weren't sure if Devon floated back to the ground or not; because he landed without making a sound. Joshua grabbed his back, lifted his swollen face and crawled towards the couch where Gina was.

Joshua awkwardly rose to one knee, his legs throbbing. He tasted the blood that trickled from his nose and said, "OK...we have a forty percent chance of succeeding."

"Look at you... talking about having a chance," Gina smugly said.

Joshua pulled himself into the comfy recliner and released a long moan.

"Joshua humanity could use you," Gina said to Joshua as she handed him a bag of ice.

"So just some ragtag heroes," Joshua said, holding the bag to his head.

"How about a team?" Devon said coming over to the two wounded fighters.

"So now that we have a forty percent chance, what now? Do we gather the grazers, identify the craziphinos and craziness from the sane, or is it more stomach churning encounters and more sobriety?" Joshua asked.

Gina's noticeable grin quickly turned into a frown.

"Yes and yes," Devon said as he walked past them, his stride full of indie soul. Joshua sighed while he watched Devon move.

"Look at this warehouse, imagine what we could do together. We must stick to our principles. We must be better than this. Joshua the worlds need you. I don't like leek soup either," Gina said quickly looking at Devon.

"You hurt people tonight," Devon said to Joshua.

"Most of them were bad." Joshua said.

"...and some just needed a job to feed their families, they didn't deserve this." Devon said staring at Joshua. Joshua just lowered his eyes.

"You have to make things right," Devon said.

"I will. I had detailed files on people. I have been mapping rift points. I have been monitoring events around the world. They seem to be less random, more predictable. Also, the rifts seem to be getting larger."

"I figured as much," Devon said.

"I feel better when I'm doing something, even if it's the wrong something," Joshua said turning to Gina. "Devon shares before he teaches. We've been best friends since college; he invited me on this journey. You move gracefully, are you a performer?"

"I am a dress size larger than I would like to be. This is me and I'm okay not being perfect. I was in a pit of hopelessness. I was so used to always saying sorry for whatever reason. Devon changed everything. He gave me hope, and now you have as well."

"He does listen," Joshua responded.

"People need our help. The real stuff breaks them, they can't stomach it. They'd rather not have it. They rather allow things to get worse than have the truth. I might not have hit you so hard, if you hadn't called me a little girl." Gina said to Joshua.

"Sorry about that. Devon, maybe just maybe, I tried to impress you," Joshua said.

"So you don't go around killing people." Devon said.

"Well...sometimes I have to," Joshua said.

"How did you become this way?" Gina quizzed.

"I went to all of the community forums and the town halls," Joshua said. "I watched communities of psychological experiments move along as if they weren't a plan. I witnessed the state monetize bad behavior. I felt detached. I was falling apart so I did what anyone would do; I digitally invaded the lives of people I don't know. I lived under the bridges of the information superhighway.

"About a month ago, an elderly lady walked into a convenience store. She stumbled along with her walker, barely able to make it from the door to the counter as her walker's legs struck the floor tap, pain, tap, pain. Her age and the cancer in her bones made this simple trip; one she's done a thousand times before, the last trip before going into the hospice that will house her for what's left of her days.

"The lady said hello to the woman behind the counter and placed four cans of cat food on it. She fumbled with her purse as she opened it. The purse weakly leaned to the side. Her purse didn't carry much, but it was everything she had left. Her hands and the sides of her eyes were full of the memories.

"Behind her, a young man was annoyed that she was taking too long. And today of all days, he had enough of coming into this store on his way to work only to end up being later than he already was.

"The man grumbled as he pushed up next to her. His complaints about how valuable his time was only grew louder. The lady lowered her head, only wanting to take her cans, shuffle away from the counter and out the door.

The woman's eyes told a story of pride and heritage. The smell of cornstarch masked the urine scent that told the story of a nation that forgets it's no longer able to battle warriors.

"The man forced an 'excuse me' towards her. The woman's life experience and personal trials told her that this man, who had treated her most unkind and with such vigor, was not to be given in to. The lady turned to the man and calmly said, 'No, there is no excuse for you'.

"The man raised his hand to hit her, but he couldn't move, because I was the third person in line. After the confused look left his face, he apologized to the lady as she left the store and then I broke his hand..."

"Wow," Gina said looking at Joshua.

"I started flattening tires on the expensive cars of twenty-something men picking up their girlfriend from high schools; and then I progressed to making drug shipments disappear. I think my body count is near triple digits." Joshua continued.

"I'll say," Gina said.

"I found government documents about an illegal military weapons shipment. I traced deposits to an offshore account and then I hit the transport train. The train carried a ten million dollars worth of weapons. Once I secured the weapons I engaged in a shock and awe campaign of my own..." Joshua looked at Gina.

Gina slowly limped over to Devon, who had just put his scotch glass down.

"Ummm, Joshua has a mask... do I get a mask?"

"No. Any more questions?" Devon said.

"Yeah, how are we all going to fit on the bike?" Joshua responded the corners of his lips revealed a smile.

CHAPTER 15

While Joshua and Gina healed, Devon brought them half a dozen books to read and large portions of leek soup. He repaired the warehouse and added blast doors. He removed the missile parts, six tons of cable, most of the swords and other easily traceable items. Using more partitions, he created bedroom spaces for Gina and Joshua.

Devon bench pressed 2,000 pounds and he leg pressed twice that. Devon trained while carrying on conversations with them. He wanted them to see how far they had to go. It would be two days before they could resume training.

"How long did it take you to master all of this?" A stretching Gina asked Joshua. They both smiled as prominent dark shadows were under their eyes.

"No time at all." was Joshua's response.

Gina couldn't read Joshua's expression but she knew he was lying.

"Who did this?" Devon said when he saw the training equipment not in its proper place.

"Wasn't me," Gina quickly said and an argument between her and Joshua followed. This was their second argument over who left out the equipment; and it was the third argument over whose turn it was to clean the workspace. When Joshua lost an argument, he hummed. When Gina lost an argument there was an uncomfortable silence.

"Geez, how long do I have to hold this pose?" Joshua grumbled as he bent over.

It had been 108 days since Joshua had been changed and 60 days since Gina had been altered. The mood was considerably lighter with Joshua back on board.

"Later, could you teach me how to erase my digital footprint?" Gina asked the bending Joshua.

"I can teach you now."

"We have to finish training first," Gina said. She smiled linked her hands together and put them over her head; behind her ears and then she bent her elbows in the wrong direction. She took three small steps and put her feet in the fifth position. She stood on the tip of her toes and then jumped high into the air and beating her legs like wings before she landed back in the fifth position.

"I'm impressed," Joshua said realizing that Gina had been a student of movement long before he was.

"Now, bring the heel of your support leg forward. If you don't, you'll fall," Gina said to Joshua.

"Like this?" Joshua said contorting his body.

Devon was in the middle of the warehouse marking points on the map, but he heard everything. The noise from them falling over made Devon smile. It wasn't long before Joshua had enough of the splits and left the warehouse to train by himself.

Gina turned on some music and began stretching. Devon vaulted over three partitions to land by her side. She quickly stood up and approached him. Devon grabbed her and she performed a backward dip.

She turned her back to him, swayed her hips and lifted her arms. She let her arms slowly fall against Devon's neck. Devon spun Gina and then tossed her high into the air. She flipped to land with her feet on his shoulders. Devon slowly lowered her down in front of him. As soon as she touched the ground, she began to salsa.

Devon danced around her. He jumped, turned three times in the air and landed with a slow split. Devon had already attended Ms. Lawrence's ballet school.

Gina looked at Devon. "You're getting pretty good."

"You ready to work out?"

"Always."

Devon lay on the floor and she put her hand in his. Devon bench pressed Gina, while she did pushups on top of him, occasionally lowering down for a small kiss. Gina always kept eye contact whenever she trained with Devon.

Gina was easily clearing six feet on her jumps. "Show off," Devon said grabbing a towel to wipe the sweat from his neck. Gina walked toward him and pressed her lips to his. They molded into one as their tongues wrestled for dominance. Her lips seemed connected to lower parts that tingled. She released him.

Devon continued to pat himself down. Gina turned, took the towel from him and said, "The show's not over." She pressed her butt against him and wiggled. She turned to face him, lifting her leg onto his shoulder and leaning forward so her chest touched his.

Devon held her as she slowly moved her body into the sexiest position in the universe. The look on her face told him that this was a pose she could hold for some time. The closeness, the eye contact, the back arching, the positions, the breathing; Devon's natural reaction was arousal. He swallowed hard, clenched his jaw and backed away from her. Devon quickly got dressed and left the warehouse. Once Gina had the warehouse to herself she spun around and continued training.

An hour later, Devon was gave his business card to the court clerk. After lunch he was always tried to be first on the docket. When Devon wasn't training or engaged in his profession of pretending, he worked on a compact bandage that used red light to scan through skin and bone down to the neuron to gather information. This information would be refined and decoded by Joshua's computer chips.

Two weeks had passed since they had all been together. Devon instructed Gina and Joshua to take the Soul Stirrer and meet him at the airfield at exactly 3:15 p.m. They were at the airfield on time and waiting. Their glasses shielded them from the violent way the sun peeked through the clouds.

Looking towards the sky, Joshua saw something quickly dart into the clouds. The object wasn't falling because it changed direction and speed. Again, the object darted back into the clouds and this time Gina saw it. She put on her goggles, but they gave her no information.

They tracked the object as it rapidly descended out of the clouds. Joshua walked to the motorcycle and pulled out his rifle. It was too late as the blue and silver object was upon them. It slowed down and quickly retracted its wings just before landing. The object was now recognized as Devon slowly came to a stop a few feet from them.

Their eyes hung open wider than their mouths. Joshua put the rifle back into the motorcycle mount and said, "When do I get to do that?" Now Joshua understood why Devon had him hack the FAA database a week ago.

"Today," Devon responded.

"This is incredible," Gina said feeling Devon's wingsuit.

"It's not easy. Pushing off of a jet going four hundred miles per hour is dangerous, even for me. A wingsuit is constricting and it magnifies the slightest movement. These suits come with a safety parachute," Devon said handing each of them a wingsuit. "soon you won't need one," Devon said as they admired their newest upgrade.

"Does yours have a parachute?" Joshua asked.

"No."

"Hey. I want one like yours," Joshua said.

"Mine is customized, now, who's first?"

Devon had spent so much time in the air. He could see air currents they way birds do. He used natural thermals and updrafts to dynamically soar. He mastered downwind descents and could turn a gust into a climb.

Most thrill seekers could slow down to about forty miles per hour before landing. Most experts dream of landing speeds of thirty miles per hour or below. Devon had just slowed to ten miles per hour out of a dive and hit the ground running.

Gina was the first to try. Devon watched her stumble around before jumping off a crop duster. They way these two hit the ground and hangars made the prospect of riding a microjet seem like a lifetime away. Devon could glide for miles using these twenty thousand feet lily pads.

Every day for two weeks, Gina and Joshua returned to the warehouse with tales of their accomplishments and every time Devon responded with, "Try landing with zero speed", or "Try a faster jet" challenges he knew they would accept.

With his student's abilities growing Devon was still torn by guilt. Would the practicing, the training and the altering be enough? It would all mean nothing if they couldn't get to the other side and to the council.

In the morning, Devon closed the door behind him and quietly left. He had placed a small note on the bulletin board. The note read, "I'll be back." Ten minutes later, Joshua angrily snatched the note off the board. A confused Gina woke to see Joshua loudly repeated, "Not again, not again."

A frightened Gina searched the warehouse for Devon. She didn't eat waiting for him to return. Her sadness prompted Joshua to stop hitting the heavy bag. He gave her Devon's note. This information caused her to hyperventilate.

"Hey, he left me too," Joshua said trying to calm her down. "So... Devon said he had to revive you twice," Joshua said changing the subject. "I've even been to a rift site," he proudly said.

Gina stopped hyperventilating and said, "I've been to six." Joshua frowned at this and returned to hitting the heavy bag.

When Gina was with Devon, she would just look at him whenever a happening occurred or whenever otherworlders appeared. When he wasn't around she made always had a book or notepad handy.

With Devon gone she struggled not to react to the devastation and destruction that otherworlders often caused. Those glowing silver eyes cutting through the environment are hard not to look at. The lights on the otherworlder's coats commanded attention; it was up to Gina and Joshua not to draw the attention of them.

Gina initially didn't travel far from the warehouse, which was near the city, but she needed to know her surroundings. Joshua didn't like reading, but he read what Devon had brought. Reading became one of Gina's passions.

Joshua didn't train much, but he did like to spar. When they sparred, Gina didn't always avoid his punches and kicks. Gina needed to see the angles, the routes and she needed to feel the hits. When Joshua got the better of her, which was every time it was as if her ballet coach had just told her no. She would dress her wounds and continue her lessons with renewed effort.

Twenty minutes into Gina's workout with the heavy bag, Joshua stopped holding the bag. Often Joshua would just stop mid-workout. When he did he would say, 'Mass times velocity equals momentum', '1/2 times mv2' or 'I keep it ten squared'. Sometimes he would randomly leave, but this time was different.

"Do you every think about your father, like where he is? Why did he leave?" Joshua asked.

"Nope," Gina said.

"Hmmm," Joshua said and then he held the bag so she could continue her workout.

Gina's body wasn't far behind her will. Joshua was ahead of her, but her skills were catching up. The speed at which Gina learned annoyed Joshua. He took his frustrations out on her when they sparred, sometimes he would add more weight to her bar and more reps to her sets.

Sometimes when the two weren't training, Gina could get Joshua to a book reading at children's hospital. Joshua would go but he mostly talked with the nurses.

Holding on to an airplane, battling the winds and pressure at 30,000 feet; while enduring thirty below zero temperature is no easy task. Joshua loved drifting between the white puffed cotton candy clouds that at times looked like snow.

If Joshua wasn't in his wingsuit; he was getting lipstick smeared on his collar. Joshua liked to have one in the chamber, so to speak. Gina opted to master the bow and arrow, nunchaku, throwing stars, daggers and the staff.

Gina held the katana in her hands. Its long grip, squared guard and curved blade fit her hand. She was lost in thought as she drew the blade. She watched how Devon's eyes glazed over every time he drew the weapon from its covering on his back.

Devon was running his hands over his hand-polished Damascus steel dagger. When Devon noticed Gina was watching him he said, 'This is for meditation purposes only.' Gina now understood why Devon always had his blade on him.

Gina and Joshua mastered the sniper rifle, the shotgun, the assault rifle and the handgun. They could switch hands; flip and pull the trigger with their eyes closed and still hit the target. Their skill with any firearm was beyond the standard known as 'expert'.

Their fighting skills quickly surpassed physical limitations. Gina saw Joshua looking intently at himself in the mirror and she went over to him.

"What do you see?" he asked her.

"I see you." Gina responded. Joshua backed away from the mirror and started to wrap his hands and Gina slowly wrapped her toes.

"People look at me and think I have privilege, like I'm some kind of unicorn." Joshua said as they approached the arena.

"Right. Any privilege I have is muted by existing. There are a lot of people who wish to be like me, like us…" Gina said stretching.

"…without the work, without the stress and without the heartache. People pick and choose the parts of you they want; the parts they'll accept." Joshua said.

"They only ask 'where are you from?' so they can be offended by whatever your response is."

"I try not to think about it. Like you said, people are the victims." Joshua said.

"Does a person have the right to take a life?" Gina asked Joshua before they started training.

"Yes?" was Joshua's response.

"Uncertainty is not permission," Gina responded. These guns we have provide the least amount of thought time between action and consequence. Whenever I carry a gun, everyone is transformed into a potential target. There are many inferiority complexes behind squeezed triggers." Gina finished.

Gina always put her weapons into the locker. Joshua liked to have a firearm near him. In violent situations, Gina thought out every hit, she worked from the end to the beginning. To Gina it wasn't about fighting; it was about results.

"Strike, enforce, control," Joshua said tossing Gina to the mat for the twelfth time. "Don't wait, leave no openings."

Judo was used for tossing and immobilizing, aikido backed opponents off without injuring them. Wing Chung was used to control distance and Krav Maga solved unique problems. Muay Thai gave them eight limbs and Jeet Kung Do gave fluid grace to it all.

"The high left kick shuts down the weapon of the right punch. Attack what attacks you, arm, leg or body," Joshua said trying to sound like Devon. "Anger is pain's successor."

Gina lunged with a knife and Joshua tightly grabbed her knife hand and twisted her body to the ground. "The more you resist the greater the risk of injury," Joshua said. He let her go and said, "Now again."

Joshua and Gina had a regular routine of bedtime stories and chokeholds until there were no schools of thought. The majority of Gina's cuts and bruises were earned by realizing that martial arts is less effective in parking lots and crowded malls.

Everyone was working within The System and anyone could snap at anytime. Gina and Joshua could accidentally be injured, but more importantly they didn't want to be discovered.

"I see everything as art." Gina randomly stated.

"How is everything art?" Joshua said pushing away from his computer.

The leaves blowing in the wind; the waves on a beach, the flying bird. The traffic, the people walking, the unoccupied street, all of it hung in invisible frames on my mental wall. I see the beauty in a movement or a color broken down to its layers. Everything has depth; everything is like strokes on the canvas of life. Can't you see it?" Gina said.

"I see it, but it's not art. It's mechanical."

"Mechanical..."

"It's flawed mechanics that somehow still manages to operate. What I see are once shiny mechanisms that have rusted with age. I see gears of bones that need to be oiled from time to time. I see squeaky hinges that become loose no matter how many times they are tightened. If there is beauty, it is in its flawed precision."

"I actually like this side of you." Gina smiled.

Joshua gave Gina half a smile before he slowly walked towards a beam in the center of the warehouse. Joshua scaled the beam and disappeared through the sky roof without saying a word.

Joshua constantly grumbled about giving the money he obtained to charities.

"They aren't trying to cure anything, eighty percent of the money goes to administrative costs and I've seen the records."

Joshua grumbled less once he saw the lines of people that were being assisted by these organizations. The more they gave the less he grumbled.

"These organizations do a lot of good for people," Gina responded to her whining training partner.

"And what happens when the people can't do anymore?" Joshua said. "What happens when they can't score, can't tackle, can't catch and can't shoot? What happens when they can't do? Who'll be there for them then?" Joshua said.

"We will," Gina responded.

"That's right, good or bad," Joshua said smugly.

Joshua's research determined which organizations were worthy of receiving funds. He also made sure he helped the families he had harmed. Through this giving Gina and Joshua learned that helping one person escape horrors is how you help rescue others.

Joshua removed their existence from the internet and built firewalls into software preventing identification. The Otherworlders still caused happenings but didn't bother Joshua and Gina; perhaps they had seen Devon with them. Gina and Joshua still had to resist the urge to try to speak to them.

These two are the reason items are missing from unregistered flights. They are the cause of lost cargo from transport airplanes. They thought of themselves as salvagers, but considered themselves pirates. As for these missing items, let's just say that there's a lot of dangerous shit in this country and it's better that Gina and Joshua have them.

"Is fear a commodity?" Gina said to a barely waking up Joshua.

"What?" Joshua said pouring freshly squeezed orange juice into a glass cup.

"I mean, why do people believe their choices and opinions should be respected, but they don't do the same for others? Why do they believe the state shouldn't find diversity threatening, while the individual certainly does?"

"Oh...the isms," Joshua said sitting at the counter and playing with his glass of orange juice before taking a sip.

"The isms..."

"Their mission statement is that they have to fight all constraints originating from traditions, authorities or institutions."

"Radicalism."

"Basically," Joshua said pointing at her, acknowledging the correct answer. "See all 'isms' are radicalized forms of the original intent. The ism allows the fringe to move beyond the original intent and into areas that aren't related. When the ism's wins all the battles and its mission accomplished; will it disappear into the background?"

"Probably not." Gina said.

"Victories will only to lead to new challenges. It's not enough to win; you have to be at every party, every event and the subject of every discussion." Joshua said.

"So the platform is really just freedom for you…"

"Without a platform many people would implode; so the platform must continue, even if they have to prop up foes by giving them victories. That's why they attach agendas to the artist, the performer and the politician. The platform is another way The System controls people." Joshua offered as he climbed to the ceiling.

"In this way, there will always be another battle to fight and a platform to stand on," Gina said.

Joshua again pointed to Gina and then he disappeared through the open sky roof. At night, Joshua could often be found high above everyone, but for some reason he seemed angrier in the mornings.

These altered two were both outcasts from their family, both were the product of mixed blood and both were viewed as less than the sum of their parts. Joshua was obligated to train Gina, but he was under no obligation to like her.

CHAPTER 16

Ten bodies fell to the ground; the gunman apologized each time he squeezed the trigger. He dropped one magazine and inserted a full magazine. He yelled, "It's not you, it's The System." ...squeeze... squeeze... twenty five hundred screaming children ran through the hallways, a hail of bullets at their backs.

He waved the gun as if were a flag, to those he knew. This was his way of taking back control, his way of drawing attention. Shooting up this school was his suicide.

The buses are parked, the soccer field is empty and the news crews were parked just off school grounds. The school was staffed with two police officers, during the rampage one ran and the other hid, but that was yesterday's story.

The bodies, the blood, the screams and the news crews were gone. Those that escaped didn't sleep; they were up wondering why more wasn't done to prevent this tragedy. Today the school is closed; Gina and Joshua were too late.

On the bus ride back home, Joshua reflected on what they had seen, "They'll spend years trying to discover why this happened. They'll give money to security firms and pass laws to prevent it from happening again, but it won't matter because nothing moves the needle like death."

Normally, Gina would join the march or participate in the rally. Her eyes had been full of tears since they arrived at the school. Joshua turned to Gina and said, "The sellers, builders, hospitals, architects, politicians, the board members, the wood and steel manufacturers all profit from this.

"We have allowed ourselves to be desensitized by video games, movies and TV. Look at the news, death brings attention to people, if only for a day. Death stirs the economy, it motivates people. The only card more powerful than the agenda card is the death card." Joshua said. He looked out the window of the bus and didn't say anything else until they returned to base.

Gina was purchasing manager grade four, which meant there were two more levels before she was made an executive. She privately complained that she had been passed over by others not as good, not as talented and not as smart. She had told herself that these slights had something to do with her part-time Americanism.

She convinced herself the swoop neck sweater, beaded clutches and colorful cutout cocktail dresses were for her and not for wayward eyes, but those things were for those eyes. She convinced herself that wearing uncomfortable clothes two sizes too small wasn't to play up her body features.

She would put her hair up and wear a strapless dress, accompanied by forty minutes of make-up to go out and all of it made her feel good for an hour. It made her feel good for the moment. She was unaware that she had been beautiful all of her life. The truth is that people hated on her long before 'hated on' was a term.

Now she wondered how she could have ever been viewed as fragile or weak. How society treated her had a lot to do with behavior, her behavior and the behavior of others. Why did the decision to wear a ponytail weigh so heavily? Why did it matter how her abs would look in a mid-riff? Could this product make her small pouty lips, into large pouty ones?

All of her life society had inflicted subtle wounds, now she realized that it was The System making her consume; making all of us consume. None of the items she had ever purchased made her feel any better than the form fitting tank top she had on right now.

"I have behaved badly and blamed it on hormones," She admitted to herself. "I did act helpless in the face of unpleasant or physical labor. I have threatened to harm myself if my boyfriend broke up with me. I did force him to have sex with me, when he didn't seem to want to. I watched and enjoyed porn. I hid alcohol in fruity drinks and used it as cover for bad character actions.

"I judge people. I was jealous of my friends. I have regrets. I have been in uncomfortable situations, made even more uncomfortable by me. I have given my power away, but no one ever took my power," Gina thought these things. She wanted to blame the system, but the truth was they blame was hers.

The only glass ceiling was the one her mind created. Gina complained but she made more money than her male counterparts. She didn't get a promotion because there were no openings. She was a willing participant in her own victimization.

Gina traced most of her life's slights back to her own mental errors; a series of survivable wrong choices. The truth is a hard pill to swallow, but her growth demanded that she swallow hard.

"The wrong choice can't lead to the right outcome." Gina thought to herself while walking through the warehouse. "It can only lead to an outcome you can or cannot live with."

Joshua no longer needed insulin twice a day and the insomnia that had been part of Gina's daily life was gone. Whenever Joshua was around, Gina would ask him as many questions as possible.

"You know I used to take a tablet for this, a capsule for that and a cream for what itches. I can't remember if there was a time when I didn't have to take something, just to feel normal." Gina said.

"There is something about this world that is a mirage, a fantasy dangled in front of us to make us comply," Joshua responded and then he showed her how to navigate the sewers. She didn't like the smell.

Fairhaven, Massachusetts is a dock town, complete with an old stone school house. It's a beautiful town in the day, surrounded by petty thieves, poverty and scams at night.

This is a city where rudeness was normal and babies are dosed with cough medicine until they sleep. Here emotional abuse, rape and politics are natural bedfellows.

"They said it was a freak accident. That awkward landing, that over-extension that moves a player's leg just enough to strain a groin or pull a muscle." Joshua said as he met with Gina very late at the local park.

Gina sat on a bench reading under the soft lamp post light. She hadn't seen Joshua this depressed since he discovered the lottery was a voluntary tax designed to generate hope.

"Didn't your team win the championship… You're supposed to be happy…" Gina said putting her book down.

"Spatial temporal, probability, likelihood and the crowd went wild, I didn't. Missed layups, horrible calls and timeouts when the clock isn't running…somehow sport has lost its passion."

"Why?"

"Them." Joshua said sitting down next to her.

"You said yourself that otherworlders have caused balls to not reach the intended target."

"I did but it's disheartening to see these otherworlders working inside The System. Do you know how disturbing it is when you're watching the biggest game of the year and you look up from your popcorn and see an otherworlder float onto the court?"

"That sucks…"

"On the way here, I calculated all of the time I wasted on sports, how many times I left church with a happy heart, eager to look at a screen to view some spectacle, some athletic circus.

"I calculated all of the money I spent on clothes, shoes, apps and game tickets. I've even counted the neurons I spent talking about sporting events. I calculated how many Saturday afternoons I spent getting schooled by the 70 year-old sweatpants wearing hooper at the gym."

"How much did you spend?" she asked.

Joshua looked as if he had just sucked down a lemon, but he kept speaking, "When my team took the floor, it was like I had entered that mythical arena. The banners, the clipboards, the invites and the video games ushered in a new season of overtold stories and nonsensical lists; about petty, chemically aided, abusers and over grown divas that I was brainwashed into celebrating.

"I cheered and booed violence perpetrated for good reasons and for none; because context matters until it doesn't and it all sells. I bought and wore my team's jersey, but I never really had a team. I thought sport was truth; the one escape left. Sport is just another system of control with its hits, ankle breakers and miracle catches; bookended by whistle blows and culminating in a superhero finish all staged for maximum effect.

"All of it dispensed in digestible bites called games full of lightning shock satisfaction, but only for a moment—just enough to leave you wanting more," Joshua said as they got on the train headed back to base. Gina smirked because Joshua was always bothered by something.

As Gina became more comfortable she ventured farther. She would return flushed with new data to process.

"No matter what is done, justice is still for the few who can afford it," Gina offered to the reclining Joshua.

"Justice is only the advantage of the strong," Joshua replied not looking up from his novel.

"We should assess social institutions from a position of ignorance," Gina countered.

"Private property and markets benefit all. They maximize the opportunities of a randomly selected member of society," Joshua said as he turned a page.

"Inequalities between social positions should benefit the worst off now."

"Capitalism raises the position of the worst off in the long run and in future generations," Joshua said closing the book.

In the dim light, Joshua's half read Doctor Zhivago lay on the floor and he was gone. Gina didn't know Joshua before, but she did notice that he looked at his reflection in the mirror the way one does when they are trying to figure out something. Joshua spent countless hours staring at and touching his body.

Joshua and Gina spent a lot of time watching people. Part of their training was observing people so they could avoid nasty entanglements. Gina enjoyed breaking up criminal enterprises and ending the plans of crooks. They gathered a lot of information, by simply observing people.

Gina would sit on the A-Train and watched people from underneath her glasses. Northbound she listened to enraged parental arguments with six-year-olds. Southbound, she overheard a twelve-year-old racist, correct an eleven-year-old one.

"You know the first amendment?" Gina asked Joshua as they made their way downtown. They were traveling on top of buildings.

"Freedom of the Press," Joshua responded.

"I submit to you that these news agencies are not the press."

"Yeah, that was one of the first things I discovered. The System, these uninvited beings; it's all just managed chaos," Joshua said climbing up the building.

"Is that why most people are only people moral if something is offered to them?" Gina said. "Does the society a person is born into determine morals? Does it determine whether or not an individual becomes good or not? "Why is it not considered child abuse if a physician signs off on it? Why can't people think for themselves?" These were the questions Gina fired off as they sat on top of the tallest condominium complex in the city.

"Why would the system give people the information needed to overthrow it?" Joshua said finally responding squinting as the sun lowered.

"So, children aren't being educated?"

"They are being educated, just enough. The authorities tell you the changes are being made because it's the right thing to do. If they knew what the right thing to do was; why did they do the wrong thing to begin with? Why did it take so long to stop?

"Because they don't feel it's the right thing to do. They only stop doing a thing when it becomes obsolete," Joshua said. Tonight there was no happening and all was quiet in the city. They returned to the warehouse.

"What do mean, obsolete?" Gina said when they entered the warehouse.

"Obsolete, like our ancestors saw how technology would make slavery obsolete."

"So they ban it and say 'it's the right thing to do'. I never thought about it that way." Gina said.

"That's why I'm here."

Joshua pulled out a golden bottle of Bruichladdick X4 quadruple whiskey. This whiskey had been matured with bourbon in new virgin oak barrels. It was one of the strongest alcoholic drinks in the world. The affect it had on Joshua was that of a mixing wine. He sighed as he poured a glass.

Joshua slowly rolled the glass through his fingers rousing the black charred oak, almonds, vanilla and grapefruit. He breathed in the malt and then sipped. He lowered the hot liquid, his eyes searching the glass for meaning.

"What's on your mind, Gina?" Joshua said walking by Gina as she sat on her bed staring off into the distance.

"I'm surprised how people become friendlier and more open when you speak their native tongue. It's like night and day, how people who would never speak to you will speak to you if you speak their language." Gina said.

"Wait until you find out that things are only true if the masses are entertained by it. Their feelings have taken the place of facts, reason and objectivity. The echo chamber is; it exists but not to change, grow or understand. Should we just let them have the lies?" Joshua asked.

"Speaking opposite of truth is the worst kind of wrong." Gina said. Disagreeable people are more likely to be incarcerated, but is their disagreement biological or environmental? Some people are good, some people are bad; a person can be both from minute to minute. One moment can shape or empowerment a person." Gina stated

"Even most enlightened people operate in bad faith and narrow minded ignorance. They create words and phrases so herds of agendamongers can maintain sanity. They'll call it being specific or speaking up about long held societal problems, but it isn't.

"They push laws they haven't read and hold on to damaging recordings, images and paperwork until it's politically opportune. They can't help but to hide fascism inside romantic comedies." Joshua responded.

"You'd rather give might to injustice."

"I never said that."

"What has surprised you?"

"That these otherworlders hardly blink."

"I know, it's weird," Gina said.

"I was surprised how, in any group real talent is the least distributed quality," Joshua said.

"See, hiding and fixing the IT problems places of worship isn't exactly noble," Gina incredulously responded.

"If their prefrontal cortex isn't fully developed, people will imitate anything."

"Not anything."

"All of those 'Go Natural', 'Love Your Body' and anti-shaming campaigns are really just a way to buy more."

"All of them?"

"Pretty much. Without the prospect of gaining money would there be a campaign? Every news article, every campaign begins with the goal of profit…"

"I don't think the situation is that bad for people."

"I thought like that before this grand adventure turned into homework," Joshua said sarcastically.

Joshua went over to the computer and with a wave of his hand he updated the calendar, but he went back and forth several times on the changing of a punctuation mark on an unsent message.

"You have adjusted to this better than I have." Gina said.

"You think that because I don't have nightmares like Devon does. I have to watch humanity quietly whimpers as it chokes down every morsel of chemical laden food that they pay a premium for. They wash down detergent packs with blame and regret.

"They never apologize. They never admit guilt. They have gotten rid of shame and they never get enough. What happens when you remove luck and innate talent from dreams and goals? The responsibility of solely owning your life is terrifying." Joshua said.

"I get confused when they use words like diversity, but mean assimilation. It's not fair to define people by their edges. You want to shove them all into one psychotic box...I don't." Gina said.

"Do you ever feel like letting them drown or get taken advantage of?" Joshua said slowly.

"What?" Gina said shocked. "Aren't mistakes and insecurities the real villains?"

"Where are those things housed?"

"How about we crack down on detrimental behavior?"

"Not possible without injuring..."

"Then what?"

"I don't know."

"Joshua, don't let all of this consume you."

"I haven't. I meant what I said, I'm sorry I said it. I wasn't trying to discourage you."

"You and I being here is encouragement to me."

Joshua took another sip of whiskey. "You see people lift the few, the exceptional upon their shoulders, so they can at a later time, watch them fall. I know you've seen them grab products willed into being by marketing algorithms. You've seen them gloat over their ethnic food product labeling. How can that not make you depressed?

"People are worried more about musical paragraphs than the paragraphs of their children. They crave digital approval, more than mental approval. They worried about what a celebrity is wearing more than what their child is wearing. They hurry home in time to catch a show, but make excuses why their child isn't in a show.

"They have been inundated with chaos until chaos is normal. My nightmare is being estranged from society that disgusts me," Joshua said moving his mouth as if he had a tasted something bitter.

"They can't see," Gina said.

"You don't know you can't see until you can see."

"What we are doing will help free them from these illusions."

"These people fight and die over neighborhoods where they own nothing. These people will kill over an illusion because it's all they have."

"None of this would occur were it not for the system. People are only half the problem," Gina said.

"The enemy was never at our door. They enemy was always in our hearts," Joshua said.

Joshua looked up from his glass and abruptly stopped speaking as they were in the middle of arguing like two drunken philosophy majors. He took a few more sips and got up and left; leaving his empty smoked hazelnut bottle on the countertop.

Observations and these conversations caused Gina to question her very humanity. She complained about too many straps, zippers and underwires. Her closet held a gorgeous, chestnut cashmere cape coat, and a dangerously fitting gold and majestic blue dress.

Today, she was wearing green turnout leggings and dark green knee length boots. Gina trained in a mesh racer back sports bra or long sleeve bra top. She did love her moisture wick leggings.

After training, she would slip into a semi-sheer cardigan wrap, a crisscross sweater, orange cotton leg warmers, or a farfalla top. It was not unusual to see her wearing colorful fishnet stockings. She had over-knee boots that she would wear with an assortment of spandex.

Mostly she wore sleek leather moto jackets, but she also had leather trench coats similar to Devon's. Recently she added a hood to the bodysuits she wore those the most.

Tonight, she was wearing corduroy pants, a button down shirt, and a belted black coat. Her belts and bows were more like shields than accessories. Gina changed outfits four to five times a day and she still had time to craft a black bodysuit with green accents.

Gina double stitched nylon straps to hang ten wood suspension rings from the ceiling. She set up four adjustable horizontal bars, three ceiling to floor poles and an adjustable ballet bar. She was good with her arms and hands, but she was great with her feet.

For over a month, Joshua had sparred with Gina. He got the better of her over every square inch of arena. Today, Joshua's best efforts couldn't put Gina down on the mat. She caught his hand and he became agitated; he intensified his attacks.

She was cornered. Joshua swung at her; she leaned forward ducked under his punch and her foot smashed against his face. Gina stood on one leg while bringing her other leg up backwards over her head to deliver the blow. It was a perfectly placed, perfectly timed scorpion kick that caught Joshua by surprise. He could only admire it while looking up from the mat.

This was the day Joshua decided they had sparred enough.

"Why even put up a pedestrian bridge, if you aren't going to build it right?" Joshua said as they prepared to help the wounded.

"Was it Them?" Gina said as they geared up to leave.

"All I know that we have to clean up another bloody mess." Joshua said.

"Still I just don't understand why harass someone that doesn't agree with you." Gina said washing her hands.

"To harass is human." Joshua said. "Without it, there's no political discourse and no media. Professors harass students with opinions. People in relationships harass each other, parents harass children. Nations harass other nations; people harass animals, we just use other words for what it truly is.

"I see people fall to their knees and thank us after we disrupt the system and I like that. But we have leave; we have to remain in the shadows. I am more unseen now than I ever was." Joshua said

"The human heart is the most powerful thing in the universe. I kinda like being the 1st responder."

"Don't mind me not agreeing with you on that but some of my people were only citizens by law, not birthright. Where was the human heart then?" Joshua said closing the door as they left.

Last week, Gina and Joshua were helping clean up a fuel spill at the oil refinery when a fuel tank exploded. Joshua pulled up a floor grate and they jumped down into it as the air ignited around them. Joshua covered them with concrete as fire engulfed the structure.

Joshua was terribly wounded and bleeding. He dug them out of the debris, Gina was semi-conscious. Joshua wrenched off a manhole cover and took her through the sewer system as flames and sirens dominated the night. The orange glow of the fire could be seen for miles. The explosion damaged Joshua's right eye. Gina helped him attach a small cybernetic eye attachment and his cells regenerated around it.

This cybernetic piece was not connected directly to his brain, but rather linked to his eye. He could pull up overlays, range findings, orientation and holographic data over his normal sight like the heads up display on jet fighters. After two weeks it wasn't noticeable.

Joshua sat in the training area staring off into space. Gina set the treadmill to its highest setting and began running.

"I almost touched one," Joshua said.

"Touched one of what?" Gina said

"You know..."

"One of ..."

"Yes."

"When?"

"Today, I landed a few states west. Tornado was there, it looked like he was practicing. When he was finished he ran by me towards the rift and my arm reached out, but I pulled my hand back."

"He had just finished making twisters?"

"He made a few different sizes. They were pretty amazing."

"The subflux was present so he would have felt you. What were you thinking?"

"I was thinking of no longer hiding, of not looking the other way," Joshua said and then he paused. Joshua turned and looked at the only thing still in the loot box, a one hundred dollar bill.

"My loot box...my loot box. Make things right," Joshua said mocking Devon and then he kicked a large dent into a steel beam.

"What else is bothering you today, Joshua?" Gina questioned, getting off of the treadmill after running twenty miles in two hours.

"What bothers me is that this ark we are building isn't big enough." Joshua said. Gina laughed.

"Today I wrung a few necks, but it didn't produce the desired results," Joshua continued.

"Tell me about it," Gina said grabbing a towel.

"Every day the world becomes ten times more complicated."

"Only ten times?" she said quietly. Gina went to the opposite side on the beam and kicked it back into form. "You can't manhandle everything," she smiled. This was the first time Joshua smiled back at her. After the explosion things were different between them.

They played monopoly in Italian. Gina beat him the first time they played and he grumbled something about the female IQ bell curve being higher and taller than the male IQ bell curve. This was a backhanded way of saying there aren't as many female geniuses as male ones.

"Male distribution of intelligence is flatter at the bottom, which indicates there are more male idiots," Gina said smiling to herself.

They broke into the local pool to see who could hold their breath the longest underwater. They swam with their arms to the side using their feet similar to a fluke. This gave them underwater thrust

The more flexible their legs and feet the more efficient swimming this way was. They needed more room so they planned more trips to the ocean, where they could fly through the water without limits. Gina loved the way sand felt under her feet.

"I've thought of trying to go into a rift," Joshua said coming out of the ocean.

"Did you also think of what would happen if you were caught on the other side?"

"That's why thoughts of it are all I have."

"I couldn't imagine doing that on my own," Gina said as they returned to the warehouse.

Gina's eyes widened as she narrowly evaded his fingertips. A large hand reached out as she ducked under a platform. She jumped over a bar; she turned left and ran right. She dodged, rolled and then jumped to grab a ring. The hands kept coming after her. She flipped, bent and twisted, but the hand had her. She was jumping to an overhead bar when her foot was grabbed.

Joshua tilted his head; inhaled, raised a finger, and said, "You're It!", then he ran away. They had three thousand square feet to play Tag in and they used all of it.

When it became easier for Gina to ignore the otherworlders, she stayed out all night. Joshua and Gina were in the middle of blizzards, cold waves, power outages, mudslides and other happenings. They tested water for contamination, provided food and went on search and rescue operations. They never stayed long and were gone before too many questions were raised.

Gina and Joshua were conducting the most extensive research project ever. They'd sit unnerved in the middle of bar brawls. They'd wander around yellow crime scene tape and conduct their own investigation.

They watched otherworlders whisper into the ears of thousands of people. Some people would just keep doing what they were doing; others would suddenly cross the street or get off a bus. One otherworlder actually pulled a person out of the way of a speeding car.

Gina and Joshua walked through the Mall of America, observing and speaking to each other in a number of languages Hebrew, Latin, Russian. They used crisp accents and perfect pronunciation unless the audience called for something less.

Joshua would angrily move his hands through the air as he signed, and Gina would elaborately gesture a response. This is how they remained anonymous and it provided them with some humor.

"Those three pretty women walking together, what do you see?" Gina said, her nose filled with their perfume.

"I see smiles, a slow deliberate gait and a subtle sway. I see what they are wearing."

"They are all ovulating."

"You can tell that just by looking at them?"

"I can."

There was a time when Gina and Joshua would have done anything for money. The absence of currency made them look at the world differently. People were more than a series of ones and zeroes.

Gina now saw people in their natural states, the state they find themselves in when they think no one sees. Gina saw a thousand copies of herself in the masses. She had crushed her share of candies, built her share of empires and raced her share of karts to victory.

For years Gina and her seasonal friends couldn't wait to decorate and dress up for the next holiday, the next event and the next challenge. They gave no thought to their boyfriends; holidays aren't for males anyway. This mall was full of holiday trappings and holiday themed music.

"False belief in one's own significance causes despair. Look at them," Joshua said pointing down to the crying youth. "The more I understand people, the less I like them."

"Joshua, we watch them not because they've done something. We watch them because they've done nothing."

CHAPTER 17

Gender is marketable. It is something that can be used to move a person, but it doesn't define anyone. Humanity is too complex, too dynamic to be bound by something called gender.

Gina had spent over two dozen years on Earth and today was the first time she was free. Free from rules, free from responsibility and free from being human.

Joshua and Gina helped people, but they weren't sure if they had simply been making allowances for group mind control. People didn't want context or perspective they just wanted to believe what they believe.

The presence of otherworlders was terrifying. Gina and Joshua could see them, this made them terrifyingly familiar. They could see what they were doing, even if they didn't know why. The results and the actions of the people within The System are things that could be seen and understood. This made people more predictable.

The System was elegant. Simply by discussing it or watching its programs made the possibilities of it spread. The System was everywhere, yet nowhere. The System was more terrifying than the otherworlders.

For Gina and Joshua sometimes the falling whiteness was ash, other times it was snow. For three days they helped fight a wildfire. Fifteen wildfires has stated simultaneously. These were wildfires otherworlders did not create. A giant wildfire is powered by combustion, like a hurricane is powered by water, both are unstoppable.

Their goggles allowed them to see in the dark. At night they made the most progress in putting the fires out. "Isn't there usually a report detailing how the fire was started?" Gina quizzed Joshua as they returned home.

"Usually…"

"So, they don't know?"

"They know."

"Well, what started the fire?"

Joshua pointed skyward and then he walked over to the computer. He waved his hand and the screen came on. His fingers fluttered over the keyboard as a file about a direct heat weapon opened. The file showed that the government had placed a weapon in orbit that triggered heat waves and fires.

"This is a weapon they are getting better at using," Joshua said.

"Why wildfires?"

"Remember the school shooting? The System has its reasons."

"The people we helped today weren't simulations. These people mattered; what we did affect them. What's this?" Gina said pointing to a file with the heading, 'Bio Neural Interface'. Joshua opened the file. This file detailed a program that used ultrasonic sound to control people.

"Parts of that program will soon be marketed as instant learning," Joshua said.

Below an essay labeled 'The Wizard of Oz: The First Team Up' and next to a 200-page essay on 'How the Common House Fly is the Most Technologically Advanced Flying Machine Ever Created', was a file on the military's newest jet fighter.

This was an airplane full of programmed weakness. This warplane will be sold to other nations for millions of dollars.

"Are you going to eat that?" Gina questioned as Joshua sat at the table eating a meal he had prepared.

"Yeah," he said, stirring his spaghetti. "I mean, it tastes like shit, but its dinner." He took a few more bites, rubbed his chin and turned his head to the screen saver. Joshua's novel was half open and face down on the couch; nothing in the warehouse was where it should be.

The next day Gina hooked up a stove, with plenty of utensil porn and made a nice kitchen in the middle of the warehouse. Gina bought food and cooked leek-free breakfasts and dinners.

Gina usually sat on the countertop with her legs crossed; she quickly read novels until she fell asleep. While sleep she imagined she was still among her novels urgent, unnerving characters. Gina always had old fiction, scattered about the warehouse.

Joshua left the warehouse at 2 a.m., perhaps for language lessons. Once he left, Gina put down 'Desde La Sombra'. She cut off all the lights and found her way around the warehouse, mentally mapping obstacles as she moved. Gina had started losing weight and her monthly cycle now lasted only fourteen hours.

Sometimes Gina convinced Joshua to take bus rides with her. On these rides they would try to guess a person's profession first, what stop a person would get off on or if a person was single. Of course, they'd have to follow the subject to find out if their assessments were correct.

Gina preferred to travel by busses or light rail. There were always interesting people on the train. The lady to her left had pumpkin color hair; the one to the right had a sharp tongue which she used liberally. Gina sat in the middle of the power suit wearing, tailored dresses having throngs of unraised children.

Max Kensington was a regular on this line. He always sat in the same seat, looking out the same window. He sat in that seat and imagined that instead of going to work he'd watch black and white films all day.

Micha Ludden was tall, had long curly hair and small brown eyes. She rode the same train every day. Micha watched people as much as Gina did. She pretended to be reading but she wasn't. Today, she looked as if this six-mile stretch was her only escape of the day. She was slow to get up at the end of the line; maybe she didn't want to go home.

While everyone watched performers sing, dance and flip, Gina watched four young girls steal from people who sat next to them. The train stopped and people, like Max, Micha and these girls got off and disappeared into more faces.

As Gina watched people, she realized that no hierarchy is without tyranny and that by being altered she had been liberated from a society where everyone is guilty and no one is responsible. On the way home, she watched a press conference; she searched the police chief's eyes trying to determine where he fell on the spectrum of racist.

She once had a kinship in this place where the police are executioner and tax collector. Maybe an otherworld happening was nearby; maybe Joshua's words had gotten to her, either way Gina was sickened.

Gina was once moved by movements and terms like equality. She needed these causes; they gave her a sense of purpose. She donated to animals before she would humans and she volunteered.

"I campaigned for causes that would never affect me," She thought. "I fought for people who never asked for my help. I shamed people who didn't leave the correct tip percentage. I was two steps from being offended by everything. I was one of the offended masses.

"The System used conflict as currency within me. It used me to force others to conform. I helped to create society's largest brand, consumption."

She listened to the rest of the police briefing. When the chief said, "we're just doing our job", she knew it was just the company line. She had seen the police look the other way, she watched them harm and injured when they were supposed to protect and serve.

She watched police kill because it meant less paperwork. She saw how they inflicted pain on the poor masses. She watched the courts sentence poor people harsher when the rich, who knew better and did worse. It had almost three months since Gina had been altered and everything she knew was an absolute lie, yet The System moved along smoothly without her.

At night, Gina watched humans fighting the power of these otherworlders. The only options were to try and stay up or try to stay sleep. The subconscious mind actually sensed these intruders. The mind sends out countermeasures that prevent a person from sleeping, resulting in insomnia. This is a subconscious signal to the conscious self that something was wrong.

A person could stay up partying, working or doing just about anything in order not to sleep, not to dream. If the otherworlders wanted you, they would keep trying, until they got you. People think insomnia is because of stress or worry. They never think a war is raging within their subconscious. So, people consume pills that make them sleep.

These small chemical concoctions handcuff their subconscious and cause suicidal impulses, sleepwalking and depression. Once the mind's defenses are down, the psyche is defenseless.

The System moved people with numbers, statistics and official sounding reports. The purchase of devices forced the masses to shuffle off dutifully. On their way to these forty hours, people are assaulted by every psychological ploy ever devised.

These ploys—suggestions if they could be called that—were easily adopted by the obedient; even the strongest minds eventually succumb to the onslaught. The System uses these ploys to release its ultimate weapon, called 'want'. This want caused people to manage interest rates, credit scores and most importantly their time.

People did this to pay a mortgage on a home they only slept in, and to pay a note on a vehicle they hardly drove. They happily spend because they want. The more they wanted, the more want grew. Want held them at gunpoint and forced them to go to work; it forced them to scheme, to lie, to be pathetic.

Gina could probably get whatever from whatever man or woman. She was simultaneously watched and overlooked. People watched her walk, her body, how she sat, how she spoke or didn't, what she wore, what she bought and how she bought it.

Gina was privy to private conversations and was never seen as a threat. On this train, her glazed over look caused other people to observe her, so she lowered her eyes to wrestle the black and white quirks within "The Tale of Genji".

Gina watched the anthem kneeling patriots and the eye batting scammers. She watched as throngs of people waited in line for the latest product intended to add more convenience to their lives but somehow resulted in a loss of loss of time.

In cities like this the inhabitants were willing to become unpaid ads. More faces were buried into devices than to anything made from a tree.

Today had been particularly tedious for Gina. On a fifty-foot screen in the train station, a commercial played with a banner that read: "Technology is your salvation." The next commercial didn't show the face of any male. Another commercial implied that any woman that doesn't use their product isn't free. The commercials that followed showed people suppressing a virus, having sex and finding happiness with soda.

Gina overlooked otherworlders as if they were sign spinners and she ignored their pull on her. The System was something she could not avoid, something she could not ignore. She rushed into the bathroom and promptly threw up.

Gina had consumed 400mg of racism, 200mg of sexism and 565mg of four other isms, just by traveling from one end of the city to the other. There were groups here that fought for social dominance, but all Gina saw was one predator fighting with the other. She saw victims that were also oppressors.

She came out of the bathroom and got on the train. She planned to go home to detangle, blow dry and dye the front edges of her short bob hair purple. That was her plan.

The System kept the chaos going through protest, fueled by adding money. The System made people reject truth because the messenger was flawed. The belief in a higher power, works against free enterprise. Corporations charge the individuals for its sins. God is bad for the economy.

In this train station, it all of it rose to a crescendo of dog shit, crying babies, loud conversations, discarded syringes, coughing, the rubbing of thighs, the grinding of wheels and endless braying. Gina got off twenty miles away from the warehouse.

As she walked home, the coming night turned downtown buildings into nothing more than blighted cement rectangles covered by glass. These grey blocks were smudges against the dull blue skyline. For a few seconds, her thoughts were deflected by the whirl of an electric blue bicycle.

The billboards and neon signed storefronts eerily beckoned her attention. The flickering reds and blues surrounded her as she patrolled the streets. The array of colors fit together like a perfect jigsaw puzzle. In-between blaring sirens and shotgun blasts, the night city appeared to be created by one act of inspiration instead of thousands.

Gina walked into the warehouse and headed to the bathroom. Yesterday's bangs grazed her forehead. She turned the faucet on and threw cold water on her face. She used a hand towel to dry her face. She exhaled.

She reached into her purse and pulled out her lipstick. She took the cap off and was about to calm her mind with it. She paused and looked at the accessory in her hand; it was no longer pink lipstick it was power. It had always been power.

Her lipsticks were red, green and brown shaded bullets of attention. Her hair dyes, fragrances and scents were look-at-me projectiles; these are the things she would get rid of. She would no longer wear another person's shoes, another woman's dress or purse. She would not drive another corporate logoed vehicle.

Next week, her hair would have been a vibrant blue, with green strands, an asymmetrical bob with side swept bangs. A week after that, her hair would have had metallic purple roots that fade into flamingo pink along the ends.

This is what would have been if Gina had still allowed The System to blur the line between consumption and what makes a person valuable to society. Gina realized that all of these things were icing on an incomplete cake that made her who she was.

Later that night Gina arrived early as she had for the last two weeks, but tonight would be the night she went in. This theater was having an evening performance of 'The Prince of the Pagodas'. The lights from passing vehicles made the cocktail dresses, long sleeved, button down shirt and blazers stand out in front of the theater.

Gina perched herself high across the street on a facade like a gargoyle. She scanned the crowd of black suits, sequin clutches and colorful heels. This production was a casual affair, still, some wore watches. One woman had on a blue knee length taffeta, others wore floor length silk gowns. It was quiet, cold and dark. Gina never went in the theater.

She ended up on a rooftop in one of America's Chinatowns. Every night since she could be found in a Koreatown or some heavily populated Asian town. She felt at home surrounds by the vibrantly colored towers and grand dragon gates. The ornamentation, logograms and dragon arches where backdrops to glassy floor storefronts.

These towns weren't theme parks, they were homes and workplaces. Gina quietly made her way past the conversations at the bar and deli. She listened to the music and the siren of the passing ambulance as old men played elephant chess. This live action tourist attraction had chartered buses that took dozens to casinos. It also had blight, disease, pollutants and crime.

Here boundaries were crossed every second, every minute and every hour; here is where she needed to be. Gina targeted places where the female only housekeepers came and went weekly. They rotated the women to keep customers happy and the authorities guessing. Some of the girls and boys were as young as eleven; some arrived without passport or visa.

Some families paid tens of thousands of dollars for this journey to a better life. Immigration documents complete with forged passports that read Japanese, South Korean or some other ethnic group that didn't raise suspicions with immigration officials. They would arrived and vanish from the foster care which they have been assigned. They would soon be found in massage parlors or suburban basements.

Otherworlders were present in these cities but didn't cause many happenings here as they did elsewhere. Some children were abducted; others had simply left home. Society had told them they didn't have to listen to anyone and that parents are to be ignored. Much of this went unnoticed like the many Americans who travel abroad to indulge deviancies.

Here there were no platforms, no movements and no job offers. They were being trafficked like a bag of potato chips. These children were trained to perform, to please and to go back to their small cage rooms when done. They were merchandise put into service after being starved, drugged and beaten into compliance.

Storage rooms were grooming way stations; she would intervene here before the products were shipped across the nation in semi trucks. In the middle of this large storage room, Gina fell to her knees among the caged masses and cried. There was no hope for these lost souls, until now.

Gina dressed up in traditional Chinese garb, applied makeup and customized her mask. The respectable establishments were run by a headmistress. Mistresses that turned pale when they saw Gina float in through a window or bust through a door. They believed her to be Huli Jing, a fox spirit.

Spirit Foxes are believed to be capable of magic, make people sick or drain life energy. Foxes are thought to be a demons or ghosts. These spirits are often seen in flowing white dresses, a light blue half cap with white and red faces. Asian communities believe in spirits more than other communities, Gina used this to her advantage.

The spirit floated into these spaces with grace. The head mistresses offered food and drinks to the spirit, but the spirit wanted lives, the enslaved. Gina didn't speak, she pointed and gestured to get her point across; and when those points were not taken a well placed blessing across a face adjusted points of view.

This fourteen-year-old girl and her younger sister disappeared from a social services hotel nine months ago. This fifteen-year-old ran away from his home two years ago. By the end of the day their new lives would begin. Gina spoke to each in their language; it was these moments when she felt alive again.

No more earning as much as you can, as fast as you can. No more just trying to get through it. Gina dosed them with antibiotics and handed them school transcripts and gift cards. She gave them a care package of new clothes and a spot in the runaway shelter two cities north.

These three will be free, but they won't become a witness against their controllers. Their heads were full of horrific stories; some of them had been abused by the police. Gina made it her business to be at the ports, the projects and inner cities also helping from the shadows.

She didn't want them to say, 'She freed me.' Gina knew that in order to truly be free they need to free themselves. As they walked away, Gina climbed to the top of a pagoda where she was reminded of the wrongs that she couldn't make right. She thought how it all came to this...

"The Emancipation Proclamation prompted southern states to hire Chinese people to replace slave labor. In Rock Springs, Wyoming, two hundred armed white miners drove my great-great-grandfather and other Chinese immigrants out of town. Those miners murdered and set fire to homes. No one was ever charged.

"In the 1900's, there were hundreds of riots against the Chinese the worst being in Seattle, Tacoma, Washington, Denver, and Los Angeles. Those riots forced many to go east; my great-grandfather stayed and he fought. Others like him knew that numbers brought them safety and that's how Chinatowns were created.

"My grandfather had to deal with Asian exclusion laws and other legal practices that excluded Asians from American life. Still, my grandfather managed to get married and have four children. One of those children was my mother.

"In order to survive my fashion worker mother, in one of the biggest Chinatowns, became the ethnic playground for a rich white man. He was married but he had a penchant for egg rolls and fortune cookies. Once he found out that I would be born; he left my mother.

"He gave her five thousand dollars and she never saw him again. She only knew to always call him Mr. Lawrence. That's all I knew of my father.

"All my life I was ignored for my lack of heritage and teased for not having enough heritage. I used to wonder why Miss Molly would not acknowledge my heritage through her magic mirror.

"I only watched that black and white video of a lady gracefully twisting and performing for thirty seconds, but I knew I wanted to be just like her. I found out that her name was Dai Ailian. She was Chinese and born in Trinidad; she was an outcast like me.

"I endured the verbal school yard daggers meant to sever Asians like me from their American citizenship. When I looked at myself, I saw a round face, a long neck and pale skin. I didn't go to the bathroom in school because I didn't want to cry. The kids saw me as the tall, thin, outcast who couldn't speak Mandarin.

"After middle school, my mother and I moved outside of the shadow of Chinatown and became the docile modern minority, willing to pay gentrified prices. And like that my mother went from having an illegitimate child to the respectable title of single mother.

"We were the perfect, model family complete with the children who never get into trouble and love to study. When I danced all my troubles fell away. What I am doing right now is my finest performance to date." Gina finished her thoughts as she took one last look over the neighborhood

Gina knew that no matter how many people she rescued, it would never be enough. This was the first time she allowed herself to be furious with her mother for giving up. Gina closed her eyes and she was again on stage alone, slowly spinning the lights growing brighter with each spin. In the crowd, there were no applause; just silent faces waiting on her to fail.

Her fall punctuated by a surrounding scream. The auditorium filled with gasps as she tried to lift herself up from the hard to the floor; the eyes looked at her. She felt the heat from the ever brightening lights. She grabbed her ankle as pain surged through her. Her tears dotted the stage and then the lights went out.

Gina left Chinatown and walked a long time before reaching the warehouse. She put a large towel around her and prepared a hot bubble bath. Joshua saw her in her makeup and said, "Where have you been?"

"Out being foxy," Gina responded.

CHAPTER 18

Gina's study of biology and horticulture, lead her to created a plant based hair dye. These were cocktails of grapefruit, lemon fruit oils, natural sunflower seed extract and jojoba oils. She used apricot and grape seed to activate the color. She used chamomile tea and sunflower petals to lighten, calendula, rosehips and hibiscus for the shades of red; rosemary and sage to darken.

She used walnut shell, henna and wheat protein to give her hair volume and a high gloss shine. Gina created these applications; she no longer had to worry about bladder cancer, lung, kidney and nervous system disorders from hair dyes. She also didn't want to dull her senses from chemicals. It took her three hours to shimmer, strain to get the color the way she wanted it, now it took thirty minutes.

"Maximizing average photosynthesis," she said to herself while looking through a microscope. She started a bamboo garden. It was comprised primarily of azaleas, primrose with ginger and licorice scattered about. If water was the earth's arteries, then rocks are its skeleton. Interspersed in her garden were grey Taihu stones and volcanic yellow stones ones from St. Helena Island.

Hand trowels were against the wall next to the pruners. The Dutch hoe was beside the shears. The crops would be near her workstation. On her workstation were notepads, a box of gloves, a compound microscope and a stereo microscope for up close inspection.

She needed the crop to grow quickly. She had to figure out how to avoid the poor crop yields that shortening the regeneration process. She went through hundreds of pages about of sexless breeding before she began.

She used grow tents to increase light intensity and improve light distribution. Gina spent half a day attaching LED lights above the tents. LED lights use half the electricity, produce less heat and are shatter resistant. Gina used adjustable intensity lights with a spike of blue light to stimulate stronger root growth and enhance photosynthesis.

Joshua was interested in the Fibonacci sequence present in the petals of the plants Gina grew. He helped her install solar panels. He installed a rooftop tank to harvested rainwater. This water would be cold filtered through the irrigation system. Rainwater is slightly acidic; once it soaks into the soil it releases copper, manganese, zinc and nitrogen.

Joshua never interfered with her indoor greenhouse. If you saw the way she bent over microscopes and jotted notes down, you wouldn't interfere with her either.

Gina carefully managed the air temperature, humidity and radiation quality. She adhered to specific plant spacing and water irrigation. She elevated carbon dioxide and nitrogen, which speeds growth. She used artificial light to extend day period.

Each crop species has a genetic code. The onions and carrots had to be kept away from the potatoes and peas and so forth. She clipped leaves and plucked stalks; there was a strategy to quickly growing crops. In the raised black locust beds, she mixed alluvial and iron rich soil, which drains excellently.

She replaced RuBisCO the most abundant protein on the planet with a 3-hydroxypropionate pathway to catch and use green light. This increased crop photosynthetic by fifty percent.

Gina's snap beans and lettuce were ready to harvest in fifteen days. Her green onions grew into good size scallions in twenty days. Radishes were ready to harvest in a week and a half, spinach in two weeks and chives in ten days. After three weeks she pulled the green stem out of the juiciest strawberries imaginable.

Gina always had bunches of oregano, thyme, basil and other herbs hanging to dry. Everyday Joshua's nose filled with the rosemary. His mouth watered ever time she started preparing meals. The meals she created were the only thing that regularly pulled Joshua back home.

Sautéed snow peas, spring onions next to chive and garlic mashed potatoes were placed in front of Joshua, and he would listened to anything and Gina had to say.

"I believe that people are special," Gina began as Joshua ate. "How else could humans wade through the forty million viruses, thirty million germs and eleven million bacteria in each cubic meter of air? How else could loud, inconsolable babies have survived the most primitive of times?

"Most people risk little but act as if the world is upon their shoulders. They have spent all of this time formulating solutions to hide problems. They have created medications that work so well they think they no longer need them.

"The streets are filled with strangers that I once knew. Look at their faces while corporations force them to eat term papers," Gina said giving Joshua a second helping.

"Communication is the currency of ideas and we have some ideas to spend," Joshua said as he finished his meal. He thanked Gina and disappeared into the night.

When Gina and Joshua weren't exploring, or people watching, they would race each other home. Their parkour scenes rivaled any Hollywood production as they tried to beat each other's time from the previous race. Kong Gainers, Arabians and vaults through small openings were commonplace for them the world was a gymnasium.

In this big city, there was no shortage of mass transit lines and eight lane highways that cut through pedestrian friendly cities. Train stations, buses and subways were where they usually found themselves wedged in-between people and otherworlders. Gina usually ran on rooftops and Joshua took the street level, they never took the same route home twice.

They were halfway through a long dark alley when they heard glass softly being stepped on. Without hesitation Gina grabbed a shadowed crook and slammed his face through a glass window.

Joshua knocked the gun out of another would-be-attackers hand, prompting the thief to pull a knife. Joshua's quick back flip sent the weapon flying straight into the wall behind him.

More teeth gritting assailants came into view. Gina quickly turned, scanning the shadows. She broke an arm that reached at her. The next guy received a broken nose for flaring his nostrils. She finished him off with a double eagle kick.

She kicked a broken chair into the face of the guy who puffed out his chest; this stunned him. She dodged gunfire by running up the wall. The limited light helped conceal her. She flipped behind this gun toting thug. She seized control of his weapon, shot an assistant robber in the leg and then she broke the gun holder's hand.

Everything about Gina and Joshua told these urban marauders they would be two more victims in the wrong neighborhood at the wrong time. This information caused them to shove out their jaws; only to have them shoved back in. If your muscles twitched, or your pupil dilation you were quickly dealt with.

Three young women followed the attackers into the alley. They were dressed in different colored leather skirts. These women yelled encouragement to the assailants. Gina did three successive flips over to the women and smiled them into silence. As she did this, a large man emerged from the darkness and tried to grab her.

The man gave himself away by his loud breathing. Gina turned sideways; she was less visible. She repeatedly avoided his attempts to grab her. Once he showed signs of frustration; she delivered several surgical hand strikes to his chest. She took him down by chopping to his face.

Gina's eyes moved past the concrete and metallic structures to a tall aggressor that shifted weight from one foot to the other. Gina reached behind her and pulled the strings that tied her modified recurve bow to her side.

A ruffian advanced with his partner. She slammed the bow into one man's head; he wailed and dropped to his knees. She jumped to a wall, pivoted and smashed her foot into his head, this put him down. She ducked under the punch from the other man and twisted until she was behind him. She kicked the back of his knee; he stumbled forward hitting his head against the brick wall.

In the middle of the alley, the hand of the man who had been shot pressed his injury, blood welling up between his fingers. Six capable would-be robbers were incapacitated on the cold wet ground. One last man confronted Joshua. Gina tapped Joshua on the shoulder. Joshua moved and gestured for her take the lead.

The man's stance showed that he was unaware that Gina's whole world had been a lie. The man lunged at where Gina stood, she was no longer there. She was just out of his reach and readying a punch.

This punch rose from her toes, braced in her legs, accelerated in her hips, twisted through her torso, surged through her shoulder, expanded in her arm and exploded out of her fist. Gina landed an uppercut that elevated this two hundred pound person off of his feet. He landed ten feet away on his back with a thud.

"Is that all you've got?" Gina yelled. The young women ran off into the night.

Gina didn't have on gloves and would have to ice her knuckles for several hours. That's the thing about Gina; she could have gone unnoticed longer than Devon or Joshua. Her skills would be overlooked easier than theirs would be. A woman fighting and escaping into the darkness would not ring many alarms.

But Gina stood there with those that could not run away. Her chest slowly heaved; she wanted more. Joshua came behind her and she threw a punch at him. He caught this punch in the palm of his hand.

"Hey, you don't always have to give out the punch; sometimes you reach the goal by taking the punch." Joshua smiled. Gina sighed and leaned against the wall next to Joshua. As soon as she did, Joshua took off running. He was headed home. This is a race he would win.

It was Saturday and Gina had on a shirtdress, belt and motorcycle booties. Joshua seemed nervous as they walked the street in the Broadway Theater District. There were large crowds of tourists and locals who were looking down at their devices. These tourists searched for restaurants, train stations and waited for vehicles to pick them up.

"Remember that night you kicked me in the face and I left and went out into the night," Joshua said as they walked the streets.

"You mean the night you stopped sparring with me," Gina said without looking at him.

"I didn't really leave. I was on another warehouse and I watched you. You turned on this delightful music and danced. I had never seen jazz, tap, hip-hop and ballet rolled into such a gracefully broken performance. You finished with a forward flip. It was inspiring, I wanted to clap, but I didn't."

"I needed a partner," Gina said.

Joshua smiled and unexpectedly stopped walking. He took off his blazer and started loudly humming a George Benson singsong tune. Joshua's humming had polyphonic overtones. The beauty of this impressed Gina.

While Joshua hummed, he ran and happily danced in his black slacks and baby blue button down shirt. Gina put her hand to her mouth slightly embarrassed.

Joshua's shiny shoes shuffled over to sit a stumbling drunk down; he frowned on a few ill-mannered children, helped an old man cross the street and stopped two pickpockets… with heel, toe, step and jazz hand precision. He ended his performance by hopping onto a light pole.

"Who do you think you are, The Dancing Cavalier?" Gina said smiling ear to ear. "Maybe you should leave the dancing to me," she said as they walked off into the night. This was the first talk they had that didn't end in a debate.

***

Eight hours ago across the Atlantic Ocean, sunrays coated the mountain as fires ignited. The fires burned out of control on either side of Athens. Wind whipped flames tore through dense forestland as Devon glided down from the clouds. Wildfire was in top form; he was in the middle of two towns setting flame to cars, to farms and to lives.

Thousands of people were trapped on the narrow cobblestone roads. Wildfire took a break from his mission to watch a smoothly gliding Devon. Devon darted in and out of the columns of smoke as he surveyed the area. Devon's arrival prompted Wildfire to raise the temperature. Devon landed and began to move the blockages. Wildfire frowned and he sent embers out as far as he could.

"This way!" Devon shouted after busting through the wall of the town bakery as intermittent ocean water fell from two air tankers. Devon led hundreds of people through a burning basement labyrinth. To prevent a collapse he quickly braced his body against the wall.

As people ran by him, two old women stopped and said, "Iraklís... Iraklís." These two women used wet rags to clear Devon's face of ash before moving on. Devon held the building up until the last person was through and then it collapsed on top of him. The collapse caused ash to fly across the harbor.

A woman grabbed her husband and whatever belongings she could. Once the flames burned a hole in the roof of their summer home; they ran for their lives.

"Head towards the sea!" Devon shouted while opening the singed wings of his wingsuit to shield them from the approaching fire. These two and a thousand others stumbled and plunged into the sea.

Just being in the water wasn't sufficient; they swam out some distance to avoid the suffocating fumes. The water current took the frightened masses further from the coastline.

From the highest rooftop in the town Devon saw the shadows of people underneath the waves; he heard screams coming from the water. Devon immediately jumped into the water. He grabbed as many underwater bodies as he could and took them to shore. Behind him, coastal towns were slowly being consumed as fire billowed the smoke of its digestion.

The winds subsided as a battle weary Devon crawled out of the water to find twenty bodies huddled together on the beach, the smoke slowed them; the flames did the rest. They didn't make it to the water. Coast guards and Navy vessels picked up those who were still in the water. The mast of sunken fishing boat jutted out of the blackened water as fire crews battled fire pockets.

Wildfire burned two towns off the map in half a day. While Devon fought this fire, a warplane was shot down, a dam collapsed, a village was flooded, a heat wave sent 20,000 people to hospitals, 103 people were cooked in their homes from a Guatemalan volcano, a place that never had a mass shooting did and all over the world people plotted to harm each other.

Devon was severely burned and bleeding; his breathing was labored, yet he moved down the coast searching for survivors. This victory; if 112 dead and 600 injured could be called that was a reminder of a larger goal.

Devon made it to The Parthenon, where he spent two days recovering on the fine white marble, before he returned to North America.

On Devon's trips to the other side of the rift he didn't just pushing his body and mind. He tried to locate a city, the people. Devon had traveled dozens of miles from the rift openings. Four hours was the longest he had spent on the other side and he never saw a city, just creatures and ruined structures.

It had been over 300 days since he had been altered, Gina and Joshua were evolving, still Devon didn't feel any closer to carrying out this mission; more would be needed.

Devon returned and searched for her, the one that defied Prime's orders. She was the only otherworlder that refused to complete a mission. This insubordination had been shown to the council as part of humanity's defense. Perhaps, that one incident is what stopped him from being killed at that meeting in Alaska.

Devon rode pass the taverns, tidal creeks, wine tastings and condominiums. Beaufort, South Carolina was an inviting clash of past and present. In the fleeting warmth of the sun her dress looked like aged white leather painted with gold. It had a platinum colored neck holder and it was accented with golden metal.

The tight fitting, contoured dress lovingly hugged her curves. It appeared to be made from snakeskin, but it wasn't. Devon recognized her from behind. The opening in the back of the dress showed the curved nature of her spine. In a world of supermen she was regal. Devon recognized her from behind.

Her neckline swept low to enhance the curvature of her breast. The sides of her dress showed her wide hips and a small waist. This battle dress lacing went up the backside. Shortly after the sun went down Devon came out of the shadows. He went entered the white five-bay home and headed to the bedroom.

"After all that has happened you show up here," a startled Influence said.

"I saw what you did at the trial. How you refused orders."

"So."

"So your kind don't always have to follow orders, you can think for yourself."

"I got demoted in the process of thinking for myself," Influence said walking around the room looking at her sleeping subject.

"You did that because it was the right thing to do."

"In a way, it was liberating. Now my 2nd in command Will Power, is in charge."

"I met her."

"You have?" Influence said coming closer to Devon looking him over.

"I need you to show me the rift you came through," Devon said.

Influence bristled at this and walked away from him. Devon grabbed her by the hand. She quickly turned and motioned to slap him. Devon looked into her eyes and her stern gaze softened. She lowered her hand and he let her go.

"Take me to the rift," Devon repeated.

"I'll take you to the rift, if you can keep up," Influence said. Before Devon could say another word, Influence opened the window and hoped out into the night. Devon quickly followed her. Influence floated from rooftop to rooftop. Devon knocked over people and trashcans as he tried to keep up with her.

Influence hid in a corner as Devon ran past, chasing misgivings. Once he was out of sight, Influence made her way down one block and glided over the next until she reached the outskirts of town. She was six miles away from her mission.

Influence was disappointed that Devon had not offered more of a challenge. She drifted down the road until she came to the rift. Ten feet from the portal she stopped, frozen in her tracks. Devon was there reclining on a worn log as if he had just woke up from a long nap.

"You just don't quit, do you?" Influence said. Devon just sat up and smiled. "Humph," Influence grunted and walked towards Devon. "Well, you got me here, now what do you really want?"

Devon hoped off the log and entered the rift opening; he disappeared from view. Influence's eyes widened and she lightly sat on the log. A minute later, an unharmed Devon exited the rift the same way he had entered it. Influence was speechless. Devon dusted himself off looked at Influence and said, "It's a recent development."

"I don't understand this," Influence uttered her battle dress gave off a subtle glow. A gust of wind brushed up against Devon. "This cannot be." The silver in her eyes waned and dark pools of reflection returned.

"Why show me this?" Influence suspiciously questioned.

"I need your help," Devon said pulling out a map of the rifts he had visited in. "I need you to tell me where to go."

Influence came closer to look at the map and she slowly breathed him in. He smelled familiar he smelled like home. Devon started walking through the small forest and Influence followed him.

"Whatever you are planning forget about it," she said. "How many times have you been to through?"

"Eight times," Devon said as they went deeper into the brush.

"Eight times!" she said. "What have you seen?"

"Your world is absolutely beautiful. I have seen mostly forests and deserts. The swamps are biological wonderlands. I have seen the effects of the yellow rain and black pools, as creatures were blistered or dead near the rift," Devon began. A silver tear left Influence's eye and wandered down her cheek.

"There are fire trees with leaves that fall to the ground as embers. There is a cactus that causes rashes upon contact with skin. I encountered a green berry that causes temporary blindness, a mistake of mine.

"There is this juicy spiked plant that causes the most vivid hallucinations. Luckily there is a colorful spicy fruit that counteracts the effect of the blindness and hallucinations. I saw a lot of desolation."

"Those places weren't always desolate," Influence said following Devon down a shallow ravine.

"There was a single orange leaf plant that coiled up and retracted to the ground when I touched it," Devon said. "There was this bird like creature that has scales and the tail of a dragonfly. It can fly in any direction."

The way Devon described Influence's home brought a smile to her face. They stopped walking just outside of a small cabin. The cabin was set against the small forest. Behind the cabin was a trail, a peach grove and rocky cliffs; below the cliffs was Lake Oolenoy. The porch was inviting and the red pine ends fit snugly as if they had grown that way.

"What I haven't seen is a city and I don't know where Prime is," Devon said forcing the cabin's door open. Influence followed him inside.

"I could help you, but I won't," Influence said as Devon checked the cabin for occupants. The cabin was dusty but in good condition. Devon took fire logs and kindling and placed them into the fireplace.

"I need a guide to take me where Prime is," Devon said without looking in her direction.

"You want me to do what?" Influence said.

"Be my guide," Devon said. "I need to meet with the council."

"I have been demoted and only Prime can call a council session…"

"Where can I find Prime?" Devon asked moving the kindling around.

"You won't stop, will you?" Influence said.

Devon stood up and said, "Look at all you have gone through for the sake of your world; will you stop?"

Influence shook her head slowly. "I can't be a part of this."

"You already are. Are you going to report what you have seen today?" Devon said crouching down. He placed his hands on the logs and increased the heat in his hands until they ignited. Devon used the poker to move the burning logs around.

"How can I report the impossible?" she said standing close enough to touch him.

"The impossible is why I need your help," Devon said standing up. He could feel her hot breath on his skin.

"And if we are caught…"

"We could change everything."

"My mate was killed because he altered you. He must have seen something good in you. You were the last to see my mate alive. I never thought I'd be without him." Influence said slowly gliding away from him. "I've seen how you watch me, is it more than curiosity?" she said, her gaze firmly meeting his.

Devon's face showed striations from going through the rift. Influence's thoughts ran down these subtle lines, her eyes settled at the hollow of his throat. The growing flames illuminated her fascination. She lowered her hand and placed it on his chest. Her eyes grew wide and she quickly put her hands around his neck, choking him.

Her hair moved as if she were an angel in a painting. Devon was stunned as Influence rose above him. She put her mouth to his. Her imperfect lips were cool and smooth, the longer they kissed the warmer her lips grew. The thought of "Can we?" drifted out of her mind as she took the armor from her body.

Her hair fell against his face. Her toenails were light blue. The pores on her neck opened. Devon tasted her. She was slightly sour. Devon pivoted his hips in an effort to move away, but her hands were around his throat. Breathing in only drew her further into his mouth. The fine sandpaper feel of her lips smoothed out the edges of his lips. Her lips parted and her long tongue touched his.

It was like the finding a nerve you didn't know you had. A jolt was sent through Devon. The sour taste was gone and he slowly, willingly kissed her back. Their mouths clung together and every time they pulled apart a tear dropped from her almond shaped eyes. Devon felt the rapid beating of a heart; it was his own. She pressed into him and removed her hand from his throat.

Her breath came fast and she began to lightly tremble. She straddled him and placed her hands on his chest. "I can feel you," she said. "Don't be afraid," she urged as she ran her hands along his arms and legs.

"I'm not afraid," Devon said.

Influence was aware that Devon could leave if he wanted to, a part of him was curious, every part of her was curious. She kissed him again and then she ripped open his shirt and unbuckled his pants. She reached between his legs and he grew in her hand.

The honey hued logs kept in the cabin warm. She had to be one hundred years older than Devon. This was probably the first time he really saw her. "Soft, warm," she whispered as her hand moved on him.

She kissed down his stomach, causing every hair on his body to rise. She hesitated for a moment, then pressed down harder on his chest and pulled down his pants. Through a vague series of moves and counter moves, this physical pleasure exceeded foreplay.

She excitedly explored him. Her head lowered and she put her mouth to him. He seemed to be nowhere and everywhere, as her coarse hands gripped his flesh. Her hands wandered his body as she sucked harder. The texture of her skin produced a unique pleasure that caused Devon to warmly throb in her mouth.

"There you go," she said as Devon's moans broke the silence. Devon threw her from him. His chest glistened and his thighs were wet from where she straddled him. She stood up, allowing what was left of her clothes to fall to the ground.

How could she be a monster? Her body was beautiful, her hips were voluptuous. She had a confident way about her and right now she was less monstrous.

She stepped toward him, focused on his large erect member. She got down and again straddled him. She put her long fingers around his throat. "Relax your mind," she said as her eyes outlined in silver. She infiltrated his neural pathways as she put him ever so slightly inside of her. Devon's eyes outlined in gold, they were connected.

Devon could feel what passed inside of her for blood, twisting through pumpless channels. It had no beginning and no end to its movement. It felt like a double heartbeat, but it wasn't.

"Can you feel me?" she said taking more of him. Devon wanted to stop, but his flesh made the choice for him. Influence did not hesitate. She put her hips over his thigh and pressing down as she raised and lowered her body. Her hip was sharp, her hand was blunt.

She moved her hips faster. Her double heartbeat quickened. Her body was tense with anticipation as he felt the familiar shape of her bones. Inside her there was a secondary suction as she moved up and down with surefooted traction. She screamed and clamped down hard on Devon. She wasn't soft, or gentle, yet her passion dripped all over him. The texture of her skin wasn't alien or foreign, it was different.

"How was your first time?" Devon said reaching up to touch her face.

"How dare you touch me!" she said. She slapped him hard across the face. Devon rolled over on top of her. She tried to apply pressure to his neck but Devon no longer allowed it. Devon slowly spread her legs, she was still wet and she held her breath as he fully entered her dampness.

Her body temperature was lower than a human's. She squirmed, adjusted and accommodated every extraordinary inch of him. What she felt was somewhere between ecstasy and death.

The flow of dominance between their two bodies was a tug of war that descended deep into the flesh. Devon lost himself inside of her.

Influence pulled him closer; she held him tighter. His body convulsed from pleasure but he was unable to withdraw. Her legs gripped him tightly as her body filled with a gentle light.

She released him as she faded in and out of consciousness. In the air was a faint vanilla scent. Her stomach tensed, her back arched and her moans intensified. The three line light tattoo on her shoulder grew brighter with each convulsion she made. Each successive heartbeat was faster, stronger and louder than the last.

She let out a low hollow roar. Her fingers dug into his shoulders as a wind blew through the cabin extinguishing the fireplace fire. Her silver eyes cut through the darkness. Her moisture covered him as the room filled with echoes. Whispers of Devon's plans tumbled out of his mind and lay silent in the darkness of spent want.

When she was able to move again, her fingers massaged the broken floor wood back into place. The sun was on the other side of the planet. She was drained; this was the longest Influence had been on this side of the rift. She had a subtle glow to her. The full glory of Influence's other beingness had been revealed by the fire's absence.

Devon opened the cabin door and Influence stared at him. Her long arms reached for her battledress. In the subtle twilight, Devon eyes followed the curve of her ass all the way down to the cliff of oblivion, then he made sure the cabin fire was out.

Influence picked the map up from the floor and weakly reclined. The scratches and bite marks on Devon's chest had healed. After she dressed, Devon hoisted her up on his back and quickly carried her into the darkness, through the forest, to the rift.

Influence's weakly touched his shoulder and handed him the map. She placed one foot inside the rift, cleared her throat and said, "I might be able to find out where Prime will be."

CHAPTER 19

The warehouse was organized and clean. A plaque that read, "Manibandhan bahirmukham" which is Sanskrit for "wrist outwards" hung on the wall. These were the first things Devon noticed when he entered the warehouse.

An apple appeared out of nowhere and floated in front of him. Devon looked closely at the apple. The image seemed to rest in his hand as if it was a real thing. He studied it for a few seconds and then flicks his thumb to move the image around, then the apple disappeared.

Further inside the waterfront base the new wingsuits hung neatly in the closet. Electronic keypads glowed as Gina and Joshua stood at attention. Devon continued to examine the living space. Devon thought Gina would shriek with joy when she saw him, she didn't.

"I see you have redesigned the wingsuit," Devon said.

"We have done some things," Gina said.

Devon simply smiled. Joshua pointed to the repaired the server and the see through computer screens with dark tinted backing. Devon had interacted with the apple, a 3D projection from these devices.

"All designed to enhance what we do," Joshua said.

Gina added a micro weave mesh to the lighter, thinner wingsuit. The boots now had energy dampening technology, to make them quieter. The goggles had navigation features, file hierarchies, video and text panel layouts. The goggles heads up display had green and yellow indicators with layered lines down to sub-levels to show readings such as height and speed.

Devon walked over to the weapons cabinet and opened it. The cabinet held a XM25 CDTE, an AK-47, an APC9K and various other weapons. Gina's modified recurve bow and arrows hung on the all.

Devon went to the corner and looked through their supplies. He could see that they had toyed with the idea of using Potassium Iodide and Propylthiouracil. These substances stop radioactive isotopes from invading thyroid glands and they flush toxic particles from the body.

"Gina came up with the idea to add a couple teaspoons of sea salt to each gallon of water; that we drink after rift encounters," Joshua said.

"We should be able to stay in longer and make quicker recoveries," Gina added.

"I've modified to a few things," Joshua said, his iris outlined in gold as he waved his hand over a computer keyboard and the desk monitor lit up. He accessed files and pages without touching the keyboard. Each time Joshua suffered an injury; he integrated custom built microprocessor into his body. His body healed quickly around the ultra thin titanium chipsets.

The chips allowed Joshua to squeeze more power into less space. He had three in his left arm, one in each knee and digital processors on each hand. He controlled devices by moving his hand near them.

Joshua could manipulate traffic signals. He could use a cell phone to track locations and he could loop camera feeds. He could remotely trigger an alarm and engaged fire suppression systems. While he was hooked into a machine; he could project information from his hands to a wall. He could do this at short range, but he needed more power to tap into distant systems.

"And the eye?" Devon said. He was able to see the small cybernetic prosthesis near Joshua's left the eye.

Joshua gulped and said, "I may have overdone it. Right now, there are currently thirty six entrapment operations and thirteen murder investigations underway by local authorities. We just restored the power this morning." The only remnant of the injury was a periodic eyelid twitch.

Gina used the polymer replicator to make their clothing more durable. She used the 3D printer to make the nanofibers smaller; everything else, she hand stitched. Their clothes were not just stylized, they were bulletproof, waterproof, heat resistant and wafer thin.

Devon tried on the green and black biker suit. It fit him perfectly; his well defined muscles could be seen underneath. Joshua had on what could best be described as ninja casual. Gina wore a green lace, high neck, open shoulder dress. It had a dark leather harness cut across the body. Her line work was exact yet sexy.

Monograms of their initials laser were cut into these new uniforms. Devon's had a 'DH'. Joshua's was 'JD' and Gina had 'GAL' prominently embossed across her chest.

"Looks good, feels better," Devon said, moving around in his new clothes. His attention was drawn to the pair of gold eyes subtly woven into the hip of his biker suit.

"What's this?"

"That's our symbol," Gina said proudly.

"I like it," Devon replied. "But what have you learned?"

"Humans are only smart because humans say we are," they said simultaneously.

"Instead of asking what it is, ask what can I know?" Gina said.

"The more hands that benefit from preventable tragedies; the more likely systemic manipulation is involved," Joshua said.

Joshua pulled up a holographic map that was dotted with hundreds of red dots; these are the rift locations that we know of. Joshua's read outs hung in midair like three dimensional sand paintings.

"Who did this?" Devon asked, noticing the improvement from the barely readable grainy holographic from before.

"We did this together," Gina responded with a smile.

"Were you expecting red pins on a map attached by yarn?" Joshua said.

Gina quickly pulled her gun from its holster and fired six bullets at various angles, a centimeter from Devon's skin. He could feel the heat and was tempted to flinch, but didn't. Gina picked up another pistol and began firing both weapons at the same time.

Two empty magazines bounced on the smooth concrete. She popped in two fresh ones from her inner jacket sleeve into the guns and continued firing uninterrupted. She used angles and room clearing tactics.

"The handgun is just an extension of your hand," Gina said holstering her weapons.

"Anything else?" Devon said.

Gina went to the weapons locker and retrieved her bow; the bow assembled and extended it with a quick flick. She shifted slightly in her stance, ensuring she was in the right position before she reached for her quiver. She pulled out an arrow and nocked it.

She let one loose in calibration, it landed forty yards on target near Joshua and Devon. Over the next minute, she sent fourteen more arrows towards the target. She lowered the bow and looked at Devon.

"You can do better," Devon said.

Gina slowly looked at Joshua, who looked away into the vacant middle distance. She filled her quiver with fifteen more arrows and took a position seventy yards from the target. She looked at Devon, who shook his head. "From there," he said pointing to the delivery door, which was 150 yards from the target.

Gina looked at her bow and made her way to the service door. Joshua, who had stood a yard from the target, took a few more steps sideways. Her bow was adjustable, lightweight and had near zero vibration. She looked at the target and then at Devon.

"Focus." Devon said.

Gina looked at the target until she could no longer feel the vibrations from passing trucks. She could no longer feel the cold draft that came from underneath the door. Her face showed determination. Her eyes had a faint golden tinge. She felt nothing, there was no target, there was no bow, there was only her.

She inhaled deeply, the air moved through her like a calming balm. She used the corner of her eye as an anchor point as she nocked an arrow to the string, then she carefully exhaled. As the last of the air left her, the arrow escaped her bow.

The first arrow was quickly followed by eleven arrows, all clustered near the center. She didn't bother to aim the thirteenth arrow, but it flew truer than the first had. The last two arrows were shot together and landed near the center.

"I knew you could do it," Joshua said clapping as he slowly walked forward. Devon let out a subtle 'humph' as he examined where the arrows landed. Gina now held arrows in her drawing hand. She could fire five arrows in ten seconds and hit targets while on the move.

Gina opened a small case which housed special arrowheads. A four-prong grappling arrowhead, it was sturdy enough for a thin tension cable to be attached. An incendiary arrowhead, which on impact, mixed plant based chemicals these could explode or melt materials. A mechanical shrapnel arrowhead that shot fragments in a circular pattern after hitting a target, this one was particularly nasty.

Gina collapsed her bow, below the handle and midway down each limb, into a compact form. She put her equipment into the cabinet and grabbed a sword. Devon smiled as she swung her blade around in powerful arcs as if she were cutting out space in time.

"How is the sparring going?" Devon said interrupting her. Gina looked at Joshua. Joshua was already entering the arena.

Gina entered the arena. After they bowed they unleashed a rapid series of kicks queixada, martelo de negative, meia-lua de frente on each other. These were followed by escapes, flips and leaps. The two fought in a magnificent violent tango of flexibly, grace and power.

Joshua absorbed Gina's hits as she leaped and spun away from his strikes. She executed a flying omaplata which Joshua caught; he tossed her twenty feet away and she landed with a cartwheel into a backflip. They bumped into everything but they never let anything break.

"Enough," Devon said.

"Impressed yet?" Joshua said breathing heavily.

"I would be, if this were real world situations," Devon said. He didn't say it but he was pleased to see that Gina's gracefulness had rubbed off on Joshua and his power was harness by her.

"I think we could take on Tornado or Avalanche..." Gina confidently stated.

"You two aren't ready."

"Who would they send?" Gina said.

"Everyone..." Devon responded. "We train together; we keep the element of surprise."

"So why are you talking instead of training us," Joshua said. A smile briefly appeared on Devon's face. Gina stared coldly at Devon and then went into her garden. Devon followed her.

"You look good," Devon said looking around.

"Don't give me that."

"You started all this, you don't just leave like that!" Gina said examining her plants.

"I had someplace to be."

"That's no excuse!"

"You had to find your own way. I didn't want to get in the way of that. There is only so much I can tell you, only so much I can show you," Devon said walking around her crops. "So, you're responsible for keeping things clean in here?"

"It was tough, but we've been keeping each other in line," Gina said smiling, no longer able to hide her happiness at his return. Gina changed her clothes and went into the kitchen.

Devon had returned just in time for Gina's carrots to be harvested. For the occasion, Gina prepared four herb roasted carrots and potatoes and sweet strawberry smoky chipotle chicken wings with a balsamic vinegar base glaze.

Devon and Joshua sat at the table and watched Gina happily danced around the kitchen tossing wings in baking powder and salt before putting them into the oven to crisp. While the wings air-dried, Gina presented them with a creamy avocado and blue cheese dip.

She served a tangy spinach and apple salad; she added radishes for crispness and pomegranate seeds for an explosion of freshness. The salad was dressed with a mixture of pomegranate molasses, lemon juice and virgin olive oil. It was topped off with a generous amount of feta.

She grabbed a black bottle with white writing from the cabinet. She poured a glass of this botanical vodka made from wild elderflower and milk thistle. She slowly moved the liquid around inside her mouth with her tongue. She watched Devon and Joshua eat two layers meringue beds topped with fresh strawberries and sliced almonds; this dessert was dusted with confection sugar for sweetness.

Other than Devon smiling and saying, "A hint of vanilla...vanilla bean..." They ate the wonderfully delicious meal in silence. Joshua thanked Gina for the meal and he disappeared into the night. Devon washed the dishes and cleaned up.

The abundance of plants made the air cooler, cleaner. Gina sat on the stool and slowly rubbed her ankle. It had not escaped Devon that her hips were fuller and that her thighs tightly pressed against the bodysuit.

"Still mad?" Devon said coming over to sit next to her.

"A little."

"We don't have time to be mad," Devon said, rubbing her feet.

"Are we leaving?"

"Not yet."

"You have a lot of cuddling to make up for," she said looking at him.

"I know," Devon said. Gina got off the stool and hugged him.

"You feel like home," she said burying her face into his neck.

Gina pulled the pins that held her hair in place and threw them ten feet away. They landed on the countertop and slowly turned parallel to each other. "Viens couche avec moi," she whispered into his ear. She felt the muscles in his arm as they wrapped around her waist. She pressed her body against his. Her nipples tightened when she felt her chest on his.

She kissed him. Her lips were more succulent than the strawberry topping. He slowly dragged his lips to her neck as he cupped the back of her head. She shifted her weight slightly and thought if this was what he could do with the mouth, she was willing to see what could be done with the rest of him. She allowed her ripped jeans to slide down her legs.

She stood there as his fingers rubbed her in ways she had never experienced before. This, this was better than anything she'd been doing to herself. His confident grazing made her twitch in compliance. Her hands clung to his back, as she reached new heights.

She dug her fingers into his back; the desire rose as her ankle pain was forgotten. Devon grabbed her leg and pulled it up, his other arm underneath her. This allowed him access to every part of her. His soft, warm hands slowly moved from her toes, to her knees, to— gasp. Her body shivered.

His hands applied pressure as they probed her back, stroking her shoulder and lower back. There was something about this lower area that caused her to relax. She quickly got up and turned away from him. Devon got up and followed her out of the kitchen.

Gina walked confidently and unsnapped the buttons on her crotch bodysuit. Before they could reach the bed, Gina turned and jumped on him. They fell backward onto the floor. She weighed less than he did, but her force made her heavy.

Her hand slid into his pants. He stood at attention, like a monument to her presence. She couldn't help but smile. Her other hand held him down as she placed her lips on his chest. She pulled his pants down and off in one motion. There would be no middle ground to this renegotiation of the gender contract. She was a bow with its string pulled back.

His man wick wandered between her thighs. Her moisture allowed him to easily slide inside of her. She slowly eased half his length inside of her. Specks of gold dotted her eyes, every sensation was magnified. Her body was a lightning rod of instinct, every fiber trembled. She let out a cry of happiness as her secrets dropped to the floor.

She clamped down on him. Sweat dripped from his forehead and ran down his naked back. Gina lay there, gently stroking his hair, waiting for her heart to slow. His weight was on top of her, she enjoyed that, this is the closest she had ever been to him.

Devon pulled away enough that he could look at her face. A thin gold outline was in his eyes. Gina looked different. Devon grabbed her waist and brought her hips to his. He moved in and out of her hard and harder, she preferred this. She cried every time his torch warmed her deep insides.

She met every one of his thrusts with one of her own. Devon turned her around and entered her while they knelt. This position required that she hold her breath. The entire lower half of his body was a matchstick that had set fire to the structure that was Gina.

She focused on pushing back, not on rhythm; doing anything other than allowing her body to tingle was pointless. Their breathing became heavier, their movements grew faster.

Gina trembled as her waves of need hit the high water mark. She couldn't think as they slammed against each other. A new level of heat surged deep inside of her. She was over the edge, in the middle of a waterfall of desire and need. Her back arched. Her eyes closed. She licked her lips as her insides squeezed and twitched.

Gina grabbed the metal bed frame and squatted over him. Devon's eyes widened as she slowly lowered. She began to rise and fall on top of him. Sweat beads wandered down her shoulders. Her chest heaved as collapsed on top of him.

Her screams hid the sound of the bending metal bed. A few more movements and Gina was again released from her desire and she cried out again. She dug her nails into his thighs as every inch of her body tightened. She pulled him close, so she could feel him throbbing.

She looked up at Devon and kissed down his stomach. Gina put him in her warm mouth. He vibrated from her delicious movements. There in the shadow of the garden, Gina proceeded to blow out his candle.

They lay there; having made love like it was their last day on earth. The last time he touched her like this she hadn't been altered, but this felt better. She lay there on top of him, running her hand down his head. She could still feel him surging through her.

Gina was more furious than any tidal wave or hurricane he had ever fought. This was the first time Devon slept without nightmare. This was salvation. Gina woke up and seemed lost in thought as they lay in the bed.

"What's on your mind?" Devon asked.

"Just... thinking," Gina responded.

"Thinking about what's next?"

"I'm following you."

"You know we won't be able to stay under the radar much longer. I am sure that we can end this."

"When it's time, you'll lead us to where we need to be..."

"I have to go," Devon said getting up.

"If you have to," Gina said turning on her back, slowly spreading her knees spread apart. Devon looked back at her and put his head underneath the sheet. Gina's morning laughter could be heard throughout the warehouse.

Devon kissed her lips until she went back to sleep. Once she was sleep he went out into the rain and was slowly swallowed up by mist. The afternoon rain woke Gina; her mind still drenched with passion. She reached down as if his lips were still there, she smiled.

"This time it won't take two weeks to recover," she thought.

They trained as usual, and they would cuddle. Gina determined when and where she would take more of Devon. Quite often Devon would wake up with her scent on his lips.

Gina had just helped authorities find illegal prescription drugs hidden in a tractor trailer. She stepped into the riverfront base quieter than an expression of thought. She sensuously took off her gloves and stockings in front of him.

It was unnerving to Devon in all the right ways. Devon's invincibility waned when it came to her. Devon's eyes focused on her as she stood near the window bent over her work. There was something about her confident stride that inspired his imagination.

Devon's nightmares were often interrupted by Gina's soft lips and fiery wetness. The warmth of her mouth lingered on him for hours. When Devon's hands moved over the computer keys, she thought about his hands moving on her. She could feel him up her spine and his mind had built an altar to her round backside.

Sometimes the two of them would dance for hours. With Devon she could express herself, she could let go. Being with an average man would have reduced her to an underpaid actress in an award winning film. She never said anything about the two of them being lovers. They pretended nothing was going on, but the moaning, screaming and the broken furniture and gym equipment replacements were dead giveaways, but she never said anything.

"Two fists, two elbows, two knees, and two feet, use your stance to defend. Now... Again," Devon said, demonstrating how to use the whole body as a weapon. Devon was up and instructing them as if he had never left.

Devon told them the story of how he had been in the Sahara Desert so long that he found the city of Atlantis. Devon began his stories by telling of terrain only accessible by horse. He stories were full of how he defeated enemies, only defeatable by guns, with his hands. Each time he began a story he would follow with, "but that's a story for another time…" and then he'd tell them pieces of the story throughout the day.

"Did you really travel the world in three months?" Gina asked.

"I did more than travel the world, I learned the world." Devon said.

"So, you know the biggest secrets now?" Joshua quizzed.

"Of course."

Joshua stopped the treadmill and eagerly pulled up a chair. He sat down and said, "Tell me one."

"OK," Devon said leaning close to Joshua. "Zebra stripes are black and white because they have different temperatures, it creates little breezes," Devon said smiling. "Now back to practice."

They were running at least 100 miles per week, reaching speed of twenty five miles per hour. They had equipment in the warehouse, but they preferred to run outside so the cities could be mapped and people could be watched. They maintained more common speeds when people were near, so they mostly ran at night bouncing hordes of mosquitoes off their skin.

They cycled 100 kilometers to and from various training locations. Devon rode BMX and always allowed Joshua and Gina to race each other. Joshua squatted 400 pounds while Gina punched and kicked his abdomen, most of these he absorbed. Joshua and Gina knew each other's habits; it could be said that they were friends.

Gina and Joshua looked forward to Devon's tales of smoke winding up from piles of burning debris and narrow escaped from grenades of shrapnel. During today's training Devon detailed the week he spent teaching in Atule'er Village. A poor Chinese village, where children have to climb half a mile ladder to class.

Yesterday, Devon told them how he narrowly escaped exploding landmines in Cambodia. His altered students listened quietly as he guided them through his adventures in the rainforest where he was bitten by a green mamba snake. Joshua's favorite story was how Devon led twenty people through the desert. He had wandered through the desert for fourteen days, digging up root and straining water through t-shirts.

Devon denied them the darker stories of dead bodies that collected at the border of nations. He wouldn't detail the foam that rested at the edge of mouths and the trail of ants that crossed lifeless bodies. These were memories he could not forget. Devon remembered all the faces in his nightmares.

In the middle of a story, whenever Devon said something like, "Straight jab into the face, if they block it, their field of vision is lost." or "Once a person can catch flies, they realize they don't need to," they knew that story time was over.

Devon had been back for three weeks when he gave Joshua and Gina a mission. The mission: sneak into the building, override the system and download the files—simple.

"Gina, you don't have to go," Devon said.

"Why not?" she said her left foot impatiently tapping. "A queen has been behind every decision a king has made. Skirts are every bit the weapon, suits are…." she said.

When Gina set her mind to something she couldn't be reasoned with. They couldn't take any weapons on this mission, there would be no killing. The building was in the heart of the city. It had a State-of-the-art security system and a small army of paid security enforcers.

Their gear hid them as vehicle lights probed the dark streets. Joshua and Gina were in the shadows, but they weren't the only ones. They entered the building from the sewer. Joshua disabled the building's camera system and they went up three flights of stairs. On the fourth floor, Joshua waved his hands and overrode a series of time locks on the door, and they made their way towards the clean room.

Gina followed Joshua into the ventilation shaft. They scuttled and squeezed through the narrow space. They navigated the building like they were the architects. They lowered themselves into the clean room. Joshua sat at a desk and hacked into the computer system.

"No fuss...no muss. A piece of cake," Joshua said.

Gina pulled out a small device, pushed a button and the files started downloading. The white progress bar purposely moved across the screen. This progress bar was around ten percent when the red strips on the wall of the clean room started to flash. There was series of clicks; as the door locks snapped back into place. The security system had been reactivated.

Joshua jumped up to the vent and reached out his hand for Gina.

"Sounds like it's time to go," Joshua said pulling Gina up.

Gina followed him into the vent. This security detail was full of ex-military, law enforcement and Special Forces types. Joshua and Gina backtracked but saw a dozen heat signatures moving in their direction. Small flashing red lights danced in dark stairwells. The download continued but they were trapped.

"I think their sensors are picking up my body heat," Gina said. She wasn't very good at regulating her body temperature.

"We can go up to the roof," Joshua said pulling up a holographic schematic."

"You go to the roof," she said.

"And you?" Gina just nodded. Joshua went up a ventilation shaft and Gina crawled down until she made it to the lower cafeteria. The only way out was down the hall and through the front door. Security officers filled the hallway, moving towards the heat signature.

The forces breached the doors of the cafeteria and tossed flash bangs grenades inside. Their training told them to enter with speed and aggression. They did as they were trained; they entered the cafeteria one by one, clearing the corners as they moved towards her. Gina sat on a bench in the center of the room holding a cup of yogurt.

"Don't move!" were the shouted instructions.

Beams from flashlights locked on her but also gave away the position of the guards. The first officer grabbed her arm; she quickly slammed his face into the table. When the second officer came to assist the first officer she slid on the ground between his legs. Silent red emergency lights briefly illuminated the floor.

As the guard turned, Gina jumped and launched two center sternum kicks to his chest. She jumped over the kitchen counter and swung a hanging plant against the skull of her closest pursuer. A waffle iron, rolling pin and barbecue tongs were called into action by her.

Gina quickly looked at the progress bar; it was at sixty percent. The files they were downloading would prevent this company from putting a virus into one of the largest banks in the nation. A security officer grabbed at her and she sent him flying through the glass door. This bleeding guard wrapped his hand with a towel from his pocket and picked up the large shard of glass.

Picking up this glass was a mistake. She kicked the guard in the abdomen, and then jumped off his bent over body to kick another attacker in the face. She ducked under two swings but was knocked to the floor by a third. Gina fell on her back and several security agents were on top of her hitting her with batons and flashlights.

This snapped her mind into a tigeress. The four other animal styles of Shaolin Kempo Karate are the snake, the leopard, the crane and the dragon these techniques used blocks or parries before striking. The tiger's existence does not involve defense. The tiger is at the top of the food chain, the strongest and deadliest in the kingdom.

Gina pushed the human mass off of her and into chairs and tables. She formed her hands like claws and launched herself at the nearest moaner, digging her fingers into the bicep of his swinging arm. She put her boot into the face of another man. An approaching guard received a straight palm heel, a paw as it were, to the chest. The baton he was holding dropped quickly to the ground.

Gina struck with frightening confidence; she rolled forward and struck his neck. She ripped down the cheek and landed another strike to his throat. She scrambled beneath another attacker's flailing arms and elbowed upward into his abdomen. She hit the groin of another man, an elbow to the chin of this guy and a rising helicopter kick to the bridge of that one's nose.

Blood from his nose and mouth splattered against the walls. His eyes closed and he made a gurgling sound as he impotently fell. Gina took a step towards a recovering guard and clasped both of her hands. She shouted a 'Kiai' and issued a double palm heel strike. She made contact with his bladder and then the underside of his cheekbone. He dropped were he stood.

She jumped on the big one, the last one. She spun all over his body raining blows to his face. He dropped to one knee and the fell over as she walked down the hall checking the progress bar. Half an hour later than expected, Joshua entered the waterfront lair and flopped down on his bed.

"Joshua, where is Gina?" Devon asked.

"Isn't she here?" Joshua said looking around. Devon immediately started putting on his gear. Joshua scanned networks on any word of the building breach. Devon and Joshua hurried to the door on their way to look for Gina, when she dropped in from the sky roof.

"Do you have any idea how worried I've been?" Devon said quickly running over to her. Gina handed him the micro-drive and he hugged her long and hard.

"Whatever is in that file won't make things better," Gina said letting him go. "Tonight, we stopped one company from doing what another one will. Because of what we did tonight, tomorrow an arch-criminal disguised as a humanitarian will be publically removed, but the corporation will go on.

"Are the only victories left, the ones that only slow the enemy down?" Gina finished. She sat down beside Joshua.

"How are you feeling? Do you need a break?" Devon asked them. Gina smirked back at him. "Good, clean yourselves up and pack your things." Joshua jumped up and threw open the weapons locker. Devon looked at him from the side of his eye.

"Are we going in?" Joshua said closing the locker.

Devon smashed the micro-drive in between his fingers. He looked over his shoulder at them and said, "Training is over."

On the table, Devon left the key to the motorcycle and the coordinates where they were to meet him in twelve hours. Then he walked out of the warehouse. Joshua and Gina spent the next two hours packing supplies.

"Do you feel like driving?" Gina asked outside. Joshua nodded his head and Gina tossed him the key. Joshua throttled the engine and they rode towards their destination.

CHAPTER 20

Familiar groans came from their tents, it was morning; the rift called to them. Two Creeks, Wisconsin is where the coordinates led Gina and Joshua. They arrived in the night and scouted the area surrounding the rift.

"The altitude's 7,159 feet and it is 50 degrees," Joshua said as Gina stomped her feet to keep them warm. "The wind blowing left to right at 13 miles an hour."

Devon couldn't shake the notion that Prime was somewhere watching, even allowing all of this. Devon removed anything he didn't need. Devon stepped in the rift first, the others followed. They had breached the barrier. They had built up a tolerance to rift energy. Devon was the first through the portal followed by Joshua.

"What's next?" Joshua said stumbling out of the portal. "More danger, right," he said not waiting for an answer. Gina followed Joshua out of the portal. She immediately threw up and then she threw up again.

"This is the second time this year I've have to learn to walk this year. Joshua said trying to steady himself.

"Do you want to go back?" Devon said. It was mildly humorous watching them stumble and fall as they grappled with the stronger gravity on the other side. Gina regained her composure, wiped her mouth and pulled out a notepad. She began taking notes on moisture levels and humidity. She was always taking notes.

Soon they were able to stand and from standing they began to walk. While they walked, questions without bodies formed around them.

"So, this is it," Joshua said wiping fluid from the side of his mouth. It was colder than they had anticipated. Out of their mouths came an icy fog. Their eyes bulged as a finless creature breached the water of the lake. This otter-like creature just looked at them as it glided along. Seeing this made Gina want to see more, Joshua wished he had his guns.

A yellow raindrop fell in front of them and soon there were other raindrops. The raindrops left small blotches on the ground. The rain stopped shortly, briefly turning the lake a light orange. The dark orange color of this creature was a type of camouflage and camouflage meant that there were also predators.

The surf made shorebirds scatter against the clay, silt and sand erosion only to regroup as it receded. The sand felt porous and was home to crab-like eels and other ground diggers. A whole community lived here, and everything went about its business oblivious to the intruders.

"What do you think they eat here?" Joshua said.

"Eat?" Devon shot back.

"Yeah, eat. I'm not saying I'm hungry but..."

As the tide retreated, a colossal starfish-type animal surfaced near the shore. It had fourteen arms and was larger than a compact car. It was badly injured. Its dark gold blood ran into the water making it look like fire.

Devon wondered what scientific name he could give to such a creature. It was covered in thick spines and was emerald green along the edges. It had thousands of transparent cilia; these must help propel it underwater as it searched for its prey.

The sight of this magnificent creature brought Gina to tears. The longer they stared at it, the more alien it became.

The large overhead leaves cast a shadow over the area. Joshua and Gina were as amazed as Devon pulled at tree bark which turning to fire. Devon called these flying ink-blots birds, but these colorful flying creatures that gliding above them weren't like any bird they have ever seen.

Gina's hips shifted as she lay on the ground next to Devon. Joshua zeroed in on a creature through his display. Devon saw beads of sweat trickle down Gina's forehead. He could smell the deodorant Joshua wore and he could taste the bitterness of yellowing grass they had flattened.

Something moving fast in the distance snapped them out of their amazement. There was a noise that sounded like ice crystals shattering. The buzzing that they heard earlier stopped the water creatures disappeared below the surface of the lake. There was the noise again. The noise began to take on a melody and rhythm that filled their brains.

The explorers were overcome with unease. The loud thrashing sound was now directly in front of them. Devon was sure he could make it back, but Gina and Joshua might not. Devon hesitated, a part of him wanted to see the creature.

Devon was curious when all that mattered was survival. On Devon's left the reeds parted as a large hairless blood orange bear-like creature ran towards them. Joshua pulled Gina out of the way of the lunging beast.

Gina crumpled to the ground and rolled into a ball like she anticipated an encroaching winter of dark ice. Before they had time to absorb what happened; the blue eyed beast turned and came at them again. Before Devon could yell, "Don't touch it!" Joshua reached out towards the beast and his fingers received a shock. Joshua rung his hand in pain and jumped to his feet.

The shock Joshua received was a mild electrical shock but the pain was drifting up his arm. Then that same unnerving noise came from multiple directions. The tree line revealed vague shapes moving in the distance. The movement stopped for a moment as blue eyes floated in the shadow. Joshua stopped shaking his hand long enough to register his terror.

"We have to go back!" Gina yelled.

"Yep," Joshua responded as he ran past her on his way back to the rift.

The creatures breached tree line and ran towards the nearest intruder. Devon's mouth was still half open as he got up. The first beast's musk clung to the air; a high pitched growl came from its mouth. Devon ran but he could feel the beast's breath hot on his back.

Joshua made it back to the entrance first, followed by Gina. When Devon came through the clearing; Joshua and Gina peered down at him through the portal as if he were a tadpole. Their eyes widened as the creatures were closing in behind Devon.

Devon cleared the brush and jumped head first into the rift. Once past the threshold of the rift they ran out into the light of their world. Fear filled their eyes.

Once they were all out of the rift there didn't speak. They just poured water down their throats. They stood outside the rift opening and wondered if their behavior had caused the beast to attack.

The returned to their camp and went over their errors. Their clothes were minimally damaged. This rift was merely a test to see how well they adjusted to the rift's energy and to make sure they worked together. Their real destination was much further.

Devon borrowed a vehicle and Joshua and Gina rode the Soul Stirrer for eleven hours to Matagorda, Texas. The landscape on other side of this rift was flush with the pop of multicolored explosions burping up out a river. The water was reddish orange, a reflection of the sun. There were no sirens, no voices, no clatter, just water gently lapping at the banks as Gina scribbled in her notebook.

"What do you think?" Gina said looking at Joshua.

"I think it's horrible. You prefer this place, don't you?" Joshua said to Gina. This wasn't a question; there was pity infused disgust in his voice. He was still upset about the shock he received in the last rift. Joshua didn't think of these rifts, as portals of understanding.

Joshua wanted it known that coming here, for him, was not the finger tipped obsession it was for Devon and Gina. One hour into their trek when Gina said, "Look," pointing her quivering finger to toward the sky. They knelt down.

Joshua squinted against the sunlight counting in his head as a large moving object appeared in the sky. They could not make out what it was; they knew it wasn't human.

"What are those marks on its side?" Gina asked leaning forward to point again. She was whispering, which at this point seemed useless. Her voice had a catch in it. Every time she spoke, Devon noticed she was becoming more unnerved. Her panicked tone made him calmer.

"Have you ever seen anything like that?" Gina asked.

"Yes," Devon replied.

"What about that?" Joshua said pointing to a small squirrel-like creature chasing a larger squirrel-like creature.

"No. I have not."

They held this new information inside of them as they pushed deeper into the dark brush.

"Now there are more of them," Gina said.

"Male or female," Joshua said.

"It's something," Gina said in response to his question.

The black color of the creatures was faded but life still powered through them. The explorers watched for a few more seconds and then moved up the mountain side. The shadow of this mountain was like the petal of a monstrous flower that blossomed within the skull only to expand the mind beyond what any person can bear.

At the crest of the mountain was another strange creature. This one had no arms or legs. It was a large eye socket. It was the blackest pit of an eye and it saw them. It had a dozen smaller eyes surrounding it. The main eye was so large that it sees the thought you just had of getting away from it.

These creatures glided along smoothly hardly leaving tracks, but they did leave some kind of slimy residue. The mountain area was largely covered by red earth. On the southern of the mountain was an ocean of green water.

On the downside of the mountain, the landscape slowly grew meaner. The blue plants gave way to patches of brown grass and weeds. The weeds gave way to ditches; the ditches gave way to dark canals. The dark canals gave way to dreary paths and those gave way to mounds of yellow colored soil.

In the middle of their path was another creature. This one was like a large mouth, but it had no teeth or tongue. Its skeleton seemed to be without bone, tendon or muscle, yet it had huge whispering wings that beat against time. This creature roared, not in anger, but in despair.

The creature quickly scurried out of sight. This was the quietest Gina and Joshua had been. Devon was excited but he had to be calm and provide balanced for all of their sakes. As the sun climbed down the trees began to subtly glow. The wind changed and started blowing east then west. This below against them and made their hike longer.

They all paused when they heard a small, tight sound. This could possibly be another creature beyond their imagining. They stood motionless, listening for a minute, maybe two; there was nothing. Then they continued to descend the mountain.

Little lights started to appear, hundreds of them. These firebeetles had a pair of slender antennae, forewings and a puffed out thorax. It emitted light from its abdomen, green for female and blue for male. Dancing green and blue lights playfully surrounded them, lighting their path as the group moved forward.

At the bottom of the mountain, the three stopped near a field and viewed this world of dotted light through the tangled branches. Near them a creature's squealed. This prompted Gina to run a few yards in front of them. Her heart raced, she wasn't easily upset, but this was new territory.

Another sound approached them from behind. This sound was headed towards them and it captured their attention. In the dim light, there was a shadow— nothing clearer than that; there was no sign of what it really was. From behind the black brush came Influence.

"We came for Prime, but you're just as good," Joshua said lunging at her. Devon quickly stepped between them and held his hand out.

"She's with us," Devon said. The ominous weight of those words infected their unspoken thoughts.

"She's one of Them!" Joshua responded trying to get around Devon.

"What do you mean, she's with us?" Gina asked.

"Hmmm… Three of you," Influence said coming closer to them.

"What were you expecting?" Gina said.

"Devon is full of surprises." Influence raised her small veiny hands as she spoke softly. Her almond eyes focused on Devon.

"I've heard a lot about you?" Gina said as she warmed to the presence of Influence.

"I've heard nothing about you," Influence responded.

"Influence, nice to meet you," Joshua said extending his hand towards her. Influence raised her hand to slap him. Devon again stepped between then and caught her hand. Joshua stood there with a confused look on his face.

"He tried to touch me," Influence said incredulously.

"I told him not touch anything, but… We didn't see you on the path behind us." Devon said.

"I took the shorter way around the mountain," Influence said.

"We hiked for two hours, running from those eye and mouth things through disgusting contaminated water when we could have just gone around?" Gina said irritation filled her voice. Influence weakly smiled at her; Gina was not amused.

"You think Prime will see this coming together as beautiful? That he will hear the spirit of redemption when you speak and give you his blessing complete with an Amen…"

"We are here as proof that people are more than what he thinks," Gina said.

"Most cities have been pushed back from the rift area. There is a city not far from here. Prime is there; this way," Influence said pointing them down the path. Behind Influence, the group marched across the wasteland shielding their faces from the direction changing winds.

With Influence as their guide they walked quicker. As darkness grew; their attention was on getting to the distance lights.

"No posted warnings," Devon said as they went deeper into the long black grass.

"We don't come to the Radiated Barrier unless we are on a mission," Influence responded. "With all those books you carry around, have you been mistaken for a teacher?" Influence asked Gina.

Gina stopped scribbling in her notepad, "What do you mean?" she shot back at Influence.

"There are a lot of warm bodies out there, why were you chosen?"

"I'm not Devon," Gina said putting her notepad away as she approached Influence.

"I accept that you are in fact, not Devon."

"You can't do anything but accept it," Gina snapped at Influence.

"You display anger to me but not to your mothers who are reading porn and raising generations alone..."

"What do you even know of my world?" Gina said now almost within arms-distance of Influence.

"I've seen what dominates your screens. These screens show faces, hair and upper bodies. They use bodies for identification, as if they couldn't advertise a product by showing legs in pants and feet in shoes. They show the things that have tribal connections; they promote sexual possibilities. Your kind is far too easily swayed," Influence said looking at the smaller Gina.

Gina took a deep breath and another step towards Influence. Up to this point in their journey the order they walked in didn't matter; now as if by instinct they switched position. The nature of their exploration changed as a result of the exchanged between these two.

During Gina and Influence's conversation a new protocol was established. Influence led, followed by Joshua. Devon was at the end and Gina was in-between Devon and Joshua. They continued to move and spoke in hushed whispers as if someone might overhear. The red skies extended into the distance as if it was rendered just for them. They continued to get closer to the city.

"The way politics in our world works is," Joshua said. "If a nation declines an invitation to join, The System takes the rejection graciously. It keeps a peaceful diplomatic posture; it invites the nations that surround the declining nation to join it. Soon simple partnerships become expansion and expansion becomes encirclement.

"There will be barriers to trade that cause economic problems and soon that first nation will be the odd nation out. The System might allow that nation's ships and airplanes limited passage through partnership controlled space. But only as that nation agree to play by The System's rules and submit their citizens to being occasionally violated.

"Without knowing it that nation's aspirations for growth became predicated on acceptance of The System's rules and values."

"So when The System shows up on your doorstep prepare to be assimilated?" Influence said.

"Ummm…Where's your vehicle?" Gina said.

"On the other side of the city; only authorized vehicles are allowed near radiated areas," Influence said without looking in Gina's direction.

They had walked for some time now, they could see lights but the city seemed distant. Devon thought that perhaps Gina and Joshua weren't ready and that perhaps they should have turned back, but at no point did they speak of turning back.

Laser lights pierced the sky. They were now on the outskirts of the city. They saw trees and beyond the trees they saw bushes. Beyond the bushed was a grey fog. They night sky slowly moved in above them.

When the trees and the bushes seemed the thickest and the sky was blacker than a sky should naturally be, that is when they made it to the street. There were no sentinels to greet them as they came out of the brush. The four of them moved forward as nature gave way to broken roads and remnants of curved linear homes and structures.

"This is the edge of the city," Influence proclaimed. "Here everyone has a home and is provided for."

"This place doesn't seem so different," Gina stated.

"There is a kind of beauty in human delusion. Twenty percent of your water is wasted. Forty percent of your food is wasted. We don't have any of that here," Influence countered.

They saw the streets and heard the laughter of playing children. In a haze of fading sunlight, they stood in awe of a land in decline.

"You will see that our culture is the superior culture. There is no fear of being coiled up by multiculturalism. We are Them. We are one." Influence stated.

"Maybe we won't be noticed," Joshua said as they slowly walked down a street.

"You'll be noticed," Influence responded looking back at him.

"How do you know?"

"You look different, you all do."

"What do you mean?" Gina said.

"A light glow outlines you, like you don't belong."

"Then there is no sense in hiding," Gina said.

Gina went to the door of the nearest home. The door slid open and the lights turned on. They all entered the dwelling. Inside the structure was like a giant metallic snail shell, with sculptural curves that all lined up beautifully. A vehicle was attached to the side of the dwelling.

Inside this unadorned home, were floating interactive holographic monitors. These manipulated silvery grains into images, diagrams and schematics. Everything in this home had a strange tactile feel but they couldn't access anything.

They walked back outside in to the sprawling expanse of the city. Their vehicles rested on silver pentagon shaped panels that lined the street.

"What are these?" Joshua asked.

"They are Dendrite panels. Long ago we learned how to harness the sun's energy. Our streets and homes are made from Dendrite. These panels are like your solar panels but far more efficient. This is why our cities are self-sustaining." Influence said.

The air was clear, but it felt damp on their face. Joshua closed his eyes until the dampness passed. They continued to move through the city staring at the shimmering domes and the gleaming spires above them; above that were flying crafts that at times seem to float like jellyfish.

These flying vehicles had insect-like hulls. Some were winged ships with bodies that looked like coral; some hulls looked like crab or beetle shells. The faster ones created shockwaves of speed. Each craft was a sculpted work of art crafted by an enlightened society.

The crafts had clean curves and were devoid of ornamentation. The skylane intersections were not filled with barriers. The air traffic was constant, but uncrowded. In the distance, stately vessels and midsize ships zipped around slow moving vehicles that seemed to be carrying cargo. Vessels large and small cruised around the washed out neon pink and blue city.

Most of the vehicles were driverless. They traveled in all direction and changed direction seamlessly. Each flying craft was surrounded by a black tinged light.

"What's that black stuff in front of them?" Joshua said looking at the flying crafts.

"Our vehicles use dark matter particles like strings to pull it towards a destination," Influence responded.

"So, this is Shangri-La... No wars, no murder, no violence and no cable?" Joshua announced.

"Look at all those black rainbow windows," Gina said still looking up.

"Those viewports are made from black steel ore that we refined until it's transparent," Influence responded.

"Hmmm... metallic glass," Joshua said.

As they got closer the laugher and playing stopped. The children were larger than their human counterparts, other than their height and shape of the eyes they were indistinguishable. As the four approached children squeezed their parent's hands, crossed the street or ran into their home.

The city's gathering center was three stories high; it's only two stories if you don't count the spire on top. Most structures weren't over two stories and much of that was design. Night had arrived and the citizens were still going about their business.

"Much of this is biomechanical, a union between the mechanical and biological. We grow some of these objects." Influence said touching the side of a building.

"You grow ships?"

"And some of the buildings."

Influence explained that they grew vehicles and buildings in a 3D printing way. It's controlled biomorphic architecture. Their organic philosophy rendered the straight line useless. These materials behaved like metal or stone but looked iridescent and shiny.

They could tell that this had once been an advance city. There were large black patches on the walkways, grassy areas that gave way to dirt and color had faded from the buildings. The inhabitants seemed resigned to their drab existence.

"It's like this all over my world," Influence said as she led them deeper towards the middle of the city. Influence was a legend, to all here. Several eyes followed Influence and the strangers, but they were not bothered.

"Prime is here," Influence said pointing to large structure that occupied its own zip code. The Chamber was just across the central plaza.

CHAPTER 21

They looked for a way to enter the building. Influence said, "Turn this contact plate." Devon opened the panel and turned it as Influence instructed. There was a draining sound as the silver panels powered down. The snap of locks confirmed that the building was now open.

When they opened the door to the building a wave of dark matter ran through them. They quickly moved through several rooms, before the dendrites powered back up. They entered a colorful crystalline hallway. This corridor led to the chamber doors. They paused and then opened the door of the main chamber.

This cathedral-like structure was a darkly congealed celebration of life made of metal and stone. The huge crystal sculptures that decorated the walls were designed to make an impression on all who looked upon them.

Devon was more impressed than when he had roamed Hagia Sophia, Sagrada Família and Saint Basil's Cathedral in Europe. The chamber was unnaturally larger inside. Here, space collapsed in on them and they closed ranks. The four walked towards the center of chamber as a beam of light rifled through it. The light made the walls almost translucent. This light reminded them to breathe.

The floor was full of gold streaks and in the middle of the chamber was a large hexagon medallion. At the opposite end of the chamber was a giant door. Joshua started to look around the room.

"Joshua what are you looking for?" Devon asked.

"A singing choir, a French horn..." was the reply.

In truth Gina was also listening for dramatic drum beats. In the center of the hall etched banners hung. The ever-widening beam of light cut through the silence. From that doorway a single robed figure emerged. The figure's face was too far away to see. The chamber became brighter as the figure approached. Devon gulped; he recognized the shape.

The sight of the gray haired, pale eyed advancing figure caused Gina and Joshua's stomachs to churn. The chamber was now fully lit. Devon's face showed respect so the faces of those he brought would show the same.

"How dare you enter our world! How dare you enter this chamber!" Prime said. His lantern jawed eyes were full of fury; his echoing voice struck fear into their hearts. Prime reached for one of the gold seals on his unicoat.

"Prime, we merely seek an audience," Devon said knowing what happened the last time Prime flipped a gold seal.

Prime could have been hundreds of years old. His resting expression was a sneer. His robe was unfastened and draped about his shoulders. His eyes crinkled around the edges.

Prime was slightly taller than Joshua, but he was the smallest one of otherworlder they had seen. He wore an ornate headdress that seemed gothic. In the front of his outfit was a white breastplate. Prime's was subtly overwhelming.

"I am impressed that you pulled this off and I am disturbed that none of my citizens tried to stop you," Prime said his voice cautious; deliberate.

"He certainly isn't underwritten," Joshua mumbled. Gina nudged him in the ribs.

"Who are these two?" Prime inquisitively questioned.

"Joshua and Gina," Devon responded.

"Ahhhh… this one is your friend who escaped us?" Prime said looking closer at Joshua.

"And who the hell are you?" Joshua asked.

"Don't question me!" Prime said his voice rumbled through the chamber. Prime quickly turned to Influence. "You have gone on unauthorized missions and now you have escorted humans here. I'll deal with you later." Prime's voice was colder than his eyes. Influence lowered her head and she stepped back as far as respect would have her.

"Resourceful…"Prime said. "I am not accustomed to accepting unknown visitors. I trust that you've been treated well," Prime said.

"We have," Gina said.

Prime looked over the group and said, "How human of you to sneak up from behind and club us over the head."

"That's not why we are here," Devon said.

"Why are you here?" Prime said.

"We seek an audience with The Council.…"

"You had an audience with The Council. Humanity had its trial and humanity was judged to be unworthy. What has Devon told you?"

"He told us enough," Gina said.

"The rest we discovered for ourselves," Joshua said.

"Still handing out stuffed animals to children?" Prime asked Devon.

"I am."

"I can see the rift effects in your face," Prime said to Devon. "Devon, you had a tour… Do you mind if I show associates around?"

"By all means," Devon confidently said.

"This way please," Prime said motioning them to the end of the chamber where a door opened to a hallway. Joshua and Gina entered into the hallway followed by Prime. Influence and Devon would wait for them inside the chamber hall.

"I am sure you worked incredibly hard to get here," Prime said. "Fate altering is hard work and there are so many of you. What we do here is see the path. We see how things connect. Sometimes people don't get the job they want and they don't get to be with who they love. Sometimes our missions nudge a person; pull a group or change the course of a life and its all part of a plan."

"You are intervening in a person's destiny," Joshua said.

"No. We are destiny," Prime responded and the door sealed shut behind them. "We are your biggest cheerleaders. We push for you."

"And those you killed?" Gina said.

"Sometimes people need a little convincing and sometimes they need a lot of convincing." Prime said walking ahead of them.

The hallway walls showed images of otherworld inhabitants living peacefully. They were happy, a glowing sun thundering in the distance. Gina and Joshua watched as amber rain fell on the populace, black pools formed as it landed on the ground. There were screams were everywhere. Joshua and Gina's faces couldn't hide their horror.

"Our towers once shimmered, our streets once bustled and our grassland once sprawled, before man and his civilized knowledge," Prime said. "Walk with me and don't open the doors."

"It must terrify you to see us here," Joshua said breaking the silence. "You can't blame all people for this. It's not their fault."

"Not their fault but it is most assuredly their responsibility! Your kind never ceases to amaze. You support those that actively plot to keep citizens grounded, medicate and misinformed. Your representatives get rich by fear not by record. No matter how immoral your leaders are, no matter how flawed your celebrities are and no matter how many people your scientists hurt, your kind worships them for centuries."

"This…is madness," Joshua stated.

"Humans have been oppressed by armies, firearms and sticks, far more people have been oppressed by nothing. Human existence is at odds with the existence of other creatures. We are a nation of brothers, sisters, sons, daughters, mothers and fathers that seek to be avenged." Prime stopped walking and looked the tourist up and down and said, "Why does she have more Hypernium in her than you?"

"How much more?" Joshua incredulously asked.

"More…" Prime responded.

"How do you know about Hypernium?" Gina said.

"It's the rarest metal on our periodic table. I don't know how you got it or how it's inside of you…" Prime turned to Joshua and said, "You have the look of a hero, the jaw, the poise. You have the body of a hero but you lack faith."

"The fact that we are here should let you know that people can change," Joshua said.

"There are small suicidal impulses programmed into your kind; you call them behaviors. You drink, smoke and jump off mountains with nothing but cloth. You inject substances into your bloodstream and spread disease but that just normal behavior for your kind. It is the energy your kind carries that's corrupt. You see energy cannot be created nor destroyed, only…"

"Transferred," Gina said.

"Each action lowers the threshold for the next action. This is why your kind is so willing to throw a rock through the nearest window at the slightest offense."

"What do you mean?" Joshua said.

"Some of these actions are due to your meddling or The System," Gina retorted.

"Still these acts are carried out by people. Like with our happenings; don't look at the events separately, they are dependent on each other. Each action builds to the next action. These things building up until even the best are tempted into acts of social disregard. This contagion spreads until senseless acts are carried out by otherwise normal individuals. Each act is a flare shot-up to warn an indifferent society."

"So it's like a virus that builds up immunity as it infects the next body?" Gina said.

"The energy of an action can be transferred into the next action." Prime said.

"So it good thoughts and actions could also me magnified?" Joshua offered.

"Your kind promotes the immoral, the contrary, the negative..." Prime replied. "A human changing is a fantasy..."

"Yesterday, it was." Joshua said.

"Look what we have become. Humans have to be allowed to evolve..." Gina said, as she choked down the horrific images that painted the walls.

"You think that by coming here you have proven that change is possible. I know that you can't and I'm positive that you won't," Prime said as he walked toward the end of the hallway.

"You have proven that you want to would adopt our language, wear our clothes, steal our name and take our mates, but you would never adopt our understanding or our ideals. If nothing else, you have proven that you would come here and drive us from our own home.

"It's not enough that you have caused the slow death of our great race; you want us to commit suicide as well. You two stand before me having been altered. You've motivated yourself with thoughts of my kind wanting to take your world from you."

"Well..." Joshua said.

"Your kind calls this projection. All Devon did was created a version of you that can withstand what you could not and then you ventured into a place, despite its active hostility towards you, all to realize that you are fighting a thing called time..."

"We have done what we must to protect our planet," Joshua said.

"You think that we have merely overreacted. You think this is reflexive recoil to the extinction of our race; a grotesque wartime denial in the face of our genocide. You think that the presence of genetically and culturally inferior intruders, please me...Do you wish to continue?" Prime responded.

They followed Prime to the next hall. The corridors were warm. The corridors were a sprawling series of interconnected passages, connected to the central chamber. The sheer enormity of it made them wilt.

"Joshua, you feel that you are in this big world operating with interconnecting systems; systems normal minds can't quite understand. You feel you are controlled by beings that are like you but are larger, more powerful and never seem to be telling you the whole truth."

"That's exactly how I feel."

"That there's a huge system is in place that chews up everything in an effort to sustain itself."

"Right..." Joshua said.

"That's how a child sees a world they are powerless to change. Why are you really here?"

"To save our world," Joshua responded.

"No, you are here because this fulfills your fantasy. You have abilities that would have fascinated you as a youth, overly praised as a teen only to realize they don't hold up as an adult.

"Let me guess. You thought you'd travel to exotic places, with no financial, politics or national limitations, inflict violence on anyone who opposed you using your newly acquired abilities, have as much consequence free sex with whomever you wanted and be heralded a hero for doing so..."

Prime's words left Joshua speechless. He turned to Gina and said, "The effects of what your kind have done to my world are irreversible and now you just want us to do the right thing. The right thing is to manage the end of your world. You have my condolences."

"We don't want your condolences we need your help," Gina said. "Can you forgive us enough to work with us?"

"You expect too much from us. Help you and how long would it be before your kind places us in internment camps? A year. Two." Prime said.

"The best of us working with the best of you is how we correct what's wrong," Gina offered.

"We are correcting what's wrong," Prime said. "Your kind isn't bad because there is no good in it. Your kind is bad because the good in it can't help." Prime turned down another hallway.

"Talk about crushing pretense," Joshua said.

"You humans are so hot you have to be hosed down and you are so vile you often spit back at it. Your people are so demented they put bird feed in bug zappers. An enlightened people don't drop bombs on weddings. They don't debate gun control. They don't list torture tactics like it's a wine list."

"And enlightened people don't murder babies with tornadoes either," Gina retorted.

"Enough!" Prime commanded holding up his hand to silence them.

"We have been altered. We have been to your world and we have survived. We are more powerful than you think. In an all out conflict maybe, we prevail," Joshua said ignoring Prime's command for silence.

"Maybe not," Prime said confidently.

"Losses would be heavy on both sides, but war isn't going to help this plan of yours, right?" Joshua said.

"Get the council together and we can talk about our new options," Gina said.

"The council won't approve," Prime said.

"How do you know?" Joshua said.

"Because I don't approve," Prime responded.

They turned down a corridor appeared to extend forever. The wall screens now showed happenings around the world. The floor was charged with electric particles. Gina reached out to touch the wall. The surface of the wall sensed her and blue energy ripples swept across it.

"Devon mentioned something about an Astroprojection room?" Joshua asked.

"He also mentioned Volcano and White Ocean Dragons," Gina said half looking in Joshua's direction.

Prime stopped walking and looked at them and said, "Devon told you of the habitable planet we discovered beyond the reaches. He told you about our efforts to cultivate the untainted DNA. Here you are a month before the deadline of the offer we made Devon."

"What offer?" Joshua said.

"To send him to this planet to help life grow...of course," Prime responded.

"He didn't mention that," Joshua said. Gina had a puzzled look on her face.

"I didn't expect that he had," Prime said.

"What you offered him doesn't matter. This is the only home we know and we are here in defense of it," Gina said.

"It seems that Devon has more sapien in him than we thought."

"Is there life on this other planet?" Joshua said.

"Yes, stop interrupting," Prime said.

"We can't trust your reasons," Gina said.

"You may have picked the wrong side," Prime growled.

"Depends on where you're standing," Gina snapped.

"And where are you standing..." Prime said snapping a goal seal on his coat. The corridor darkened and they were engulfed by a mist-like hologram. This cosmic hologram was full of unusual shapes and organic curves.

"Look..." Prime said his graveled voice vibrated the corridor.

In the middle of the hologram, one planet showed destruction, sickness, masses repeating slogans, old men pounding on podiums and women on platforms giving speeches.

Joshua and Gina walked around this display of trillions of shining stars. This map of the universe was littered with neon molecules, symbols and floating equations. As the electric lettering faded a small craft left the dying planet.

This tiny technological chip; this craft quickly made its way past purple nebulas, black holes and planets with high energy radiation tentacles. The ship corrected its course in the face of outgassing, nebulas and fragmentary shaped planets.

"Now this is amazing," Joshua uttered.

The craft pushed past planets and rode on bent waves of light as it moved through the starscape towards a double star planetary system.

"How?" Gina asked as she took a closer look at the vehicle.

"Planets are like boats in a lake floating on the ripples. The ripples cause them to bob up and down," Prime said.

"Is this stardust going into the ship?" Joshua interrupted.

"It's dark matter."

"Is it bending the universe?" Joshua asked.

"Our dark matter reactors will allow the craft to travel waves faster than the cosmic speed limit. The reactor generates highly energized plasma. We have allowed for the possibility that gravity is not a primary force."

"What does all of that mean?" Gina said.

"It means they have created a faster-than-light craft that shrinks space and time." Joshua said. "See the universe doesn't rotate, it expands. This expansion is a combination of quantum forces and gravity. Harnessing the differences in plasma should create electricity."

"Right," Prime said. "We have tested theories humans never could. In a year we will reach a planet that would take you eight hundred thousand years to reach." Prime walked to the end of the hall. "What you see before you, is the plan."

"Not if we stand together and unite our worlds," Gina said.

"…even if we did…even if we did…" Prime said.

CHAPTER 22

"Our altering has changed the natural order of things. It has stretched the human's capacity to know, to learn, to believe and to go beyond the possible." Gina said this knowing that people were all victimized but she also saw how individuals contributed to the victimization of others.

"You're fighting us, The System, people, yourselves where do you find the time?" Prime responded.

Joshua used his hand to pull up the schematics for the botany and engineering sections of the ship and said, "I thought the ship would be bigger."

"Larger doesn't mean more power." Prime said. He looked into Gina's sad face and said, "Humans aren't so unique after all."

"We are unique; we are human; we can't be anything but human," An animated Gina continued to speak to Prime as she walked through the hallway. "Humans are connected to each other; this is an essential part of our being. We feel things deeply, we get sentimental and we make mistakes. We name our boats, our cars, our guns and our private parts.

"Our uniqueness is why we have keepsakes and heirlooms; it's why we build memorials, it's why we give out nicknames to the things we love." Gina finished.

"You're right that's why you give acronyms and nicknames to your deviancies. Once your kind rid itself of only the most fit passing on genes, you became a selection most unnatural. Today, we march towards this plan, before all genes are tainted," Prime said.

"Why can't we just get rid of people who pose a threat?" Joshua abruptly said.

"Joshua, what are you saying?" Gina said quickly turning her head.

"….More than half of your population…" Prime said with curiosity in his voice. "You are willing to do what's necessary to accomplish this?" Prime asked as the hologram and ripples faintly paused as Joshua's suggestion was contemplated.

"No… No, we are not." Gina responded before Joshua could answer.

"We came here to negotiate, didn't we?" Joshua said as Gina pulled close to him. Joshua shrugged his shoulder as he protested her words, but not her outrage. Prime looked at them with interest and then he moved a few blue ripples on the wall.

"We came here to stop the bloodshed not participate in it," Gina said angrily pulling away from Joshua.

"You're right," Joshua said relenting.

"We call this craft Genesis and it will travel to furthest reaches of space. The Earth is beyond its tipping point," Prime said.

"Our cities aren't being washed away by flood, buried by sand or burned to the ground. The sun isn't imploding; an asteroid isn't hurling towards us. The ground isn't crumbling beneath our feet." Gina said.

"How would you know?"

"Even if it were, somebody has to be around to defend it."

"The world is beyond saving, how did things get this way?" Joshua asked.

"Electricity," smiled Prime. "In the time after Columbus rediscovered that the world was round, people fought each other but they also rose up to fight for what was right. People stood against bondage and stood up for truth, but that time has passed long since.

"After electricity was harnessed you split the atom and landed on the moon. Then the system helped you create the information super highway to gather information on people. Humans are trapped in digital alchemy as nothing more than animated data in a synthetic dream.

"There are data vaults that store this information. And there are virtual versions of everyone. The System runs tests to see the outcome of various scenarios, so it can predict what a person will do.

"The System's reach is beyond buttons on suit or stars on a shoulder. The System is beyond countries and borders, beyond months on a calendar. It respects no such notions as morning or night. Every now and then The System allows things to go haywire, just to remind you how much they need it.

"When we discovered the carnage, you were not just doing to your world but to ours. We had to act. The end is coming and we are the only ones doing something about it."

"Prime your society has advancements that ours doesn't, so why not help us. What if you overlooked something?" Gina said.

"We haven't," Prime responded.

"What if you're wrong?" Gina said.

"We aren't wrong."

"What if you are?" Gina said. "Is it getting hot in here?" Gina asked. She felt a little disoriented.

"We aren't wrong," Prime said drawing their attention to the planet the craft sped toward. "Life doesn't grow out of want, it grows out of need. Sending the building blocks of life into the cosmos is the ultimate act of hope. We are erasing corrupted genes and harvesting perfect ones."

"And how many decades will it be before you can do this?" Joshua said as the bold craft crashed into the planet as a ball of fire.

"Mankind's reckoning will be far sooner," Prime quipped as the hologram ended.

"And if we rally people to work against this plan?" Gina responded.

"Human tendencies precede any platform," Prime said. "Platforms are cover for frailties. The people won't hear you. They won't rally to your cause. The System's official report will tell them how to see you."

"Maybe humans are that sick," Joshua said.

"Hmmm... I thought you couldn't recognize the same sickness amongst your own. There is just enough dark matter in our worlds to provide the fuel for one launch, one trip."

"You said this trip will take a year...right?"

"Give or take."

"So, you get there and then what?" Joshua said.

"Then we seed."

"And the fallout?" Gina said.

"The collision will punch a hole in the crust of their world. The inhabitants will choke on dust as we reform RNA."

"RNA?" Gina questioned.

"RNA is complex but it will be the catalyst for the bonding process. An RNA molecule contains information and the ability to copy itself. Silica will attach thermally to unraveled DNA..."

"Causing the strain to spontaneously form," Gina said walking closer to Prime. "…That should break the covalent bond of the phosphate groups and the hydrogen bonds of nitrogen bases."

"Right," Prime said. "The free strands will pair with other molecules and those will pair with the planet's genetic building blocks, whatever they are."

Listening to Prime and Gina talk about DNA, phase shifts and methylation points was similar to listening to intellectual elites repeat phrases like Gage theory, electromagnetic potential and sea level, when there is no sea. Joshua found the ripples generated by the wall's quantum computer of greater interest.

"It's smart to allow RNA to naturally bond and reconnect," Gina said.

"Once paired the strands will be put inside cells for fertilization and then incubated. Once this lifeform is created and we see that it is good. This blueprint will get copied over and over again, a template for its own duplication. These lifeforms will evolve and another kind will rise.

"When their numbers are plenty, curiosity will lead them out of the safety of the lush areas. They will carry this biologic blueprint to every corner of the planet—this is the beginning."

"Playing God, are we?" Joshua said.

"For people, God is their own opinion."

"It's basically horizontal gene transfer," Gina said. "What you described should allow for pockets of diversity. Still, multiple and designs could be created."

"I am starting to be impressed," Prime said leading them further down the hall.

"As you should be," Joshua said.

"You may have distanced yourself from people, but you are still people." Prime uttered.

"This plan of yours is beautiful, imaginative and creative," Gina said. Joshua looked surprised as Gina continued to speak. "What if migration caused them to develop into two different species that contend for limited space?"

"What if everything goes right?" Prime countered. "People fear sharks, but cows kill more people than sharks do. You know why people don't go crazy over killer cows?"

"Because they can see them," Gina responded.

"People close beaches, post warnings, have news reports, make movies and create location machines so they can hunt down every shark that ever lived; all because one wayward shark. The fear of not being able to see one lost shark, causes the murder of hundreds. No. The human mind won't take to learning about our presence well," Prime said.

"Humans weren't made to be logical," Joshua added. "What's in here?" Joshua asked as he touched the nearest door. As the door slowly slid open a darkness started to fill the doorway; darkness so thick it had physical form. This was accompanied by a howling sound. Smoky tendrils of this darkness crept past the threshold of the door.

Joshua quickly moved away from the door. "Never mind," he said. He quickly walked past them as the door slid closed.

"What about you?" Prime said looking at Gina.

Gina's eyes were still full of tears from the wall images. Prime expected her to abandon her neon gothic façade and reveal her internal passions. The memory of loss was etched onto her psyche like an ancient hieroglyph.

"When I performed," Gina began. "I not only made the audience forget but I forgot. I forgot everything; I even forgot who I was. I had some dreams that…" Gina's words trailed off and she continued to walk towards the end of the hallway. She had no desire to entertain Prime. Prime's subtle smile disappeared as he waited on her to continue, she wouldn't give him the satisfaction.

"And you Joshua?" Prime said, half turning toward him.

"I'm just glad that I now know how this plan works. How are these premature deaths part of any sensible plan?" Joshua said.

"Trust the process," replied Prime. "All Devon did was reach down and lift you out of a lake that you thought was the entire world. Now you've learned that your world is only a small lake. There is another lake with more trees and more sky.

"You are now a part of a much larger and more mysterious reality than you had ever dreamed. And just like fish in a like, some are thrown back by the universe."

"With so much information being changed, I just need to know exactly how long we have." Joshua said.

"Not knowing is what makes tragedy so tragic. Not just what happens, but how it happens. The end is a sucker punch that comes out of nowhere. You don't have time to flinch or brace and you always think you've done enough to prepare. Extinction just happens that's the nature of the things.

"All you need to know is that you are on the edge. There will be no bells, no alarm, no warning when the end comes. Where you see flesh, bone and tissue; I see virus, disease and schism. You…can't know," Prime responded.

Prime's response caused the invisible set of responses appear in Joshua's mind.

"The only alien on Earth is the man," Joshua stated.

"So you know," a surprised Prime said.

"Bad backs, sunburns and people out of balance with the planet. It wasn't hard to figure out," Joshua said.

"Chimpanzees walking on their hands and you still need an official report," Prime said.

"What do you mean chimpanzees walking on their hands?" Gina said.

"Chimpanzees have four feet or four hands. That's how evolution works. The lower animals vocalized first then universal trial and error made it possible for us to speak," Prime responded.

"Ohhh," came from Joshua and Gina.

"How did we get here?" Joshua said.

"There have been an infinite number of big bangs, each creating their own universe. The creation of our two verses is evidenced by the background radiation that saturates each verse."

"How did these verses develop?"

"This planet's early settlers, The Ones from Before."

"The ones from before?" Gina said exchanging a puzzled look with Joshua.

Prime continued, "The Ones from Before came to this planet when the magnetic field was weaker. They brought the best of themselves to add to this world's biochemical reactions. They harvested from the hot vents of metal and sulfur of this planet. Their experiments created our kinds.

"Our races are offshoots of a different humanity. The Ones from Before planted old bone and aged feathered imprints in preserved amber. They left a fossilized egg here, a tooth there and old shells embedded in rock just to keep the human mind wondering."

"We aren't just extreme expressions of complex chemistry?" Gina said.

"Imperfect people create imperfect systems," Joshua slowly said.

"More perfect people create more perfect systems," Prime said.

"However we were created, however, we got here... it doesn't matter now," Gina stared at Joshua. "Prime, share your technology and methods with us. We will build a bridge between worlds."

"You want us to serve man?" Prime sardonically remarked.

"That's a cookbook," Joshua said half-listening. "So no matter what, everyone on this planet dies?" Joshua said walking faster to keep up with Prime.

"Some, sooner than others," Prime said looking at him.

"I don't think I like this plan," Joshua said.

"Like it or die human," Prime said turning down the corridor that led back to the chamber. "You are the invaders here, but don't worry, we won't imprison, torture and dissect you. We are civilized, unlike your kind."

"What you are doing is morally indefensible," Gina asserted.

"Save your grand notions and your impractical ideas. The System isn't a created program. The System is human nature and you infected by it. You dare talk to me about morals when your kind has turned the aborting of innovators, curers and real leaders into a fashion." Prime offered.

"But we tell people not to kill one another," Joshua said.

"That's political," Gina said.

"It's hypocritical," Joshua retorted.

"Josh stop!" Gina pleaded.

"I'm just saying that when people started thinking about legal liability before obligation, we probably weren't going to make it as a society," Joshua said frowning.

"Your society doesn't value its most precious resource— its people. Look how easy you gun down people while they pray and children while they learn?" Prime pressed.

"We love our children. Our children are freer than they everywhere," Gina retorted.

"He has a point. Children are free but they aren't working or helping to till the field. They down bring a dowry, build bridges or get married to make peace between nations."

"Times change…"

"Yes, times have changed to using children as political set pieces, forcing them to play sports. Children are the entertainment for bored minds."

"Parents want the best for them, they love them," Gina said.

"They have to love them. I call that adding value," Joshua said.

"See, Joshua understands why we are doing this. It's not the individual that needs the therapist."

"It's society that does," Joshua said finishing Prime's sentence.

"Our missions help manage the chaos," Prime continued.

"Ummm… the murders?" Gina interjected.

"…by slowing the unavoidable," Joshua said once again finishing Prime's sentence.

"The new generation inherits from the previous one. You suggest that we leave them the corrupt and the fallen. Our morals are as indefensible as your politics." Prime said.

"Something has to be done," Gina said.

"Something is being done!" Prime said waving his hands.

"You can't scare us. People have a right to know, a right to act in their own future," Gina said.

"Such noble lies," Prime said. "How will you convince them? When every affiliated killer has more written about them than those receiving doctorates? Human equality is a lie, it renders no one special.

"What your history books read as Western Expansion our history books read as Human Infection. History has shown that your kind will cause disorder, even injuring themselves to break free of this social equality of yours."

"Prime, I am asking for something that hasn't happened since humans rose from the primordial ooze, something that hasn't happen since Them ventured through the first rift. I am asking for something that may not have happened in the course of history, this one chance," Gina stated.

"Are you ready for the world to see you; are you ready for your world to see itself?" Prime said almost gleeful in his presentation. Prime flipped a seal and the horrible images on the walls vanished. "You still haven't figured it out yet," Prime said drawing his grotesquely face near.

"That we've been fighting ourselves," Joshua said. Prime quickly turned and revealed a grin.

"Telling others of this will drive some mad and others murderous. Humans do more abuse to themselves than we ever could. People need to kind of motivation that comes from being left in a dumpster or a dying mother," Prime said his calmness was particularly annoying.

"People...Them... all of us... I have faith that we can figure this out, without more death and destruction," Gina said.

"Of course you would think that. Before coming, you tried to reassure yourself that you were in good hands, that politicians, the military and scientists would come to the rescue, that they would be trustworthy, competent. Now that you are here you realize that you are alone.

"Youkind's faith is nothing more than scriptural anthems and radicals and you come here to change us..."

"The System is too big to fight alone," Joshua said.

"We need your help," Gina whispered.

CHAPTER 23

"Devon, your masterpieces are flawed," Prime announced as the three of them reentered the chamber. As soon as Gina and Joshua joined Devon in the middle of the room the chamber doors opened. Confusion and Monsoon entered the chamber.

Confusion had abilities that weren't element based. She wore a sleeveless midriff with an elevated back collar. She had a different sense of warrior fashion. Monsoon was colossal; almost 7'0" tall. His trench coat was adorned with blue raindrops.

When Confusion saw humans in the chamber she ran to defend Prime. Monsoon turned to the visitors with aggression in his eyes. Devon, Joshua and Gina were unsure if a defensive posture was necessary. Influence stepped between her guest and the two returning agents with her hand outstretched. She said nothing, but motioned that she was the guide for the humans.

Confusion and Monsoon looked to Prime who nodded his head. They both looked pensively at Influence, who lowered her head. Devon unclenched his jaw and relaxed the toes that tightly flexed against the insoles of his boots.

"I'm surprised to see you, Devon!" Confusion said. Devon simply nodded. She looked at Gina and Joshua, "Primates" she growled.

"Every time he returns he inspires," Joshua said sarcastically.

Monsoon walked up to Prime and bowed his head and said, "A soccer team went into a cave in Mae Sai, Thailand and that's when I struck. I used half of my energy dumping torrential rains on them. I flood the cave with water. The other half of my energy was spent chasing them through the dark cave."

"Your target?" Prime said.

"I dropped two inches of cold rain on that cave. They scurried further inside, to higher ground. I dropped another inch of rain and they managed to squeeze through small passages. They remain in the cave, alive... I have failed you," Monsoon said almost cowering.

Prime put his hand on Monsoon's shoulder and said, "You haven't failed me."

Monsoon looked up surprised. Prime looked at Gina and said, "We don't always kill. Sometimes purpose is found by keeping humans busy and away from their own humanity. Sometimes lives are rewritten to entertain, instruct and guide.

"We have done our part to write the plot lines of history, to pencil in interactions and to ink the thought balloons of intelligence. Life is scripted. Humans need undebatable reasons why they should work together."

Prime waved his hand then images of rescue crews pumping water from the cave materialized before them. "You did well my friend. Tell Tsunami, Earthquake and Volcano to prepare for the Indonesia mission," Prime instructed. Monsoon quickly stepped back.

Confusion walked towards Prime and slightly bowed. "The airplane was on final approach to Tribhuvan International in Nepal when I struck," Confusion started. "The controller's voice rose as he told the pilot to turn again. The airplane swerved low over the runway and then nose-dived into a nearby field, erupting in flames."

"Survivors?" questioned Prime.

"One," Confusion said finishing her report.

"Leave us..."Prime said.

Confusion and Monsoon slightly bowed and Prime nodded. As they left the chamber; Confusion saved a constipated facial expression for Influence.

"More missions, happenings and murders... You kill, you don't kill. What is this?" Gina said.

"Mercy." Prime responded.

"You call this mercy?" Joshua said.

"Who are you to tell those who mourn how to mourn?" Prime said.

"When I first accepted your meeting invite in Alaska," Devon said. "I told myself that would be the day I avenge my wife and daughter. I came for vengeance and left with a greater understanding."

"I actively despise that you are messing with world. I came here to look into the face of the monsters at our door," Joshua stated.

"Every step of life is a step towards death, yet all hope is not lost. Hope is the only magic humans have," Gina said.

"There is still time for you to accept our offer," Prime stated to Devon.

"There will be no offers," Joshua said.

"We are your answer," Gina replied.

"As you can see, I do not stand alone," Devon said.

"Devon, how many have you saved?" Prime offered. This question brought a look of surprise on their faces.

"Thousands," Devon responded.

"Have you hurt just as many? Tell me would Brianna be proud of you right now?" Devon was speechless at this line of questioning "And Sarah, would she be proud of what you've done in her name?" Prime said.

There was an uneasy quiet in the chamber as Prime waited for answers that would never come. A slightly disoriented Gina looked down.

"There have been reports of apartment complexes with rivers of blood in the hallways, dozens slain. Could that have been you?" More silence came from those assembled. Devon had a shocked look on his face.

"You thought we wouldn't know. We needed some of those people, no matter what crimes they may have committed. Which of you was it?" Prime said looking into their faces.

"Does it matter?" Devon said breaking the silence.

"When you've come all this way, when you've asked these two lives to risk life and limb against us and when you wish to offer us a different way that looks a lot like the old way—it matters." Prime again turned to Devon and said, "Why did you really alter them?"

"I altered them to save humanity to give the world a chance!" Devon said.

"No. You altered them because you didn't want to be alone. Take them back to their unnamed source leaked stories and high-paying jobs, so they can say a company's name every time they turn the lights on."

"That's called psychological market..." Joshua interjected.

"Who asked you?" Prime's said his tone was now unsympathetic. He was once again rendering a judgment. "The most dangerous place to be is in the human imagination. Your kind recruits enemy scientists to help advance a cause, meanwhile you vilify their leaders. Your leaders are nothing more than war criminals with security clearance.

"Your kind applauds its forefathers for crafting a society not for them to be adults in, but to behave like infants in." Prime's voice boomed over them as his teeth chewed up every word that came from his mouth.

"You fight for beings of want and little self control. You extol the virtue of beings who, over breakfast, loudly ponder what nation to launch missiles at. Your appetite for violence knows no bounds.

"Only a creature so flawed could convince people to raise an individual to be, unindividual. How dare you come here and rebuke us?" As Prime spoke the walls showed a future world of violence and despair."

"You know I have some ideas," Joshua said.

"People are full of ideas," Prime said. The floating screens now showed animals lying dead, explosions and gun fire. "People and their ideas. You thought you'd come here with your recruits and impress us. This little insurrection of yours has accomplished nothing. Joshua and Gina are extraordinary but that won't bring back our dead."

Their collective attention shifted to the horrors presented by the screens. Devon would not entertain Prime's notions. He didn't even want to think about it. For Devon fighting this fight was the only sensible option.

Devon knew that getting Them to stop their plan would be easier than telling humans the truth. To this end, Devon would keep coming back until he had spoken to everyone on the riftside. Joshua and Gina knew that Devon wouldn't stop, and so did Prime.

"Your plan is now just one possible future; we just need one meeting with the council," Devon pleaded, "After all we've gone through to get here."

"All you've gone through? Not only are you asking us to rewrite the characters, the setting, the world building, the structure, the answers, the questions, the challenges and the puzzles. You want us to change the sequence of events, the clues, the emotions, the payoff and the entire point... No!"

Coming here, talking with Prime and asking for help; they knew there would be a line they either had to back away from or cross. This line was now before them as Joshua and Gina looked to Devon. Devon's stone face hid his emotions.

"We will still send the craft to deliver the package and hope for the best. The council will be disappointed they missed your little cultural exchange program. When you leave here Them will be more efficient, which will cause The System to be more resourceful.

"And now that we know who these two are; this incursion will not go unpunished. We underestimated man's curiosity..."

"And our courage..." Joshua said sounding defeated.

"The world you return to will be different one from the one you left. It and you will know a new level of destruction. I hope you're ready..."

"Influence, escort them back now." Influence nodded her head and joined them in the middle of the chamber.

"What kind of destruction?" Gina said.

"More," Prime retorted. "On one side of the world a typhoon will make landfall, followed by an offshore earthquake that will crush houses. In another part of the world a hundred landslides will buckle roads. For good measure a hurricane will sweep across North Carolina and another one will flatten an island and that will be followed by The System causing a gunman to shooting 500 people at a concert.

"You humans live without believing the words you utter. Humans apply their guilt and shame to one person or organization hoping that will free them, it never does. You sex-positive, sex-negative, shirtless beings don't know how good you've had it and that's all about to change."

Prime's words showed that the novelty of humans in his world had become an annoyance. Influence walked silently over to Devon and urged them toward the exit. Prime continued his sermon as they turned to leave.

"They call themselves parents but what are they doing for their offspring besides collecting taxes from their existence? And even after hundreds of centuries, parents are still sacrificing their children to gods.

"Heaven, hell, good and evil, all created by man and the only thing bigger than man's ego is his capacity for self-deception. People think they deserve a pat on the back because they paid for the treatment and the addiction to the treatment. Your kind is a sickness better removed," Prime thundered on filling the visitors with dread as they walked toward the large hall doors.

"Your kind can pick up all the trash they want, they can conserve all day. They can go green while name dropping purchased snacks bought with their reward points. The System will make sure it all contributes to your destruction. Your kind has to study for decades to understand things that children understood millions of years ago.

"Ancient people understood that species die off and something better came along, but not you. Humans have hindered the planet's progress with unchecked human progress." Prime flared open his robe and said, "This is the policy and Them are the instruments of that policy."

"You are right energy can be transferred, but it can also be transformed. You can't take hope, optimism and the human spirit and boil it down to flawed mechanics, broken calculations and bad ideas..." Gina said as Influence led them towards the door.

"Your people are quick to put on a uniform to die in battle for surrogate father's approval." Prime said. "Your kind communicates with bullets, missiles, insults and pop culture references. Your kind displays radical tribalism as a badge of honor. Your kind is unable to distinguish useful from pathological. Your kind may not believe in religion but all of you worship something; it gives your lives purpose.

"You have used our lore to satisfy your idle minds and is the worst kind cultural vandalism. You burned the library of Alexandria for a printed t-shirt. Your futile arm failing is nothing more than rectum puckering after hitting an infield foul in Tee-ball.

"Your greatest successes are at rejoicing required moral of the story moments. Your actions in this case are a clear declaration of war," Prime said his robe fluttered.

"We free people. We help people. No nation volunteers more than we do. No nation donates more than we do. We have done great things together. It is the system that keeps people from unifying!" Gina said under her breath.

"You can't cheat your nature and your nature fuels The System." Prime replied. "Only a people as detached as yours could create an Information Age, that doesn't allow information to age.

"Humans specialize in deviancy so much that criminal, immoral and absurd behavior are but baselines. You stand here while the gatekeepers of the truth gladly rally to the flags of liars. The oppressed embrace the flag of slaveholders. They fought and struggled only to smile and take an order."

"We were made to carry one another. We reach out for each other." Gina said her words were swallowed by Prime's fury.

"Every war, shooting and conflict is a slow motion riot against the social order, yet you stand here trying to convince me that humans are just unlucky and the circumstances of their affliction made them the way they are.

"Do you think my mate and sons would understand what you are trying to do?" Prime said veins popping out of his neck as he spoke. "They can no longer hear anything so I will no longer listen. This plan is all that's left. I won't allow anyone to take that... anyone.

"Your kind has convinced itself that they are not consciously evil but composed of infinite layers of small lies, justifications and micro cruelties that sit atop each other, just a whisper at a time until it builds to a scream you are too numb to hear.

"We've managed you barbarians for quite some time. Were it up to me, I wouldn't give humans another day, another hour, another minute. I warn you, do not return." Prime said with righteous anger as the visitors reached the door. Prime's speech made Joshua frown.

"You humans attack terms so you can redefine them into useless structures. You have think-tanks pumping out new-think words and new phrases just so you can't have a conversation. Even you illogical, unpredictable humans must you realize the futility of resistance. We have the benefit of purpose. Each mission is for the benefit of this one goal." Prime said.

"We are proof that humans and your kind can coexist. We can reverse this, please allow..." Gina responded.

"You are proof that human can do more damage than we ever imagined." Prime said. "Go back to your streamed live and alcohol brewed with wind power. You don't have to convince us, like those promise squandering generations that you'll be less restrained and more transformative in your second term.

"No. We will no longer listen to your belligerent cries for attention." Prime said the punctuation in his monologue produced a coldness that weakened body and spirit.

"Your list of transgressions includes inquisition without evidence, ascension without earning, self-righteousness, condemnation and censorship. You bombard students with misread texts when real progress is achieved by dreamers, madmen, rebels, skeptics and outcasts.

"Your kind is so blinded by trust in titles that they make promises they can't keep and go halfway out on limbs they can no longer find. Leave this place!

"Go back to your sonic, electronic, computerized creations. Go back to giving them the bombs and calling them terrorist. Go back to providing drugs to them, but calling drug dealers. Go back to leading with gender or race because you can't stand on your own. Go back to shaming anyone who doesn't agree with. Go back to hiding behind your bulletproof pews.

"Go back to violence for little or no reason. Go back to your people farms. Go back to your distractions. Because not a single landmark; not one building will remain. When all of this is over, nothing of you will even be found in the ashes!

"Say another word, just one more word and I will have you unkindly escorted from this realm now..."

Suddenly two hands came from behind and grabbed Prime's head. These hands forcefully twisted upward in a counterclockwise motion. A single pop shook the chamber followed by silence.

A long pronounced shout of 'No' vibrated the walls as Prime's body slumped about Joshua's ankles. Gina's constant smile disappeared as their goal lay broken before them, being set to flame.

CHAPTER 24

Gina, Influence and Devon ran toward Joshua. Joshua discharged a blue pulse. This pulse tossed Gina against the wall, knocked Influence to the ground and stopped Devon in his tracks. Joshua's arms had a blue glow to them.

Devon stood there looking at Joshua; his mind was already questioning everything that had been done.

"What have you done?!" Devon shouted.

"I took care of this," Joshua said kicking Prime's body off his shoes. "Did you know that the human brain allows the finger to feel vibrations on 16/1000 of an inch. It allows the eye to see ten million different colors. The human being by design and function is magnificent, the crown jewel of creation and somehow you made it even better.

"For all of Prime's authority, all of his condemning and all of his preparation, he never saw me coming," Joshua said. His smug intensity somehow fit the moment.

"We came here to save lives," Devon said his eyes full of tears.

"He was never going to listen to us."

"I never gave up hope," a shaken Gina yelled.

"That was easier than I thought it would be," Joshua said still looking at his hands.

Joshua realized that on this side of the rift, Hurricane wasn't a hurricane. Avalanche wasn't an avalanche. Tsunami wasn't a tsunami. Tornado wasn't a tornado. They were just beings that had homes, families and friends and they didn't have any abilities. They couldn't control elements here.

"Was your plan to try to demoralize them with all this talking?" Joshua said looking up to Devon.

"What are you doing?" Devon said cautiously approaching Joshua.

"What am I doing? I'm liberating myself, from this growing war. I have found what so many before searched for— freedom."

Devon had taken a boxcar and a jug of wine and made them into a straight razor. Being altered, venturing into the rift and killing Prime was a mistake born from resentment. A subtle conscious thought can make a person do anything. This act wasn't desperation; this was a calculation on Joshua's part. Reality had started to melt away the corners of his mind.

"I'm a product of Reaganomics, crack pipes and music television. I had to endure the badly lit, over the top costumes and this cheesy sanctum—this…this just feels right," Joshua said with a smile on his face as the blue light dissipating in his forearms.

"I always thought that when I died, I'd be in a better or maybe a worse place. I never imagined that once I opened my eyes from death that I'd be exactly in where I was, do you know how disturbing that is? I never wanted this responsibility."

"Did you ask these people what they wanted?" Devon said.

"From the beginning, we've been dealing with 'what if' scenarios, what if the world can't deal with the truth, what if mass hysteria ensues? We never dealt with the biggest what if of all."

"Which is?'

"What if we can't deal with it? You see if people think in a straight line, they'll walk in one."

Influence recovered from the blast and stood up. "You... human!" she cried.

"I'm more than that," Joshua said staring back at her

The Joshua's increase in knowledge caused him to become unhappy. The more things he saw and heard the angrier he became, and Joshua saw and heard everything. He hadn't learned how to turn the world off when it grew to be too much. He would sit on top of church spires and meditate. From those heights, he could look down at the world.

He saw people waiting at the corner, impatiently looking around, pressing the walk button for a fourth, fifth time. He watched the light change from red to green. He watched their arms and legs move as they crossed the street. On top of these buildings, he would close his eyes and he was normal again.

Influence was stunned but rage grew in her eyes at seeing Prime's body lying at Joshua's feet. No guards rushed in, Prime did not live in fear. Upon seeing Devon, Joshua and Gina, humans on this side the Themasarians hadn't taken the necessary precautions. Maybe it was arrogance; perhaps Influence's presence gave them a false sense of security. This would be an unforgivable lapse.

Influence's heart raced and her stomach tightened as she realized she had brought fear to this place. By now Confusion and Monsoon had told others and everyone would know that humans were here.

Soon the elders would wonder why Prime had not told them about the invaders and they would discover that prime had been murdered. Treason would be the least of her charges. Influence's worry extended beyond her family and her own life, it extended all the way to the chaos her society would be thrown into.

Tears ran down Influence's face and landed silently on the chamber floor. She took a step towards Joshua; he turned his head and growled at her.

"When we were in the hallway with Prime and wall stopped moving for a millisecond. I knew Prime was integrally connected to the quantum computer and that taking him out could end all of this," Joshua said.

"We provided for you! We took care of you! And this, this is how you repay us? Prime was right!" Influence said looking directly at Devon.

"Devon, you've been here many times. You spoke to Prime before, but you weren't listening, you were reacting. The information was always there, every religion, every group, blacks, whites Asians, women, men, children—people; they all had their shot at rulership, it never lasted, and it was never good, all of it lead to this."

"You are people as well," Gina responded.

"I was people. In our world they are viewed as monsters. In their world we are viewed as Neanderthal."

"Prime needed to recognize our right to live but we also needed to recognize his," Gina said rubbing her forehead.

"I wasn't a good teacher. It wasn't good enough," Devon said.

"It wasn't enough to know what I know. It wasn't enough to have abilities. It wasn't enough to fight them. You see when I finally got here and heard Prime; I realized that nothing would ever be enough."

"Joshua, when the world is tearing itself apart, we hold each other together…remember?" Gina said.

"This is Battleship and we know exactly where their fucking battleships are!" Joshua exclaimed his voice booming off the walls. "I'm not like you. You want to save a world that doesn't want to be saved. You want to spread belief and she wants to give hope." Joshua looked at Devon and laughed.

"You took the most hopeless cases, fought the most uphill battles and helping those most in need, for what? You're the hero of this story, you are better than the Wizard of fucking Oz. You gave me what I needed. You took me where I wanted to go. I'll do the talking, now."

"They can't be negotiated with. They won't listen to you," Devon said.

"Why not? You did."

"Why did you do this?" Gina said.

"Why…why…why? Because Prime is right!" Joshua said coldly. "I have done 65,458,502 permutations and they all ended the same. I am tired of living in warehouses and barns. I'm tired of the knee deep mud, the rising flood waters and raging fires. I'm tired of feeling like I'm hiding in a foxhole but most of all, I'm tired of losing.

"When I was younger I would walk into a crowded room, knowing that I wasn't unique. I used to think, how could I stand out among these copies of me? I was afraid to go to dinner parties, solely due to the conversations.

"I avoided the invites and the questions, because I thought that everyone was trying to take something from me and they were. I was surrounded by thousands and I was still alone. I faded away even if no one saw. Even before I met you, I was nothing more than a victim of molecular circumstance."

"Those were darker times," Devon responded.

"That was last night! You thought you transformed this blank page by moving bones like commas, slicing sections together like word constructions and suturing membranes like odd paragraphs. You thought your creation belonged to you. How long did you debate with yourself before deciding to alter me?"

"What?" Devon said with frustration on his face.

"Glowing insignias and light tattoos… who could resist that? I was amazed by you and what you could do. You wanted to alter me, so how long?"

"We did this, so we could save humanity, so we could change the future." Devon said.

"Admit it; you altered us just like Prime said." Joshua stated.

"No," Devon said. Gina regained her strength and slowly moved towards the middle of the chamber with Devon.

"You expect for us to believe that?" Joshua said looking at Gina.

"I was alone, resurrected as a different person, with a story that no one was going to believe. I couldn't defeat Them. I couldn't defend the planet alone. If I couldn't change you I may have taken them up on their offer. You gave me hope, both of you."

"You needed co-conspirators…psychological manipulation that's your forte. Here we are in the midst of a global plot and it's just us. We nearly died being changed into this. Look at this." Joshua said. He had remotely jacked into the quantum computer and produced a large screen that hung in the air.

That screen showed a hurricane hit the Gulf of Mexico; on another screen a hurricane struck the southern states, followed by a tropical thunderstorm that rocked Puerto Rico as eighteen wildfires blanketed California.

"We are not alone. We have to stand together," Gina stated looking at the images.

"We are in a battle we have no hope in winning. When you said a biologically similar enemy, I didn't know you wanted me to star in just another monster movie, you could have just given me the residual checks."

Devon stood there weighing the loss of his family versus the lives he had saved.

"And every time you close your eyes you relive the worse moment of your life," Joshua said. "While we are trying to save this world, these otherworlders are just getting stronger and The System is preparing new weapons of war and new things for us to argue about.

"The System moved the homeless from the aqueducts to in front of your house. It doesn't allow children to flunk. Human must be pushed forward, like you said the industry must be fed."

"When we come out of the rift this time, The System will likely identify us as a threat. Before we were irrelevant; specters it couldn't identify, beings it couldn't trigger, anomalies not worthy of its time, but now..." Gina said.

"What The System is able to do is only possible because people are predisposed to deception. Freedom is whatever people are told it is. The powerless are easily demonized for effect. Poverty is human-made. People are manufactured into existence. There is no heaven, no hell, just wherever you happen to be." Joshua stated.

"I told both of you that nothing you believed was correct," Devon began. "I can't walk through the multicolored leaves on my lawn. I can't walk into my home to my family after work, that's all gone and can't be recaptured."

"You may have been an unexpected outcropping, but Gina and I were not. You came around seducing me with your flips, toys and feats of strength. What you did was no better than what these otherworlders or The System does."

"I never had a choice. I gave you a choice..."

"Did you really... you were just great at making it sound like a choice. You and I both know that the worst case scenario is that people will create a new much worse system."

"People may react no better than Prime did, but we can prepare them. We tell them the truth no matter how unpleasant it is time and we can guide them," Gina said.

"Gina, you free children because it makes you feel good about yourself. What do I get?"

"We are saving humanity, people need our help, that's enough," Gina said.

"I thought it would be, but it's not."

"It should be," Gina responded.

"What did Devon offer you?"

"He allowed me to be myself. I'm here because I choose to be. We are better than this."

"Are we? Why don't you ask Devon about those unauthorized missions Influence has been going on?" Joshua said staring at Gina.

"Josh... don't." Devon said.

"There is no moral high ground when everyone is knee deep in mud," Joshua responded.

"What about these unauthorized missions?" Gina said turning her attention to Influence.

"Gina...you are the most valuable of all of us," Joshua continued.

"Josh Stop!" Devon said talking a step towards Gina.

"You're a replacement. We both are," Joshua said.

"You are not a replacement," Devon said shaking his head.

Joshua had laid the truth was before her. Gina looked at influence and then at Devon and she despised them both. Devon was all she cared about. He meant something to her and now she wanted to be anywhere but there. If she could vanish, she would have. Her inner happiness held on to a cliff in her psyche.

The normal questions didn't apply; Gina swallowed all that made her human. Instead of slapping Influence's face, Gina turned and stared at her and said, "I saw how you looked at him. I saw how you touched his shoulder…"

"It's not like that," Influence said reaching out to Gina.

"Don't you dare touch me!" Gina said as green sparks came from her hands. Influence was shoved to the ground. "Joshua is right, on this side you are as weak as we are on our side," Gina said surprised by the powering surging within her. She frowned at Influence and her eyes became golden.

"I didn't really have a choice." Devon snapped. "If I hadn't we wouldn't be here now. Humanity wouldn't have had a chance. So I took the only option left and I'm sorry I hurt you, but it was the only way.

"You didn't have a choice." Influence said over Gina's sobbing. "I was your last option…" Influence said the disillusionment in her voice was like a knife being jabbed into Devon's side. "I meant nothing, the things we did, the time we spent together" Influence said as she got up.

Gina and Influence's words hit Devon harder than any otherworlder ever had. Behind him Joshua was shooting electrical charges from his hands into the walls. The chamber was disintegrating.

"I never said that, never." Devon said to Influence "You act as if I wasn't a means to quell your fear, your doubt. As if I didn't satisfy your curiosity. It wasn't meaningless," Devon said rubbing Influence's shoulder.

"How is it even possible?" Gina said squinting as she continued to stare at Influence.

"Oh it's very possible." Influence said squinting back at her.

"Day after day of watching my mother's body fail and I still had hope. It was the tiniest sliver of hope, but it was hope. Have I lost you to this thing?" Gina said. Tears filled her eyes as she Devon's face for an answer she could believe.

Gina suddenly weakened and leaned against the chamber wall. Her cheeks were losing what little color they had. She put a hand over her eyes. Devon quickly reached for her wrist. He rubbed her brow. He cupped her face and she closed her eyes.

This weakness was partly due to the revelation that Devon had been Influence's unauthorized missions and partly the effect from the rift. They had been here for six hours.

"As long are you were there, I knew who I was," Gina said. Gina didn't just bring hope into the rift; she brought her love as well. She turned her head and put her mouth against Devon's palm. Her lips were soft. He kissed her forehead as the ground shook as the chamber broke apart.

"You get high marks for the music, less so for the lyrics," Joshua said interrupting Devon by clapping. "I am sure that you've written beautiful prose but who is going to sell this narrative to the people." Joshua was the lone heckler in an empty theater. "They murdered your family and you're acting like we are supposed to be some kind of dysfunctional family now," Joshua said.

"You're not the only one who has sacrificed," Devon fired back at Joshua. "We were misfits, broken things that came together. I needed both of you," Devon said quietly to Gina, ignoring Joshua's taunts.

"I've lost my family again," Gina said putting her hand over her heart as she tried to pull away from Devon. She wanted to say that she loved him, but she wouldn't, she couldn't.

"See what you've done!" Devon said standing up after setting Gina down.

"See what I've done. We all know of your Job-like suffering, but even you thought you had lost everything, until right now," Joshua said. Joshua's hands started to glow as Devon angrily approached him. Blue beams of light arched out of his hands ripping apart the chamber's ceiling. These electric bolts of destruction tore through the night sky. The falling debris caused Devon to jump out of the way.

They heard footsteps quickly approaching. Without hesitating, Joshua punched through the wall. As Joshua stepped out of the building an onslaught of weapons fire hit him. These hits pushed Joshua but were little more than an annoyance. He stepped into the street swatting bystanders away.

"Your love for your friend blinded you!" Influence angrily said as she grabbed Devon's arm.

"Take care of her," Devon said. Influence nodded as he followed Joshua out into the screams.

"See Devon," Joshua said holding one of their vehicles over his head. "Here we are gods. We have the power. We are the executors of fate and we are the destroyers," Joshua said throwing the vehicle into another section of the chamber collapsing it.

"This was not the way things were supposed to go," Devon said.

"Your way was an ill-conceived attempt to persuade a council of overlords of our worth. I have a more mathematically sound approach. Instead of going into battle as three people armed with the truth. I intend to allow people to believe the hoaxes, lies and uncomfortable myths if it makes them happy. It won't be fair but it will be equal."

"If you stop now maybe we can salvage this…."

"How long have you known?"

"Known what?"

"I noticed that you stepped in whenever one of us got close to Influence. I was too caught up by your stories, too awed by your superhuman abilities and too intrigued by this other world to see it what was right in front of me.

"All this time I thought you didn't have a tell when you had the biggest tell of them all, you actually care. How could something so obvious have slipped by me for this long? You didn't think I would notice?"

"I suspected that being this side would affect our abilities."

"And now we are the overlords, look at this," Joshua said while shooting electricity from his hands to set fire to a home. A blue fireball rose up as the structure was quickly engulfed in flames. The inhabitants ran out into the night screaming.

"See...they fear me," Joshua said smiling walking through the destruction. Joshua was in the center of the city, the best spot to exact maximum damage.

"Joshua, this is..."

"Crazy?"

"I wasn't going to say that."

"Crazy is when you and those monsters showed up at my condo. I couldn't think straight. I couldn't believe what I saw. I viewed Them with reverence. I thought there had to be divinity in them that they had to be sent from a higher power.

"The explosion, the investigation and the closing of my company...all of it was trying to tell me something..." Joshua chuckled, "That's why I was in those churches, trying to find purpose, trying to get closer to divine power.

"Then you popped up and you showed me that they weren't divine at all, that planets didn't form in the vapor of their breath, that they were mortal." Joshua's spoke in an amused tone as if they weren't standing in the middle of a small war.

"Not long ago you were lost and afraid of your own shadow, hiding in places of worship... and now I found out that you don't believe..."

"Don't believe? You think I could be conceived by people who hated each other and not believe? That as a baby I could be left for dead in a dumpster, and not believe. I absolutely believe, I believe in me. Creation is a savage process. Take it from someone born by violence and pushed out into confusion."

Joshua was angry. He was ripping up panels, throwing people and vehicles. Devon threw a vehicle at Joshua. Joshua moved out of the way and allowed it to crash into a building behind him.

Their armed forces were unable to tell the difference between the two men. The citizens ran away from Devon as he tried to move them out of the area. Troops closed in on both monsters.

"I am the future!" Joshua yelled. "I used to matter. I can matter again," Joshua said. "People work long and hard for titles, awards and positions that mean nothing and you're fucking trying to take it all from me. I can't allo..."

Joshua experienced a moment of weakness and he leaned on a large building, knocking the metal from it. Joshua regained his composure and stood up and continued his lecturing. "We have judged our executioner, they'll think long and hard about continuing this plan of theirs."

"Or they'll intensify their measures against us," Devon shot back at Joshua.

"Prime is the being that organized the slaughter of our people, no thanks is needed."

"You of all people know the odds of succeeding."

"The odds have been stacked against me since I was born."

"This is not like you?" Devon said, advancing towards Joshua, motioning to onlookers to leave the area.

"How would you know?" Joshua said maintaining his distance from Devon. "How would you know? You helped me overcome, it was up to me to become. You and me, this is pulling of light and dark gives everything direction," Joshua said.

Influence brought Gina out of the crumbling chamber, her condition was getting worse. "Get your hands off of me," Gina said pushing away from Influence.

"I'm trying to help you," Influence said chasing after her.

"Get away from me," Gina said slapping Influence's face.

"What's this?" Joshua said again feeling lightheaded.

"It's the effect of our stay inside the rift. We are breaking down, just as our world does to them. Josh, we have to get back..." Devon said and he offered his hand to Joshua.

"And go back to being weak, back to living in fear, back to hiding?" Joshua said declining Devon's hand and kicking holes in two more buildings.

"We came here for an audience; the only way this works is if Them and humans to work together."

"When is that going to happen, Neverurary 1st?"

"It happens with patience and it happens with the truth."

"The truth doesn't bring people together, look around you the truth separates us," Joshua said regaining his strength. "The second time you left; I grew angry waiting on you," Joshua said jumping to the other side of the street and away from Devon. "You know the first time I killed I washed my hands for days, I trembled for twice as long. I couldn't sleep. The blood never seemed to wash all the way off.

"I tried everything; all the soap and hot water in the world couldn't wash it away. The next time I killed it was easier and then I found my parents."

"You found your birth parents?" Gina said. Influence had found shelter nearby. Influence was in the streets directing people to safety.

"Joshua, you didn't…no…no…no," Gina weakly said.

"My father was a janitor in a school in Alabama; he lived alone in a small apartment. My mother had a nice family and a three-bedroom house in Philadelphia. I waited, until they were alone…" Joshua held out his hands and opened his fingers and a video formed between his hands. The grainy video showed Joshua busting through doors to pummel each parent.

"When you made it college, I…" His father pleaded as he scrambled on his back.

"Look at me!" Joshua commanded as he stomped him.

"I kept tabs on you," his mother pleaded her battered body leaning against the wall.

"You don't even know me!" Joshua responded.

Joshua had exacted revenge on those the Catholic teachers that hit his hands with rulers, the foster care center owners that sexually abused him. The last image was a bloody knuckle dominating the screen. Gina held her hand to her mouth.

"I didn't even ask them why they did it." Joshua said rubbing his hands as if he were trying to remove a stain from them.

"Killing my parents, killing criminals and other blameless people? None of it made me feel any better, none of it made me feel as good as I do right now, you were right Devon… it's not my fault."

"Joshua, you have to stop this right now!" Devon's said his voice tilting towards anger. There was a beast locked away inside of Joshua, a beast that breathed at the window panes of his mind, a beast that would no longer be ignored.

"I believe in destiny and I am destined for more," Joshua said pacing in the streets. "When I was in those foster homes hiding those cigarette burns on my arms, I felt like it was only happening to me. All my life I've been without, but now I have something—something no one can take from me, not even you."

CHAPTER 25

Junior year while in their dorm Devon told Joshua that he had mapped out his life. Joshua nodded while he thinking that his admission to the university had a racial component to it. Devon told Joshua that Sarah was the one, that they would get married, that they would buy a small home and have a beautiful child. It was Devon's simple fairytale, Joshua congratulated him, but he envied him.

When Joshua saw Devon stand up to Them in his condo, he envied him. When Devon returned stronger, faster and better, he envied him. When he saw Devon stand unflappably in the middle of a level four tornado, he envied him. He envied how otherworlders acknowledged Devon. He envied how Gina hung on his every word.

Before they were altered, Devon had asked Joshua countless questions; Gina was asked even more questions. Devon had run every test known and unknown. There were no neurological disorders found; they were both in excellent physical and mental condition. Before they were altered they had passed all the metrics used to determine personality traits and predict future actions. Still, all of this was there bubbling just beneath the surface.

"You'd accept being their House Sapien, if you though it would bring you closer to your goal. You want your words to come out of my mouth. You want me to listen as you two make the beast with two backs? No, thank you," Joshua said tossing more attackers away from him.

"Do you have any idea of what you've done here?"

"I had this idea before we came here."

"Joshua, you can't go back to the way things were!"

"See that's where you're wrong. You can't go back… I might be able to."

"What do you think you're going to do?"

"Maybe I'll water the lawn, put up decorations and pretend there is justice. That's how people get by," Joshua said and then he ran through a series of homes, leveling them. The rift had become a slot machine handle to Joshua. He had tasted real power and he liked it.

Devon wished that he had not asked him to join. He wished he had not altered Joshua. He wished he had done something different.

"I'll slowly take control of this mistake they call the internet."

"The what?" Devon asked.

"The Internet. From there I can control content, behaviors, buying patterns…anything."

"So you want to replace The System?"

"All I want to do is change this one but first I have to crush some people." Joshua said. His cynical tone revealed that he had no desire to be just another altered being.

"You did all of this, so you can be the biggest cog. You are going to render judgments based on what's best for the new system?"

"Oh that's right, it's always thy will be done." Joshua said sarcastically his face partly illuminated by the fires.

"What's that supposed to mean?" Devon said shielding those fleeing from debris.

"How could anyone compete with the stoic, gravely serious, somehow somber daddy-type; so burdened by the terrible righteous of this that must be done, that only he can thanklessly do on the behalf of people. A moment in time this big requires bolder direction, stakes this high deserves braver vision, an existence this grand shouldn't seem so small."

"You haven't learned anything," Devon said as Joshua's slide into cynicism would not be slowed. Devon continued to speak to Joshua as he bought time for Influence to evacuate the area. Still there were those that wanted to look and Joshua wanted the audience.

"Only in a world where truth sounds like nonsense can people believe evil comes from ignorance," Joshua fired back at Devon. "They believe people are more often good than bad, even though that is never the question. They believe that bad people are merely giving in to vices; the most common vice being ignorance; an ignorance that knows everything and permits itself to commit any act.

"There is no true goodness without the greatest possible degree of short-sightedness. There is no good person list, no bad person list, just a list. How those names got on the list is the doing of system controllers.

"Just like sheep people can't see what's in front of them, they get easily lost and they need guidance from time to time. They'll internalize the narrative, the lie; they'll accept it, because it's easy, it's necessary to survive. But something inside knows, something warned them, they can sense the errors.

"And yes, people want conflict; they'll look for anything that produces even a sliver of it, so they make purchases not because of want, but because it produces desire in those they have relationships with. These purchases, no matter how insignificant they seem, mean they can keep their relationship, they can keep on loving. They want to feel important.

"Everything in society tells someone to hate this person, mute this person even if that person made what they love. Now they can't love it because society makes people conform to the mob's fickle whims. So, this person who loves now must hate because this unrelenting society demands it.

"A shot, a throw, a punch, a catch, these are things that last only a second for bystanders, but those actions for the person that made then took a lifetime. Growing up my power, my control was seeded to others; they said it was necessary, that it was ordered by a court. Now I have power and I have control. It has taken me a lifetime to find my way.

"Them aren't evil, Humans aren't evil. You see I have learned. I have been victim and oppressor and those that oppressed me were also victims," Joshua said tossing another citizen out of his way. "For a long time, I questioned whether these things balance out, one night I was sitting on top of a church watching people go into the strip club across the street and that's when I knew good needs evil to survive.

"Devon, you are the good and the evil and well..." Joshua said putting his hands out. "It's an unwritten law in the universe, balance. The Ones That Came Before learned the hard way. For every action, there's a reaction. For every pole, there are an opposite and opposites don't push away...no...no...no... they attract. Like you said when you found me, it was fate. Things had to happen this way. I just wish I could have been a better friend."

As the area cleared the two men stood there sizing each other up. Devon looked for a better way to end this worsening situation. Each man was no longer recognizable to the other, each was somehow different. The rift had been an ever beckoning void that promised finality that the world couldn't offer.

"I am only alive because fate determined it. Isn't that right?" Joshua yelled feeding of Devon's disappointment. "You never lose, you left school early, but you got a good job. You were a womanizer, but you married a great woman, you lost everything but got superpowers. You're not the only one who has loss. I know what it's like to lose."

Influence looked at her devastated city. She turned to Joshua and said, "You come here and this is what you do? This is what your kind has always done." Joshua looked at her but didn't respond.

"So you want to shape narratives by being just another soft spoken sociopath at the top of the food chain," Devon said.

"A mosquito feeds on lions; head lice feed on people a food chain isn't linear. The mandibles of the trap jaw ant, the speed of Saharan silver ants, the power of the bullet ant, these abilities evolved in ants over millions of years. Evolution is the key to survival, I am that key."

"You went through all the pain of being altered, all the training— you agreed to this undertaking..."

"I only agreed because it seemed like the right thing to do. I agreed before I knew that phrase was just another systemic slogan drilled into my head. The Right Thing to Do, what a joke."

"You aren't thinking clearly; the rift is affecting you," Devon said. He wanted to believe that Joshua was simply overwhelmed by the weight of this responsibility.

"You're right, the rift is affecting me," Joshua said as blue energy surging through his arms. "But I've never thought more clearly. Humanity needs an upgrade," Joshua stated.

This action by Joshua wasn't a swing vote by a high court playing politics. There was a mental panic room inside of him where he put all the people and things that hurt him; while in this box, Joshua could no longer be hurt him. When Devon left him the first time, this box sprung a leak. Joshua's mind had gone back to an earlier save state.

"What are you going to do?"

"You sent me out in this wilderness and now you are concerned about what I am going to do? Don't look at me like that," Joshua said looking intently at Devon. "Leaders trade a few thousand; a few million lives to save a billion live. I see it as a simple math problem; the history books call them visionaries."

"You are gambling with the lives of people."

"You gamble with lives all the time as a surgeon, and they call you a hero. I thought...what kind of hero gets paid... All of them... A hero's reward could be anything...money...fame...worship... People can't distinguish hero from villain, they have to be told who to hate and who to worship."

"Because they there are no hero or villains, just people. That doesn't give you the right to do what you are doing."

"Here's the thing about that though... I don't care."

"Shouldn't we care?"

"Why should I? Prime already showed us how all of this ends."

"If you run a simulation enough times, the impossible becomes a certainty."

"No. You'll just drag us from one rift site to another, just cut scene after cut scene from a game I have no desire to play."

"This was the right way to go about accomplishing our goal. What you are doing is unjust."

"It isn't right and just, to kill our enemies. My every dream has been realized, everything except love. Never had love...like sure, real love. I was never blessed with having to feel the pain...the joy...the gut wrenching heartache...of real love," Joshua said bending over.

Joshua righted himself and let out a moan. The ringing in his ears was an indication that it was time to go. Joshua shook his head and kept speaking as he punched holes into the walls of a learning center.

"I was right there with you when you hung from the cliff. I was with you for the dead that are reposted and hashtags. I have been there for the things no one sees but us," Devon said.

"When some smiling suit wearing guy drains off retirement plans and there is no trail to follow, who finds them? We do. In the middle of sexpionage carried out in five-star hotels, we are right outside the door. Those brush-by package handoffs; who is there in the dark, watching? We are. For me they are all just more nightmares, you know that." Devon finished.

"Ahhh, your nightmares. Dreams are hard to interpret, but they never lie." Joshua said with a half hearted chuckle. "People dream about things like making love, being naked in public, but you, you don't have to worry about that. I mean you made it through a sweltering desert without water. You have been physically attacked by aliens and you're still here.

"When you close your eyes you get your family back. You don't have dreams because; your mind doesn't need to invent fantastical places, events and creatures. You don't have to fantasize about being with someone sexy. You have nightmares because you don't need dreams." Joshua's voice trailed off as he again felt the effects of the rift.

"We have to get Gina back," Devon said grabbing Joshua's arm to steady him.

"I taught myself how to tie my shoes, how to ride a bike, how to shave, how to fight and how to survive in that hellscape that was my life," Joshua said. "When they touched me, when they hurt me, I held my breath as long as I could. My heart pounded louder by the second. Now I have the power to never feel empty again. I have the power to stop pretending. God's don't need to pretend.

"These brown eyes, coarse hair, brown skin and aquiline nose, are not the things adoptive parents' prize in the blending of two races," Joshua said pulling his arm away from Devon. "No, none of them deserve to be saved. They deserve to be ruled."

"So, you are the revolution?" Devon said as animals barked in the distance. The fur of these dog-size creatures' turns into blues flames when they are angered; and the fur of these creatures were blue now. Several of these creatures ran towards the conflict.

"Examining their why, forced me to examine our why not." Joshua said. "Prime was right about humans, but wrong about the mission to save humanity. Human nature, these destructive genes would manifest wherever any molecule turned up. A different being would just do what has been done here only somewhere else."

"We don't know that," Devon said.

"Don't we?" Joshua said as Themisarians troops from all angles converged on Joshua and Devon firing their energy weapons. They accurately hit their targets. These energy bolts left Devon undamaged and produced a grimace from Joshua. Joshua issued another energy blast, just as bright as before smaller.

This blast hurled body parts and knocked city's power out. Devon grunted as he sailed backward landing down the street. Next to the jumble of screams was sadness and fear. The golden light of the intruders' eyes cut through the darkness as Joshua continued to destroy the city.

"You conquer evil; it just comes back rebranded. The same thing happens with good. Sarah, Brianna, this world, that world, let it go. When I saw you in that tornado, when I saw you saving people who were being abused and trafficked—it was the most powerful thing I had ever seen. I wanted that kind of power for myself."

"That's selfish," Devon yelled.

"It's human."

Devon turned towards the main street as three silently floating drones flew over him in formation. These drones headed towards Joshua. Joshua was fighting off more Themasarian troops.

"You can't escape the system, a system," Joshua said and then he used a slab of wall to crush the drones. The largest two large fire animals raced towards Joshua. These two were ahead of seven others. Their loud barking alerted Joshua.

One of these animals jumped at Joshua. He caught it by the throat with his hand. The other creature dug its teeth into his groin. Joshua howled and quickly reached down. He grabbed the other creature by its neck. He breathed in deeply and then slammed the creatures to the ground extinguishing their flames.

Whimpering caused the trailing animals to stop and run back the way they came. The animals slowly crept away as Joshua as he bounced a few bystanders off a building. Joshua pulled a radiator size engine out a vehicle and tossed it through the wall of what looked like a place of worship.

"They thought they were superior!" Joshua roared.

"All of this serves a purpose, it has to." Devon said walking closer to Joshua. "Amino acids came together in an exact sequence to create you…none of this was random. The chance of these processes happening by pure luck is mathematically impossible."

"Those that don't believe, will again," Joshua said ignoring Devon.

People from distant towns could hear the explosions but only saw glowing lights over the hills. Above Devon and Joshua in the backdrop of a city partially engulfed in blue flames a fleet of airships approached.

The airships were quickly propelled through the night sky by glowing thrusters.

There was a loud bang as Joshua had run into several vehicles sending them lurching in Influence's direction. Gina got up, spun around and put her arms out shielding Influence. The vehicles dented and then flipped over them causing an explosion a hundred yards away.

"How many unauthorized missions?" Gina said seeing fear in Influence's eyes. She knew Influence would never tell.

"Once you stop trying to change the world, everything becomes simpler. If there are enough dead bodies, no one looks too closely at any one of them," Joshua said. Several explosions occurred around them. These explosions destroyed homes, vehicles and the street but Devon and Joshua remained standing as the blast from energy weapons cratered the ground.

"Why do this now?" Devon said as debris fell around him. His voice oddly dispirited.

"You're still asking why...why...why anything? You want to know why? Because you love them. You love this place. You never loved me they way you loved Sarah, Gina...the world," Joshua said.

"You can't rationalize all of this destruction, all of this death," Devon said maneuvering into a better position.

"Everything people touch, we infect. Where it was green, blue and red we turn it grey and lifeless. Prime said, this can only end one way. So if you have something else to say, say it now." Before Devon could respond Joshua grabbed him and tossed him half a block away. Devon crashed through a series of homes and into what must have been a school.

To the citizen, the glowing eyes and outline around these unwelcome visitors made them look like demons. Some of the residents appeared to be praying, but there were others who were ready to defend their world.

These were elite armored, mission hardened troops to be sure. They had been born to defend their culture. The technology, the knowledge that created this place was now under attack. In defense of this city hundreds were ready to die, thousands if necessary.

In the distance engines lightly whined as the fleet of flying crafts accelerating towards their position. Glass shattered somewhere close by as energy beams sprayed across the sky like an outburst of liquid fire. These beings responded to Joshua's aggression in full force. Defenders screamed as they were crippled or engulfed in flame.

These defenders attacked like a colony of ants would on a threat. This time the number of assailants besieged Joshua. A large otherworlder blindsided Joshua with punches to the back of the head, this was a mistake.

Joshua's foot came up from the roadway, to kick him in the face. Joshua shook off the other ants. He lifted one up with one hand there was a rasp as the collar ripped from his shirt. Joshua used this body to assault the others and then he threw him over three houses.

The leisurely pace of the skylane was gone. No less than seven matte blue crafts hovered into position. Previous energy bolts annoyed Joshua and succeeded in reducing walls and vehicles into colorful piles of sand.

The gunners took their position and squeezed the trigger and bolts of tremendous power issued from their terrific weapons. Red bolts of destructive energy tore through the blue moonlight to hit their target. These beams heated the surrounding air, burned through Joshua's clothes; his howling could be heard for miles.

From the mouth of the gunships other guards fired their weapons at Devon. They concentrated their barrages on both intruders. Plasma and charged neutrons streaked through the air. Devon and Joshua were knocked off their feet.

Joshua slowly got up, his chest heaved; the look on his face showed that he was only enraged further. He glanced back over his shoulder as onlookers ran for cover in the avenues and arteries of the city as debris rained throughout. There was little safety to be found anywhere. Emergency sirens contended with explosions and screams. Lights flashed as the battle continued beneath the muted red sky.

Devon found himself on a ledge looking over a horizon of chaos. The screams of the dying assailed his ears. The smoke stung his eyes. The wind blew hot against his face assaulting him with the stink of death.

The chamber was nothing more than a gaping crater, surrounded by streets littered with the lifeless, wounded bodies of patriots. From flying crafts more bolts were fired, Joshua used his hands to shield his face from the explosions, but the blue and white flames engulfed him.

Joshua grabbed a nearby vehicle; he looked at Devon and said, "Give me a moment." The lights in the sky above them flickered and rapidly disintegrated into darkness as he hurled vehicles into the sky. By morning there would be no city left.

CHAPTER 26

"This is the only moment, there are no other moments," Devon shouted over the thunder. The flames from the burning city danced in their eyes. The silence that hung in the air was only broken by the sounds of boots on the dendrite pavement and the crunch of shattered glass underfoot.

The two remaining flying vessels retreated; leaving the sky quiet, except for the breeze whistling through the ruins of the city.

"See I don't want to be a god; I just want to watch from a safe distance," Joshua said pushing his way through wrecked vehicles.

"Joshua this isn't about you!" Devon shot back.

Joshua stepped over the bodies that lay in the street, pacing like a predator stalking a kill. Here, he was a god, they all were. Wordless screams were all that was left as Devon clenched his jaw; Joshua curled his hands into fists.

Nearby a green bolt of lightning struck and set fire to a line of trees as the two jumped at each other. The growing flames gave warnings to any that remained to leave the area. The two shadows fought and splashed in the cold yellow water that filled the streets.

Joshua's thoughts now came in the form of blows to Devon's abdomen. Devon loudly groaned as he scrambled to his feet. Devon sidestepped his lunging opponent. He avoided one flying fist only to collide with another.

"Joshua you may be right, but people don't need to suffer," Devon said as he threw Joshua off him.

"What?"

"We can find a way to change the system, together?" Devon said. Joshua's brief pause allowed Devon to quickly grab him and throw him across the street. Joshua's back slammed hard against the wall.

The otherworlders that had not run from the destruction watched the battle in disciplined silence. The two combatants' breath rose in a vapor before them. Joshua flew across the street and hit Devon in the face. Hitting Joshua's body was like hitting concrete bricks. Joshua struck accurately and didn't waste movements. A blow glanced off Devon's ribcage; the sharp sting faded fast.

Joshua grinned as Devon jabbed into his abdomen. Joshua pivoted and struck Devon harder. Devon growled; his shoulder was dislocated.

"Without absolute fear, they won't accept the program. I'll give them the fear they require." Joshua said circling around Devon.

Devon moved sideways and said, "Remember when you said, 'A rational view of others isn't possible without a rational view of self? That was the truth, but now you'd rather live a lie. You can't reject the world."

"That world is an illusion!" Joshua exclaimed.

Again, lightning struck as a hundred leaves blocked the vermilion moonlight. The steam rising from their skulls gave the impression their heads were on fire. Devon looked down to where the stuffed reminder of his daughter would normally be attached to his belt.

Devon popped his shoulder back into place. He moved his arm around and then flew at Joshua. Devon landed a flying double kick followed by an elbow in the middle of Joshua's back. Joshua dropped to his knees. Joshua elbowed upward into Devon's abdomen and rolled into a strike to his groin.

Devon's eyes came alive with a golden fire that cut the darkness. All cohesive thought left Devon's mind. Back and forth Joshua and Devon struck each other; each blow caused them to lose more pieces of clothing. Each hit felt like a bomb went off.

Joshua's skin briefly shifted green as he reached for Devon. Joshua's arms coiled around Devon's midsection. Joshua's grip was so tight that Devon's flesh ripped.

"You were right; once the gatekeepers were removed new programs were installed. The only way to fix it is to tear it all down, can't you see that!" Joshua said squeezing Devon.

Joshua flung Devon against a large fire pine, which split his head open. Devon landed on a tree root. Devon howled like a wounded coyote as blood ran down his side. There was a slow trickle of blood from his head. Water, branches and leaves splashed about them. Each drip of blood sounded like a dull thud as it hit the water.

The streets were filled with debris from flying crafts and overturned transports. Shards of glass, broken bodies and deepening water covered the sidewalks. Every home was damaged or destroyed. The smoke winding up from the burning debris could be seen for miles.

The rift was the barrier that separated the two kinds. It was also a mirror to Devon, an opportunity for Gina and a strainer of truth to Joshua. They had changed place with their reflections.

Joshua reached down and said, "This dirt is all around us. In it we find the bits and pieces of other evolutionary test; the other evolved machines that were manipulated by the universe. This flesh, our flesh is just a different kind of machine.

"Gina likes to talk about how special humans are. For all her talk of specialism and uniqueness, humans do a lot of following. We are the byproduct of evolutionary processes that never had us in mind. The Ones From Before saw the villainy in their creation.

"You suspect just as I do that The Ones From Before lost control and were killed by humans because we're just machines, elaborate but flawed machines. Just dots connected by lines. People can't be cured, they can't be saved." Joshua said his blood turned the water around him orange.

"Stop them before they destroy my world! Stop them before they kill each other!" Influence yelled at Gina.

"I can't," Gina said looking up.

"You can't or you don't want to?" Influence scowled.

"I can't," Gina said trying to walk; Influence caught her before she fell to the ground. The horror within her tone acknowledged the severity of the situation.

A hundred feet away Joshua had grappled Devon to the ground and was on top of him landing powerful blows, but he failed to control his breathing, a mistake. Devon was able to turn as Joshua's grip was weaker now.

As the fight continued Devon made adjustments as if he were being coached, he countered and landed kick after kick to Joshua's body. Two jabs down the middle were followed by a beautiful right hand which made Joshua backpedal. Joshua loaded up a right hand and struck, but Devon was out of range.

Joshua tried to circle into position, but Devon swept his leg. As Joshua stumbled Devon loaded up a punch and hit him. Joshua sailed through the air, knocking down several trees before landing face first in yellow water. Devon soared through the air, flying half a block to land with his knee squarely in between Joshua's shoulder blades; this produced a loud, dull roar from Joshua.

Devon placed Joshua in a chokehold. Joshua took several deep breaths and let out an unearthly noise that only called attention to his breathing which sounded like the liquid rattle of congested lungs running through tiny speakers.

"You left me when you got married," Joshua groaned as blood dripped down his side.

"Joshua, I never left you."

"You never really came back," Joshua said flipping Devon. As Joshua scrambled to his feet, he briefly caught a glimpse of his face in the churning orange water. His fingers felt the small striations forming on his face as he looked at his reflection in the water. He looked at himself as if he were a monster that had been stitched together.

Joshua's hands struck his image in the water. "You did this to me!" Joshua yelled as he stood up and faced Devon.

"You did it to yourself," Devon yelled back.

"I'll take ending it here over being thrown into a pile of punched through heavy bags," Joshua said his eyes glowed gold and then he ran fast towards Devon.

Joshua furiously lunged at Devon. Devon did a middle split to avoid Joshua, as he did he reached back and pulled out his dagger, slicing Joshua down his back, piercing his spire. The dagger vibrated slightly on contact.

"You just got here, I've been here," Devon stated sheathing his blade as he stood up.

Joshua cowered for a moment in anticipation of a finishing blow that never came. He fell to his knees as a small puddle of water gathered around him. He reached behind and brought his hand towards his face. Underneath this scarlet moon, he could see his fingers were covered in blood.

"Coated in Hypernium, I should have known," Joshua said. He quietly hummed a few bars from 'I Feel the Earth Move'. His eyes narrowed as the floating percentages of success decreased before him.

Joshua had offensively weighed his next words in his mind like a rock he was about to lob. He looked up at his opponent, smiled and said, "That's what I get for wanting superpowers." then he fell over into the water.

"Sometimes terrible things have to be done, you told me that," Joshua groaned as he rolled onto his back. "Just leave me here." He coughed as Devon approached him.

Their troops had regrouped and were closing in on them. Devon momentarily looked at Joshua and then he vaulted where Gina and Influence had been sheltered from the chaos.

"Did you come for me, or her?" Gina said struggling weakly against him. Devon grabbed her and lifted her to her feet.

"We have to get back, now!" Devon said sternly blood still trickling down his face.

"Who's going to answer for all of this?" Influence said with impending dread in her voice. She ran toward Joshua, "Who?" Influence said lifting Joshua out of the water. "He has to pay for this!" Influence started punching him repeatedly in the face.

"Everything is hackable, given time," a barely conscious Joshua said.

"Influence, Influence is there a closer rift!" Devon said pulling her off of Joshua. She stepped away from Devon shaking.

"Your hand is bleeding," Influence said. Devon looked at his hand; she gave him a small towel to wrap it with. She kissed him on the cheek and pointed in the direction they should go and then she disappeared into the night.

Devon put Joshua across his back and held Gina's hand as they quickly moved in the direction Influence pointed. Explosions were heard behind them in the distance. Gina's semi-conscious mind brimmed with questions.

On the outskirts of the city a large creature with slit-like gills floated above them. It made the sound of old wet windshield wipers moving across the glass, this sound permeated everything.

Prime was dead, hundreds murdered and the city was in ruins. The flames from what still burned marked the night behind them. Another fleet of flying vessels quickly advanced on their position; Gina's questions had been subdued by chaos.

The rift was halfway up the mountain. Devon neared exhaustion as they moved towards the opening. Soft yellow rain began to fall as they pushed up the mountain; plasma weapons ignited several trees near them. Joshua hummed a distinguishable 'I Am Blessed'.

Devon dodged several more energy beams before carrying them into the rift. There was no sign that they had been followed but that was wasn't permission to slow down.

The three of them tumbled out of the dark abyss, a week after they had entered. Each of them violently threw up in the dirt. Steam rose from the clothes, even with the alterations their clothes disintegrated around them.

The back of Joshua's shirt was split from the dagger. Joshua's back had been exposed to radiation. He was bleeding and vomiting. They had come out of the rift twenty miles away from where they had entered. Their vision was blurred, their ears rung as a cold breeze covered them.

Devon looked over to Gina and Joshua and he coughed a few more times. He wiped the blood from his hand and face, he nodded at Gina and he ran into the night as if he had been propelled out of starting blocks.

Joshua began to convulse. Gina blindly edged through the darkness to hold him. The color returned to her face as she slowly rocked Joshua. His eyes finally opened but he was couldn't speak.

Devon slipped over an embankment, swam across a river and followed an invisible path. He stumbled through a quiet town as he hurried back to camp. It took him almost an hour to get back to their camp. He dropped a few salt tablets unto his mouth and drank two gallons water as he packed up the supplies.

The Soul Stirrer growled as a profusely sweating Devon returned to the others. Devon pulled himself off the motorcycle and crawled over to them. Gina had dressed Joshua's wounds and the radiation burn. They forced water down Joshua's throat.

They went through ten gallons of water and depleted the salt tablet supply. Devon quickly set up the tents as Gina packed Joshua's shivering body into a sleeping bag. Joshua immediately fell asleep. Gina fell asleep after Devon tended to her wounds, they slept for two days.

They were finally awakened by storm warning sirens. Rain lightly fell in front of the sunlight. There was a growing noise of clicking of rocks being pushed downhill by water. The gentle rustling of leaves told Gina it was morning. She reached over to feel nothing, Devon was gone.

Her heart sunk as she sadly looked at her tattered clothes in the corner. She came out of the tent and into the sunlight. The last bits of water from the sky landed on her face. She felt heavy and slow but otherwise normal.

Joshua was awake; rustling leaves also disturbed his sleep. His fever had finally broken. Redness had left his eyes. He sat up and was slowly drinking water on his own.

Gina stretched as a glimmer of hope stirred inside of her. She started a fire and began to prepare a meal. There was the rustling again. Gina slowly ate the toast and strawberry jam. Joshua nibbled on his toast and groaned. There was the rustling again, this time it was closer.

Joshua's eyes widened and his mouth opened wide. Gina turned her head and looked directly up, dropping her plate to the ground. Her face turned pale as it glided through the trees towards them.

The Earth has a different electrostatic charge from the ground to the sky. When sweat evaporates on soaked hair, it cools the body. Hair is a defense against bugs, dust and other irritating things. Hair protects the body from ultraviolet radiation exposure. Hair can detect rain or a breeze.

The hairs on an altered body could detect these electrostatic charges. By alternating the internal charge, this electrostatic force could provide lift. Devon came through the trees and hovered twenty meters above them.

"Oh my God!" slipped from Gina's lips.